7/3/12

"Jordyn Redwood makes quite a splash with her debut novel. *Proof* is a hard-edged mix of medical thriller and crime chiller that grabs you on the first page and doesn't let go until the end. This one will keep you up way past your bedtime."

—Rick Acker, best-selling author of *When the Devil Whistles*

"From the very first chapter, the first page even, Jordyn Redwood pulls the reader into a story that won't let go. *Proof* is proof enough for me that Jordyn is the real deal: an author who knows how to weave a tight story, write descriptive, authentic prose, and deal with some pretty hefty issues. I'm a fan!"

—Mike Dellosso, author of *Frantic* and *Rearview* (a 7 Hours story)

"Debut novelist Jordyn Redwood has used her experience as an ER and ICU nurse to craft a blend of medical thriller and police procedural with twists and turns to keep fans of either genre turning pages."

—Richard L. Mabry, MD, author of *Lethal Remedy* and the
Prescription for Trouble series

"A rollercoaster of a story. Jordyn Redwood's *Proof* has everything you could want in a thriller—believable characters, a villain who makes your skin crawl, a touch of humor, and a twisting plot—all bound by fascinating medical and scientific details. A fabulous debut!"

—Sarah Sundin, award-winning author of the
Wings of Glory series

"Jordyn Redwood may be new on the scene, but she writes like a seasoned pro. *Proof* is one of the best books I've read in a long time, with well-drawn characters including a villain I despised and a hero and heroine I rooted for. I thought I would just take a peek at the first chapter and finish the story later. I thought wrong. I read late into the night, lost sleep, and put off my own writing to finish this book. I'm eagerly awaiting Jordyn's second book and will be first in line to purchase it the day it releases."

—Lynnette Eason, best-selling author of
The Women of Justice series

"I love a great medical thriller and I'm glad to add another author to my list. Jordyn Redwood writes like the medical insider she is: a gripping tale laced with realism, sleep-robbing excitement, and something every reader loves—hope."

—Harry Kraus, MD, best-selling author of *The Six-Liter Club*

"*Proof* by Jordyn Redwood is a gripping medical thriller written with vivid detail from an author who knows her subject firsthand . . . Just when you think you can relax, the stakes get even higher."

—Donna Fletcher Crow, author of The Monastery Murders

"Jordyn Redwood's debut novel is a page-turner with an ingenious premise and solid Christian values. A satisfying read."

—Frank J. Edwards, Medical Director, Delphi Emergency Physicians, author of the medical thriller *Final Mercy*

Bloodline Trilogy 1

PROOF

A Novel

JORDYN REDWOOD

Kregel
Publications

Proof: A Novel
© 2012 by Jordyn Redwood

Published by Kregel Publications, a division of Kregel, Inc., P.O. Box 2607, Grand Rapids, MI 49501.

Library of Congress Cataloging-in-Publication Data
Redwood, Jordyn.
Proof / Jordyn Redwood.
    p.   cm. — (Bloodline trilogy; 1)
1. Women physicians—Fiction. 2. Rape victims—Fiction. I. Title.
PS3618.E43538P76   2012   813'.6—dc23   2012004188

ISBN 978-0-8254-4238-4

Printed in the United States of America
12 13 14 15 16 / 5 4 3 2 1

To the three teachers who read my early stories
and encouraged me to keep writing:
Penny Stewart
Doug Reeves
Troy Williamson

Acknowledgments

FIRST AND FOREMOST, to my husband, James, thank you for supporting me in your quiet ways and helping me pursue my writing dream. Second, to my friends and family for all those times you read varying versions of this story and gave me pointers along the way, thank you.

My thanks go to many others as well:

To Greg Johnson, agent extraordinaire, who took a chance on an unknown novelist and worked great magic in helping this manuscript find a home.

To everyone at Kregel, for supporting debut authors and having a heart to make the story shine yet keep my voice clear. Cat Hoort, Steve Barclift, Dawn Anderson, and Leah Mastee—it's been a pleasure working with you.

Since it's impossible to be an expert in all things medical, to my medical reviewers: Crystal Bencken (and all those who work with her), Heidi Creston, Frank Edwards, Laurie Kingery, and Holly Picone (and Andrea Boeshaar for hooking us up).

To my police review team: Keith Howland, Karl Mai, and John Mueller, who made sure Nathan and Brett acted like real police officers. Also, to Aurora Police Department, who taught me many things and answered several interesting questions during their Citizens' Police Academy.

To the people who edited early phases of this book: Heather Burnem and Susan Lohrer. Working with you helped everyone else see the story and not my horrible grammar.

A shout-out to SECC Book Club and my first group of beta readers: Marcella, Kelly, Judith, Rosemary (and her handwritten notes), Natalia, Linda, Jan, Marcia, and Catherine. Thanks to you, Drew will see new life in the subsequent books.

Lastly, to every reader: I'm eternally grateful and would love to hear your thoughts. Please e-mail me at jredwood1@gmail.com when you finish.

Some of the places in this novel are real—names of several police departments and towns. That's as far as it goes. All the rest—characters, procedures, incidents—are fictional, except the mention of John Mark Karr and the Green River investigation.

Chapter 1

THE CEMETERY WAS closing in ten minutes, and Lilly Reeves was going to be late. She searched through her black tote bag for the third time and riffled through medical reference cards, hemostats, and lipstick tubes, frustrated that her means of escape had disappeared. An alarm toned at the bank of ECG monitors that sat at the nurse's station and a quick glance assured her that no one was dying.

"Is everyone sure they haven't seen my keys?" She secured loose strands of black hair behind her ear.

"Dr. Reeves, you need to keep your bag locked up. Someone may be trying to teach you a lesson," her senior attending said. The man who'd hired her onto the ER staff at Sage Medical Center.

She eyed him evenly. His gray hair and washed blue eyes did little for his pale skin. Was the look on his face amusement or condemnation?

"Wouldn't be you, would it, Dr. Anderson?"

The ER pager at her hip vibrated. Lilly pulled her lab coat aside and checked the message. "Trauma Code—one minute out."

"You might as well take that." He closed the chart he held in his hands.

"My shift is over. I have other plans."

"Like what, Lilly? Family event?"

She let the comment drop. "If you're understaffed tonight, I'll stay."

"My guess is you won't be going anywhere for a while anyway. Maybe in the interim, your keys will turn up."

Lilly blew the stray hair from her eyes and then left her bag under the desk before she made her way down the corridor. From the hall cart, she gathered her safety equipment and pushed through the swinging doors. Two nurses were on either side of the bed. Towering over all of them, Luther waited with one hand holding cords for the monitor. Regan, petite, with brown hair and eyes, hung IV fluids into the rapid infuser.

Sonya, one of their newer nurses, stood near the head of the bed. The paperwork from the trauma folder slipped to the floor as she worked to organize it on the mayo stand.

"Someone get that? I don't like to bend over unless I have to." She stroked her pregnant midsection.

Lilly pulled her stethoscope from under her gown. "What do we know?"

"Not much." Luther offered Sonya the stray chart sheets.

"Twenty-eight-year-old female involved in a high-speed MVA," Regan said.

"Vital signs?"

Luther shook his head. "Their radio cut out. Don't think they had time to try cell phones."

"Fabulous."

The EMS crew pushed through the doors.

The patient's breath misted inside the oxygen mask, eyes closed, blonde hair snaked and tangled around her pale face. Thick, clotted blood covered the left side of her head. As the medics transferred the patient to the bed, a rounded midsection on the thin woman caught Lilly's gaze.

She frowned and pushed the blanket to the side.

"Hey, Mike . . . Raul. She's pregnant?"

Mike yanked the oxygen tubing from the transport tank and connected it to the wall source. They tilted the backboard up so the patient rested on her left side.

First responders used the left-side position to prevent compression of the vena cava by a pregnant woman's enlarged uterus, thereby improving blood flow to the growing baby.

"Two for the price of one." Mike, the shorter of the two men, confirmed. "This is Torrence Campbell—"

"Torrence?" Sonya's startled gasp paused Lilly's movements.

"You know her?" Regan asked.

"She's a friend. Our babies are due on the same day." The color drained from Sonya's cheeks. She fanned her face with the chart.

"Can you do this?" Lilly asked.

"I'll be fine."

"Twenty-eight-year-old restrained driver was T-boned by a truck moving at a high rate of speed," the paramedic continued. "Her car then slid into a lamppost at the corner of the intersection. No air bags. Significant incursion of the vehicle into the passenger compartment."

Lilly looked down at the woman on the table. What was going to happen to the little one inside? Experience had shown her there was no guarantee for either of them. Would she have to choose which one lived or died?

"Her head hit the side window—shattered the glass. Initially alert and oriented but now we can't get her to wake up. Both femurs with obvious deformities. Splints in place. Heart rate 130. Respiratory rate 32. Blood pressure 90/50. Pelvis feels stable. She stated on scene she is 28 weeks pregnant. Was able to get fetal heart tones at 140. Two large-bore IVs in each AC with saline wide open."

"Thanks, guys. You're clear," Lilly said to the EMS team. She helped Regan pull off the layers of linen, placed her palms lightly on the woman's abdomen, and pressed inward at various stations, her practiced hands testing for firmness that might indicate a collection of blood. The muscle tensed under her fingers. A contraction?

"Sonya, I need a page out to OB for an imminent delivery."

"Got it."

"Luther, let's get a couple of liters of Lactated Ringer's running in. See if that helps her blood pressure and fast heart rate." Lilly motioned to one of the ER techs. "Pull the bedside ultrasound in here. I don't see it."

"The cops are right behind us." Raul tossed the dirty linens into the laundry bin. "They don't think it was much of an accident."

"What do you mean?" Luther connected the ECG cords to the patient's chest. Lilly watched the tracing come up on the monitor.

"They're saying someone was after her. That she was hit on purpose." Mike followed his partner out the door.

Lilly catalogued the comments in the back of her mind. The patient's clothes lay on the floor in a shredded heap. Trauma protocol dictated a systematic approach to assessment so nothing was missed. First, responsiveness.

She shook Torrence's shoulder.

"Torrence, can you hear me?"

Not even a flicker of an eyelid. Lilly pulled a hemostat from her pocket and pushed the metal into the base of her patient's fingernail.

Nothing.

"Sonya, she's unresponsive."

"I don't have a good feeling about her, Lilly," Luther whispered as he secured a blood pressure cuff around her flaccid arm.

"Regan, we're going to need an airway." She positioned her stethoscope in her ears. Techs began placing films for X-ray.

Next, breathing and circulation. Breath sounds quick and shallow. Heart tones distant. Pupils were unresponsive black discs as Lilly shone her penlight into the vacant stare.

One was larger than the other.

Reaching to the wall, she grabbed an otoscope.

Blood behind the left eardrum.

Lilly's years of practiced training edged over the panic that enticed her heart into a faster rhythm. She began an injury checklist in her mind.

Head injury probable. The blown pupil could indicate an epidural bleed. A torn artery near the brain could be devastating. That meant a CT scan and neurosurgery consult. The lower blood pressure and increased heart rate could be blood loss caused by the presumed femur fractures or other internal bleeding. Add an ortho doc to the list. Disruption of blood flow to the uterus was Lilly's next concern as it could mean death for the baby. OB should be on the way.

"Where are ortho and neurosurgery? Is anyone getting their pages today?" Lilly asked.

"The system's been a little twitchy," Luther said. "I'll call the desk and have the service specialist page it out again."

A man unknown to her entered the room. Regan pulled a stand of airway equipment near the head of the bed. Lilly tested her patient's jaw to see how easily she could get it open to place the tube.

Tight.

"Luther, I'm going to need a dose of Etomidate."

"Got it."

"Is she coherent?" the stranger asked.

Lilly glanced his way. His height topped hers by a couple of inches. Tousled brown hair and bloodshot blue eyes alluded to his lack of sleep.

"You are?" She guided him back toward the door as they shot the last X-ray.

"Detective Nathan Long."

"You know you can't be in here until we give you clearance."

"I know, I'm sorry. I just need to ask her a few questions."

"What's your interest in my patient?"

The radiology tech tugged Lilly's gown to get her attention. "We'll have these in the computer soon."

His voice drew her attention back. "We think she was intentionally hit by the man she was going to ID as her rapist. Can she talk?"

"She's not responsive, and we're getting ready to stick a tube in her throat. I doubt he'll show up here." Lilly turned back to the patient.

"He might be crazy enough." Long stepped closer to the bed.

Lilly took two strides and faced him, putting her fisted hand in the center of his chest. "Since you were wondering, I'm her doctor, Lilly Reeves. Perhaps you didn't hear me when I told you she's not responsive. I need you to wait outside."

"I have to try. She's the only one so far who's come close to identifying this man."

"Meaning there are multiple victims?"

Detective Long was silent.

"The police department is keeping quiet about a serial rapist?" She pushed her nose within an inch of his face. "You need to release that information to protect other women." He stood his ground.

"I'll keep someone outside this door." He turned and left. Lilly watched as he spoke with a uniformed officer.

"Her pressure's dropped into the 70s," Regan said.

It was much too low for mom and baby.

"Have the two liters of LR run in?" Lilly asked.

"All the way," Luther noted.

"Let's get some blood running."

Lilly unlocked the bed and pulled it away from the wall until she could step behind it to access the patient's airway. "Luther, we're going to roll her supine."

They eased the backboard down.

"Ready for the Etomidate?" he asked as he pulled the metal stand with airway equipment within her reach.

Lilly looked over the tray to ensure each piece of equipment was ready. "Give it now."

Luther injected the medication. A respiratory therapist pulled the oxygen mask off and began to assist the patient's breathing.

Reaching into the patient's mouth, Lilly opened the jaw and placed the blunt metal blade, visualizing the airway. The vocal cords popped into view, two thin pieces of v-shaped muscles. She slid the breathing tube into position. The respiratory therapist gave several quick breaths with the anesthesia bag. Lilly watched the patient's chest rise and fall.

Luther listened at the chest and gave a thumbs-up. "Breath sounds clear and equal."

"Good color change for carbon dioxide," the RT noted.

Tension eased from Lilly's shoulders. One problem fixed. "Let's secure this. We need a tube into her stomach to decompress before we get the post-intubation film." She grabbed the ultrasound machine. A quick check showed the baby's heartbeat steady but slightly lower than reported by the EMS team. No obvious internal bleeding. Vessels and organs looked good.

"Sonya, page OB again. Get them down here. If you have to drop tackle an obstetrician, I want you to do it."

"Come on now, Dr. Reeves. You make it sound like OB never wants to come and play with us." Sonya reached for the phone near her charting station.

"Heart rate is dropping," Luther noted.

Lilly glanced up at the monitor. She watched as the complexes began to widen apart.

Slowing down.

"Is the blood going?" Lilly asked.

"Two pints in." Regan knocked at the small plastic door on the rapid infuser.

A low heartbeat was a poor prognostic sign for the pregnant woman. The problem may not be blood loss from her leg fractures but brain swelling that was causing the low heart rate. Their patient was sliding from shock to death.

"I've got the X-rays here for you." Sonya turned the monitor. Lilly walked up to her computer. She scanned through each of the films.

Cervical spine, okay.

Lungs expanded. Heart normal size and position. Thoracic spine, okay. She opened the pelvic films. No fractures.

Several fractures to each femur.

"Let's secure an OR. It's between ortho, neurosurgery, and OB. They're going to have to figure out who gets first dibs."

"On it."

She looked at Torrence's skin tone and thought back to all those times she had referred to a patient's color as "ashen." Now she saw the definition clinging to life in front of her.

Another blood pressure popped up. At least it was improved from before. "Luther, let's get some Mannitol in here. I think her low heart rate is her brain swelling."

Lilly rechecked the baby's heartbeat. Now, it hovered at 100.

"Let's get her back on her left side and see if the baby's heart rate picks up."

"She's going to code, Lilly," Luther said.

"Give me a suggestion."

The mother's pulse had dropped into the 50s.

"Luther, go ahead and give the Mannitol."

A cool rush of air from behind caused Lilly to turn around. Her breath paused in her chest as the OB attending strode past her to the patient.

Lilly followed him to the bedside. "Kadin, I didn't think you were on today."

"Lilly." Surprise erased the tension in his face. "Didn't Drake come down? I'm really sorry. We're falling apart upstairs. Nurses are spread thin. What do you have?"

Two nurses and a neonatologist followed with an infant warmer.

"Pregnant trauma patient. She stated at the scene she was 28 weeks. Probable head injury and cerebral edema. We're giving Mannitol for that. Two femur fractures. She's had two liters of LR and two pints of blood. Thus far, her heart rate is not responding to treatment. I suspect the big problem is her head. The baby's heart rate is running 100s."

Kadin glanced at the vital signs on the monitor. "Let me take a quick look at the baby with the ultrasound."

The trauma door slammed into the wall.

Dr. Davis, the neurosurgeon, rushed in.

"What's the story?"

Before Lilly could start, Dr. Strevant, the orthopedic surgeon, walked in as well.

"OB and neurosurgery. This is not a good combination." He stopped next to Dr. Davis. "I got the report from the EMS guys out front. Femur fractures?"

"And head injury. Pupils unequal and she's unresponsive," Lilly said.

"We'll need to get her in the CT scanner," Davis replied.

Kadin motioned to Regan and Luther to help him slightly ease apart Torrence's legs, which were constrained by the ankle-to-thigh splints the paramedics had applied. Lilly worried at the patient's lack of response to the surely painful movement. She was surprised he'd be checking the patient's cervix.

Unless he thought she was going to deliver.

Luther's eyes widened at something Kadin said and he began to wave at the neonatologist.

"What's been the treatment thus far?"

Lilly turned back to Dr. Strevant. "We've given her fluid and blood which helped her low blood pressure but not her heart rate. I think her brain is swelling to the point where she's going to herniate. I've given her a dose of Mannitol."

"She needs to get in the scanner now. What quality of life will she have if we don't fix her head?"

"She could hemorrhage and die if we don't fix those leg fractures," Strevant countered.

"Clearly, she's stable from that point."

The belligerent voices of the two surgeons intensified in stereo.

"Five minutes in the scanner is not going to make a difference!"

"It will when she codes!"

The weak cries of a newborn stilled the room. Kadin cut the umbilical cord and settled the baby into a nest of warm towels. The neonatologist hurried the bundle to the infant warmer.

"Wow . . ." Dr. Davis whistled.

"Well, at least we don't have to worry about the baby anymore." Strevant unlocked the bed's brakes. "I'll make you a deal." He turned back to Davis. "Five minutes in CT and directly to the OR. Let's make sure that baby has a mother to come home to."

The nurses prepared to move Torrence. When they'd left, Kadin let out a long breath and turned to face Lilly.

"Why don't we step into the workroom for a few minutes before I have to go to the OR. There's a woman getting prepped for her C-section."

"What happened?" Lilly tore her gown off. "We don't like to deliver babies in the ER."

"When I went to check, the baby was sitting right there."

"I thought she might be contracting."

"Trauma can make the body do strange things."

Kadin discarded his bloodied gown and gloves in the biohazard bin and turned to Lilly, his mask still in place. She reached up and threaded her finger through the elastic and slipped it from behind his ear, the stubble scratching her thumb as she eased it from his face. She wanted to linger with her hand against his cheek. There was something about Kadin, something that came from within, that tapped against the shell she'd built to keep people at bay.

The more they were together, the more she felt her will to keep him at arm's length slipping.

After tossing the mask into the trash, Lilly placed her hands on her hips. "I wish you would have told me what was happening."

"I thought I said something along those lines."

"All I saw was Luther's panicked face." She signed the trauma chart for Sonya.

"While everyone else was arguing, I did what needed to be done." Kadin led her down the hall.

"How do you think the baby is?" Lilly asked.

"It's a girl, and she's gorgeous by the way. She's going to have a rough start, but the neonatal team will take great care of her."

They entered the central work space. Lilly stopped at the sight of a four-foot rose tree, its trunk slender with a rounded crown of dark green foliage set off by full white blooms, standing near her things. Kadin cupped her elbow with his fingers and eased her forward.

"It's for you, kind of."

"What did you do?" She reached up and fingered the leaves with the tips of her thumb and forefingers. Bending down, she inhaled the distinctive scent.

"It's for your mom, Lilly."

Kadin stepped to the other side of the plant and stuffed his hands into the pockets of his scrub top. "I was hoping to do this differently. Be all dressed up. Not be on call . . ." He pushed his fingers through the sun streaks in his light brown hair. "Dana told me about today."

"I see."

"She said white roses were your mother's favorite flower. I thought we could plant it, and then it would be there for her all the time."

"Kadin . . ."

"I asked the groundskeeper if it would be all right."

"I . . ."

"Is it okay?"

"How did you even find one so late in the summer?"

"I bought it in May. I've been trying to keep it alive ever since."

Lilly was mute, trying to search for the right words to express her shock at his generosity, her utter thankfulness at his tenderness, her confusion about the wisdom of entering a deeper relationship with him. Was friendship enough or was she looking for something more? Before she could speak, she was elbowed in the back and nearly fell into the tree.

"There's a detective looking for you." Dr. Anderson nudged her as he breezed by on the way to his computer.

"What's up with that?" Kadin asked.

Lilly shook her head, unsure whether Kadin meant Anderson or the detective. "Long story."

"Are you upset?"

"Not about this." She cradled a bloom. "I can't go to the cemetery tonight."

"I know it'll be hard. We can go together soon as Drake turns up. I'll help you plant it."

"That's not it. The cemetery is closed and my keys are missing."

"Aren't they right here?"

Lilly looked down.

They were posed on top of her bag.

Chapter 2

DETECTIVE NATHAN LONG perused the series of manila folders open on his desk. He knew in his heart his city was in trouble. There was a monster in their midst. Frustrating though it was to admit it, he needed help on this one.

That meant asking the FBI to consult.

Before his demise from the Bureau five years ago, he'd been a lead hostage negotiator assigned to the Denver, Colorado, office. He was well known and respected by local law enforcement for his calmness under pressure, which he considered an honor as his age at the time was just shy of thirty. Nathan's attention to detail and his quirky ability to surmise a situation quickly, determine a course of action, and have the issue resolved in under an hour solidified his reputation.

Most of the time.

That was before he met John Samuals. Initially, it had seemed like any other ordinary day—at least for a hostage negotiator. According to reports, Samuals had been holed up in his rural home in south central Colorado for several hours, threatening his wife and six children. He was well known to Teller County Sheriff's office because of the anti-government literature posted on his property. This included several large plywood, spray-painted signs asserting his right to privacy and weapons. Due to concern that he may be stockpiling guns, he was flagged as a potential terrorist bringing him onto the radar of the FBI and Homeland Security.

Nathan and a few other agents neared the property after a two-hour drive from Denver. Upon arrival, on-scene law enforcement had been unable to make contact by phone. All utilities had been disconnected the previous week. No phone. No gas. No electricity. The temperature was nearing 105 degrees in the mid-afternoon July sun. Combine the record-breaking heat and humidity, and the temperature felt closer to 120. A hot temper fueled by oppressive heat was like a fuse lit on a barrel of TNT.

Nathan wore the famous bureau–blue, button-down-collared polo adorned with the FBI seal on the left breast, which was always his choice for fieldwork. His pants were heavily stitched khakis with large cargo pockets cinched with a department store brown leather belt. The only trick was finding one wide enough with a sturdy buckle to properly support his holster, one spare magazine, handcuffs, badge, and cell phone. Nathan learned a long time ago to spend the money for comfortable, protective footwear. Tired, sore feet could be a mental distraction during a marathon standoff. Baseball cap was snug on his skull to shield from the heat.

The FBI bare necessities.

Nathan exited his vehicle and surveyed the front of the structure. Dilapidated would be a compliment for this home. The roof had several areas of missing shingles. One side of a porch swing had broken off and the free end scratched against the porch, the pull creating an incessant squeaking on the chain that rattled at Nathan's nerves. Old wood siding showed from beneath the chipped white paint, making the house look gray and brittle. Three windows faced his direction from the upper level, and two large windows framed either side of the front door. Nathan noticed a flimsy white curtain pull aside from the middle window on the upper level. A young girl with raven hair and curious eyes fluttered a wave. He returned the gesture. Her fingers lingered on the glass before she was pulled away by someone unseen. The curtain closed.

Raven—that's what he would call her.

Nathan found the on-scene commander, who was the local sheriff. He extended his hand, and they shook hands briefly.

"George Benson. Glad to make your acquaintance."

Nathan smiled. Southern charm was like ice-cold beer to his nerves, smoothing his frayed edges. The sheriff smiled back, his chocolate brown eyes echoed the rich tone of his skin.

"What do you know?" Nathan readjusted his baseball cap, which was already slick with sweat after a mere two minutes outside.

"Seems Mr. Samuals has run into a bit of financial trouble," Benson explained. "Lost work at a biomedical firm several years ago. His job was the family's only income. Been in a downhill slide ever since. He'd been eking out a living by doing odd repair jobs in town but seems his reputation caused his customers to shy away. Last week all their utilities were turned off. So no landline we can use." He wiped his face with a dark blue bandanna. "His vehicles have been repossessed. Today two of my deputies came to evict them from the property, and all hell broke loose. He grabbed a shotgun, got off several shots before they were able to take cover. They knew there were kids inside so they didn't return fire. All they could really do was get somewhere safe, begin observations, and call in the cavalry."

"Was anyone hurt?"

"One deputy took a couple pellets from the shotgun blast to the arm. He'll be all right. That was a couple hours ago."

"Where is the injured deputy?"

Benson pointed to a vehicle near the front of the house. "He's behind there."

"How far out do you think SWAT is?"

"Seems like the devil came to play today. Our SWAT team is on another incident but El Paso County has offered assistance. Their tactical team should be on scene in another twenty minutes."

"When was the last time you spoke with him?"

"Can't say we've done much talkin'. We've tried to make contact through a megaphone. He doesn't respond."

"Has there been any additional gunfire since the initial encounter? You sure he's still alive in there?"

"Oh yeah, he's still kickin'. He's been peekin' from the windows."

"Do you know for sure how many people are in the home?"

"At this point it's an educated guess. We talked to several people he goes to church with and know he's married with six children ranging in ages from twenty-three on down to three months. Several different children have been spotted looking out as well, so we think they're all in there."

"Do you believe they're centralized in any one area?"

"Not sure, but I doubt it."

"You have any floor plans for the house?"

"My deputies are workin' on that as we speak. This house is older than Abraham, and there may not be any plans on file. We're talkin' to some neighbors to see if they've been inside. Bad part is he's an isolationist so even that is doubtful."

"What kind of weapons?"

"We know he has a shotgun for sure. Out here, people generally have quite a few long guns, and there's no requirement to register what they got. It would be hard to say 'xactly what he owns."

"When you're interviewing the neighbors and friends from church, make sure they're asked what kind of weapons he has in the home."

"Not a problem." He ordered the command through the radio.

"What does he look like?"

"Grizzly Adams on crack would give you a good mental picture."

"He's using drugs?"

"Not illegally, but when he lost his job, he came undone. I heard he caused some strange accident. People died." Benson wiped his brow. "We've been in contact with the family before. A couple of times related to domestic violence issues. Wife called once because he tried to commit suicide. That was about a year ago."

"Maybe she should have let him," Nathan said. "Did you make an arrest on any of the domestic complaints?"

"Nope. From what we could gather talkin' to the oldest child, the incidents were all verbal. He apparently threatened to off the whole family and himself, but the wife wouldn't cooperate with the responding deputies. She never acknowledged that he made the threats, and she would just say he was all talk, anyways. I guess she needs him around more than she needs him in jail."

"So your deputies have been inside?"

"Actually, no. He always came out to meet 'em. When our guys would insist on checking the welfare of the rest of the family, John would just yell for them to pile out, and they all came runnin'. He's pretty territorial, and he's got this family under his thumb."

Nathan slid his pen from behind his ear and flipped his notepad onto the burning hood of the command vehicle. The heated metal would have seared his palm in a heartbeat, but the paper provided a barrier and would take a while to burst into flames.

Maybe.

A glint from the front of the house caught the corner of his eye, and he turned to look. Raven was in the upper left window, flashing him with a mirror. Once their eyes met, she placed her palm on the window before easing back.

Not distressed. *She's playing hide-and-seek.*

Nathan took off his cap and wiped the sweat from his forehead with his bare hand, swiping the saltwater on the thigh of his cargo pants. His hat was soaked through to the point that the sweat band was little more than a worn speed bump for all the fluids that were leaking from the top of his head. Confirming the roll on the bill with a quick squeeze, he dipped his head and seated the hat back into place.

"What happened with the suicide attempt?"

"That incident landed him in the county's psych ward on an involuntary hold. He's supposed to be on some meds, but who knows if he's actually taking 'em."

"Can we talk to a doctor—anyone who has provided treatment for him?"

"We can try."

"We need to get him a phone. I've brought a couple of cell phones with me. Let's see if we can get him to take one."

Nathan prepared to expose himself from behind the cover of the command vehicle. He preferred his life before comfort, so he grabbed his tactical vest from the ground where it had been resting against his shins while he spoke with the sheriff. The vest was heavy from armor plating, his police radio, and additional spare magazines for his assault rifle, which was leaning within lunging distance against the side of the SUV. He slid the vest over his head and secured the one open side. The weight and lack of airflow would become cumbersome in less than thirty seconds, but the protection was reassuring. He grabbed the rifle next and threw the specially designed strap over his head and right shoulder, passing his right arm through as well. This allowed the light weapon to drape across his chest for quick access and fast target acquisition. Nathan physically and visually verified his selector switch was on SAFE, and he pulled the bolt back all the way and released it to seat a round into the firing chamber. Pulling the bolt back again, only about an inch, he verified he'd chambered a round and the weapon was hot. Never before had he found it empty, but he always checked twice. Maintaining this ritual in every situation ensured he wouldn't miss a step under stress.

Nathan grabbed the megaphone off the bumper and leaned out from behind cover, exposing himself as little as possible.

"Mr. Samuals. John Samuals! My name is Nathan Long, and I work for the FBI." He paused, waiting for the gunfire that could ensue from announcing that federal law enforcement was present.

Only stillness.

"Sheriff Benson was kind enough to call me in. Said you and he were having a little trouble."

A window slid open and the barrel of a rifle poked out. Nathan's instincts forced him to pull back a little at the sight of the subject's weapon.

"Are you a man in position to help me?"

"Hopefully! I want to try my best to do so. Can I get you a phone so we can stop yelling?"

"I have one!"

Nathan turned to Sheriff Benson, who shrugged in response. Nathan rubbed a drop of sweat out of his eye. "What's the number?"

Samuals rattled it off. Nathan grabbed his own phone and dialed. Samuals picked up immediately and pulled the shotgun from the window.

"I don't want to be forced out of my home."

"All right, Mr. Samuals. We can work all of this out. We'll get a call into the bank, see what we can do. Can I call you John?"

"That'd be all right."

"I need to know how everyone is doing. Who's in there with you today?"

"My whole family and Lucent."

"So your wife and all your children are there?"

"Yes, and Lucent."

"Who's Lucent?" Nathan asked, not only over the phone but to Benson as well. Another shrug. Nathan shook his head in disbelief.

Lord, a little help here. Just a little.

In the right upper window, Raven held up a picture of a big red heart.

"He's a man. Tells me what I should do."

"What's he telling you to do right now?" Nathan watched the SWAT team truck bump its way down the dirt driveway.

"To kill my family. Says to get rid of them since I can't take care of them anymore."

Nathan's spine tingled despite the heat.

"John. We're going to help you take care of your family so you don't have to do anything like that. Can you promise me not to hurt them?"

"I don't like to make promises I can't keep."

"Are they hurt now?"

"No, not yet."

"Can I talk to Lucent?"

"I'll put the phone to his ear."

Nathan wiped his neck with a towel. "Hello? Lucent?" Dry static was all he heard.

"Did you hear what he said?" John asked.

"No. What did he say?"

"That you don't have too long."

"John, I need you to promise me you won't hurt any of them. And that you'll tell me if you're thinking about hurting them."

"I'll try."

"John, I understand you have a baby in there. Is she okay? I'm concerned about her because of the heat and all."

"It's a boy, and he's doing fine. He was crying pretty good earlier, but he's quiet now."

Nathan was appealing to the man's fatherly instinct to protect his children, but John's description of the infant caused him concern. Was the baby too weak to make noise, or had he merely cried himself to sleep?

"Are you guys hungry in there? Can we bring you some food and cold drinks?"

"Yeah, we haven't eaten in a few days."

"All right, John. I'm going to get some things together for you, and I'll call you back." Nathan disconnected the phone and disappeared behind cover.

"I've got his psychiatrist on the phone." A uniformed deputy handed him another cell.

"Hello, this is Nathan Long. I'm a negotiator with the FBI. With whom am I speaking?"

"Dr. Lucy Freeman."

"I understand John Samuals was under your care recently."

"Yes, he was."

"Can you tell me, specifically, what for?"

"That would be a breach of his patient confidentiality. If you'd like to present me with a warrant, I'd be happy to release his records to you and have a conversation with you then."

Nathan slapped his hand on the top of the car. The searing heat fueled his frustration.

"Dr. Freeman, I understand your need to wrap this all up in a nice little package. I also understand patient confidentiality issues and HIPAA violations and such. But let me explain to you that John Samuals is currently holding his entire family hostage. Yes, that would be his wife and six children, and he's armed with a shotgun at this very moment. Oh, and there seems to be a man named Lucent involved. So if your conscience is fine with him killing these individuals, which he is currently threatening to do, without aiding me in any way, then I guess we can end this conversation until I get you that warrant you requested."

"He says Lucent is there?"

"Yes, and that Lucent is telling him to kill his family."

"That's a problem."

"No kidding."

He heard a heavy sigh on the line. Nathan kept quiet, hopefully allowing the silence to give her mind time to make a favorable decision.

"Can I get some kind of documentation after this is all over, no matter what the outcome, detailing these exigent circumstances which are forcing my cooperation with you due to a life-and-death situation?"

"Yes, ma'am. I will get you an FBI letterhead memorandum that will most certainly protect you."

"Lucent is not real. He's a hallucination. He's the one that prompted John's suicide attempt."

"How did he try to kill himself?"

"He stabbed himself in the abdomen. Knives are a fascination for him. We started him on some antipsychotics. Under the medication, the hallucinations were kept at bay, and we discharged him home. Obviously, he's not taking them anymore."

"It may not be his fault. The family has run into significant financial difficulty."

"You're right. These medications do tend to be expensive."

"Do you have any advice on how to handle him?"

"He takes Lucent's advice very seriously. If Lucent is telling him to kill his family, I'd be very worried about that. You're not going to be able to control the hallucination unless you medicate him."

"All right, we'd appreciate you keeping close to the phone. Please give this deputy a number where we can reach you at all times if we need more help."

"Certainly."

Nathan handed the phone back. A tall man with bright blue eyes and military-cut blond hair in full SWAT dress approached him, extending his hand.

"Lee Watson, TAC team leader."

"Nice to have you here. Do you know Sheriff George Benson?" Lee nodded, and they shook hands. "I'm Nathan Long, FBI negotiator. I've got a handful of agents with me spread out in a loose perimeter right now. The sheriff's got himself and a couple of deputies, one of whom is injured. He caught the edge of a shotgun blast and needs to be evacuated."

"Okay. We'll make that our number-one priority right now. We passed a staged ambulance on the road in. We'll get the wounded officer to them. The situation is too active for them to come up here. Sheriff Benson," Watson said, "if it's all right with you, I'd like to start deploying my guys in a perimeter around the house and have my snipers start scouting out some good observation posts. I'll have my entry team grab a couple of shields, and we'll get your wounded man safely to a vehicle and bus him out to the ambulance."

"Thank God. Just let me know what you need."

Watson clapped his shoulder. "Don't worry. My guys can handle the evacuation of your wounded deputy."

Nathan lowered the brim of his sweaty cap, shielding his eyes from the sun.

"Actually, Sheriff, I need you to put together a box of sandwich fixings, soda, water, and juice boxes for the kids. Get a bag of ice in there, too. I don't want these sandwiches already made. I want them to have to do it. And throw in some chips and candy."

"I'll get to work on that." Benson walked away and signaled a few of his deputies closer.

Watson squawked something brief into his radio, and Nathan saw an eager young SWAT member sprint over to their tactical vehicle. Watson gave his secondary a brief but meaningful order, and he was off in no time.

"I haven't gotten the full details yet, Nathan. Can you fill me in?"

"John Samuals has taken hostage his wife and six children. He's suffering a psychotic break, likely brought on by his financial difficulties and inability to purchase his antipsychotic meds. It all started when the sheriff's deputies arrived this A.M. to evict him. Apparently the bank has foreclosed on the property. He says he wants to stay in his home. He produced a shotgun and cranked off a few rounds, most likely birdshot. As you know, one deputy suffered minor injuries. I think that's the least of our problems."

"We need to try to get eyes and ears," Watson said.

Nathan watched as several of Watson's team members set up a perimeter. "Our major issue is Lucent."

"Who's that?"

"This is the not-so-good part. Evidently, Lucent is an imaginary friend, a hallucination. About a year ago, Lucent told John to kill himself and the subject actually stabbed himself in the gut. Now, Lucent is telling him to kill his family. According to his psychiatrist, John loves knives. She says Lucent is as real to him as you and I standing here in front of one another, and we need to be very concerned about Samuals' interaction with him."

Watson nodded in silent concern. "This is bad. Hallucinations and a knife as a preferred weapon are a silent, deadly combination."

"Agreed."

"What's your approach?"

"I'm going to try to trade the three youngest children for food. We've got an infant in there who may be in the early stages of heat exhaustion. I'm hoping when they have to work together to get lunch made, he'll look upon them more favorably, be less likely to want to hurt them. Also, so far it looks like he's letting the family roam freely in the home. We need to watch for opportunities to coax them out individually. I don't want your guys to approach the residence without approval, but they are free to coax these people out with hand signals, smiles, chocolate bars, whatever."

One of Watson's boys approached. "Nathan, this is Ryan. He's the entry team leader."

He gave a quick nod to Nathan before turning to Lee. "Sarge, there's a window on the north side with good cover up to about the last three feet. Oscar was able to approach without being detected, and he slipped a microphone inside. Snipers say there hasn't been anyone in that room since they set up. All we're picking up on the mike is the voice of one male. He seems to be talking to himself or to someone who's not talking back."

"What's he saying?" Watson asked.

"'Please, Lucent, don't make me. I don't want to kill them.'"

Watson adjusted his Kevlar vest, and his shirt remained unmarred by sweat stains. Nathan's eyebrows hitched upward.

How does this man not sweat?

Lee shielded his eyes from the sun and glanced at Nathan. "Looks like your assessment is on target."

Nathan watched as three more of Lee's men, two protected by heavy shields, the third man behind, reached the injured deputy and dragged him to the edge of the perimeter. Once at a safe distance, the team put him in a car for transport to the ambulance down the road.

John Samuals remained quiet.

Watson pressed his ear piece tighter and nodded.

"Is your deputy okay?" Nathan asked.

Ryan smirked, amused at the radio transmission as well. "Yeah. Poor guy wanted to be Superman. He didn't want to leave the scene. The sheriff had to give him a direct order."

"Well, I'm sure he'll get a nice medal for that. Do we have our building sketch done yet?" Watson asked.

"Yes, sir. It's posted on the backside of our vehicle."

"Good job. We'll need to plan to go in heavy with shields and masks. Figure out where Joey needs to set up with his gas gun in order to get that whole house with CS." Watson turned, surveying the crew. "Sheriff! Got a second?"

"Just wrappin' up the food. What's up?"

"Sheriff, as you know, our subject has already used deadly force against one of your deputies, and we don't have any reason to believe that he won't react the same if we attempt to make entry. Can I give my shooters permission to take this guy out if the opportunity presents itself?"

"Nathan? What's your assessment?"

He was relieved Benson was willing to listen to more than one point of view considering his own man had been shot. Tactical decisions were best made by a group of seasoned officers rather than one stressed out sheriff who wanted to ensure his injured deputy got justice.

"Sheriff, I agree with Watson. I think this guy will shoot right now if we attempt to make entry. But the negotiations have just begun, and he's expecting a call from me. As long as I feel like Samuals is actively participating in the process, I have a hard time agreeing with flipping this guy's switch at the first chance. I want to keep him talking, use the SWAT team to observe his movements, and maybe come up with a solid plan to catch him off guard and take him down without killing him. However, at the first moment I perceive he is giving up on the negotiations and becoming unpredictable, I will let Lee know, and he can give the order to shoot on sight."

"What do you think, Watson?" Benson asked.

"We can work within those parameters. Ryan?"

"I'm clear."

"Okay then." Benson grabbed a blue-and-white handkerchief from his back pocket and mopped the sweat from his brow. "Those are the rules of engagement right now. Watson, unless your shooters think someone's life is in imminent jeopardy, they will not shoot. Let's give our FBI negotiator some time to get inside this guy's head."

"We should try to get the bank manager on the phone. Have him talk directly to Samuals and let him know he can keep his home," Watson offered.

Nathan folded his arms across his chest. "No. Absolutely not. What do we do when John finds out he's lying and goes ballistic? Besides, I don't want him talking to someone he's contentious with. One of my guys will get in touch with a bank representative and try to work up a real relief plan on John's behalf. Maybe if he can get him a couple of months' worth of deferred payments, he'll put his gun down. Then we just take him into custody on the attempted murder charge for shooting the sheriff's deputy, and he goes away forever."

A sheriff's deputy came to a quick stop in his marked unit near the command post. He leapt out of the driver's seat and then scrambled to retrieve something from his trunk. The cumbersome box made it difficult for him to see the ground and he stumbled as he ran.

"There was a mini-mart close by. Had everything you asked for," the man said, placing the box on top of the hood of the car.

"Looks like it's time to talk to Mr. Samuals," Nathan prompted.

Benson inhaled and held his breath.

"Ryan, get your team into position." The young man trotted off. "Stand by." Watson spoke in even soft tones into his tactical mike confirming that his team was positioned. He turned back to Nathan. "Ready when you are."

Nathan dialed. Samuals answered on the first ring.

"John, everyone okay in there?"

"Yeah."

"I have the food and drinks for your family as I promised. I want you to help me out with an act of good faith. John, I want you to put the three youngest children, including the infant, on the front porch. I'm concerned for their health in this heat. I'll send some nice police officers up there to get them. Then they'll leave you the box of food. Okay?"

Nathan waited. John talked in pressured speech, though Nathan only made out muffled garble as he must have placed his hand over the receiver. Nathan tapped his fingers against his chest.

"Lucent doesn't think that's a good idea."

"John, it's your family. You need to make the decision. Think about what's best for your kids. I'm really concerned about your baby boy. I want to get him out of the heat. Don't let Lucent force you to do something that will hurt your kids."

More silence . . . everlasting silence. The black-haired girl peeked out the left, first-floor window.

Peek-a-boo.

"All right. He says it's fine."

"Great. Just do everything slowly. All right?"

Samuals had disconnected the phone.

"You ready?" Nathan asked Watson.

"Absolutely."

Grabbing the box of food, Watson approached several of his comrades. Watson spoke into the mike wired to his ear and circled three fingers in the air behind the other hand, which was stretched out flat. Three SWAT members ran over to Watson's position, one of them hefting a ballistic shield weighing more than seventy pounds. The importance of his job was set in his face. Every man behind him was counting on his stamina and ability to remain steadfast, especially under fire. He was the bullet catcher, and he wouldn't let them down.

Watson passed the food off to Ryan, who took the middle position. The third man was there to cover Ryan because his hands would be full. The three set off for the front door at a steady pace. Taking it too slowly would put extra strain on the lead man. The front man stopped a couple of feet from the door, and then the small unit swung to the right, taking up position along the exterior wall, crouching beneath the picture window before inching closer to the screen.

From Nathan's vantage point, he could see a woman framed in the doorway. He grabbed his binoculars for a closer look. The right sleeve of her dress was torn and several long scratches made their way down the length of her arm.

Scratches or knife marks?

Nathan couldn't be sure from this distance. The screen door opened, and out through the crack was borne a two-year old and a young woman holding a small baby, struggling to keep him contained in her arms.

Ryan set the box of food down to the side of the shield. When his hands were free, he lunged forward in a slow but sure motion to brush the threesome back behind him.

The small child scurried out of his reach and back to the house. Her little fists pounding on the aluminum screen cut through the stillness.

Nathan felt panic rise in his chest.

Ryan grabbed her by the shirt and pulled her back behind the barrier. The child fought to get away. Her cries fed Nathan's anxiety.

From the corner, two additional SWAT members came forward and waved the children to come toward them as Ryan tried to scoot them away from the house. Concern propelled one officer forward, and he snatched the infant from the young woman, tucking the boy into his chest like a linebacker heading for the goal. He offered his back to the residence as a shield for the child and jogged off at an angle that offered Samuals a limited target. The second perimeter man scooped the toddler up in one arm, pulled the young woman away with his free hand, and headed off in the same direction. Once everyone was concealed in the thick trees, they were moved to an additional ambulance.

Nathan's heart sank. Raven was not among them.

When was the last moment he'd seen her look through the window?

With the number of promised children out of the house, the approach team pivoted left and began retracing their steps back toward the perimeter. When they were halfway back, Watson called out that the screen door was opening. The woman Nathan had caught a glimpse of before, presumably Samuals' wife, crawled out toward the box of food. Nathan, along with everyone else, could see that John held the shotgun's muzzle in contact with the back of her head. The further she got out the front door, the more he leaned, hanging onto the door frame so he wouldn't fall forward.

"Sniper one has a clear shot right now. What do you want to do?"

"Hold! No fire! No fire!"

Watson relayed the order.

"This is progress, Lee. He's not going to shoot her because she's bringing the food in. He's just letting us see that he's in control and he's not letting his guard down. He won't kill her. No fire."

The moment passed. The woman crawled back, dragging the box inside, and they both disappeared into the shadows.

"Three down, four to go," Watson said. "EMS is checking out the kids now."

"Good job." Nathan slapped his shoulder. "Your team executed that perfectly."

It wasn't too long after they stopped congratulating one another that Watson received a call from one of his team members who had taken the children to the ambulance.

"Nathan, my SWAT medic wants us at their location. Something's wrong with the kids."

It was rare for people who worked as first responders to become nervous. After all, they had seen the worst of the worst and past that point every day, many of them for years. It was usually children that caused distress.

And usually something that shouldn't be happening to children.

Nathan and Lee hurried to the ambulance that was stationed about five hundred yards away and entered the back. The two older children were seated on the pram, the younger girl clinging to her older sister. Fresh tears made clean wakes down their dirty faces. Another paramedic held the infant to his chest, stroking the back of his head to calm his cries.

Each girl was dressed in tattered tank tops and shorts. There were several open lacerations on each of them. Nathan took a knee before the young woman. He guessed her to be in her early twenties.

"I'm Nathan."

"Keelyn." The water bottle she held in her hands shook as much as her voice trembled.

"I want to be sure I know how many are left in the house. Can you tell me?"

Keelyn's hand clenched the thin plastic, causing water to geyser through the top and onto her legs. She swiped at her knees, mixing the fluid with dirt sending small rivers of mud down her calves. Nathan reached forward and placed his hands over hers to still her. She took a deep breath and closed her eyes.

"Keelyn?"

"My mother, step-father, and three more kids."

"Where is Lucent?" Even though John's psychiatrist claimed Lucent wasn't real, it was Nathan's job to ensure he had the most accurate on-site information.

"Lucent is nowhere. He's a ghost."

"Why did he let you go when I asked for the three smallest children?"

"He wanted me to take care of the baby."

"What are these wounds, Keelyn? All of you have them." Lee bent in for a closer look.

Nathan scooted on his knees a few inches, positioning himself in front of the younger sister. He lifted up her shirt, revealing puncture wounds that dotted her abdomen and chest.

"They're hesitation marks," Nathan said. "He's been practicing with his knife on them. Trying to get up the nerve to do as Lucent asks."

"The baby?" Lee asked.

The paramedic gently lifted the back of the infant's shirt.

He was the worst of all of them.

"Keelyn, did your step-father do this?" Lee asked.

Her trembling became so severe that Nathan eased the water bottle from her hand. Lee sat next to her and placed a protective arm around her shoulders.

"Why?"

"He does as Lucent asks."

"Why do you let him?" Nathan persisted. Lee's piercing look told him he'd crossed a line.

"If we didn't, he said he'd kill my mother."

"He promised me he wasn't going to hurt them." Nathan stood.

"We've got to get in there." Lee eased away from Keelyn and waived the SWAT medic over.

"Wait, Lee. Let me call."

Nathan grabbed the phone. It rang. This time there was a delayed answer. It stopped ringing, but there wasn't any salutation.

"John? Can you hear me?"

"I'm sorry . . ."

"John, what's happened?"

"I couldn't take it. Lucent said they would at least be in heaven."

"What did you do, John!"

The response sounded like a prayer, broken by loud sobbing.

"Lee! Hit the house now! Take it down!"

Lee jumped from the back of the ambulance, landing solidly on two feet, barking orders through his earpiece. Ryan's team sprinted for the front door. At the side of the house, three members of the perimeter group busted windows by pitching flash-bang grenades. The sound was like thunder, deafening even at a distance. The entry team poured through the front door, which had been broken in half by a well-aimed kick.

A shotgun blast rang out.

Nathan was troubled by what he didn't hear.

No screaming or crying from frightened children.

Please, Lord.

He stepped down from the rig and walked slowly to the house. He could hear the men shouting as they cleared the residence. The commotion was over in seconds and there was a cloud of dust caught in the humid air. Waves of heat distorted his vision as he continued to walk forward. Two officers half fell, half pulled John Samuals out of the front of the house.

"Get the medics in here!"

Nathan ran forward and crossed over the threshold.

The wife and remaining children were piled up, a hill of bodies bathed red in the middle of the living room, duct tape over their mouths so their screams of pain would be silenced. He eased limp forms off the pile, placing them on their backs; each had wounds incompatible with life.

Raven was at the bottom.

Picking her up, he placed his cheek next to her lips and felt the flutter of her breath whisper against the side of his face. Her brown eyes opened and settled on his before she twisted from his embrace, crying and reaching for her mother.

He felt something inside himself shatter.

Sometimes it's hard to identify a man's breaking point.

But Nathan knew it was this day for him.

As he held the young girl in his arms and rocked her gently, stroking her head and pulling her eyes away from the mother she longed for, Nathan knew this was his last day with the FBI.

This day, he started his list of unforgivables.

And this was number one.

Chapter 3

September 3

Kadin hovered over Sara, the baby he'd delivered from Torrence Campbell in the ER a week ago. She was snuggled in lamb's wool, lying within the clear walls of the Isolette, her black hair combed and parted to one side. A pink bow with pearl center was secured to her head with a drop of corn syrup. A tube parted her pale lips.

He glanced at the monitor and watched the infant's heart rate dropping despite the efforts of Dr. Kerns, the neonatologist who now looked down with a defeated countenance. Nancy, Torrence's mother, held the small baby's hand between her fingers. She caressed the ivory skin, tears threatening to breach her lower eyelids. Paul, her husband, seemed to sink within himself and leaned against a chair one of the nurses had brought for him. He refused to sit down.

"There is honestly nothing more we can do," Dr. Kerns said, his voice breaking pitch.

"Won't you try to restart her heart if it stops?" Paul asked.

"Sara is already on the maximum amount of medications that we can use to keep her heart going. Again, as I've told you, the issue is not with her heart. Her problem is the large bleed in her head. Because of it, her brain cannot control the functions of her body anymore. That's why she's dying."

"What about taking her to surgery and taking the clot out?" Nancy said through stifled tears.

"The blood is diffuse and can't be removed. I think your time will be better spent saying good-bye."

Kadin rested a gentle hand over Nancy's arm. She gripped the baby's hand tighter and closed her eyes. Tears split caverns down each cheek. Paul withered into the chair, dropping his face into his hands. His shoulders heaved.

"Do you mind if I say a prayer for Sara?" Kadin asked. With her free hand, Nancy dabbed each of her eyes with a crumpled, torn tissue as she nodded her assent. "Lord, we pray for Sara. We ask that you swaddle her in your comfort and ease her suffering. Give peace to her loving grandparents as you come today to take her home."

In his peripheral vision, Kadin saw the woman swoon and reached for her arm to hold her steady. One of the nurses sensed his plight and rolled an additional chair to the bedside. He eased her gently into the seat.

For several minutes, each was quiet. Dr. Kerns watched the monitor. Paul was stoic, eyes wide and unblinking. Nancy wept without making a sound. Kadin prayed silently, both of his hands covering the baby through the portholes.

Finally Kadin secured the closures and turned from the Isolette. He lowered himself to his knees in front of the grandmother. "I want to take Sara to Torrence."

"That will kill her!" Nancy pushed up from her chair. Kadin stood as well, stepping back.

"I think it could help her. She's never had a chance to be with the baby." Dr. Kerns turned away from the monitor, arms folded across his chest.

"Do we have to tell her the baby is dying?" Paul asked.

"We can leave that to your discretion," Kadin answered.

"I think we should, Nancy. Just bring the baby to her and see what happens. Torrence is strong."

"The baby is the whole reason she's dying!" Nancy clutched her shirt in her hands. "If Torrence had done what that monster asked and done away with it, she wouldn't be in such straights!"

"Nancy, we will not travel down this path. I know you don't mean it! The only guilty party is the man who victimized her."

"And we still don't even know that. Nothing good has come from her keeping the baby."

Paul stood in defiance and approached Kadin. "Take the baby to Torrence." He turned to Kerns. "We give you permission to stop your efforts to save Sara's life."

After those words, he left. Nancy followed with slow steps in his wake, once glancing back with pain-ridden eyes. "Forgive me," she mouthed.

Dr. Kerns was at the Isolette. He opened the side access door and pulled Sara toward him. He made quick work of disconnecting the monitors and removed the breathing tube from her lungs. One of the nurses approached Kadin, a white patchwork blanket with pink stars folded between her hands.

"Is this one of my sister's quilts?" Kadin asked.

"We've been saving this one for the right baby." She unfolded the blanket and placed it over Kadin's outstretched arms. His throat thickened. Dr. Kerns placed the infant in the middle, bundling the edges around her and bringing the top down to cover her face.

"Steve, thanks for letting me do this."

"You're going to need to hurry," he said.

Kadin turned to the nurse who'd brought the quilt. "Call the ICU for me—."

"Already done." She smiled, nudging him forward.

Leaving the neonatal ICU with Sara, Kadin rounded the last hall and waited for the elevator. Sometimes his determination in bonding babies with their mothers, even if they were dying, defied logic. In reality, it was penance for an act that had caused unending suffering to someone close to him.

Early in his career, his sister miscarried a baby at twenty weeks that was disfigured from a rare genetic mutation. Fearing the trauma it would inflict on Ellie's psyche, he refused to let her see or hold the baby, convincing her she would heal better if she never connected to the infant.

It resulted in the exact opposite.

Ellie grieved the baby in every quilt she made for other sick infants. The nursery was a kaleidoscope of her tears. Even after five years, she didn't stop sewing through her despair.

It was always the unknowing that festered open wounds.

A woman tapped his shoulder. The elevator doors opened in front of him.

"Can I see the baby?" She reached forward, attempting to pull the corner of the quilt up to see Sara's face.

He swiveled his body, and the cloth slipped from the woman's fingers.

"I'm sorry, she's got RSV. No harm to you, but we don't want to spread the virus around the hospital." Scurrying into the elevator, he pushed the button for his desired floor. The woman's blank look was framed by the closing doors. He leaned against the back wall, letting his held breath escape slowly.

He made his way to Torrence's room and saw Lilly at her bedside. Joy edged into his sadness.

"Not enough mayhem to keep you busy in the ER today?" Kadin hugged the infant close to his chest.

"I came to check on her. The nurses told me you were bringing the baby. I thought I'd sit with you."

"How is Torrence doing?"

"Her parents made her a DNR. The neurosurgeon believes she'll be in a persistent vegetative state from her head injury. Her organs are failing. It's not likely she'll live much longer. The baby?"

"Kerns let me bring her here to say good-bye."

Lilly crossed the room, grabbed the wooden rocker that sat in the corner and pushed it closer to Kadin.

"The baby may be what Torrence is holding on for. Her injuries are so devastating that there's really no reason she should still be alive."

"Maybe we should call her parents," Kadin said.

"They were just here and made it clear they don't want to come back. They've already said good-bye."

"I guess we better not waste any more time. Shall we introduce Sara to her mother?"

Kadin stood and approached the bedside. Tubes snaked out from beneath Torrence's covers. The ventilator and dialysis machines hissed and hummed in the background. He rested Sara at the foot of the bed and unwrapped her from the quilt. Removing the blankets nearest him, he pulled Torrence's arm away from her body and with one hand, scooped the baby and laid her in the crook of her mother's arm.

"Torrence . . . this is your baby, Sara." Kadin edged the rocker closer. "She's the most beautiful thing I've ever seen, and I've seen a lot of babies." He encircled Sara with her mother's limp hand. Watching closely for several minutes, he saw the baby breathing only intermittently.

Lilly pulled a chair up and sat down.

"He's right, Torrence. She has lots of black curls, and somehow they managed to get a pink bow in her hair. Those neonatal nurses have some tricks up their sleeves."

"I think they use corn syrup."

"Well, I don't think they could make your baby any sweeter." Lilly cradled Torrence's free hand between hers.

A shrill triple beep sounded from the monitor. Kadin noted Torrence's heart rate converting into a lethal rhythm. Lilly stood, reached up, and silenced it.

"You're right." Kadin rocked gently in his chair. "She was waiting for her daughter before leaving."

"At least they're together," Lilly said softly.

Her eyes drifted to the floor, and Kadin felt her emotionally pull back as if she'd physically walked away.

"This is hard for you." He ached for her to connect with him instead of choosing the hollow well she often retreated to.

"I should go. I'm meeting Dana at my place." Lilly stood and strode to the door.

"I'll stop by later," Kadin called.

He wasn't sure if she heard his words.

Chapter 4

DETECTIVE NATHAN LONG rested the phone in its cradle and leaned back in his leather chair. Tufts of padding sprouted through several tears in the cover, irritating the skin under his pants. Slamming his feet on top of the desk caused his five equally sharpened pencils to roll off to one side, clattering to the ground.

"You know, you break one of those leads, you'll be sitting here for hours trying to even them up in that electronic sharpener of yours. We don't have time for that," Brett Sawyer observed, sitting in the worn metal desk that faced Nathan.

Taking a pen from his inner suit pocket, Nathan flicked it at his partner. Brett dodged it easily.

"At least you won't have to sharpen that."

"That was SMC on the phone."

"You only have one concern there, and it's Torrence." Brett leaned forward.

"They just pronounced her and the baby."

"They both died?"

"One of those cosmic events. The baby wasn't doing well in the nursery so they brought it to her. Nurse said within ten minutes they were gone."

"Funny how humans are," Brett said.

"Yeah, funny."

"What's got your feathers ruffled?"

"Other than the fact that my one witness who could ID this serial rapist just died?"

"You're ready to call him that?" Brett crossed his arms. "A serial rapist?"

"That ER doc was right. We have to notify the public about this creep."

"Speaking of her, did I notice something between the two of you?"

Nathan paused, his silence a giveaway. "You weren't even in the room."

"I was hovering."

"I don't know how to say it. No doctor has ever been that protective of a patient."

"She wouldn't let you get your way."

"Something like that. I can't get her out of my head."

"Let's get back to your theory. We only have DNA confirmation on semen samples positively linking Heather Allen and Jacqueline Randall."

"But we have suspicions linking this guy to four women."

"Yeah, but the evidence isn't strong."

"It isn't that weak, either." Nathan crossed one foot over the other on the desktop. "I think the first victim in the series is Celia Ramirez."

"Because her keys were missing?" Brett asked.

"No, because she stated that his eyes were different colors—one blue and the other brown. That unusual physical characteristic links her to Heather Allen, the third victim, who reported the same information in her original statement to the responding officer."

"Just to keep playing, who else are you thinking of?"

Nathan leaned to one side, pulling a slim manila folder from the center of a stack at the side of his desk, straightening the remainder of the pile before consulting his notes.

"Torrence, of course. She stated her keys went missing but then re-appeared. She remembers an odd tattoo of an animal creature, but she couldn't describe it in great detail. I think this is the same tattoo that Heather Allen was also trying to describe."

"The lion's head with a dragon's tail?" Brett ran his knuckles over his three-day stubble.

"Have you ever wanted to do something in law enforcement that was unusual but you thought it would play out in the end to your advantage?" Nathan lowered his feet.

"Are we talking legal or illegal?" Brett asked, one eyebrow ridged.

"You've done an illegal kind?"

"I'll plead the fifth on that one."

"Have you ever done much reading about the Green River Killer?" Nathan asked, closing the folder and realigning it with the rest.

"They use that case a lot in teaching about serial rapists. I can't say I've done any reading on my own about it."

"Gary Ridgeway was convicted of raping several women in the SeaTac area of Washington. Early in his crimes, he left semen behind. At the time, they weren't doing DNA typing, and what they could do wasn't very effective at identifying a single suspect. One of the detectives came across Ridgeway several years into the investigation during a prostitution sting. He had him chew on a cotton ball for evidence even though they were limited in what they could do with it. When DNA typing came along nearly a decade later, they matched that saliva with semen at several of the crime scenes. It's what led to his conviction."

"And how does this relate to our case?" Brett rested back in his equally abused chair.

"It's Torrence's baby I'm most disturbed about."

"Why?"

"Our guy is very interesting in the type of evidence he leaves behind."

Nathan stood from the desk and approached a large, dry-erase board with photos of several women aligned vertically to one side. He ran his finger slowly over each one.

"I made this link chart to illustrate what I'm proposing as his series. We'll start at the beginning." Nathan pointed to the photo at the top of the board.

"Victim one: Celia Ramirez. Victim two: Torrence Campbell. Victim three: Heather Allen. Victim four: Jacqueline Randall. Semen samples positively link the last two victims as having the same perpetrator. It's what's missing from the crime scenes that I find unusual. No hair, no saliva, no skin scrapings from under their fingernails that would otherwise identify him."

"We know he spends time bathing them. It's likely his ritual versus him trying to clean up evidence."

"Victim one, Celia Ramirez, likely destroyed the semen sample. She states that she showered and douched several times before notifying police of the rape." Nathan paused a moment before placing his finger next to Torrence's photo. "Torrence did the same thing—showered and douched. No recovery of a sample from her, but she ends up pregnant."

"Obviously sperm was left behind in Torrence, but you also think there would have been in Celia?" Brett clarified.

"Yeah, and I wonder why our criminal doesn't care that he leaves it behind. He's highly intelligent. It's not him being sloppy." Nathan turned his back to the board.

"Maybe he doesn't like to wear his raincoat when it's raining." Brett smiled.

"I don't think that's it."

"Then what do you think?"

"I don't know. Why would he hunt down the only victim that became pregnant?" Nathan pressed.

"We're not sure it was him."

Nathan hit the board with an open palm. "She was run off the road on her way here!" Several sticky notes drifted to the floor.

"All right . . . all right. I'll give you that it likely was him. He could have caught wind of the ID."

"That's even worse—it would mean we have a mole tipping him off."

"You're right. That would be worse and an unlikely possibility."

"It's not just the hit-and-run. It's that he made contact with her, telling her to get rid of the baby."

"Doesn't want to be sued for future paternity."

Nathan ignored the comment. "It's perplexing me, but something within me wants a DNA sample from Torrence's baby. I just want to have it to hold in reserve, like that Green River detective did with the cotton ball."

"So get a sample."

"I'm trying, but there's a problem."

"What?"

"It's the grandparents," Nathan sighed, leaning against one edge of the display. "They flat-out refused. They want Torrence and the baby cremated."

"We'll have to get a court order."

"I know. I already have a judge on board. I know this has to be done, but I don't want to traumatize the family anymore."

"Catching this guy will be good for them in the end no matter what they think. It's not going to be that invasive getting the samples we need."

Nathan nodded in agreement. "This guy is very crafty. He takes his time. He watches them long enough to get a copy of their house keys." He turned back to the board. "It's odd. They don't even resemble each other. He starts with Celia, a Hispanic woman. Torrence is next—the all-American girl with blonde hair and blue eyes. He follows with Heather Allen; a young woman, early twenties, brunette with brown eyes. Last is Jacqueline, an older mom with four kids. They have different occupations, social status. The attacks are spread all over the city."

Nathan returned to his chair and placed his palms on the desk. Brett returned his gaze.

"I think he leaves his semen because he doesn't believe it will connect him to the crime."

"Well, that just proves he's another dumb criminal. Science is way too advanced to let this guy get by. We just need one ID."

"Unfortunately, we'll probably get our chance." Nathan leaned into his chair. "If I'm correct in the fact that these are all his victims, then there is a pattern. The last attack was Jacqueline. He usually strikes every other month, sometime within the first week."

"And that would be any day now."

Chapter 5

LILLY RETURNED FROM the kitchen and sank deep into her pillow-covered couch. Grabbing her drink from the glass-topped table in front of her, she stirred it thoughtlessly, staring at no point in particular.

"That must have been Kadin on the phone," Dana said.

Focusing on her best friend, she gave a weary smile. "He's coming over."

Dana set her drink down, nestled back into the opposite mission chair, and twisted her hair about her index finger. A habit that hadn't left her in the years Lilly had known her. Sometimes it was hard for people to believe Dana was an accomplished surgeon.

"I just don't get the two of you," she continued. "There's obviously an attraction. You've been going out for months . . . as friends."

Lilly chuckled as Dana made air quotation marks around the platonic word.

"Neither one of you are seeing anyone else. You should see the nurses swooning over Kadin in labor and delivery. I mean, they're all wrapped around his little finger." She held up her pinky and tapped the end of it.

"You know the reason." Lilly took a sip of her margarita.

"For the swooning? Well, of course, that's obvious. I mean, he's gorgeous, kind, thoughtful, considerate. He bathes the NICU in these quilts his sister makes."

"No, as for why Kadin won't make it official."

"His faith and your lack thereof."

"I think things might be changing between the two of us."

"Is this a joke? It's not fair getting my hopes up . . ."

"I feel peaceful around Kadin. Like all this chaos I try to control could stop. I've never had that with anyone else."

"What about his faith?"

"One step at a time. Isn't wanting to move past friendship enough for you?"

Dana's eyes darkened. "You know I don't take your atheism lightly, and

Kadin won't either." She gathered her shoulder-length brown locks and formed a knot behind her head. Small wisps of hair fell around her face.

"I'm open to his thoughts about God."

"What did you think about the tree?"

"I was shocked, and I've forgiven you for divulging personal information."

"How was your annual graveside visit?"

"We never made it." Lilly rolled the ice in her drink. "That was the day Torrence Campbell came into the ER, and Anderson dropped the case in my lap right when I was supposed to leave."

"That was an ugly day. The OR was a mess for hours."

"I didn't tell you that I stopped to see Torrence today. Kadin brought the baby to see her."

"How did it go?"

"They didn't make it."

"Strange . . . both of them dying the same day."

"The baby wasn't doing well in the nursery. Kerns agreed to let Kadin take the baby to Torrence."

"Not like Kerns to be such a softy."

Lilly nodded, tracing the drops of condensation.

"Have you gone to the cemetery? Did you know Kadin planted the tree?" Dana pressed.

"It doesn't seem right unless I go on the day."

"You drive me nuts, Lilly Reeves. You claim I have certain peculiarities, yet you won't visit your mother's grave unless it's the exact day and you have the right flowers and you can bring a tape of her favorite song. It's not about the ritual; it's about the visit. It's about your healing from her loss. Lilly, it's been over fifteen years."

"To me, it's always just yesterday."

"This is one of the issues with your lack of faith in God. You try to hold everything together in your universe. How much energy does that take?" Dana asked.

"A lot."

"Yet you believe all life came from chance, without external energy forming it. Does your house ever clean itself? Have you ever come home and, by chance, found it was in an orderly state? This peace you feel from Kadin doesn't come from him but from Christ living within him."

So where did that leave their relationship? Was she attracted to him or just to his inner peace—his faith?

"This is not the time to get into this."

"It never is for you." Dana stopped and reached for her hip. "I'm vibrating." Pulling the pager up, she noted the number.

"This is why you should have gone into emergency services." Lilly pointed a finger. "You could have a life."

"Good thing I was just drinking water. I'll call you tomorrow to hear how it went with Kadin. I'll want explicit details."

"Yeah, yeah," Lilly said standing. She followed her friend to the door. They hugged briefly.

"Don't forget your triple locks."

"I never do." Lilly secured the door after Dana left.

Chapter 6

THE FIRST THING that alarmed Kadin was the fact that he found the door to Lilly's town home open. Lilly was preoccupied with her safety. Triple deadbolts protected this entrance, each with a different key. He'd been unable, as of yet, to ascertain why.

He rapped the wood three times and stood, waiting for her tender voice to invite him in. A cool autumn wind whistled through the entryway. He rubbed his hands over his arms to cut the chill. The breeze pushed the door open another few centimeters. The hinges creaked.

"Lilly?"

Kadin worried about protective barriers two and three—her black belt in martial arts and her gun. "Hey, Lilly! It's Kadin. I'm at your front door."

He reached into his pocket and grabbed his cell phone. Taking a few steps back, he leaned against the iron railing. The lights were on inside.

She should be home.

Ringing echoed throughout the living area.

Voice mail.

Kadin disconnected the call and returned the phone to his pocket. Eerie tingles crept up his spine. He neared the door and pushed it open with a single finger.

At first, he didn't see anything out of place. Taking three steps in, he stopped cold. The glass table that sat between the overstuffed couch and chair no longer glistened under the lights. Four more steps and he figured out why.

The glass was missing. He put his arm through the surface and raked his fingers through the carpet below.

There were no shards. The carpet looked vacuumed with organized strips lining the floor. Stepping into the kitchen, he opened the cabinet beneath her sink and pulled out the trash.

There wasn't any glass here either. Not even a plastic liner.

He exhaled, releasing pent up anxiety. Feeling certain Lilly had stepped out to empty the trash, he returned to the living area and sat down on the couch. One of the pillows toppled to the floor. A bloodied handprint showed prominently against the light fabric, like a warning in a crosswalk. Grabbing it, he traced a finger over each chenille ridge.

Damp.

Standing, the pillow falling to the side, Kadin raced to the hall that contained her study and an additional bedroom. He burst through the door to her office.

Empty.

He turned and threw open the door to the closet.

Nothing.

Racing across the hall, he entered her guest suite. It remained untouched.

"Lilly!"

He took the stairs, stumbling several times. Standing at the top, he paused indecisively between the two doors. The first door on the right was the bathroom. He entered. The shower curtain was closed. He flung it to one side.

It was empty, but wet from recent use.

"Lilly, this is not funny! You need to answer me!"

Exiting, he turned to the master bedroom. The door was closed. His chest was heavy with fear. Placing his hand on the latch, he paused.

He withdrew it and knocked.

"Lilly, it's Kadin. Are you sleeping?"

He pounded harder.

"Lilly!"

The metal knob was as cold as his feet.

The fear of changing all he knew and all he hoped for paralyzed him.

Lord, I am begging you . . .

He opened the door and stepped in.

Lilly was on her bed, posed as a corpse in the coffin. She was nude, but covered in a crisp white sheet that was folded over her breasts and tucked beneath her arms. He swallowed thick mucus and walked to the bed.

Reaching down, he placed two fingers on the inner aspect of her wrist and waited. Her warm skin reassured him. The fast, steady pulsation beneath his fingertips proof her heart was beating. The rise and fall of her chest confirmed she was breathing.

He grabbed her shoulder and shook her.

"Lilly!"

Her black hair covered her face. With gentle motions, he smoothed it away and tucked it behind her ears as she preferred to wear it.

It was then he noticed the bruising—anger-inflicted patches of red and blue. Grab marks surrounded both her upper arms. Her right eye was tense with edema. The swelling so tight he couldn't examine the pupil. The left eye appeared untouched.

He pried it open with gentle fingers.

The pupil, swallowed in a blue halo, was small and pinpoint. It ticked back and forth like a fast-paced metronome.

He knelt beside her.

"Lilly, I need you to wake!"

Reaching again for his phone, he dialed 911. The numbers blurred through his welling eyes. At that moment, his heart racing from massive adrenaline release, he realized he could no longer stand in judgment of any patient's family member when they acted irrationally. His close emotional connection with Lilly superseded his years of medical training.

"Police, fire, or ambulance?"

"I don't know . . . I need everybody," he said, choking back tears.

"What's the emergency?"

"My friend . . . she's been attacked." He wiped his eyes with the back of his free hand. "I think she's been drugged. She's not responding to me."

"Sir, is she breathing?"

"Yes."

"What's the address?"

"1225 Aspen Circle."

"Is the intruder still there?"

"I don't think so. Please, can you hurry?"

"We are sir, we're coming."

"I'm scared for her."

"Stay on the phone . . ."

He muddled through the rest of the questions. The next thing Kadin registered was the firm hand of a police officer on his shoulder and the 'man gently easing the phone from his grip.

Chapter 7

NATHAN RACED THE stairs two at a time. He paused at the crime scene entryway and began a cursory exam of the door. Pulling on a pair of latex gloves, he ran his hand lightly over the frame, noting receptacles for three deadbolts. Every edge was clean and untroubled.

The day he was expecting had arrived.

He had no doubt that victim number five was inside.

Two paramedics with a woman secured to their gurney neared him. He stepped to the side, placing a firm hand on her shoulder.

"Hey, Mike. How is she?" Nathan asked, the woman unmoving under his touch.

"Hanging in there. Looks like he hit her with some weird drug. Blood pressure and heart rate are sky high but stable."

"Got a name?"

"She's one of ours," Raul answered, securing the belts tighter.

"What do you mean?"

"Dr. Lilly Reeves. Works in the ER at SMC," Mike answered, shifting the free-flowing IV bag to his other hand. "We run into her all the time."

A vision of this woman in a different dress and manner flashed into his mind. She had stood in front of him with a fist firm to his chest, preventing him from questioning Torrence Campbell. Bringing his hand to his forehead, he rubbed his fingers hard over his eyebrows.

"You've got to be kidding me," he said, his arm falling.

Lilly's question to him about the lack of public notification came to the forefront of his mind. If he'd released the facts of this assailant's MO, would he have this sense of guilt?

This would near the top on his list of his unforgivable acts.

Mike continued, "She was there the day we brought that woman in— the one you thought—"

"I know who she is," Nathan interrupted. A uniformed officer paced a few steps behind.

"You okay?" Raul asked.

"What hospital?"

"The guy that found her doesn't think Sage is a good idea under the circumstances. We're going to Blue Ridge. It's closer anyway." Mike nodded to Raul to continue on.

The waiting officer nearly bumped into him in his anxiousness to speak. Nathan didn't recognize him. He sighed at the thought of working with a rookie.

"Sir?"

"What have you got for me?"

The young man pushed up his fingerprint-smudged glasses and flipped opened a notepad, running a pinky over his notations. "Victim was found at approximately midnight by that man"—he paused, pointing—"Kadin Daughtry. Man states he came here and found the door open. Says he didn't want to surprise her because she's a black belt and has a gun—"

"Is the weapon accounted for?"

"Not yet. He says he doesn't know where she keeps it."

"Have you looked?"

"In the process, sir."

"Let me talk to him on my own. We'll compare stories later. Why don't you make sure the techs are on their way?"

The officer nodded, closed his pad, and retreated to the kitchen. Nathan approached the man at the couch, who appeared to be praying. Even though Nathan cleared his throat and coughed a few times, several moments passed before the man acknowledged him.

Nathan offered his hand. "I'm Detective Nathan Long," he said.

He remained sitting, his hands clasped together. "Dr. Kadin Daughtry."

"Are you a colleague of Dr. Reeves?" Nathan took the chair opposite the pensive man.

"You don't remember me, do you?"

Nathan remained quiet, taking time to weigh the potential trajectory of this conversation. He wrote consequential observations, waiting for Kadin's next move.

Interview of Dr. Kadin Daughtry. Male, approx early 30s. Six feet, brown hair, brown eyes. Unshaven. Tired. Angry.

"You were there the day they brought Torrence in. I delivered her baby," he continued, now sitting as if a schoolmaster had reprimanded him for sleeping in class. "Lilly thought you were hiding a serial rapist from the public. Was she right?"

Angry at me.

"That's not information I can divulge at this time. The investigation is at a very sensitive point."

"If you can't speak honestly with me, then maybe this interview will become very difficult for you."

Nathan stopped writing and set his pen and pad on the armchair. He leaned forward, deflecting Kadin's anger in as peaceful a manner as he could muster. "I know that you must care for Lilly very much; otherwise you wouldn't be here. The best way to help Lilly is to answer my questions. As far as the investigation as a whole, there will be decisions forthcoming that will likely allay your fears about public safety." Nathan picked up his pen. "Can we continue?"

Kadin sank into the sofa. The man's eyes shifted out of Nathan's line of sight as two crime technicians entered the living room.

"Start up in the master bedroom," Nathan pointed to the stairs.

"You know there's likely only one drug that could cause her symptomology."

Nathan turned back to Kadin. "What's that?"

"An anesthetic agent called ketamine. Causes nystagmus, increased heart rate and blood pressure."

"Nystagmus?" the rookie asked. Nathan turned, his glare causing him to retreat.

"The same finding you guys check for during a roadside test for drunk driving. Where the eyes tick back and forth like one of those old, obnoxious cat clocks." Kadin shifted his index finger like a single windshield wiper.

"Where do you think the perpetrator would get that?" Nathan asked.

Kadin shrugged, remaining silent.

Nathan continued. "What's your relationship to the victim?"

"She's a good friend of mine."

"Dating?"

"I would like to, but no."

"What brought you here tonight?"

"I'd had a rough day at work. I called her and asked if I could come over. When I got here, the door was standing open a few inches."

"That surprised you?"

Kadin returned his gaze to Nathan after the two other men disappeared from view. "Lilly never leaves her door unlocked."

"I noticed the three deadbolts."

"She's very security conscious."

"You know why?"

"She's never really spoken to me about it. I know she and her father are estranged, but I don't know why. Her mother is dead."

"Do you know how she died?"

"Cancer when Lilly was quite young. She doesn't elaborate on the specifics," Kadin replied, speaking each word with brisk division.

Nathan paused, thinking through his line of questioning. He discarded some of his more provocative questions in hopes he would get responses to the ones that remained.

"What did you do after you found the door open?"

"I tried calling out to her from the porch. When she didn't respond, I called her on my cell phone."

"Why didn't you just come in if you thought she might be in trouble?"

"One time, I surprised Lilly and found myself flat on my back in the next second. Got the wind knocked out of me. My back hurt for weeks. You only do that once if you're sane."

"What happened after the call?"

"When she didn't answer, I came in. I noticed the glass missing from this table." Kadin tapped his foot on the metal edge. "I went to the kitchen and found the trash clean. I assumed she'd gone out to empty it."

"But obviously not."

"I came to wait on the couch. When I sat down, a pillow bounced off. There was a wet, bloody handprint on it. That's when I started looking for her."

"Did you find anything else odd?"

The man shook his head, looking away, fidgeting his feet against the floor.

"Where did you first look?"

"Here on this level."

"Specifically?"

"She has a study down here and a guest suite. They were both empty."

"What did you do next?"

"Ran up the stairs and found her."

"Kadin, I need you to back up for me and be very specific. Even the smallest details can help solve these crimes. What exactly did you do when you got upstairs?"

Kadin smoothed his palms over the tops of his denim jeans. "I looked in the bathroom first."

"Anything unusual there?"

"The bathtub was wet."

"What next?"

"I came to her door, and it was closed. I tried calling out to her." Nathan waited and Kadin struggled to keep his emotions submerged. "It took me a few moments to make myself open that door."

"What did you see?"

"She was posed on her bed. She was covered in a white sheet up to her chest with her arms laid over top."

"I need to know if you touched her."

"I touched her wrist to check for a pulse."

"Which one?"

Kadin paused, thinking. "The left."

"What happened next?"

"Her face was all bruised up. I wanted to check her pupils but I could only get one eye open. After that, I called 911."

"Did you use her phone?"

"My cell. After that, everything is blurry until that officer came into the room."

"To your knowledge, did you touch anything in her bedroom?"

"No."

"Did she talk to you?"

"She was unresponsive."

"Do you need a break? Get some water?"

"I'm fine. Let's get this over with. I'd like to get to the hospital and check on Lilly."

Nathan collected his thoughts.

"Has Lilly ever mentioned her keys going missing?"

Kadin's legs stopped twitching, his eyebrows arched. He rubbed the stubble on his chin for several seconds. "The day Torrence came in, there was a period of time that her keys were gone, but when it was time to leave, they were on top of her bag."

"Inside?"

"No."

"On top . . . like they were staged?" Would Kadin detect the anxious edge to his voice?

"Yes."

"Who was there when her keys went missing?"

"You know, it's the one idiosyncrasy that I can't figure out about Lilly. She constantly leaves her bag in the central workroom. She says there's enough foot traffic through there to keep it safe. They'd had a couple of thefts out of the locker area, so she didn't want to keep it there. The only doctor I saw was Anderson, one of the senior attendings."

Nathan jotted the name in his notes.

"Do you know if she had problems with anyone lately? Any patients giving her grief?"

"She works in the ER. It lends itself to being a hostile environment."

"So she hasn't mentioned anything to you."

"Nothing extraordinary from the usual weirdness," Kadin stood abruptly. "I would be more than happy to continue our conversation once I know Lilly is all right."

Nathan resigned himself to the fact Kadin Daughtry wasn't going to cooperate until his anxieties were alleviated. He remained sitting, finishing up his notes and listing the areas of questioning he still needed to cover. He stopped as Kadin's shadow fell over him.

"Detective Long, as a physician in this community, I strongly suggest you announce your concerns to the public about this criminal."

Nathan glanced up, struck motionless by the steel gaze.

"If the police remain silent, I'll call the local news myself and tell them everything I know."

Chapter 8

DRAKE MAGUIRE STOOD outside the large window to ICU room 23, debating what action would be best for his partner in practice. Through the glass, Kadin sat at Lilly's bedside, an open Bible between his tented arms and interlaced fingers. He'd been reciting passages, rarely looking at the tissue thin pages, and praying since Drake's arrival.

It was unusual for Kadin to reach out to Drake for help in covering his patients. A friendship had been hard to forge between the two of them. Several factors could be cited. Even though Kadin was Drake's junior in age, he was the head of their practice of three obstetricians. At first, Drake admired his fortitude in wanting to lead a practice so early in his career. Now, it seemed more like arrogance versus confidence not to respect his opinion in certain business decisions. Second, Kadin's emotional attachment with families unnerved him. Unlike several of their colleagues, Drake considered it a weakness.

Third was his constant referral to the saving nature of Christ.

The only one who'd ever saved Drake was himself.

Regardless of their differences, maybe this visit could create a new respect between them.

Kadin stood and left Lilly's bedside. Drake reached out to grab Kadin's hand but was pulled into a quick hug.

Drake wondered if Kadin felt his body stiffen.

"I'm surprised you'd come here. Was there a problem with one of my patients?" Kadin asked.

"No, not at all. The two in active labor have since delivered viable infants. No other interesting calls to speak of."

"Boys or girls?"

"What?"

"The deliveries. Were they boys or girls?"

"You know, I honestly can't remember at this point. Busy day."

Drake shoved his left hand in his pocket, rolling his coins. "How is she?" he asked, nodding in Lilly's direction.

"Her vital signs are steady. The guy that attacked her hit her with ketamine."

"I wonder where a common criminal would get that. You're sure she was raped?"

"The ER doc did a brief exam and stated so. They're waiting until she wakes up to get permission for the rape kit."

"Who's doing the exam?"

"I've asked Melanie. It's nice to have a partner who has privileges at both hospitals. She's Lilly's regular doctor anyway."

"Did the police interview you yet?"

"At her house."

"Have they found any evidence?"

"I'm not sure. They were still working when I left. Do you remember when I covered for you a while back . . . that pregnant trauma patient came in?"

"Vaguely."

"I think they were attacked by the same man."

Drake stopped rattling his coins. "Why do you say that?"

"Lilly suspected Torrence was among several victims. She accused the cop of not releasing the information to the public. There was something odd about the detective that interviewed me—like he was wounded over Lilly's attack."

"Great, just what she needs. A weepy detective on the case." Drake reached down and grabbed his pager from the small of his back. He looked at the blank screen, hoping Kadin would be duped by his ruse. "Looks like I need to check a patient."

"One of mine?"

"No, no . . . one of mine. She's in all the time with false labor."

"You mean early labor."

Drake leaned forward and tapped his chest. "Kadin, not everyone wants to be politically correct."

Chapter 9

September 4

LILLY SWAM IN a sea of fog, registering only a few sensations. Thick cotton had replaced her tongue. Every inch of her ached, but the sharp pain in her pelvis caused worry to creep into her waking mind—worry that she'd been raped.

Slowly, the haze lifted, and she felt comforting warmth surrounding her left hand. She could hear a voice.

First as a whisper.

Then as fervent pleading.

Her eyes opened, blinking against the bright lights. She felt dripping water cascade down her arm and felt her skin with her free hand to see if it was IV fluid. Her fingers traced the thin river to a rough cheek instead. Kadin stopped speaking. As Lilly shifted to her side, he clutched her hand until the pain of that grip brought all her senses into focus.

The memory of the attack became clear and unrelenting.

Lilly curled into a fetal position and wept. She felt Kadin lean over and bury his face in her hair.

"Lilly, it's going to be all right." He lifted his face up, running his fingers through the tangles in her hair.

She didn't know how long they sat in silence. Turning over on her back, she pulled her hand free from Kadin's and pushed the hair from her eyes.

"What day is it?" Lilly asked.

"It's Monday morning."

Lilly reached up, feeling the area around her right eye. She was unable to open it.

"Careful. It's fractured." Kadin stood from the chair and sat on the edge of her bed.

"You were supposed to be there last night."

"I was there . . . I found you." Kadin's voice broke.

"You were late." She turned her left eye in a dead stare.

"Lilly—"

She stopped him. "Whatever you say will not make a difference. What did he drug me with?"

"Ketamine."

"That's not the easiest thing to get your hands on." The bed jiggled as Kadin adjusted his weight. "I need to talk to the police." Lilly struggled to a sitting position. She pushed Kadin's offered assistance away. He stood and returned to the bedside chair.

"A detective's been waiting here since you were brought in."

"How many people know I'm here?"

"You're not at Sage. They brought you to Blue Ridge. I talked to Dr. Anderson. He said he'll personally cover your shifts until you call him. I begged him for secrecy."

The thought brought new tears. "He's never like that."

"He's the one who offered. Drake's covering the practice. I can stay as long as you want."

"I'm not sure I want you to."

"Lilly, you can blame me, but I'm not sure my presence would have made a difference."

The silence was a wide cavern between them.

"The police think he was hiding inside."

"Hiding? For how long? Dana was there with me. We came home together."

"Likely before that."

"How do they think he got in? I never heard anything."

"They believe he copied your keys."

Lilly slid down in the bed and pulled the thin, drab sheet up over her mouth. She couldn't keep the tears from flowing, the salt stung the open wounds around her injured eye. The irony of it all breeched her sanity.

All her safety measures failed.

Lilly cursed herself for not changing each lock on her door the day her keys were misplaced. Her martial arts training had proved ineffectual against the drug he'd injected. She'd never had a chance to reach her gun.

Lilly allowed the memory of the attack to play in full detail.

Dana had left. Lilly was at the sink, rinsing their drinking glasses. The warmth from the fire begged off the chill from a cool autumn breeze that drifted in through the small kitchen window. The quiet music masked any noise that might have alerted her to the presence of a stranger in her home.

It was the smell that made her turn around, an odd mixture of sweat, grease, and antiseptic.

A man, his height well over hers, was scant inches away. The tips of his shoes met her own, his face hidden behind a black ski mask. At first she paused, distracted, trying to discern why one of his eyes was blue and the other brown.

"I've been waiting to meet you, Lilly," the man said, his voice unnatural.

She replayed the memory again to that point, to ensure her findings.

There had been no sound of the door opening. She couldn't remember feeling a draft that would have signaled her that he was sneaking in from the outside.

She didn't want to believe he'd hidden like a spider in her home, waiting for his prey to cross over the threshold of his trap.

Lilly attempted to get in a protective stance when his right hand swung at her, arcing to punch her upper arm. Before she could deflect it, she felt the sting of a needle bury itself deep into her shoulder. Even in the next second as she knocked his arm away, the burn of the medicine swelled within her muscle.

Bolting from the kitchen, she ran, aiming for the front door. Within a few steps, he grabbed her shirt from behind. Her strength waning, she allowed him to draw her body into his. She then pivoted and faced him, grabbing his shoulders and throwing him back-first into the glass table. Snatching hold of her arm, he pulled her with him, the breaking glass like exploding wind chimes. His shirt pulled up, exposing his chest, in the tumble.

Before she succumbed to the medicine, she forced her mind to remember the odd tattoo of a creature with three heads; a lion, a goat, and a serpent breathing fire, joined into one hideous creature.

"You should have changed your locks when you lost your keys, Lilly," the stranger chided.

With her remaining strength, she tried to keep herself from landing on top of him. His hold on her arm kept her fixed, and the last clear thing she remembered was flopping like an earth-bound fish into the strange tattoo as his free hand came up and cupped her head, stroking it like a concerned parent.

What remained of the memory were sensations—mostly of pain, then of water, then of nothing.

Until now.

Chapter 10

"NATHAN, I THINK it would be wise if you let me conduct this interview." Brett crinkled his Styrofoam cup and banked an overhead shot into the nearest trashcan. It caught the edge of the plastic receptacle and fell to the floor.

He counted the seconds it took for Nathan to walk over and retrieve it. Exactly five seconds—right on the mark.

"Her name is Lilly."

"You're not developing a thing for her, are you?" Brett watched his partner's deep-set eyes for full disclosure.

"No."

Brett smirked at his quick response. "All the more reason I should speak with her. I think you're beginning to over-identify with these victims and their families."

"Let's go over the situation. I don't want to screw this up."

"I guess that means you're still taking the lead." Brett leaned back against the wall. "She's had a busy day. Her head seems pretty clear of the drug. She's had the rape kit done. They did find semen."

"It's going to match the other women."

Brett continued. "I'm pretty sure she took all the normal prophylaxis. I don't know for sure since they don't want to betray her confidentiality. I did see her take a slew of pills."

"Has Kadin ever left her?" Nathan paced outside the clear glass.

"Not that I'm aware of. If he's not in the room, he's close by."

"What's your take on him?"

Brett sighed, loosening his tie and releasing the button of his collar. "Personally or professionally?"

"Both."

"Personally, I think he's a stand-up guy. I did some interviews in the labor unit where Kadin delivers most of his patients. He's been there since residency. The nurses love him. Say he brings these quilts for all the sick babies that end up in the neonatal ICU. Compassionate, almost to a fault."

"And professionally?"

"Nathan, he's not our guy. There are no red flags for me in his behavior or background. None."

"I don't necessarily agree with that."

Brett pushed away from the wall. "What are you talking about?"

"Not all his actions seem to be on the up and up. You tell me. You go to the home of a girl that you want to be with who happens to be a nut case about her safety. Her door is open but you call her first on the phone before going in. Then you take time checking her garbage before you check to see if she's all right. It doesn't make sense."

"Nathan, we all know people do weird things when they're in denial. He likely never thought anything like this could happen to her."

"Did you check him for the tattoo?"

Brett approached the window, standing next to his partner. "He volunteered to show me. Nathan, he's not the guy. Why do you think he is?"

"I don't necessarily, just trying to be thorough." Brett was silent as Nathan ruminated. "I have noticed something about the two of them."

"What?"

"They seem into one another, but he says they're not dating."

"So?"

"You know why?"

"No, do you?"

"I just wonder if he would be frustrated enough to push an interaction."

Brett turned and faced him. "Nathan, you're just burning time speculating on nonsense. Let's focus on who it could really be. How did your interviews go with the ER staff? Did you talk with that guy, Anderson?"

"The other attending, yeah."

"If I had to peg someone, I would pick him." Brett leaned one shoulder into the window.

"Really, why?"

"We know from Kadin that he's in the workroom when her keys go missing and show up. He's got access to that drug—ketamine. Torrence was a prior patient at that hospital. Did he have an alibi?"

"No."

"He take his shirt off for you?"

"He refused."

"That doesn't cause you concern?" Brett asked.

"Look, I've got a court order in the works to force him, and he's being babysat until we get it. Brett, he just doesn't feel right to me. I think he views himself like a mentor to Lilly. He's rough on her to make her a better doctor."

"How did you gather that?"

"He said she was the only ER fellow worth hiring last year."

Brett looked into Lilly's room, then back at Nathan. "We need to get this interview done. We're not going to have time tomorrow. The chief is starting the task force, and the press conference is in the afternoon."

"I know."

"Then why are we hanging out here in this hallway?"

Nathan pulled his tie between his thumb and forefinger several times before answering. There were few things worth hiding from his partner. This wasn't one of them. "Brett, there is something about Lilly Reeves that haunts me. I don't know if I want to figure out what that is." He let the tie fall and placed his hand on the cool handle of Lilly's door.

In that touch, he understood Kadin's wariness to discover what he found. He turned to Brett, who rolled his eyes in mild exasperation. After raking his fingers across his forehead to restore his hair into the proper position, he entered the room, walking slowly toward her, but stopping several feet from her bedside. Brett positioned himself nearer to the door.

Lilly was alone. Nathan had convinced Kadin it would be best if they could interview her in private. He'd agreed begrudgingly.

"Lilly, I know we met briefly before when Torrence Campbell was your patient, but I would like to introduce myself properly. I'm Detective Nathan Long. I'll be handling your case."

She sat upright in bed, her body tilted away from him. A single eye stared vacantly at the blank television screen. Her hands were clenched tightly in her lap, bloodless against the neatly pressed white sheet that covered her.

He waited endless minutes for her response. Brett cleared his throat behind him.

"Lilly, I am sorry this happened to you."

Fluid leaked from her swollen right eye. Nathan's heart slumped to his feet. He felt Brett's presence near him from behind and he waved him back with small movements and took a few steps closer. After withdrawing a handkerchief from his breast pocket, he took the chair at her bedside, draping it over the side rail.

Her hand inched toward the cloth. Cautious fingers pulled the fabric into her palm.

"My grandmother makes dozens of these for me," he said. "She's an old southern woman."

Lilly pulled the garment into her palm. "I bet she's wonderful."

Her voice was soft, tired.

Nathan leaned forward. "Lilly, I know you may harbor feelings of resentment against me and the police department. It's only become clear within the last couple of days that we need to make the public aware of how to ensure their safety."

She rocked slowly.

"I can only catch him if you help me."

She turned to face him. He held his breath and forced himself not to cringe at the bruised face and stitched lacerations.

Lilly opened the handkerchief and pressed it flat in her lap. "I'll help you if you promise me one thing."

Nathan felt his throat swell as if he was experiencing anaphylaxis from a bee sting. He choked on his words. "What would that be?"

"I need you to find my father for me."

Nathan blinked several times. He grabbed his notepad from his inner suit pocket and flipped it open. "That won't be a problem. I'd like to speak with him anyway. The more we learn about you and your background, the better we'll understand the man who attacked you. What can you tell me about him?"

"My memories of him are vague, except for one."

"And the one being?"

"The day he left our family."

Nathan swallowed hard. "Let's start with something easier. What's his name?"

"Thomas Reeves."

"Have a birth date?"

Lilly shrank slightly. Nathan moved on.

"Do you know where he lives?"

"I know the address of our house where we were living at the time. I memorized his license plate as he drove away that day."

"How old were you?"

"Five."

Nathan's soul ached at the thought. He imagined her with outstretched arms as she bit her lip to stem the tears, the dust billowing from his tires as he drove away. "What do you remember about the circumstances?"

"I know he was a drunk and a thief. He has something of my mother's I want back."

"What's that?"

She kept her head down and traced her fingers lightly over the pastel, embroidered flowers. A pooled tear leached through the fibers. "He'll know what it is when you ask for it."

"When we're done here today, write down everything you can remember about him. Physical description, any known relatives, places he worked. I'll come get it from you tomorrow and we'll go from there. Okay?"

Lilly nodded and eased back into several pillows piled high against her headboard.

"Let's talk about what happened yesterday. I want to start with more general questions. Where did your locks come from?"

"I had them installed by a locksmith." Her voice gained strength with each word.

"Do you know the name offhand?"

"No, but I can get it for you."

"Does anyone else have keys to your apartment?"

"No."

"Anyone borrow them recently?"

"No."

"Kadin mentioned that they'd gone missing for a period of time at work. Do you know how long that was?"

"I can't be sure. I worked the day shift. I noticed they were missing just before I was supposed to leave. It was a busy day. Someone could have taken them in the morning and I wouldn't have known."

"Did anything strike you odd about that day?"

"Other than Torrence?"

Nathan let the remark slide. "Did anyone make you feel uneasy? Have an unusual interest? Touch you inappropriately?"

Lilly's eyes gazed upward. "There was one man who made some odd gestures. He said he wanted to be seen because he was having thoughts of killing his wife. By the end of my exam, he was asking me for my address and wanted to know what time I got off work."

"Did you give him any of that information?"

Lilly's incredulous glance answered the question.

"You remember the name?"

"He's not the one who did this."

"And you're sure, why?"

"Because he was black, and my attacker was not."

"I'd still like his name. Sometimes creeps like this will run in packs. You never know. Anything else?"

"Nothing different from the usual mayhem."

"Were there any staff there that you didn't recognize?"

"No."

"What was your routine that day?"

"I worked a twelve-hour shift. The senior attending made me stay late to take care of Torrence."

Nathan's temperature rose. "Made you?"

"I'd come back to the workroom to get my things to leave. My keys were nowhere to be found. He assigned me the incoming trauma patient."

"But you were supposed to be getting off."

"It's not unusual for him to make power plays like that."

"He does this with all his subordinates?"

"Not the male ones."

"Kadin relayed that when you finished that case and returned to the work area, your keys were back."

"That's right."

"Did it seem odd to you?"

"At the time, not really. I'd been crazy trying to find them. Everyone knew I was looking. I just assumed someone on staff put them on top of my bag so I knew they were found."

Nathan pulled his chair closer. "What did you do after work?"

"I went to a martial arts class."

"Were your belongings locked up?"

"Yes."

"I'll need the name of that place. Did you go anywhere else?"

"After that I went home."

"Did anything seem out of place at your town home?"

"No, nothing."

Nathan heard the door click open behind him. Turning, he saw Brett step aside for a nurse. He stood from his chair, closing his notes.

"I just need to assess her and get her vital signs."

"We'll wait outside for a few minutes."

Nathan followed Brett out and down the hall a few steps until they weren't in view of the window.

"What do you think?" Nathan asked.

Brett paced a small circle before him, his hazel eyes wide in speculation. "I still think Anderson could be a suspect. Other than that, you didn't get very far. We're definitely going to have to spend time tracking down those locks. We need to get someone with SMC security, reviewing tapes and seeing how they track access in and out of that department . . . and med room."

"Each of the other victims is going to need additional interviewing. We have to get going on a detailed questionnaire to determine where they're crossing each other's paths and this assailant's."

Brett nodded but stopped, mouth gaping as the elevator doors opened and their chief of police stepped out. He clamped his jaw closed, groaning outwardly, rustling up his short, brown curls with several sweeps of his fist.

Nathan stepped forward and offered his hand. "Chief Anson, what brings you here tonight?"

"Nothing good, I'm afraid. Brett, I need to talk to Nathan. Is there something you can be doing?"

The surprise in Brett's eyes pushed his receding hairline back another few inches. It was an unusual request. He stammered without forming words.

Nathan tapped Brett's shoulder with the side of his fist. "I need you to walk Lilly through the attack, forward and back. She released her ER records, so I've read through the doctor's report. See what else you can pull from her. She may be more comfortable with you for that portion anyway."

Brett nodded. "I'll see what I can come up with."

"I'll be there in a few minutes," Nathan called after him.

The chief motioned Nathan into a small vending area. Nathan took a

seat around a small circular table centered in the room. Anson busied himself at the coffeemaker, withdrawing two Styrofoam cups from a nearby
metal sleeve and setting them near the half-filled coffeepot. Nathan sat
silent, thumbing through his notes, not really reading.

Chief Anson was a distinguished man in the department, a veteran of
nearly thirty years and chief for the last ten. Most men spoke of him with
respect, and those who didn't were chastised. He was taller than Nathan
by a few inches and had salt-and-pepper hair with chocolate-brown eyes
that had the ability to draw information out of even the most reluctant
witnesses.

"Cream or sugar?"

"I've had my quota for the day." Nathan tossed his notebook onto the
table.

"How's the interview going?" Anson took a seat and faced Nathan,
blowing the steam from his cup.

"We haven't gotten very far. It's going to take time."

Anson took a sip and set his cup down. "We got the judge to issue an
order for the examination of Dr. Anderson's chest. He doesn't have the
tattoo. We've let him go."

"Brett will be disappointed. Are you going to tail the fine doctor?"

"I don't think it's necessary. He's come up with an alibi."

"Really? He didn't have one when I interviewed him."

"Well, it's of the mistress sort. He was cheating on his wife and didn't
know how to firm up his alibi without disclosing the affair."

"All this seems like something you could have had the shift sergeant
give me over the phone."

Anson took another sip, swilling the liquid around before he swallowed.

"The crime lab van was involved in an accident." Anson rocked the
Styrofoam against the table; the faint squeaks fired Nathan's nerves.

"Was anyone hurt?"

"Simms and Warner were able to crawl out before the thing caught
fire."

"That's good. I still don't get why this takes a personal visit from the
chief."

"No, you're right. It's what was in the van that I wanted to tell you
about in person."

"What's that?"

"Earlier today, they'd been at SMC collecting DNA samples from Torrence Campbell's baby. The evidence was destroyed in the fire."

"Send someone back for another sample."

"It's too late." He stilled his cup. "They've both been cremated."

"Great."

"On top of that, there's good evidence they were intentionally run off the road."

Nathan rubbed two fingers against his temple hoping the counter pressure would ease his building headache. "Just like Torrence."

Chapter 11

September 18

LILLY SLID THE key into the last deadbolt, her fingers pressed hard against the cool metal to keep them still. The first lock was easy. At the second, her heart began to have frequent skipped beats as the adrenaline released into her veins. Kadin's breath was warm against her neck, his body inches behind hers on the landing, maybe to prevent the retreat that her heart pleaded for. Dana brought up the rear, standing on the staircase. Lilly released the lock and pushed the door open. As the warm air flowed out, her back ached from the memory of falling through the coffee table. She took a deep breath, inhaling the familiar scent of cinnamon, to displace the stench of her rapist that still lingered in her memory.

Kadin stepped around her and placed her small overnight case inside the door. "Do you want me to look around for you?"

"I have to go first. It's the only way I'll be able to live here."

He stepped aside, and she entered with tentative steps. Her glass table had been replaced with a mahogany stand. She neared it, smoothing her palm over the intricate wood design.

"Do you like it?" Dana asked from behind.

"It's the one I was thinking about getting several months ago. You remembered."

"Of course. That's just the first surprise."

Dana took her hand and began leading her to the staircase. Lilly resisted her gentle pull.

"Are you sure you still want to live here, Lilly?" Kadin asked.

"We've been over this," Lilly said, her voice firm.

"It doesn't mean you can't change your mind," Dana offered, swinging Lilly's hand in small circles, her brown eyes pools of sympathy.

"I'm not changing my mind."

Dana paused, glancing Kadin's way. Lilly sensed the conversation playing between them was one of silent reluctance. She knew they wanted to be supportive. She didn't know how far she could stretch them.

"Let's go upstairs," Lilly offered, stepping in that direction.

Dana led her slowly, stopping before the master bedroom. Lilly nudged her to the side and walked through the threshold in several quick steps until she was in the middle of the room. Foreign colors swam before her, and she wavered as her vision faltered.

Kadin placed a firm hand under her elbow. She steadied herself and stepped away from him, taking in the new features. Surprise overwhelmed her as the details took form. She spun like a young girl.

"Do you like it?" Dana asked with a girlish lilt to her voice.

Lilly stopped, memorizing every niche. The room was bright and airy. A light sage green was interrupted midway down the wall by white wainscoting. Her mission-style bed had been replaced with a white, four-post canopy with layers upon layers of plush pillows in rose and lilac.

"How did you do this?"

"Kadin helped."

She looked down. The floor was now a rich hardwood, replacing the shag chocolate brown from before.

"It's a heated floor," Kadin said.

Lilly's heart swelled with gratitude. "This is why you forced me to stay with Dana for two weeks?"

They nodded at her conspiratorially.

"We didn't know how long we could keep you believing that it was a problem with the locksmith," Kadin said.

"I don't know how I will ever repay you."

"It's not necessary, Lilly," Dana said. "We did it because we love you and we want you to feel comfortable in this space again."

"It's everything I wanted. I mean, Dana, you remembered every single detail. All those times I tortured you with those decorating magazines, you were actually paying attention."

"You did bore me to death, but I was taking notes." Dana hugged her.

"No one would believe you would want something like this," Kadin said. "It's so different from your personality."

Lilly envisioned her old childhood bedroom. The boyish bed picked up off the street with faded Snoopy sheets. A white chipped dresser. The cement floor exposed through threadbare green shag carpet that would chill her feet like ice cubes dropped on the floor. "It's the hidden child I never got to be."

Chapter 12

September 20

NATHAN ROUNDED THE front of Brett's silver Highlander and waited, tapping his foot to the haunted rock ballad he'd heard on the radio that morning as it played endless loops in his mind. It echoed the anxiety he felt at his forthcoming interview with Celia Ramirez. The glare prohibited easy vision of his partner, who remained inside finishing a phone call. Turning, Nathan surveyed the business before him. Several stalls had cars up on platform jacks. The smell of grease permeated the air even at a distance. Rapid fire drills drowned out the peaceful exterior of the day.

"Ready to go?" Brett asked. It seemed to Nathan that his partner had snuck up on him.

"Are you? What's going on?"

"My ex—up to her pleasantries again. You would keep your mouth shut . . . say, if she popped up missing. Right?"

"What would I know about it?"

"Mr. Honest to a fault. You couldn't help yourself but look into it."

"Probably true. Let's say we go find Celia. You review her questionnaire?"

Brett opened the manila folder, pointing at the sea of bright yellow, green, and orange. "I see your OCD is in high gear. What's this highlighting mean? Looks like a bowl of Lucky Charms."

Nathan plucked it from his fingers as they walked toward the garage.

"Yellow is for similarities, a likely point where the victims crossed paths, with each other or with the assailant."

A high-pitched ringing sounded like someone had pulled a station for the fire alarm. "What?" Brett yelled, stopping near the main garage.

Nathan shook his head, plugging an index finger into one ear as they entered the office.

Brett approached the front counter. "We're here to speak with Celia Ramirez."

The receptionist stood and motioned to two metal folding chairs on either side of a water cooler. "Have a seat, and I'll get her for you."

Nathan began flipping through the pages again. The heavy banging was muffled in this area. Only when the glass door opened between the garage and the office did the barrage intensify.

"Are you gentlemen waiting for me?"

Nathan looked up. Her file picture had not prepared him. Tall, with perfectly styled chestnut hair, a suggestive twinkle in her eyes at her power over men.

"Celia Ramirez?"

"That's me."

Nathan stood, extending his hand. He grinned to himself at wanting to push up onto his tiptoes to regain the height advantage.

"You're somewhat different than I expected," Nathan stammered, grasping her hand within his. If he were blindfolded, he would have thought the handshake was a man's. Her grip was strong, but her fingers were thin and soft and the palm of her hand callus free.

"What were you expecting?"

"A grease monkey in denim overalls," Brett chimed in, offering his hand as well.

"How do you keep your shirt so white?" Nathan asked.

"That would be the function of those denim overalls," she said. Her pink lips formed a bemused smile. "Let's discuss matters in my office." An outstretched, toned arm indicated the direction.

They followed her, like two puppies after fresh milk. She motioned to the floral loveseat that sat in front of her light, pine desk. Nathan sat first. Brett checked over his clothing before taking his place. The cushions caved inward and they sank into one another, shoulders and thighs touching.

"I'll just stand if you don't mind," Brett relayed, taking his usual lean against the nearest wall, tipping a picture off level.

"Thanks for meeting with us this morning." Nathan spread her file open on the vacant cushion.

"I'm surprised to see you. After all, it's been nine months since my attack." Celia leaned on one corner of the desk.

"There have been some new developments in your case. I'm not sure how much I can expand on at this point in time, but your cooperation is fully appreciated."

"I've already spent quite a bit of time with another detective and that tedious questionnaire. I'm not sure what else I can do."

"I understand. I know it's difficult giving up your time, and reliving these events can be anxiety provoking . . ."

"I'm doing well, but thanks for your concern."

"Very well. I'll get to the point at hand. Mostly, I'm curious about your job here. Do you own the business?" Nathan asked, continuing to arrange papers, shuffling through photographs.

"I do now. My father recently passed, and he left it to me."

"I'm sorry to hear that. How long have you worked here?"

"You could say all my life, at least from the point where I could identify a tool correctly and be his runner while he worked."

"It was him who taught you?"

"I wouldn't say formal instruction, but on-the-job training can go a long way."

Nathan squared the edges of the photos together. The images captured Celia hours after her attack, bruised and beaten. One open laceration to her left cheek had required stitches. He studied her face for a few seconds, the scar faint under her makeup. Her calmness was odd in light of the photos in plain view. Most victims wept.

"What kind of records do you keep as far as service to the vehicles is concerned?"

"We've tightened down quite a bit. License plate, make and model, current mileage, service rendered, payment received."

"What about a copy of their driver's license?"

"Yes, but only in the last year."

"Your business is relatively close to SMC. Do a lot of physicians bring their cars here for service?"

"A fair number. I don't make it a point to inquire about people's work. So unless they bring it up, I wouldn't know."

"You must be familiar with makes and models."

"Obviously." She was calm, almost stoic.

"At the time of your attack, there was a pink Escalade parked a couple of blocks from your house. One of your neighbors stated he'd never seen it before and hadn't seen it after. Any of those come through here?"

Celia walked behind her desk and took a seat in her plush leather chair. Rolling forward, she pivoted her computer screen away from them. "I don't remember a car like that personally." She tapped briefly on the keyboard. "There is one in the database. It's relatively new. Brought in for some minor body damage."

"What was the date?"

It was the first instance where a frown drew her lips into a slight pout; her confidence cracked slightly. "January 4 of this year."

"That was the day after your attack. We'll check for hit-and-runs in your area around that time."

She nodded, continuing to scan the information. "I don't think it's related. It was an older woman who brought the vehicle in, Meryl Stipman. Nevada tags and driver's license."

"That's a long way from Colorado. May I see your copy?"

Celia pivoted the screen. "Is it the same vehicle?"

"Unfortunately, we don't have a plate number for the car in your vicinity at the time of the attack. We'll probably give this lady a ring, though. Do you mind if I show you a few pictures?" Nathan asked, finishing up his note and pulling the small stack of photos from the pile.

"Not at all."

Nathan stepped forward, placing them in a neat horizontal row aligned with the grid on her desk planner. "Do you recognize any of these women?"

"I've seen her," Celia tapped the photo of Torrence Campbell. "Her story's been on the news a lot."

"Anyone else?"

She shook her head and pushed the photos back toward Nathan. He gathered them up and placed them back in a small manila envelope.

Brett pushed away from the wall. "I'm curious about something."

Celia brushed a stray hair from her eye. "What would that be?"

"You seem so put together. Managing a business. Answering our questions without much difficulty. Are you really okay, or is this just a front?"

Nathan took a step backward, closer to Brett's position, preventing him from closing the distance, unsure how much leeway he wanted to give him.

"It did happen quite a long time ago." Celia pushed away from the desk.

"It was only nine months. Most victims feel like it was yesterday."

"I've been through a lot of therapy."

"Still seems odd to me."

"Are you accusing me of something?" Celia folded her arms, her eyes narrowed.

"Brett . . ." Nathan warned.

"Not at all. Just most victims we visit, no matter how long ago the attack was, are still somewhat tearful . . . maybe pensive."

Celia shrugged. "I've been taking an experimental drug that's helping . . . let's say soften the emotional impact of my attack."

"This would be of the legal kind?" Brett pushed.

"Yes, of course. It's part of a new treatment protocol to lessen the effects of PTSD."

"Post-traumatic stress? I haven't heard of any drug like that." Nathan reached for his notes.

"All I know is it's helped me a great deal."

Nathan interrupted. "I'd be interested in talking to your physician about that treatment. We wouldn't ask about your specific case."

"Sure. Let me get you one of his cards. Maybe you'd want a few extra for those other women in the photos."

Brett raised an eyebrow. Nathan remained noncommittal. Celia passed several to him. He perused the contact information; his heart popped a few extra beats. Brett neared him, peering over his shoulder.

Nathan tucked the cards into her file. "Thomas Reeves? Dr. Thomas Reeves?"

"You know him?" Celia asked.

"No, but we are trying to find him."

Chapter 13

September 25

LILLY SCRUTINIZED THE chart rack in front of her. She flipped through the stack, noting each complaint in the blink of an eye.

Truth be told, she was reluctant to treat any of them.

It was her first shift back, and she didn't know if she could portray compassion to any of these individuals. A deep anger smoldered within her. The only release was time spent at the firing range and hefty doses of alcohol at night to numb her senses into a fitful sleep. The bruises from her face had cleared, but what remained was the quiet resolve of a hunter in search of her prey.

She picked up the first chart and made her way to the noted room. The police presence at the hospital was noticeable, and she feared questions from patients attempting to determine the reason. Knocking at the door, she paused, waiting for muffled affirmation allowing her to enter.

An elderly gentleman sat next to an equally old woman in a wheelchair, cradling her hand in both of his. Lilly pulled a rolling stool from the corner toward the quiet couple and sat down. A laceration split the wife's forehead down the middle.

"She's mad at me for bringing her here," the man stated.

"Can you tell me what happened?" Lilly positioned the chart to take notes.

"She got up this morning to use the restroom. Next thing I hear is a terrible crash and she's on the floor . . . blood everywhere."

Lilly noted the woman's name from the chart. "Hazel? Do you remember what happened?"

"He's an old ninny for bringing me here." She yanked her hand away from his.

A true emergency and she's mad. Priceless.

"For what it's worth, I think he was right in doing so." Lilly stood and grabbed a pair of latex gloves. "Can you tell me what happened?"

"I slipped."

"The floor is carpeted," the husband interjected.

"Be quiet."

Lilly bit the inside of her cheek to keep herself from chastising their argument. "Ma'am, I can only help you as much as you help me. Did you pass out?" She watched the woman nod then look down. "Did you have any chest pain? A headache?"

"No to both. I just felt lightheaded, and then he was there."

Lilly stepped forward and placed one hand under the woman's chin, coaxing her head up into the exam light. She palpated the wound edges and didn't feel any crepitus that might suggest fractured bone.

"Hazel, you got yourself pretty good. I'd like to CT your head and do an ECG to make sure your brain and heart are okay. Then we'll get you stitched up."

"Seems like a lot of trouble for one simple cut," she moaned. Her husband patted her hand.

"When a cut runs from your hairline to the point between your eyes, it's a little beyond simple. Tell you what. You stick with me for a few hours and don't give my nurses any grief, and I'll give you a lollipop for good behavior."

Finally, a small smirk played upon the woman's lips. "I'll only behave if it's cherry."

Lilly removed her gloves and left the room, nearly colliding into Luther as she exited.

"Lilly! Nice to have a real doctor back in this place. Sorry to hear about your appendix, but it looks like you made it through surgery okay."

"Where did you hear that?"

"Anderson. Why?"

Lilly struggled to respond without raising suspicion. "Just surprised he's been saying anything. Hey, have you met my friend Hazel?"

"Yeah, I triaged her. Quite a character."

Pulling a pen from her pocket, Lilly jotted down several orders. "CT, ECG, wound irrigation, and we'll get her fixed up."

"I'll let you know when she's ready." Luther grabbed the chart from her hands.

"Oh, and see if you can track down a cherry lollipop." Lilly pulled a couple of dollars from her pocket.

"You'll owe me for making a trip to the gift shop."

"You can get one, too."

"Now that's what I like, free candy. Hey, that detective is back. The one that was here with the pregnant trauma that died. You know why?"

"I haven't the slightest."

Her quick response raised Luther's eyebrows. "Well, see what you can find out."

"Sure."

Lilly waited until Luther rounded the corner, then made a beeline to the central workroom. Anderson was there, flipping up several X-rays from an outlying facility.

"I need to speak with you, Dr. Anderson."

He flinched, and the film dropped from his hand. Bending quickly to retrieve it, he snapped it under the holder. "Not like you to be so stealthy." He sighed. "I need to speak with you, also."

Lilly took the lead in his silent wake. "Luther says you've been telling people I had an appendectomy."

"This bothers you?"

"Sometimes a lie is harder to deal with than the truth."

"So you would prefer I tell people about your assault."

"Assault seems like such a nice word. I was raped, and I would rather you tell them nothing."

He turned to her, placing the sheets back into the folder, and took a seat at his computer. "In absence of any excuse, Lilly, they'll make up stories on their own."

"Just have them come to me."

"And what is it that you'll say?" he asked, pivoting the chair toward her.

Lilly twirled her stethoscope between her fingers, looking down as tears welled up and spilled over. She watched them fall, tiny puddles of agony forming mute expressions of her grief.

"Lilly . . ."

Anderson stood and reached for her. She was stunned and took several steps back. His arms fell ineffective at his sides. Wiping her eyes, she met his troubled countenance.

"I don't know." The words were soft, like petals falling from a flower.

Out of the corner of her eye, she saw Detective Long hovering in the corner. He approached, and Dr. Anderson returned to his computer.

"Lilly, may I speak with you?"

She could feel unwarranted anger swell within her chest. Her throat tightened, and she shoved her stethoscope back into her pocket.

"I prefer we not speak here. People will begin to gossip."

"We've been talking to everyone on staff. If we avoid you, it will probably spur them more."

She paused, measuring his words. "What do you want?"

"Can we step into the med room?"

Lilly turned on her heel and approached the numbered punch lock and entered the code, allowing Nathan to enter first. She waited for the door to secure behind them.

"Next time, don't come to where I work."

Nathan held a hand up in surrender. "I'm clear on that. I guess it's not a good time to ask you how you're doing."

"It's not been a great day. I'm questioning if I should have come back."

Her response stilled him, and he seemed to search for words.

"Did you . . . contact any of the victim assistance personnel?" He tapped his pockets, then pulled his wallet from his coat. "Let me see if I have one of their cards on me."

"No!" She paused. "Not yet, I . . ."

"Let's just get through the questions. Maybe we can set up a time to speak when you're not worried about what people might say," Long offered, placing his wallet back.

"Fine. Whatever."

"I am keeping tabs on how often you say 'fine.' I get three in a row, and drastic measures will be undertaken."

The pressure within Lilly's chest eased. She bit her lower lip to prevent a smile from taking hold.

"That's better. Now, I want to talk to you about this drug ketamine. What do you use it for here in the ER?"

"I'm sure you've already broached this matter with the other physicians."

"Yes, we have. But we're looking for holes in people's stories."

Lilly sighed. "We use it for conscious sedation most of the time. If we have to reset a closed fracture . . . something along those lines."

"How do you keep track of the supply?"

"Did you talk to the nursing staff? They're the ones who would really know what you're asking."

"On my list. Just tell me what you know."

"Ketamine is kept in this machine." Lilly brushed the dust off the control screen. "You have to access it with a PIN number and finger-print scan. It's a controlled substance; therefore it must be recorded daily that no doses are missing. The nurses generally do the count in the early morning."

"Any missing recently?"

"I haven't been here for a while, Nathan." His first name slipped from her lips, and she was surprised at how comfortable she felt using it. His pen stopped mid-sentence, and she tapped her lips, unsure if she should offer an explanation.

Did she have feelings for him?

"Do you generally use all of the medicine when a vial is taken out?"

"Not usually. The extra is disposed of, but it must be witnessed by another individual."

"Any chance you can substitute the drug for something else and it not be known?"

"It couldn't happen on the patient side. Ketamine, as I'm sure you're becoming aware, has very distinctive effects. Obviously, a substitution would not bring about sedation, and questions would be raised as to what had happened."

"What about when it's wasted?"

"That could be a possibility. Anyone could say they were squirting ket-amine down the sink, and it could just be saline."

Lilly turned as the security code was punched and Luther made his way through the door.

Stepping past Nathan, she pulled Luther forward.

"Luther, have you met Detective Long?"

"Seen him. Not officially introduced."

"Consider it done." Nathan extended his hand. Luther grasped it within both of his, shaking firmly.

"Mind if I ask what you all are doing around here?" Luther inquired, not yet releasing his grip.

"He's making some inquiries into how we dispose of our controlled substances. It might be helpful in Torrence's case."

"I see." Luther released his grip. "What can I tell you?"

"I'm interested in how the remaining portion of a controlled drug is discarded when the whole dose isn't given."

Luther stepped closer to the automated drug-dispensing machine.

"When a nurse pulls out a narcotic and doesn't use it all, we're supposed to come back into this system and document what wasn't used. This is witnessed by another nurse. It should match up to what was given to the patient as recorded on their MAR."

"MAR?"

"Sorry. Medication Administration Record."

"How is the drug actually thrown away so another person doesn't take it, sell it, or use it?"

"We usually dump the vial into a specialized container. Often times, there are needles in there, too. You'd have to be a pretty desperate junkie to go for it."

"How do you know it's the drug—that it hasn't been replaced with another clear substance?"

"I guess there's a certain level of trust. I think there'd be other signs, too, that the person had a drug problem."

"Anyone like that you're suspicious of?"

"No."

"Who has access to this machine?"

"The ER docs and nurses. But, it's mostly the nurses who pull the drugs."

"What about other physicians who don't work in the ER?"

"They wouldn't be able to access this machine. They likely have their own in the area they work."

"In what other areas of the hospital would ketamine be stocked?"

"Definitely the OR. Anywhere they'd have to put a patient down quickly. Check in OB. They have an OR there for C-sections and at times will put a patient down if it's emergent," Luther said.

Soft musical tones filled the small room. Lilly checked her pager as Nathan finished his notes.

"One final matter I want to discuss with you, Dr. Reeves. Privately."

Luther excused himself after gathering a few supplies.

She placed her pager back in its holder. "What would that be?"

"Some results of your rape kit have come in. There was semen. Your case has been linked positively to two other cases—likely four other women."

"Nathan, did you really think I'd be surprised by that?"

Lilly reached into the pocket of her lab coat, pulling out a small, spiral-bound notebook. The embroidered handkerchief Nathan had given her fell to the floor. She could feel the heat rising in her cheeks as she bent to pick it up.

"I'm surprised you still have that. I thought you'd have burned it by now."

"Why would you say something like that?" Lilly smoothed the wrinkles of the soft, cotton fabric. "It's one of the most beautiful things I've ever been given. My mother used to sew—but all her things are gone. It reminds me—" Lilly stopped herself, brushing away a quick tear. "Here is all the information I could remember about my father."

She held out the journal. The touch of his fingers as they brushed against hers was soothing as he slid it from her grasp. His eyes met hers briefly, questioning, before he opened the pages and scanned the material.

"I didn't mean to upset you." Nathan closed the book. "I just thought your anger with me over these cases . . ." He paused, tapping the counter with her notes as he considered the right response. "I'm touched you would still have it."

Lilly folded the cloth and placed it back in her pocket. "Nathan, intellectually I can understand your position. However, emotionally, I'm finding it hard to fathom why you've yet to warn the public. What I can't understand is that it is within your power to save women from this man, and every day that goes by just puts them more at risk."

"Our going public with this case is coming sooner than you think. Are you ready for that?"

Chapter 14

NATHAN SAT UP from his work and rubbed the taut muscles in his neck with both hands. Several file folders were open in front of him. Brett was conferring with another task-force member at the link chart at the head of the room. He reached for his third high-priced cup of coffee, downed the suboptimal dregs, and placed his head on the cool laminate surface of the conference-room table.

The team needed direction from him. Closing his eyes, Nathan pictured each of the victims in his mind. He'd poured over Celia's questionnaire until he had it memorized. They were awaiting the surveys from Heather Allen and Jacqueline Randall.

He needed to give Lilly hers. It perplexed him that he was holding back where she was concerned, but he used the excuse that they were waiting for Brett to finish tracking down hit-and-run reports from Celia's neighborhood.

He wanted to see Lilly, but not in an official capacity.

These were the threads in a tapestry of a tale of destruction that Nathan feared was about to add an additional victim. Early November would mark the rapist's usual strike pattern.

He needed to visit Thomas Reeves.

Public disclosure of the fact that there was a serial rapist in their midst only complicated the issue. Now, the team had to separate actual leads from kooks trying to get their fifteen minutes of fame. Visions of John Mark Karr flashed through his mind. Karr had insinuated himself into the JonBenet Ramsey case. The state of Colorado could not take another false confessor.

He'd interviewed three attention seekers just this morning.

The air stirred near him. Nathan lifted his head to see Brett tapping a folder impatiently on the table.

"We've got a lot to do for you to be sleeping."

"Yeah, yeah, yeah. What do you have?"

"I just got back from dropping off Lilly's survey. I noticed you hadn't done that. Any reason you want to tell me about?"

"No good reason."

Brett sucked his right cheek in, seeming to let the question slide. "We need to go get Heather's and Jacqueline's packets. You up for stopping by their places today?"

"Sure, why not."

Brett sat down. "You seem fatigued."

"I haven't been sleeping much. I'm worried. I don't think we can stop this guy before he gets busy again."

"You know the FBI isn't going to give us much until we submit these surveys with the rest of the police work. Let's get these wrapped up today."

"Did you find any reported hit-and-runs in Celia's neighborhood?"

"It should make our trip to Nevada more interesting. Yes, a man who lives behind Celia's house reported that his car had been sideswiped, left pink all over it."

"If it was our perp in that vehicle, why is it in Nevada? Crashing the thing would mean he knew it was a risk that he was going to be discovered or he was in a hurry to finish the job. Seems unusual that he would make a mistake like that and be brazen enough to take it to the garage where Celia works. And who is this older woman, Meryl Stipman? Someone related to the perpetrator?"

Brett cracked his knuckles. "Was it that risky for him to go to her place of work? Celia wouldn't have seen the car in her drug-induced state. Maybe the woman is scoping out information for the assailant. Seeing if Celia is there. Maybe taking it to her garage was more an instance of him checking in on her, similar to when serial murderers revisit their buried victims."

"Maybe. Let's get over to Heather's."

"She's not home. She's at the local crazy house," Brett said. "I got permission from her MD for us to have a short conversation."

Nathan relinquished his car to Brett, reviewing Heather's file as they drove. In high school she'd been captain of her cheerleading squad and debate team. She'd been inducted into the National Honor Society and earned full-ride scholarships to several different universities. On the weekends, she volunteered at a dog shelter and the local soup kitchen.

Smart. Beautiful.

Kind.

Heather's assault was akin to spraying weed killer on a newly opened flower.

Next in the file were the photos taken after her assault. Her face was bruised and bloodied. One eye had a repaired laceration near the eyebrow, but her lip was still split in more than one area. Her eyes were hollow, no connection with the camera, her confidence and peace stolen, leaving a vacant look behind.

The local crazy house, as Brett referred to it, was a high-tech, glass-and-metal low-rise of seven stories tucked at the end of a long, gated drive in a grove of pine and aspen trees. Brett let out a slow whistle as he parked Nathan's car and they gathered their things.

"You've got to have some money to be put up in a place like this." Nathan closed the car door.

"It's so still out here. You can't even hear the city noise. Who can sleep with all this quiet?"

"Not everyone needs the rain forest at night to help them slumber off."

"That was a gift from my mother." Brett jokingly chopped his hand toward Nathan's face. "Just remember, you ever let it slip in the department that I sleep with that thing, your mother's going to find you dead the next day."

They were buzzed in and led to the office of Dr. Jonas. He was a short, spry black man whose bifocals hovered on the tip of his nose. Nathan struggled to keep his fingers from reaching out to push them back up. Brett stepped forward first to shake his hand.

"Thanks for meeting with us today, Dr. Jonas," Brett said, letting Nathan approach.

"My pleasure. Anything I can do to help the police."

The feminine pitch of his voice caught Nathan off guard. If he had first spoken to him over the phone, Nathan would have thought they were meeting a woman. The doctor stood to welcome Nathan, readjusting his orange-and-black striped bow tie before offering his hand. Standing did not improve the man's height.

"Nathan Long."

"Nice to meet you both. Have a seat."

"Did Heather sign the release so you could discuss her case with us?" Nathan took the chair Jonas indicated and opened Heather's case file.

"She did. You're lucky . . . not many patients would agree to do this. But this has become her new obsession."

"Meaning?"

"Meaning, Heather has always had obsessive components to her personality. When I first started treating her in her late teens, it was for an eating disorder. She wasn't anorexic or bulimic, but she restricted her fat intake to a degree that she'd stopped menstruating and was showing signs of malnutrition. After two years she switched her compulsion to bodybuilding. I was relieved in the beginning because her eating habits improved dramatically. She was putting on weight and looked healthy. Unfortunately, she was going to the gym three times a day, for two hours at a time. It was becoming difficult for her to hold down a job. For income, she started competing in bodybuilding shows. This was a vicious cycle. The more competitions she won, the more she was in the gym. She started looking into plastic surgery. Then the attack came. Everything stopped."

"As in?"

"She fractured. Her whole personality dissolved."

"You mean a psychotic break," Nathan offered.

"No, different from that. She was never delusional. She didn't experience any hallucinations. Her contact with reality was quite secure. It was that everything she valued before lost its significance. She began to drink, stopped going to the gym. Began writing in these journals trying to recall every single detail of the attack. She wanted me to give them to you along with your questionnaire."

Dr. Jonas reached behind his desk and grabbed a cardboard banker's box. Nathan noticed Heather's name, date of birth, and some other code listed on each side. Brett stood and lifted the top.

"All these are hers?" Brett grabbed the first group of papers and the most recently dated notebook.

Nathan stood as well. There had to be over twenty books. Brett handed him the questionnaire. Nathan set it on top of the glass surface and began smoothing out the pages that looked as if they'd been wadded up, then retrieved from the trash.

"I don't think that's going to help," Brett chimed in, leaning his way. "Look at this. It's full of these types of drawings."

Dr. Jonas peered over the top of his glasses. "I think that's your elusive tattoo. She draws it constantly. In these, she's told me she's getting close to the one she actually saw."

Nathan started counting the books in the box. "There are thirty notebooks in here, Doc. How long did she work on these?"

"She probably filled these in about three months. This is the second box, the most recent. Her pace has picked up quite a bit. Initially after the attack, she had moved back in with her mother. That's when she first started writing, at my encouragement. Unfortunately, her relationship with her mother was never very constructive, and it became too hard for her to live at home. That's when she came here. Now, this is all she does."

Nathan placed the journals back into the box and took the one Brett had been skimming through. He leafed through several pages. "I think what I'd like to do is just meet her today. I want to take some time reviewing her survey and these diaries and then develop the questions I want to go over. Can we come back next week?"

"Yes, that would be fine. I think that's a good plan, Detective. She's been waiting for you in one of our conference rooms."

Nathan stopped, the box in his hands. "Dr. Jonas, have you ever heard of a Dr. Thomas Reeves?"

"If you have anything to do with treating post-traumatic stress disorder, you've definitely heard of him."

"What do you think of his work?" Brett took the box from Nathan so he could retrieve his notes.

"I haven't made up my mind yet. It seems to be helping people, but its long-term benefits are unproven."

It was a short walk to the plush sitting area. A plasma-screen TV hung on the wall. The room smelled faintly of lavender. Engulfed in one of the loveseats was Heather, her formerly muscled body now soft and lanky. She was writing furiously in another notebook, dabbing at her eyes every few words with a Kleenex. Both eyes looked reddened and chafed at the corners.

Nathan walked forward first. Brett stayed back on his own accord. Nathan stood before her briefly, and she cowered before him. If the furniture could have swallowed her any more, she would have disappeared. Nathan kneeled, reducing his height to take on a more submissive posture.

"Heather, my name is Detective Long." Nathan reached his hand out. She took it limply and gave it a few unconvincing shakes.

"You're not the same officer I spoke to before."

"You're right. There are a lot of people trying to catch the man who did this to you."

Fresh tears popped, and the tissue she held seemed unable to keep up with the flow. Nathan reached to get her a new one.

"I don't mean to upset you, Heather. I wanted to thank you so much for the time you spent on all those questions. Your notebooks are amazing. I'm going to take them and review this information and come back next week and talk. Would that be all right with you?"

She nodded, but did not speak. Nathan continued. "Thank you, Heather. You let Dr. Jonas know if we can do anything for you."

He joined Brett, who held the box in his hands. Dr. Jonas excused himself, and they made their way back to their vehicle. Nathan opened the trunk and let Brett set the material inside.

"Off to Jacqueline's?" Brett asked.

"Might as well get this over. It's a short drive."

Brett pulled out of the parking lot. The day was sunny, but the cool air spoke of autumn firmly set into the base of the Rocky Mountains. Residential lawns were decorated with faux headstones, and cotton webbing hung from trees with enormous, shiny black spiders clinging to barren branches.

"This is one victim that perplexes me." Nathan pulled out several photos. "I think his other victims are these strong, independent women. But Jacqueline is a single mother of four children and a kindergarten teacher."

"You don't think you need a strong personality to manage thirty-some-odd five-year-olds?"

"Not at all. I meant, she just seems softer. More diminutive."

"Maybe it's the fact that she is a single mother. Actually, all of the women lived alone. Maybe, it's not their dominant personality, but the fact that they are vulnerable with no male presence in the home. If I remember correctly, none of them had dogs. Maybe, he actually considered them easy prey."

"That's a possibility, but two of them were obviously strong. Heather had won several bodybuilding competitions. Lilly is an expert at martial arts. He had to know that, and I think that's what he despises. Strong, confident, independent women."

"I think it's crazy how people decorate for Halloween like it's Christmas." Brett rolled his window down. "Check the address for me. I think we're close."

"Hold on." Nathan reached for Jacqueline's case file. "House number is . . . 1208." He glanced up. "It'll be on the left side of the road. Here, right here."

Brett pulled to the curb. The lawn was completely overgrown. Shrubs lined the front in snarled masses. As they got out and secured Nathan's vehicle, they could hear the chaos of playful children inside. The screen door hung off one hinge. The smell of cigarettes was pungent at the door-step. Brett knocked. The door opened to a tall, muted girl with dark hazel eyes and matted brown hair.

Nathan coughed a few times into his fist. "Hi there, I'm Detective Long. I'm here to see your mom. Is she home?"

The door opened wider. Brett covered his nose and clenched his lips at the stench as Nathan's eyes watered.

The girl motioned them inside. "She's in her bedroom."

"We'll wait here for her," Brett offered, taking a few steps backward onto the sidewalk.

"Won't do any good. She never leaves her room anymore."

Nathan ignored the look of pleading in Brett's eyes. He wished he could allow Brett to leave, but it would be inappropriate for him to be alone with this witness. They followed the girl down a short hall, peeking into one bedroom, seeing two boys clubbing one another with foam bats.

"Don't mind them; they never stop."

She neared the door, tapped softly. "Mom?" Opening it, she motioned them forward.

"Ms. Randall?" Nathan stepped inside. "It's Detective Long. We spoke on the phone?"

The bedcovers rustled faintly, and a pair of deep brown eyes turned but didn't focus. Her skin was translucent against the sheets. Nathan grabbed a small chair from the corner and sat down next to her.

"Jacqueline? You don't look like you're doing so well," Nathan reached for the nearest box of tissues. Empty. He waved it in Brett's direction, and the teenage daughter seemed to pick up on the cue first. He'd barely turned around before she was back.

"I can't do this anymore," Jacqueline choked between sobs.

"What?" Nathan asked.

"Work. Take care of these children . . ."

"Did you call victim assistance?" Nathan lifted a finger and circled it in the air. Brett reached for his phone and stepped into the hall, though still in view.

"I'm going to get someone here for you today. Are you seeing a counselor?"

"I stopped."

"Why?"

"None of it is helping!"

"All right, let's work through this. Do you have family in town? A friend?"

"I haven't told anyone," she whispered, shifting her gaze behind Nathan where her daughter must be standing.

"Jacqueline, I'm not even going to pretend to act like I know anything about this. But I do know you're going to need some help. You've got to reach out to someone."

Nathan reached for his own phone. "Do you have any family that lives close by?"

"My mother."

"You have a good relationship with her?" She nodded. "Great. I want you to give me her number."

Brett neared him. "Thirty minutes for victim's advocacy."

Nathan handed off his phone after he punched in the number. "Talk to her mother. Get her over here. If she can't drive, we'll come and get her." Turning back, he pulled the caked blonde strands of hair away from Jacqueline's eyes. "I need you to help me catch this guy. Did you do that packet of questions?"

"I can't remember the attack," she said, new tears flowing.

"I know. That's okay. The questions aren't about that. They're about you and your life. It will help us focus on where he might have found you."

Brett reappeared. "Grandma's comin' in five minutes."

"Listen, your mother is going to be here soon. I want you to tell her what happened. One of our rape counselors is on the way, as well. She'll help you. Did you do any of the survey?"

Jacqueline reached behind her, pulling apart layers of dirty bed linens. The papers were torn in half but he could see some penned responses, though not many. Nathan took it. "Thanks. This is great. It's really going to help."

A hefty knock at the door stopped the rambunctious boys in the next room.

"That was record time." Brett left briefly. In a few moments he was back, ushering in a petite yet well-muscled woman who sat at the edge of the bed and gathered her daughter up into her arms.

"Natalie, draw your mother a bath. Hot as you can stand."

"Ma'am . . ." Nathan offered.

"I know what this is. You leave us and come back in a few days. She'll be ready for you then."

Brett pulled on Nathan's elbow. Walking outside, Nathan took several cleansing breaths.

"Why the hurry to leave?" Nathan asked.

"I know mothers like that. I have one. You don't get in their way. I guarantee when we come back, this lawn will be mowed, the screen door fixed, and they'll have just as many Halloween decorations up as the neighbors."

Getting into the car, they situated themselves and buckled seat belts. "I'll tell you another thing: those hoodlum twin boys will have their hair cut and be greeting us at the door with polite little smiles. Grandma is back!"

Nathan smiled as he pulled away from the chaos, choosing to drive his own vehicle again.

"One thing I find funny." Brett tapped his fingers rapid fire on the dashboard.

"Hey, you're smudging!" Nathan slapped his hand away and grabbed a wet wipe from the middle console, wiping the finger marks clean.

"Smudging?"

"I don't know what you could possibly find funny. It's terrible what the rape has done to her. To both of these women."

"I'm not talking about the victims. I'm talking about you."

"Ooh, I can hardly wait for one of your stunning observations."

"They both start bawling their eyes out and you hand them Kleenex. Just regular tissue."

"Yeah, so, I thought it was the chivalrous thing to do. I know thoughtful male responses are foreign to you."

"Why not give them one of your grandma's embroidered hankies? I'm just curious as to why Lilly Reeves got one and not the others."

Chapter 15

October 28

DANA SUCKED THE cool air sharply into her lungs when she saw Lilly emerge from her car as she waited for her by the door to the indoor firing range. Her hair was oily and matted. Holes in her baggy clothing showed the pale, malnourished skin beneath. As she neared, Dana held the door open for her and followed her inside. Lilly failed to offer a greeting.

"Honestly, I can't even believe you convinced me to do this. Especially on my first Saturday night off in eons," Dana said. The gun club was like an undiscovered culture. Lilly stood next to her, two plastic gun cases open, loading two magazines.

"Kadin said he wouldn't come."

"Smart man," Dana replied. Lilly did not look her way. "What is that smell?"

"A mixture of burnt powder and the solvent they use to clean the weapons."

"Not quite antiseptic." The cement floor, once painted red, was chipped and pockmarked. Dana slid her feet along the floor to prevent herself from slipping on the numerous shell casings that littered the ground. Two large, wooden barrels sat in the corner with a broom and dustpan. Every ceiling tile either gaped open, showing intestinal plumbing, or was water-stained and sagging.

Lilly continued with the weapons, her movements strong and sure. She snapped one magazine into place and set the gun in front of Dana. The sound of the metal cap on Lilly's flask as it opened scraped Dana's spine like a bad violin note. Lilly took two swigs and set it aside before loading the other magazine into a second gun.

"When did you get these?" Dana handled the sidearm with cautious movements.

Lilly wiped her mouth with the back of her hand. Leveling the gun she fired off one shot before Dana could get her earplugs in.

"Hey, you could have warned me!" Dana leaned from her side of the divider and looked at the gaping hole, center mass, on the target at the end of Lilly's lane. She raised an eyebrow in mild surprise.

Lilly's eyes looked cold and resolved. "I've had the one you're using for several years. I just got this one." Lilly held the gun up and rocked it in front of Dana. "Didn't want the first edition to be lonely." She reached for her thermos again.

"I see. How many of these do you think you need?"

"I'm not sure, maybe one for every room."

Dana was amazed at how quickly Lilly aimed, this time firing off three successive shots. Her ears started to ring. Dana peered at the target. Still only one hole.

"You missed," Dana said, her own voice distant in her ears.

"Do you know what the ultimate goal is when you practice shooting?" Lilly crossed her arms and leaned against the divider.

"I would assume it's to hit the target."

"The correct answer would be to get the bullet through the exact same hole as the first shot you fired." Turning in a blur, Lilly took another three shots. Dana noted two holes in the head, another to the chest.

"What you see now is poor shooting."

"I think he'd still be dead!"

Lilly drained the remainder of her drink, reached into her duffel, and placed another silver flask before her. Dana wiggled a finger in her ear, attempting to diminish the high-pitched ring.

"Why don't you put your ear plugs in?"

"Don't yell! I can still hear!"

"Do you know you're yelling?"

When Lilly raised her weapon, Dana plugged both her ears with her index fingers. This time, she didn't check the shots.

"Well, why not?"

"What?"

"You need to get those in your ears."

"I'm not putting them in because I want to talk to you."

"I wish you'd told me that before I got your gun ready."

Dana placed a firm hand over the weapon to prevent Lilly from picking it up, keeping it in place until Lilly met her gaze. "I don't think he's coming after you."

Lilly stilled. "That's not what Torrence would say."

"They're not even sure it was him."

"I am."

Dana blew the bangs from her eyes. "When do you think you'll come back to work? One shift and you're gone for a month. Anderson's not going to cover for you forever."

"Why does there have to be a certain amount of time?"

"Because you need to move on."

"I'll be sure to say that to you after you're raped."

"All right, I'm sorry. But this is what you want to do? Drink and shoot for the rest of your life?"

Lilly turned her shoulders square to Dana. "I want to be ready. This is how I'm getting through it."

"What would you say if a patient came into the ER using these coping mechanisms to work through a major event?"

"Major event? It was a crime!"

"What would you say?"

"I'd give her the double thumbs-up and tell her to carry on because you always have to be ready for the other shoe to drop. Life is only a series of tragic events. Do you ever think about that? That's all our job is—meeting people at their lowest moments." Lilly raised the weapon, steadied her sight, but did not fire.

"You really believe that?" Dana's voice cracked.

"Why shouldn't I? My father left me. My mother left me. Now I'm leaving me."

"That doesn't make any sense."

"Ah, that's because you're not drinking enough." Lilly picked up the flask, took several quick gulps, and set it aside.

"If you want me to stay here, you're going to have to put the firearms away. All I need is a stray shot to do one of us in because your aim will be skewed with all that booze."

Dana sat, holding the spare weapon in her lap. Tracing her fingers along the cool lines of the metal, her mind whirled at how something the size of her hand held such destructive force. "I remember a patient we took care of when we were residents."

Lilly didn't face her, but set the gun down.

"The young boy who'd suffered a traumatic brain injury and wasn't going to live. Do you remember him?"

Though Lilly did not respond, Dana could see the heaviness of grief wilt her bravado. Her eyes widened and glossed over.

"At first, the family was adamant about refusing to give his organs away. It took you nearly twelve hours to convince them to surrender in the midst of utter despair. But they did, and several children are alive because of that."

"And that's not a tragedy?"

"Not for the families who received those organs. And in the end, it wasn't for the family that gave them up. Because now they know his death meant something more than just their sorrow."

"And this is helpful how?"

Dana stood, placing the gun back in its case. "Pain can be a great motivator of change, Lilly. I want you to do something more useful with this pain than do yourself in. Do you want to die?"

"Every single day."

Chapter 16

NATHAN CONSULTED THE map he held and looked down the street at the quaint row of houses.

Brett took off his sport coat and slung it over his shoulder. "It's hot. I'm hungry. I'm carrying a weapon. You know that's a deadly combination."

Nathan circled a two-block radius with his index finger. "We need to finish this area."

"Deadly."

"Stop your whining. You're not five years old."

"Come on. We've been at this all morning. Five tattoo parlors. Now, a re-canvas of Lilly's neighborhood. Feed me and I'll be a much better boy."

"There are more important things than your grumbling stomach."

Brett sat on a wooden park bench and brushed off flecks of peeling green paint. "I know you're obsessed with this guy. I know you're freaking out because it's time for him to strike. That's if we have his pattern correct."

"I just want to finish this."

"Plus, the FBI is coming. Are you even sleeping?"

"It doesn't matter."

"I'm giving you one more hour."

"Whatever. Let's do the block in front of Lilly's complex. There were just a few houses where we didn't get interviews. Let's hit 1171. Supposedly the neighborhood busybody lives there."

"Why hasn't anyone been able to catch her home?"

"Probably because she's busy. I didn't say she was a shut-in."

They approached the door. The yard was well kept. Early-style bungalow painted white with crisp, navy-blue shutters. Mums were planted along the brick path to the door in varying shades of rich autumn colors.

Brett rapped on the door. It opened up barely an inch. One unmoving pale brown eye stared through the gap.

"What is it you want?

Nathan approached, adjusted his tie. "My name is Detective Nathan Long. This is my partner, Brett Sawyer." Both quick-flipped their badges. "We'd like to speak to you about Dr. Lilly Reeves. Do you know her?"

The gap widened a few more inches. Wisps of corrugated gray hair fell over a wrinkled face that any Shar-Pei puppy would envy. "I know her."

"May we come in and talk?"

"You like dogs?"

"How many are we talking?" Brett asked.

"Just one, but he's mean. Let me put him out back."

The door closed.

"Are you sure about this?" Brett ventured.

"She could be a witness."

The house shuddered as the back door slammed. The sounds of growling, barking, and the old woman yelling seemed to incite every animal within hearing range to cry out in protest. The front door opened wide; the woman smoothed her black velvet dress and opened the screen.

"Come on in. I'll make you some tea."

They stepped into the foyer. The house was clean, void of lingering animal scent or muscle-cream rub. Nathan scanned the small living room. He stepped to the bay window and tapped his finger on a pair of binoculars.

"This is what I was hoping for," Nathan said.

Brett walked the periphery of the room. "No family pictures."

The woman returned, setting three cups on a small glass table. She motioned for them to sit on the couch as she took the wing chair.

"Mrs.?" Nathan ventured.

"Connelly." She passed the vapor flowing cups to them, took her own, and promptly threw her leg over the side of the chair. Brett averted his gaze to the side. It was evident Mrs. Connelly didn't believe in traditional, white undergarments. Nathan brought the liquid to his lips and took a large swig as Brett mirrored his movement. The burning in his mouth was not from the temperature of the liquid. Nathan let the liquid dribble back into the cup as Brett swallowed his.

The old woman eyed Nathan with a mischievous twinkle in her eye. "You don't like it?"

"Mrs. Connelly, we very much appreciate your generosity. It's just that we're not allowed to drink on the job and I'm sensing there's a little bit of alcohol in this beverage."

"A lot of alcohol . . ."

"Brett," Nathan warned.

"More and more of your gender can't hold their liquor. You just can't find real men in the world anymore."

"As that may be true, let's talk about Dr. Reeves. How well do you know her?"

"We're more acquaintances than anything. She's always been very kind to me. Checks on me when we get those five-foot blizzards and I can't get out. I told her I was not going to take my blood pressure medicine anymore. Would rather buy other things."

"Like good whiskey, no doubt." Brett reached for his teacup. Nathan cut his hand across his neck.

"Exactly! Nonetheless, Dr. Reeves came over every day for two months to check my blood pressure. Made sure it was okay so I didn't stroke out. Said it was easier to keep me alive than to have to clean my place out."

"You don't have family then," Nathan said.

"My husband died many years ago. We were both singly born. Never had any children of our own."

"I see. So you feel obligated to watch out for her." Nathan pulled his notebook out and opened to a fresh page.

"I do what I can for her."

"I want you to think back to the month of August, early September. Do you remember any odd happenings around the neighborhood?" Brett asked. Nathan skimmed his notes.

"Like what?"

"Any strange cars? Any strange events? People that were around then that don't seem to be around now."

"There was a man I would see walking around the neighborhood with one of those small, yippy dogs. I say if a dog don't weigh more than twenty pounds, you may as well call him a rat and put him in a cage."

"Not like Bruno out back."

"His name's Buttercup."

"Of course," Brett said.

"This man walking the dog . . . he's not around anymore?"

"Haven't seen him for a couple of weeks."

"That puts him past Lilly's assault," Brett said. Nathan acknowledged the point.

The woman dropped her leg to the floor and clasped her knees with her hands. "Dr. Reeves was attacked?"

"Yes, in her home in September."

"Thinking back, there was a strange thing that happened. I hadn't seen her in a couple of days. I wasn't feeling well. Had this headache for a week that wouldn't go away. I wanted to talk to her about it. Went to her door and there was a man there checking her locks."

"Checking her locks? How?"

"He had three keys and he was trying them in each of the deadbolts. One seemed to be giving him trouble."

"You didn't think he was trying to break in?"

"It was the middle of the day; bright and sunny. I could see him from the street. It would seem pretty brazen to do something like that."

"Did you speak with him?"

"I asked him what he was up to. He said he was changing out Lilly's locks. Checking to make sure the keys fit right."

"You didn't find that odd?"

"If you knew Dr. Reeves, you would know there was nothing weird about that. She's a woman living alone. Never can be too safe, I say."

"Can you describe this man?"

"He had dark brown hair."

"Did you notice anything about his eyes?"

"He was wearing those annoying mirrored shades. Kind of like what I thought you'd be wearing."

"How about any tattoos or distinguishing marks?"

"The man was covered except for his head. Wore this long, heavy overcoat. For a locksmith, he seemed overdressed and too warmly for that matter. The odd thing was he seemed annoyed that he was there. He said, 'I'm going to do all this work, and I guarantee you she's going to want her locks changed again tomorrow.'"

"Do you remember what day that was?"

"The day before Labor Day. I know for sure because I was looking forward to a senior lunch they were having at the church because of the holiday."

Nathan took out a pocket calendar. He'd been tracking the crime dates in red. His own personal timeline of the events. He flipped back to September. The day before Labor Day, September 3.

Chapter 17

November 15

Mid-November brought on cold, gray, misting clouds. The wind blew flags straight as if they were nailed to a wall. Lilly pulled into the parking structure near SMC and sat there, staring at the ER entrance. Her arms felt leaden with the thought of reaching up to turn off her vehicle. The sudden flood of tears obscured her eyes like trails of raindrops on a windshield. The thought of opening the door, walking on the wet cement into her department, taking off her coat, trying to comfort the sick and distressed when all she felt was fear and anxiety brought more despair.

She leaned forward and rested her head against the steering wheel, her arms tucked and folded tight into her body. The heated interior of her car provided little warmth against the darkness that sapped her strength.

At first, the gentle rocking of the vehicle barely registered through her drug haze. Then, a crisp rap on the driver's window caused her to lift her head and look left. A crowbar came fast and struck the window again, and fine lines spread through the dirt covered glass. She turned to reach for her purse; her fingers tingled with anxiety as she groped for the gun tucked inside.

"Lilly! Are you all right?" The baritone voice reached through her cocooned ears. Relief flooded through her and she pulled her hand off the cool metal. She waved Luther away from the door.

"Lilly! Thank you, Lord. Open up! Are you all right?"

She unwrapped the scarf from her ears and disengaged the locks. Luther opened her door and immediately brought his fingers to her wrist. She nudged them away.

"I'm all right, just tired."

"Lilly . . . the window. Man, I'm sorry but you scared me to death. I've been here forever trying to get you to wake up. The security guard brought me the crowbar and then I sent him for a gurney. Turn your car off. Do you have a headache, nausea, blurred vision?"

"All the above." She turned off the ignition and placed her keys inside her purse.

"Come on, let's get you inside and put you on some oxygen."

She resisted his arms as they reached into the vehicle. "I don't have carbon monoxide poisoning. I'm just tired. I'm not sleeping well."

Stepping out of her vehicle, she stumbled against him. Luther gathered her in his arms to keep her steady. Lilly eased him back and leaned against her car, but he maintained a firm grasp on her upper arm.

"Lilly, are you okay? Really okay?"

"I'm fine, honestly." She looked past Luther, seeing two other nurses paused at the ambulance entrance with a pram. Lilly waved them off, but they seemed wary to turn away. She tugged out of his grip.

"Luther, let me talk with her. I'll make sure she gets in okay."

Dana stood back a few feet. Luther withdrew, waving off his coworkers as well. Lilly hugged the open door for support.

"Not sleeping? Or something else," Dana asked.

Lilly pulled her body from the gap and slammed her support structure closed, surprised that the window did not continue to shatter and shower her feet with sharp crystals. She crossed her arms tight over her chest; the sound of expanding cracks in the glass like ice falling off trees sent small pulses of apprehension up her spine.

"It's going to be fun getting this fixed." Lilly turned and patted the glass, her fingers numb inside her gloves. She arched her fingers and tapped harder, trying to illicit a painful response, wanting the broken shards to score into her flesh to prove she could still feel something instead of this emptiness.

"Stop that."

Lilly shoved her hands into her pockets.

"Luther was concerned for you, as am I. Have you been drinking?"

"Not this morning."

Dana sighed. "How much?"

"Just enough to get me to sleep."

"So, essentially, you're hung over. Are you doing this every night?"

Lilly avoided her gaze and pulled her coat tighter.

"What does it matter as long as I'm sober here?"

"Lilly, honestly, I'm shocked. You know what's wrong with it! Soon, you'll be drinking at work. These are not good coping mechanisms. You need to see someone before you slip more. Do you want to lose your job?"

Pushing away from the car, Lilly stood nose to nose with Dana.

"Stay out of it. I'm fine. What do I need to talk to anyone for? To get some pity for what happened? I'll figure it out."

She turned from Dana and stumbled several steps before righting herself. Luther waited for her at the ER entrance, chart in hand.

"I'll call someone about your window."

"Don't worry about it. I'll take care of it."

"There's some guy waiting for you."

"A patient?" Lilly asked.

"Yeah, he requested you. He's been waiting for a couple of hours according to the night nurses."

"You know we don't like people to do that. It sets a bad precedent. I'm not their primary doctor. Nor do I want to be."

Luther shrugged. "What can I tell you? Two other docs tried to see him, and he refused."

"Fine, I'll take it." She threw her coat and purse over the nearest chair. Was it a dare for someone else to get her keys and finish her off?

The exam room was close. Lilly hovered in the hall and scanned over the medical information. Odd. Date of birth was listed as 00/00/0000. Sex: Male. Complaint: "Message Delivery."

A psych case. Great.

She entered the room and closed the door behind her. The man sat on the rolling stool. His clothes were without defect. Seams were pressed into his trousers. She perused her own attire. Her white lab coat resembled a smoothed-out wad of wrinkled paper, having been pulled from her clothes hamper moments before she left the house. His chocolate-brown camel hair coat was folded neatly and laid over his legs. Black polished shoes reflected the overhead lights. His hands lay folded, fingers not intertwined, on top of the garment. His eyes held hers as she stood waiting for him to give up the stool.

His emerald eyes held hers as she stood waiting for him to give up the stool.

She glanced at the chart again, more to gather herself than to refresh her mind of the information.

What little there was of it.

"I'm sorry, I don't know how to pronounce your name. What language is this? You speak English?"

"You can call me Gabe, and I think that answers your second question."

"But not the first," she quipped.

"Ah, that's true. But the story might be long for you."

"I'm Dr.—"

"Lilly Reeves. Yes, I know. I've been waiting for you."

He stood and rolled the seat her way, then took another chair as she placed herself near the low-set counter to document. Settling in, she crossed her legs and placed the chart down on the desk. She pushed herself back against the wall.

"Do I know you?"

"No, we've never met."

"Are you wearing contacts? I want to see your real eyes."

"These are my real eyes. I don't have one blue and one brown. Isn't that what you really want to see?"

"Are you with the police? It was my understanding that that particular piece of information was being held from the public."

"You're correct. It's not public information and no, I'm not with the police."

Lilly struggled to keep her nerves in check.

"Then you must know my rapist. How else would you know that?"

He pulled his chair forward, scraping the metal legs against the white linoleum floor, leaving scuff marks behind. The emergency call button was not within her reach.

"Some things are known other ways," he replied.

"So you're a psychic then?" Lilly pressed her back into the corner.

"I don't want you to be afraid." He inched his chair closer to hers. Reaching his hand out, he placed it over her clenched ones.

The sense of utter calm that washed over her was like diving into a pool of perfectly warmed water and being able to stay under without fighting for breath. It was a vision of deep sleep and blissful dreams. Of hope—fear vanished. Her thoughts crystallized.

"If you're not a psychic, then what are you?"

"I'm a messenger."

"From whom?"

"I'm not sure you're ready to know yet."

"Why pose as a patient?"

"I don't think you would have seen me any other way. You are being pursued. But not just by evil." He pulled his hand away from hers. "There's a story I want to share with you that I think will help you make some decisions in the months to come."

He paused and refolded his coat, continuing before Lilly could find a reason to object.

"Many years ago, there was a family who lived in a wooded area near a river. They had a small boy, who was frail and sick. Because of this, he was never allowed out of the house. As he grew in years, he longed for the outdoors. One rainy night he left his home and began to wander. It wasn't long before he was lost because the rain and darkness had obscured his way. He made it to the river but couldn't find the trail back home. He began to run, panicked that he was lost. He stumbled and fell into the water."

"You came here to tell me a child's fairy tale?"

Ignoring her, he continued on.

"Because of his sickness, he didn't have the strength to pull himself out. The water was cold and running fast. He realized he was dying. Two arms came underneath him and pulled him from the current. There was a fire near the bank, and he was laid there for several hours until he became coherent. When he awoke, he saw a woman sitting not far away."

"The boy sat up and asked, 'Who are you? Are you the angel of death come to take me to heaven?' The woman smiled at him and neared. 'You must pay very close attention to me. You see the light in the distance. That is your home. You must leave here and go back and never wander in the woods at night alone again.' The small boy nodded his assurance at her warning. 'You've not told me who you are,' he asked again. She smiled down on him. 'For you, dear boy, I am the angel of life.' And with those words she was gone."

Lilly gave a few sullen claps. "You waited two hours to tell me a lame story. I should place an involuntary hold on you just for that."

"Any thoughts as to who that boy might be?"

"A guessing game? Honestly, why would I care who the boy is?"

"That boy grew up and had a very eventful life. He was Adolf Hitler."

Lilly felt uneasiness settle in her stomach.

"Is this true?" she asked.

111

The man neared her. "The story illustrates how things are not always clear in the beginning. For it was the angel of death that visited this small boy, because of what she knew he would become. Life for him meant death for millions. The opposite can also be true. Sometimes, things that we believe should be given death, should be granted life instead." Nearing her more, he leaned forward, placing one arm around her in an embrace, the other over her chest. "There is a life you will have to decide this for. You must remember this story."

Unmoving, she waited.

"Lilly, there is another thing I need you to do. Please, allow Kadin to pray over you."

Through the haze of suddenly heavy eyes, Lilly watched him leave the room.

Chapter 18

KADIN'S MORNING ROUNDS had been interrupted by a distress page from Dana to meet him in the ER. Shortly into her shift, Lilly had been discovered unconscious in an exam room by Luther. Since Dana had been aware of her distress that morning and Lilly didn't have any close family, Luther had paged Dana.

The CT of her head was negative. Spinal tap negative. Lab work pointed to a viral infection. Once Lilly proved to be mentally intact for Dr. Anderson, Dana had convinced him to discharge Lilly under her care. For logistical help getting Lilly home, Dana had called Kadin.

Lilly's townhouse was in disarray. On the floor and strewn over chairs, clothes lay as lifeless victims in every open space. The smell of stale grease from old food containers was heavy in the air, and Kadin felt it coat his skin each inch he progressed forward. He stepped over several empty liquor bottles, readjusting Lilly in his arms. Dana was in front of him, trying to clear a path to the stairs.

"What do you want to do?" he asked, switching Lilly to an over-the-shoulder fireman's carry to make it up the narrow staircase.

"I think we need to get her in the bath. Her fever is sky high again, probably why she's so out of it. Plus, it doesn't look like she's bathed in weeks."

Dana opened the door to Lilly's bedroom. They both paused, taking in the pristine room. The air was clear, with a faint hint of roses. It seemed the same as the day they had presented it to her newly decorated.

"Where do you think she's sleeping?" Dana asked.

Kadin stepped past her, easing Lilly onto the bed. She moaned as her head lolled off to the side.

"Not in here." Kadin stretched his arms, attempting to wring out the fatigue. "You get her undressed, and I'll get the bath ready. I'll see if I can find some Tylenol for the fever."

Closing the door behind him, he stepped across the hall to Lilly's bathroom. Opening the medicine cabinet, he was stunned to find it empty. He latched the mirrored door back in place and turned, pulling the shower curtain from the tub. He ran the water until it was tepid under his fingers and pushed the plug down for the drain. Seated on the edge of the tub, he waited for the water to fill as his mind searched for a course of action.

What could he do to possibly help Lilly? His ceaseless prayers for her sanity were drawing a silent response. Lilly seemed impervious to all of their interventions. She shoved them away the harder they tried to assist, seemingly bent on her own destruction, or at least relentless in her resolve to fix things her own way.

He felt like she was dying, a frail leaf ready to fall at the slightest hint of a breeze.

Yet she seemed to be surviving in hurricane-force winds.

For now.

Maybe it was her spirit, the life within her, that was fading.

He turned the water off and returned to the bedroom. Dana had changed her into a bathing suit. She turned to Kadin as he approached.

"I figured she wouldn't want you to see her naked."

"I can't find any Tylenol up here. I'll help you get her into the bath and start cleaning up downstairs."

"I think I should have her done in a half hour. You can help me get her back to bed. We'll start some IV fluids."

Kadin reached for Lilly's arm and lifted her onto his shoulder.

"How high do you think the fever is?"

"High."

"You're sure all the labs were negative? This seems more than just the flu."

"They did a spinal tap, Kadin. Everything looked good. White count and inflammatory markers point to a viral process. It is flu season. We'll keep an eye on her."

In the bathroom, he moved her off his shoulder and cradled her thinning body. She was beginning to look like a third-world orphan with scrawny limbs and a protruding abdomen.

"Is she even eating?" Kadin asked. Dana shrugged. Kneeling, he eased her into the water. The soft flow of the cool liquid over Lilly's skin didn't register with her. He stood, grabbing a nearby towel to dry his arms.

"You sure you're going to be all right? She's like dead weight."

"Don't worry." She smiled, placing a hand on his arm and pushing him out of the bathroom, "I might be small, but I pack a lot of strength." She closed the door, inches from his nose.

Kadin returned to the main level. He entered the kitchen and retrieved several plastic trash bags. He set himself to work, first gathering up the dirty laundry. Sorting it into several piles on the main-floor laundry, he searched the cabinets over the washer and dryer for detergent. He found her supply, plus several boxes of gun ammunition. After starting a load, he returned to the living area and gathered up the myriad of empty fast-food containers. He placed all the empty liquor bottles on the table. Sherry and white wine were her favorite choices. He tried to remember the last time he came to check on her.

How much was she drinking in a day?

He pulled the seat cushions from the couch. In addition to food crumbs and wrappers were several empty prescription bottles.

He found ten.

Valium. Ambien. Xanax. All prescribed by Walter Henry, MD.

He'd have to ask Dana about him.

He worried over the combination. Alcohol and sleeping pills were a desirable lure for struggling souls to curb their depression and anxiety.

Meet Lilly's friends: pain, sleeplessness, and despair.

He wondered which plagued her the most. Likely, all three.

After setting the garbage near the front door, he grabbed the vacuum and set to cleaning. Dusting followed. He was in search of the glass cleaner in the laundry room when he heard Dana's steps in the kitchen.

"Bachelorhood has taught you some good lessons," she mused, holding a plastic case in her hands.

"What's that?"

"One of her guns. It was under a pillow on her bed. I didn't want to leave it up there and have her surprise us with it. I know for sure she has two. I don't know where the other one is. I think I'll take this one home with me, but you can probably take the ammo and put it with the rest."

He took it from her hands and placed it in the cabinet.

"Good thinking. Hopefully, she won't feel she needs to find the other one. Is she still in the bath?"

"No. She was a little more coherent and able to make it back to her room. She's dry and all tucked in. I have her IV started and fluids going. Find any Tylenol?"

"I found a lot of meds; nothing as innocuous as Tylenol, though."

"Great."

"Do you know Dr. Walter Henry?"

"I know a David Henry. He was a good friend of Lilly's in med school. I think he had some formal name that he didn't like to go by."

"What's his specialty?"

"Podiatry."

"Well, Lilly's friend the foot doctor has been loading her up with benzos and a whole lot of other things. And she seems to prefer them with alcohol."

"I figured as much when I saw her this morning. Let's see if there's anything I can make for dinner."

"Do you think it's too late for her?" Kadin asked.

Dana paused and turned to him, holding a box of pancake mix.

"In what sense?"

"In every sense. Physically, she's wasting to nothing. She's got a pouched-out belly like those malnourished kids get. Professionally, she's throwing away her career. Spiritually desolate. I've tried getting her to come to church with me. She refuses every time. I pray but get no clear direction."

Kadin's heart sank when he saw Dana's tears. He grabbed a tissue from the kitchen table and handed it to her. His short tirade seemed to be drawing from her well of fear. She dabbed her eyes and blew her nose louder than any man. Kadin couldn't keep from laughing.

"What?"

"Sorry, that nose blowing. Quite a feat."

"You can't say all those horrible things about Lilly and then make me smile." Dana took a seat at the table. "Yes, I'm worried. However, I think our prayers are working."

"How?"

"What I know is that God is always working around us. He doesn't just work within the walls of a denomination. Sometimes, I think we feel if we can get unbelievers through the church doors, the church will do the rest and our obligation is met. It's obvious Lilly has great resistance to anything structured. We need to watch for where God is working around her. Show her grace. Be there as much as she allows. Don't abandon her. Honestly, I think that's what she's trying to do. Make us disown her."

"Because then it will prove we are no better than those in her life who didn't believe. Upstairs, did she talk to you much?" Kadin asked.

"It was hard to make out. I didn't know if she was relaying what happened this morning, or if she was still delirious." Dana paused and looked at him. "I gave her some IV Toradol though. The fever shouldn't be an issue." She returned to rummaging through the cabinets.

"What was she saying?"

"She said someone named Gabe came to see her and told a fairy tale about Hitler. That's all she remembers."

"Do you think it could have been him? Tormenting her?"

"Today was about spiritual warfare. We easily forget that there is a real battle going on for the souls of each person, and there have been instances in the Bible where prayer has helped. Consider the book of Daniel and how prayer aided the angel Gabriel."

"You think the visitor she had today was an angel?"

Dana shrugged at the suggestion. "I don't know. But I don't think it was her rapist." She closed several cabinet doors. "Listen, there's not much here. I'll run out and get something. You feel okay to go up and check on her?"

"Sure."

Dana grabbed her purse and keys and made a quick exit. Kadin went upstairs. He opened Lilly's door with caution after his soft knock brought only quiet response. It was nice to see her peaceful, in a sense. He pulled a rocking chair up next to her bed. He was unsure how long he sat there, silently praying for help, for a way to comfort her that would bring solace instead of anger.

"All of this praying. Have you gotten any answers?"

He looked up, relieved to see her blue eyes with a hint of life renewed. He reached for her slowly, placing the back of his hand against her cheek. He felt the coolness of her flesh before she eased away. He dropped his hand back into his lap.

"I'm not sure."

She tightened the covers up around her shoulders.

"Why keep doing it?"

"I've been thinking a lot about prayer and God's response to it. It brought to mind a passage from the Bible about a man named Lazarus. He was terribly ill, and his sisters, Mary and Martha, sent word for Jesus to come. They knew he could heal the sick. However, after he received their urgent request, he waited two days before traveling. By the time he got to Bethany, Lazarus was dead and had been buried four days. His sisters were distraught, angry that Jesus hadn't come to the aid of a good friend. He essentially said no."

"That story doesn't seem to be very faith affirming," she replied. Kadin picked up a glass of juice from her bedside table and offered it to her. She seemed to consider it, eventually waving it away.

"At the time, it was known that Jesus could heal the sick. He'd already done so on a number of occasions. I believe Jesus said no to Mary and Martha because he wanted to show them something more amazing. Something no one had ever seen. On that visit, he raised Lazarus from the dead. After saying no in the beginning, he showed them in the end what his plan was. Something more amazing than anyone could possibly have imagined." Kadin smoothed Lilly's covers, thankful she didn't edge away. "I think that's why I'm not hearing God's voice now. For you, he has something amazing planned, something that I could never imagine."

Chapter 19

November 20

FROM AURORA, IT was an hour drive west to Evergreen, a small town that served as a gateway into the Rockies and the location of Dr. Reeves's business. Nathan admired the stout, gray brick building in front of him. Four white columns lined either side of the entrance. Despite the fall weather, the lawn was free from stray leaves. The bushes were manicured in perfect small orbs. The path before them was illuminated with upward lighting on each of the pillars as the sun set behind the structure. Lighting also highlighted a river-rock-framed sign that read "NeuroGenics." Nathan pulled his materials from the back of the car. As he stood to close the trunk, he saw Brett tighten his jacket.

"I hate these late-night meetings," Brett said.

"It's only five. What else do you have to do?"

"Monday night football and a beer sound pretty good to me."

"It took us weeks to arrange this interview. I want to get this mysterious item Lilly is waiting for. We're not backing out for football."

"You're sure this isn't just a glorified errand run for a woman you're pining for?"

"Let's keep this professional," Nathan warned and slammed the trunk with his free hand.

"This is his home, too?" Brett asked.

"That's what they tell me. We're supposed to be meeting him in his private quarters."

"This is a long way from the jailhouse."

"He was only held briefly for a minor felony that was later dismissed. He doesn't have a record for any conviction."

"I still don't understand why you'd want to meet this guy other than as a favor to Dr. Reeves. I mean the other Dr. Reeves . . . Lilly."

"That should be reason enough, helping her out. Plus, he has ties to another victim, as well."

"I'm looking forward to having a nice trip to Nevada next week to check up on that pink Escalade."

"We're only there for one day. You can only do so much gambling."

"There's more to do than just gambling."

"Remember, legal activities only."

"You think I would put my career at risk by doing something foolish?" Brett winked at Nathan. "I was thinking about seeing a show. Is the Blue Man Group still there?"

"I have no idea. Come on."

They were greeted at the door by an older gentleman in a black tuxedo that was accented with an ivory bow tie and cummerbund.

"Butlers actually exist?" Brett whispered, as he followed a few steps behind Nathan. Northwood's style was the decor of choice. Straight ahead, over an impossibly large fireplace, was a stuffed buffalo head. A short walk into the foyer at the right was a recessed door. The servant punched in a security code, and the doors opened to an elevator. The ride was smooth and short.

"Is Dr. Reeves a hunter?" Brett asked, stepping out of the elevator ahead of Nathan.

"Not anymore. He says there's more profit in raising them than hunting them."

"He raises buffalo?"

"As well as some other wild game."

"Does that still make them wild, if they're raised?" Brett mused. Their escort dismissed his comment with an annoyed rise of one eyebrow.

"Follow me, please."

The living area was a sprawling suite with an open floor plan. To the left of the fireplace stood a library. Floor-to-ceiling, deep, built-in cherry-wood bookshelves towered over a full-length leather sofa. Facing the couch sat an equally ornate mahogany desk with carved pine boughs on each of the legs. Music played softly through invisible speakers. White plantation shutters relieved some of the cave-like feel from the dark wood and leather. There was a stunning view of the Rocky Mountains.

"Mr. Reeves will join you shortly. Can I offer you something to drink?"

"Scotch?"

"Brett," Nathan warned.

"Make that coffee," Brett replied, a bit of mischievous play in his eyes. "Coffee for me as well, thank you."

After a small bend at the waist, the butler left them, and Nathan perused the library. Below the shelves were cabinets. Testing a few, he found them locked. He identified a number of medical textbooks dealing with neuroscience, neurosurgery, and neurophysiology. One complete section of shelves held several black-and-white photos of a young girl. Nathan could appreciate a resemblance to Lilly and wondered if they were of her or a sibling.

"She's always been beautiful, hasn't she?"

Nathan straightened and turned to see Dr. Reeves standing behind him, holding a tray. He stood several inches taller than Nathan. His brown eyes were set deeply into his face, somewhat paled by the graying full beard and mustache. His clothes were casual khaki pants and a business shirt with the top three buttons open. Nathan picked up one of the black cups, holding it between both hands, letting the heat dissipate the stiffness in his tissues brought on by the cool autumn evening.

"I'm Detective Sawyer. My partner, Detective Long." Brett accepted a cup as well. The tray was set on the desk. "We're here to speak to you in regard to two crime victims. This information will help us build a profile of the assailant."

"Yes, I'm aware. You're speaking of Lilly and one of my patients, Celia Ramirez. Celia was generous enough to sign a release so I could discuss her case fully with you."

"These are pictures of Lilly?" Nathan motioned with his cup to the photo gallery.

"I've never had any other children. At least that I know of."

"Thank you for agreeing to meet with us." Nathan and Brett seated themselves in the chairs at Reeves's desk. "When's the last time you saw her?"

"Lilly? The last time I saw her was the day I left her mother. My last memory is seeing her in my rearview mirror, arms outstretched, screaming for me to come back." He took a seat in the black leather chair, gathering up a few stray pens on the desktop.

Nathan smoothed his tongue over his teeth and counted to ten silently.

"You haven't tried since then to reconnect?" Brett asked.

"Honestly, I felt I didn't really have the right to. I consider myself responsible for her mother's death. I know Lilly would never forgive me if she knew the truth. I knew it would come out if we ever met. It was safer to just stay away."

"Safer for whom?" Nathan pressed.

"Myself, of course."

"I thought Lilly's mother died of cancer." Brett balanced his cup on his knee.

"That's what Lilly thinks as well. She actually died of kidney disease."

"How do you find yourself personally responsible for that?" Nathan asked.

"I told Lilly's mother that if she posted my bail I would go through the transplant operation and give her my kidney. I was a match, and we chose not to have Lilly tested. She was only five or six when this happened, obviously too young to give up an organ." Placing the pens in the center desk drawer, he then pulled out a white, leather-bound journal. "Lilly's mother posted the bond, but as soon as I was out of jail, I left them."

Heat rose in Nathan's chest. "Why?"

"I was a young, selfish, immature man. When Samantha got pregnant, we were both eighteen. After the pregnancy, she developed an aggressive autoimmune disease that essentially took out her kidneys. She was on dialysis within a year of Lilly's birth. We weren't making it financially. I began shoplifting things we could not afford to buy, which eventually led to my arrest." He paused, smoothing his hand over the worn cover of the book before him. "Honestly, jail was like a vacation. Samantha was so ill that when I was home, all I did was take care of Lilly. I just couldn't handle any of it. I'm not cut out to be a father."

Nathan set his cup aside and took a pen to make notes. He met Reeves's eyes.

Does he see my disdain?

"How long after you left before Samantha died?"

"It was a few years. They were able to maintain her on dialysis, but after so long, she couldn't tolerate the treatments anymore. Her veins were shot. She just stopped going. It wasn't long after that they found her dead."

"Where did you get all this information from if you haven't been in touch with Lilly?"

"Samantha had an older sister. She took Lilly in after her mother died.

Savannah kept me well informed of how my actions had essentially killed her sister and left my daughter an orphan. Lilly lived with her until she was seventeen and was pretty much on her own after that."

"Why not reach out to Lilly then?" Nathan asked. Brett cleared his throat at the accusatory tone. A warning to Nathan to back off.

"She was an adult. She could take care of herself."

"After she stopped living with Savannah, would that not have been an opportunity to reconnect?" Brett posed more casually.

Dr. Reeves tapped his fingers on the desk. "I am a selfish man. At the time, I was in the middle of my neurosurgery internship. Honestly, I didn't want Lilly to complicate things. She seemed to be doing fine on her own."

"How would you know that?" Nathan felt the sting of the question in his gut.

"I've had people keeping tabs on her. For a while, I hired a private detective to give me monthly reports. When she was in med school, it became easier because I would get information through the grapevine."

"Do you think she's been aware of this?" Nathan asked.

"I'm not sure. I wouldn't think so."

"Did you know that Lilly is, let's just say, somewhat concerned about her safety?"

"I know what the root of that is. It's why I started this research."

"The more we know about the victims, the more we know about the perpetrator."

"When Lilly went to live with her aunt, Savannah was still married. They didn't live in the safest part of the city. It was a known crack neighborhood. One night, someone strung out and needing a fix broke into their home, mistaking it for where he usually bought drugs. Lilly's uncle was shot and killed."

Nathan had known violence his whole career, but when children got in the fray, it was hard to maintain a professional front. "How did Lilly and her aunt make it out?"

"It was Lilly. Her uncle liked to shoot weapons as a hobby, and he taught Lilly along the way how to handle firearms. She got the weapon and shot the intruder. The man died."

Nathan held his breath as his mind reeled. He thought of Lilly, a young girl, the gun heavy in her hand as she raised it, her uncle's blood already black on the walls. The emotional fortitude it took for her to press a sweat-slicked finger against the trigger usually developed far past her age at that time. Taking a life was devastating regardless of the circumstance.

"You didn't object to her uncle teaching her to shoot guns?" Brett asked.

"It wasn't my place. I'd officially relinquished my parental rights. A few weeks after the incident, I started getting daily calls from Savannah that Lilly was having horrible nightmares. She was having panic attacks during the day, not paying attention in school."

Nathan dried his palms on his pants. "Why did Savannah reach out to you?"

"I think merely because I was a physician. It was clear to me that Lilly was suffering from post-traumatic stress disorder or PTSD. At that time, there was only psychiatric therapy available. You could possibly place them on an antidepressant or antianxiety medication, but for Lilly, these turned her into a zombie during the day and didn't really quell the nightmares at night. The therapies didn't seem to hit at the heart of the issue."

"What would you consider that to be?"

"When we are exposed to a traumatic event, there is a release of several types of hormones. You've heard of the fight-or-flight response?"

"Of course." Nathan flipped his notes back to Celia's interview. He wanted to refresh his memory to compare with Reeves's statements.

"The purpose of these hormones is to help our bodies do one of these two things. Adrenaline increases our heart rate and primes our muscles for movement, allowing us to either run faster or be physically stronger in a fight. Some people theorize that today we often have to think our way out of frightening experiences. Let's take a firefighter who is trapped inside a burning building. Physically, he can't run or fight. He has to keep his wits about him and think out a solution. In our current culture, more often than not, we are trying to think of a way out of our traumatic event. This lack of physical exertion may lead to these stress hormones getting stuck in flood stage like water when there's a breach in a dam. The constant flow of these hormones leads to a lot of the symptoms we see with PTSD—elevated heart rate, blood pressure. Hypersensitivity to the environment."

"Like someone who jumps at the slightest touch," Nathan said.

"Exactly. That triad is a perfect setup for someone to suffer from anxiety and panic attacks—these hormones getting stuck in the 'on' position. But the issue with PTSD is also the memory component: nightmares and flashbacks. A study done on rats looked at the role of memory and adrenaline and had quite interesting results."

"I always hate it when humans are compared to rats," Brett lamented.

"An animal lover?" Reeves asked.

"Hardly. I think a lot of humans give rats a bad name."

"You'll have to excuse him. It's hard for him to leave his sarcastic side at home."

"Well, in some ways I might have to agree about humans giving rats a bad name. I don't have to look very far for that." He stood and approached the cabinet next to Nathan. "Mind if I drink?"

"It's your home, sir."

He poured whiskey into a tumbler and returned to his seat behind the desk. He downed half the liquid in one swig and wiped the corners of his mouth with his thumb and index finger.

"The study done on rats looked at memory retention when they were given doses of adrenaline. Rats were placed in something like a child's swimming pool." He pulled a piece of paper and several colored markers from his desk and began diagramming.

"A man after your own heart," Brett chided, knocking Nathan in the ribs with his elbow.

"In the middle of the pool is a floating piece of wood." A brown rectangle was drawn in the center of a black circle. "What a rat will do is swim around the edge of the water." Taking a blue marker, he made swirls around the interior of this child-like replica. "Until he finds the wood and climbs up onto it to keep himself from drowning." Taking a red marker, Reeves swung his arm up and over, until he plopped it down into the center of the represented slab of wood. "Over subsequent days, the rat will learn that the block is in the middle of the pool and instead of first swimming in circles, he will swim directly to the wood." After making several direct lines to the center, Reeves capped off the markers.

"It's a wagon wheel," Brett mused.

"How many days does that take?" Nathan asked.

"In learning, memory retention is solidified based on daily practice. In the control group it was five days until the memory was formed, until the rat had learned that the wood was always in the middle of the pool.

"In the research," Reeves continued, "what they did next was administer two drugs; Epinephrine, which is essentially adrenaline, and Inderal, which is a drug that blocks the effects of epinephrine in the body. Rats that were given epi would swim to the wood plank an average of two days sooner than the control group. Rats that were given Inderal never learned the direct route to the wood. They would constantly swim in circles, repeating the same experience every day, not retaining what they had learned the day before. So they continued on in happenstance, swimming in circles until they stumbled upon their saving grace. Rats given adrenaline solidified the memory significantly earlier. It was curious that the rats given Inderal were not able to form the memory at all."

"And this helps humans how?"

"For one, it shows that in PTSD, the surge of adrenaline locks the memory of the traumatic event clearly in the mind relatively quickly. It was thought that, like the rats, if people were given Inderal to block the effects of the adrenaline, they wouldn't retain the memories and many of the symptoms associated with PTSD would nullify."

"This is where your research now lies."

"Yes, and Celia was one of my patients in a trial that looked at the effect of Inderal in PTSD."

"What have you been finding?"

"We've found that, if we can identify the people who are more at risk for PTSD shortly after their traumatic experience and give them a short course of Inderal, they have a significant reduction in the flashbacks and nightmares associated with the event. Many of the physical symptoms—fast heart rate, heightened senses—are reduced as well."

"So you wipe out their memories?"

"No, definitely not, but the Inderal seems to prevent the memory from having such prominence, from being so easily recalled. In the case of Celia, she will always know that she was raped. She may just have more difficulty recalling specific details, sensations, and emotions that other victims will be able to recall with ease."

"I'm not sure that's a good thing, Doc," Brett said.

"How could you possibly say that? I know my daughter must be one of these rape victims if you're here to speak with me about her as well. As a doctor, how can I not want to relieve her suffering?"

Nathan placed a fisted hand on top of the desk. "How about as her father? I would think that would come first."

Brett's mouth gaped open a few seconds before he followed Nathan's comment. "From a police perspective, excellent recall of events is what puts people in jail. The more those memories are diminished, the harder it will be to rely on their testimony. It wouldn't surprise me at all if a loony judge looked at this research and threw out the witness's testimony because her memory could no longer be considered reliable."

Nathan stood up and backed away from the desk. The pressure in his chest caused his breath to funnel hard through his nostrils. "I think the other issue is that the traumatic event, sometimes in a very cruel fashion, makes us the people we are today. Do you think Lilly would have ever become a doctor if these other things hadn't happened? Life is supposed to be hard; it builds strong people."

"There is a difference between strength and suffering. If you cannot function in your life because you are so disabled by these memories, what good is that? When we spoke, you said that I had something of Lilly's that she wanted back. This is what she speaks of." He slid a white journal forward. Grime had settled into the natural cracks of the leather, giving it a lacy appearance.

Nathan approached the desk and swiped it from the surface. "I'll be sure Lilly gets this. I wish I could say it's been a pleasure to meet you."

Reeves gripped Nathan's forearm. "I don't mind your disdain for me as long as you help Lilly."

Brett stood as well and eased the men apart. "I'm not against helping people, Dr. Reeves, but I want to be sure the bad guys go to jail for what they do."

"We'll be sure to tell Lilly about your research. Maybe she'll seek treatment . . . from someone else."

"It won't make any difference. After she reads that"—he pointed to the book in Nathan's hand—"in her life, I'll be as good as dead."

Chapter 20

November 27

LILLY ENTERED THE central workroom and ran headfirst into a bouquet of white balloons. Streamers twisted like licorice looped from each corner of the space, crisscrossing in the middle. From the center of the intersection hung a paper stork with a baby wrapped in a fuchsia blanket clutched in its beak. A mountain of presents wrapped in pink, yellow, and green accessorized with all manner of straight and curly ribbons crowded the main worktable. Someone placed a paper plate with a piece of cake into Lilly's hand.

"Today's Sonya's surprise baby shower."

Immediately, Lilly's heart sank. "I forgot her present."

"It's no problem. Bring it next shift."

In truth, she hadn't remembered at all. Sonya was beautiful, dressed casually in blue jean maternity pants and a pink cotton sweater. Her eyes moistened as she opened each gift, placing the clothes on her belly and jiggling side to side in happiness. Lilly felt ill, set her cake down, grabbed a chart, and left. Outside the door, she leaned against the wall, eyes clenched, trying to keep the tears at bay. It was obvious that she wasn't good to anyone anymore. She could barely remember what shifts she was scheduled to work. Three times in the last two weeks, they'd call, waking her up, asking if she'd remembered that she was supposed to be on duty. Dana hadn't called all week, nor had Lilly reached out to her. Every day was a cloudy, alcohol-induced haze that never cleared. She felt a faint rumble in her tummy and the threat of nausea. Biting the inside of her cheek to quell the sensation, she flipped through the chart in front of her.

"Lilly! That detective is here to see you. I put him in the family room."

"Thanks."

She went to the small room that was meant to be cozy, fitted with overstuffed furniture and soft lighting, along with tissue boxes in every nook. Lilly wasn't sure how much it helped when she told families their loved one had died.

"Detective Long, you should have called. I could have set some time aside for you."

"Lilly, call me Nathan, please. You want to sit? I brought you coffee, a nice expensive cup from an obnoxiously pretentious store." He motioned to the small sofa, and she felt her shoulders relax as she sat, putting the chart aside and taking the warm cup in her hands.

"How have you been?" Nathan sat first on the arm then eased into the small loveseat next to her. A girlish lilt tipped Lilly's heartbeat up, a short relief from its general heaviness. Was this a well-practiced move from his youth?

"Managing—somewhat poorly, my friends would say." Lilly rolled the cup between her hands.

"Did you call the person on that card I gave you?"

"No. I would say I didn't have the time, but that would be a lie. I'm just not the counseling type."

"What about a support group?"

Lilly shook her head, setting the cup aside. "Not me, either. What would help is getting this guy off the streets. Are you making any progress?"

Nathan rested his arm across the back of the furniture. Lilly's first instinct was to fit herself into the crook of it. *Where did that come from?* She grabbed her cup and took a quick drink.

"We don't have a suspect yet. We're focusing on the victims and his process, working it backward in a sense. We've contacted the FBI. We'll be meeting with one of their behavioral specialists soon."

"Any new victims?"

"Not that we're aware of. Hopefully not." He paused and took a sip. "I'm sure you know not all women come forward."

The quiet was comforting to Lilly, and she found herself wanting to stay here with Nathan. He made her feel safe. In addition to being physically strong, he had an underlying confidence that spoke of sureness and resilience. It was the first time she'd ever felt that she wouldn't want to stop knowing him after everything was over.

If it would ever be over.

"The reason I came was to give you this." He reached to the table beside him. Lying there was her mother's journal.

Lilly held her breath as she took it. White leather, gold gilded edges now faded. Opening the cover, she found a black-and-white photo taped to the inside, taken when she was just one or two years old. Her mother held her in her lap, wrapping her in a hug with a gerbera daisy in one hand, her face nuzzled into Lilly's neck. Small trembles quivered in Lilly's fingertips as she traced her mother's outline. She wanted her face to be up, so she could see and refresh her memory of every detail.

"There're more pictures. Ones where you can see her clearly," Nathan said, his voice low and soothing.

"How did you know that's what I was thinking?"

"People lose the details over time that they most want to hold onto. It's not strange you'd want pictures showing her face."

Lilly closed the cover and smoothed her hand over the top. "How is my father?"

"He's well. Very accomplished, wealthy, and lonely."

"Lonely?"

"Some of the richest people, speaking financially, are lonely. They would give up all the money for a few good relationships."

"Then why has he never come to me?"

"My sense is that he desperately wants to but is fearful that you'll reject him."

"Maybe he should be." Lilly checked her watch. "Thanks for bringing this over, but I should get back to seeing patients." She stood and gathered her things. "Thanks for the coffee."

Nathan approached her and took her elbow into his hand, pulling her toward him. At first, she wanted to resist, but his embrace soothed her. "I am here for you, Lilly," he whispered. He let her go and laid the palm of his hand on her cheek, looking briefly into her eyes as if he wanted to say something more, then relented and left her.

Lilly stood in the middle of the room for several minutes before the feel of the chart in her hands pulled her from remembering the peace she felt in his arms. Placing the journal behind the clipboard, she flipped up the top cover.

Sixty-five-year-old female with complaints of headache, right-sided weakness. Patient recently diagnosed with lung cancer.

Great. She checked the chart for the patient's room number and left, relieved to see Luther running down the hall toward her.

"Lilly, can you take this trauma coming in? Anderson is off the floor, and the other two are at the baby shower. Hate to make them leave if we don't have to."

"Sure."

She entered the room as the patient arrived. A young male was wheeled by her with C-spine equipment in place. The EMS crew and two nurses grabbed the backboard and placed him on the gurney.

"Lilly, how have you been?" Mike asked.

"Fine." Lilly put on her gown and gloves.

"It's been a few months. You don't look well."

She glanced at both of them. They looked at one another; sincere questions played between them.

"Did you transport me that night?" Lilly asked.

"We haven't said anything," Raul replied, holding his laptop computer open.

"Good, then we don't need to discuss anything here." Lilly's short reply caused each of the men to physically take a step back. "You can go on with your report."

Raul turned away.

"Lilly, we only want to make sure you're all right. You've always been good to us in here."

"Mike, your report."

He looked down at his notes, rubbing his left bicep with a gloved, bloody hand.

"This is David Lusk, a twenty-one-year-old celebrating his birthday with some excess. Alcohol on board. Wrapped his car around a tree, was ejected through the front windshield. Found approximately twenty feet from his vehicle. Presumed head, neck, and back injuries. PT has been unresponsive but maintaining his airway. Breath sounds diminished on the left side. Abdomen tense. Obvious left femur fracture. Respiratory rate 12. Heart rate 140. BP 90/40. Pulse ox 92 percent. Anything else?"

"No, that's fine, thanks."

"Lilly . . ."

"It's fine, Mike."

He shrugged her off and left the room. Radiology was just completing the bedside films. She neared the patient and began her assessment. He was a crew-cut, blond-haired boy, though difficult to tell with the dirt, grime, blood, and leaves covering his head. His age was hidden by his appearance. She pushed open his eyelids and shone her penlight at each dark circle.

Pupils were large and unresponsive.

"David, can you hear me?"

No response. Likely there never would be again. She made quick work of listening to his chest, palpating for further fractures, checking his response to pain.

"The films are up, Lilly." Luther stepped aside from the computer. She clicked through each of the series.

Spine okay. Chest okay.

"Luther, let's prepare to get him intubated. He's going to need scans of his head and belly. Page surgery and ortho."

"Got it."

Lilly pulled a blank progress report from the file cabinet and began making a few notations.

"We've got a problem here," Luther warned, and the patient's alarms sounded as Luther finished hanging up another bag of IV fluid. "Oxygen level and heart rate are dropping."

Lilly was surprised to see Dana come through the doors.

"That was quick for a surgery response."

"I was at Sonya's shower when they paged me."

"Luther, start bagging him. Let's get him intubated."

"Doesn't look like he's doing so well," Dana replied.

"Nothing an airway won't fix."

"Meds?" Luther asked.

"Not with him decompensating. Let's just get his airway secured."

Lilly took position at the head of the bed and grabbed the airway. Opening the patient's mouth, she visualized the vocal cords and slipped the tube between them. She removed the stylet, a plastic-coated piece of wire to keep the device straight during placement, as an additional nurse stepped up alongside her, placing the respiratory bag to the tube, giving the patient several breaths. Lilly looked expectantly at Luther as he listened to lung sounds.

"I'm not hearing any breath sounds on the left." Luther met her gaze.

"The tube must be in the right bronchus. I'll pull back a little. Now can you hear breath sounds of the left?" Lilly asked.

Luther continued to listen, shaking his head. Lilly could see the patient's right chest rising with each ventilated breath.

"This doesn't make any sense. If I pull this tube out anymore, I'm going to extubate him."

"Heart rate 40."

Lilly put her free hand to her head. She knew intuitively that she should be able to quickly make sense of why her patient was dying. Something she should be able to fix.

"Let me see his films." Dana turned the monitor screen her direction, quickly scanning each X-ray.

"Lilly, he has a collapsed lung on the left side. Now he's shifted. He needs a chest tube."

Luther placed his stethoscope around his neck and grabbed a chest tray. Dana stepped up to the bedside and poured iodine over the young man's chest. Brown and red dripped off of the gurney onto the floor. She made a small incision into the left rib cage, placed a hemostat into the cut and threaded a large, clear tube into the lung space. Lilly heard the rush of air. Dana began to suture the tube in place.

"Heart rate is coming up. Oxygen level increasing."

Lilly still had the breathing tube clenched between her fingers.

"Let's secure this and get an additional chest X-ray." Someone took Lilly's place. Her stomach flopped like dozens of butterflies turning within her. She clenched her lower abdomen. Dana dressed the chest tube.

"We need to talk outside." Dana pointed her to the door. Lilly followed like a reluctant child.

"What is wrong with you? A pneumo? You miss a pneumothorax on X-ray! Lilly, it's as plain as the nose on your face on that film. Your dysfunction is beginning to affect your patients."

"What can I say to you? You've never made a mistake?"

"Of course I've made mistakes, but this wasn't a little pneumo, either. His whole left chest was black. A med student could read it from a mile away. I'm trying to tell you that the way you are managing your life is affecting your work and your patients. You have to step up and fix this." She paused as the patient was wheeled by.

"We're on our way to CT." Luther pulled the gurney through the doorway.

"Great, I'll meet you guys down there," Dana said.

She waited until Luther was out of earshot. "If you don't fix this, I'm going to Anderson. I love you, Lilly. You know that, but I cannot have you jeopardizing patients."

She turned and followed Luther to radiology.

Lilly felt a quake shudder from the center of her being. She sank to the floor, placing her head between her knees and covering it with her arms as she sobbed. There was not one good thing she could claim. She was failing as a person, as a friend, as a doctor.

I want this to end.

"Lilly?"

She raised her head and wiped her eyes quickly.

"Are you all right?" Rachel, another of the ER nurses asked.

"I'm just having a bad day. I'm not really feeling so well."

"I'm so sorry. Do you want me to give this to another physician?"

Lilly had completely forgotten the chart she set down to receive the ambulance patient. "No, I can take it." Lilly pushed herself up against the wall, trying to take the clipboard from her hands.

The nurse held it.

"Are you sure? Maybe you should just go home."

"I'll see this patient and make a decision, all right?"

Rachel relinquished the chart. Lilly scanned for the room number and made her way to the opposite side of the department. Knocking softly on the door, she waited for a verbal response before entering.

"Mrs. Richards?" Lilly grabbed the low-set stool and rolled it to the patient's bedside. A bright multi-colored crocheted afghan covered her legs.

"I haven't been a Mrs. for a long time. You can call me Caroline."

"Caroline then. Did you make this?" Lilly fingered the yarn between her fingers.

"Yes, it's one of my hobbies."

"I'm Dr. Reeves. What brings you in today?"

"I've been having these headaches and the right side of my body just doesn't seem as strong. I've been tripping and falling a lot."

"How long has this been going on?"

"Probably a week or so now."

Lilly scanned through the nurses' notes concerning the patient's medical history.

"You were recently diagnosed with lung cancer. Have you started treatment?"

"No, I'm refusing treatment. My husband died of cancer. He was so sick with the chemo that he couldn't even enjoy life anymore. I've decided to let nature take its course."

"Were you diagnosed here at this hospital? I don't have your old medical record."

"No, at Blue Ridge."

Lilly set the chart down and looked up. "Why not go back there?"

"Are you a woman of faith?"

"No, not really."

"Then this is going to be hard for me to explain." Caroline adjusted the afghan, pulling it up a few inches.

"Just do your best. I'm sure it won't be the strangest thing I've heard," Lilly prompted.

"I'm not so sure about that because I'm finding it pretty strange myself. I feel I should be upfront with you. I've already seen another doctor about these headaches."

"So you're here for a second opinion? There's nothing wrong with that," Lilly assured.

"No, I believe what he told me. He said I have a tumor in my brain, something that started with an *m* . . ."

"Metastasis?"

"Yes, that's what he said. Something was now growing in my brain that was first in my lungs."

"Okay."

"He showed me the scans and everything."

Lilly waited, letting the silence spur the woman on.

"I'm all right with my decision to not seek treatment. I've lived a full life."

"Sixty-five is not that old. Treatment could prolong your life."

"For what purpose? My husband is gone. Someone said to me that if you're a Christian, living on earth is the closest you'll ever come to being in hell. I want to be in heaven."

"So, if I can't change your mind about treatment, what's the point of your visit?"

"I've had some pause about the death thing. Some doubts about what I've believed my whole life. I want to be sure that there is a God."

"I can't help you with that, but I'd be happy to call a chaplain for you to discuss these issues."

"I don't need a minister. I need you to listen. I've been praying that God would use me in a mighty way before my death, so that I could see him working and know that he is real. I've been praying for a mission."

"What sort of mission?"

"Anything. It's probably been the first time in my life I was open to doing whatever. I started having dreams about the time of Christ's birth."

"That doesn't seem unusual. We are getting close to Christmas."

"That's what I thought. Christmas is one of my favorite holidays, and you know they begin advertising the minute Halloween is over, so that's what I thought, too. I'm just looking forward to Christmas."

"There must have been something else, then."

"I started to dream about hospitals."

"That seems a little trickier."

"I'd been in a lot of hospitals so I didn't think much of it, but then I kept hearing a voice in my head, even though it sounded like my voice, telling me to go to Sage. Here. Sage Medical Center."

"And what were you supposed to do once you got here?"

"I was supposed to share the story of the Virgin Mary with the doctor I would see."

"I know the story."

"I mean in a different way. I was supposed to share that Mary was at first afraid when she saw the angel Gabriel."

"An angel named Gabriel? Could it be Gabe?" Lilly asked, her throat thickening with anxiety.

"Maybe today . . . strange how the Lord works. Anyway, I'm supposed to tell you to not be afraid, that your baby will save you. This will help you understand how Christ saved the world."

"But, Caroline, I'm not pregnant."

"That's another thing I'm supposed to tell you. Take a pregnancy test today."

"But I know I'm not pregnant," Lilly pressed as a nervous chuckle followed.

"Dr. Reeves, I don't mean to be rude, but have you looked at yourself? I mean, you're a thin woman, and you look a little swollen in the midsection." The woman pointed at Lilly. She smoothed her clothes and looked down. "He said to make sure you understood."

"I understand, but I don't see the need."

"You haven't told me your first name, have you?"

"No."

"If your name is Lilly—then this message is definitely for you."

Lilly glanced down at her hospital identification tag. Her first name was not listed.

The day dragged slowly after that.

Each second a minute.

Each minute an hour.

Lilly contemplated a way to verify Caroline's news at work. Should she steal a pregnancy test? Maybe send a specimen to the lab under a patient's name? The fear of getting caught prevented her from pursuing either of these options.

After her shift, Lilly cleaned out three stores of home pregnancy tests. The small fortune she'd spent was not the prominent thought in her mind. Foremost was trepidation. Was it possible to be in such denial that you couldn't even see physical changes that were obvious to everyone else? Upon coming home, she took her purchases and went to the bathroom. After she peed into a drinking cup, she pulled out one of the tests and watched as it soaked up the liquid. Setting it aside, she drew the hottest bath she could tolerate. Undressed, she eased herself into the water. Lilly soaped up her hands and smoothed them over her abdomen, pushing and feeling for masses. Her belly was swollen and there was a palpable density. As she pressed, she could feel the fluttering that had annoyed her earlier in the day. It was the same sensation she'd chalked up to nerves over her missed medical diagnosis that almost cost a patient his life.

If I'm not pregnant, then there is another serious issue I'm going to have to address.

She sat and watched as the bubbles leeched back into the water. Reaching for the stick, she brought it closer and saw two distinct pink lines that confirmed what her patient had insisted was true.

She was pregnant. Already three months along.

Lilly dropped the test onto the floor and fell back into the water, the force caused the soapy fluid to spill up over the side of the white porcelain. Crossing her arms over her chest, she began to weep, the thoughts in her mind colliding like clouds during a violent thunderstorm.

How is this possible?

Intellectually, she knew the chances of fertilization and implantation coinciding with the few days of the month she was susceptible to pregnancy were minute at best. Plus, she had agreed to take emergency prophylaxis.

How is it possible to love and hate something in the same breath?

Not only was this her attacker's child, it was her own. It contained her genetic makeup. What she carried from her mother was in this child as well. How could she destroy something that was part of her and her heritage? The child didn't have a say about how it had been conceived; how could she have final say in whether it lived or died? She'd seen in her work that abortion wasn't the end. Initially, there was joy wrought from relief that the situation that burdened the woman to make a choice for abortion was resolved. But then, months after, they were often haunted by their choice. The loss of that child was suffered each waking day. But was that less horrifying then looking into the eyes of your child and seeing glimpses of the man who had brought them into existence without your consent in a violent, demeaning way?

Can I love this baby unconditionally?

If not, could she act as if she loved this child without it picking up on her disgust at its presence? Children were highly sensitive to the emotions of those around them. They knew instinctively when they weren't loved. Was it fair to wait to find out which of those it would be?

Can I handle carrying this child and giving it away?

The facts in evidence were clear. Emotionally, the attack was the inciting event of her rapid downfall. Her unraveling may have been a long time in coming, the steps to the cliff marked by the tragedies in her life. But the rape was a catalyst, hurrying her along the last vestiges of the trail and shoving her over the cliff. She had turned and grabbed hold to the rocky, crumbling edge with one hand, but the depression and anxiety and her methods of dealing with them slowly peeled off those fingers. Which pain was more tolerable? Killing the child and being plagued by the loss of an innocent life, or giving it away, then wondering if each child she met were her child? What if the life it was given up to was worse than the one she would have provided?

Lilly pulled herself from the tub. Without drying off, she looked at herself in the mirror, the water dripped from her body, each pore cried the tears of her pain. She reached for the glass of red wine she'd brought with her. Pulling it to her lips, she paused, the smell of the liquor heavy in her nostrils. She breathed it in, seeing her pain and anguish clear, the shroud of denial stripped from her as she stood bare. Letting the stem slide through her hand, she grasped the goblet and slammed it into the mirror.

Chapter 21

December 6

NATHAN CHECKED HIS appearance. Brett was at his desk, finishing up several phone calls before the task-force meeting set to begin in one hour. Prior to this, however, they had another call that had Nathan's OCD in overdrive.

The FBI was here.

Nathan hated to have his work scrutinized by other agencies. Particularly one he had parted ways with in the past. And the reason for his departure was the lead slot on his list of unforgivables. It wasn't that he thought his work couldn't measure up—just that he felt they viewed his work as inferior before they even examined it. The minutest detail that he might have left untouched, that usually had no bearing on the case, would be the one thing they would hang him up by his toes for. Like a rookie who'd forgotten to Mirandize an arrestee. They acted as if all of his specialized training leaked from his head when he joined the local police.

Only a few people were privy to the fact Nathan had worked for the FBI. Even Brett didn't know about his service in that sect.

"Nathan, you've got to stop fidgeting. You're driving me nuts," Brett called, leafing through several folders on his desk.

"Don't mess those up." Nathan paced to his desk, grabbing the pile away from Brett's hands.

"You've got to chill out. That last call was the desk sergeant. Seems our savior cometh."

"Not funny."

"Let's head upstairs to the conference room."

Waiting outside the door was a towering man who looked ill fitted in the suit he was wearing. His hair was bleach blond and his eyes were pale green; a deep tan made these two physical attributes pop from his head. Brett elbowed Nathan in the rib cage as they neared the room.

"Where'd they find this guy, Miami Beach?"

Nathan glowered and closed the distance, offering his hand.

"I'm Detective Nathan Long, head of the task force."

"Joshua Reynolds, FBI Behavioral Science Unit," he replied, his handshake firm.

Brett followed suit, making introductions.

They entered the conference room and took seats at one end of the large table.

Joshua opened a folder of his own notes then, folding his hands, settled back into his chair.

"The two of you have a very nasty character on your hands."

"Tell me something we don't know," Brett said.

"I read through your preliminary report. It was quite thorough, but there is still a lot of ground to cover."

"The task force has been working this case hard over the last three months. Thus far, we've assigned one detective to each victim in the series. We developed an in-depth questionnaire for each of them to see where they cross each other's paths, as well as the suspect's. We're still sifting through those and finishing up the more detailed interviews."

"I've read through what you sent, and I think I have some thoughts. I'd like to sit in on your meeting. It will help me develop a more accurate profile. Mind if I participate in the group?"

Nathan pivoted his chair side to side. "Not at all. We're all here to help each other out and get this guy off the street."

"I'm glad you feel we can work together. I'd like to review some of my findings."

"Please share," Brett said. Nathan cranked his chair, knocking Brett's with a distinctive thud.

"I think he's our most rare kind of rapist . . . à la Ted Bundy." Joshua leafed through several pages before stopping. "I would characterize him as an anger-excitation rapist. Very charming. Quite intelligent. He learns from his mistakes."

"He doesn't seem to make any." Brett pivoted toward Joshua. "That's our problem."

"They all make mistakes. That's how we catch them."

"Then tell me what his are," Brett continued.

"Just because they're not clear, doesn't mean there aren't any. He's likely well practiced. This probably isn't his only victim series."

"He didn't pop up in CODIS," Nathan said.

"The Combined DNA Identification System has its value, but it likely won't solve your case."

"Why not? He seems to love leaving his DNA," Brett said.

"That's exactly why. For some reason, he's unconcerned with leaving semen behind, so it doesn't surprise me that his DNA profile isn't in the database. It's as I said: his IQ is high. He knows we won't catch him with that evidence. The question is why. And until we know that, we'll have to come up with a different angle. The victims will be a good place to start. Was there any match between the Campbell baby and the perpetrator?"

Brett shifted in his seat. Nathan cleared his throat. "That evidence is no longer available."

"What happened?"

"The van transporting the evidence was involved in an accident. It was incinerated."

Joshua clicked his tongue between his teeth. "That's very unfortunate. May I approach your link chart?"

"Be my guest," Nathan offered, beginning to stand.

"No, no . . . please sit. I might ramble." Joshua picked up his folder from the table. "I take it these tacks on the map represent each of your victims' homes."

Brett nodded in affirmation. "These were the places they were attacked."

"Love the little numbers on each one. Clever."

Nathan wasn't sure the tone was a compliment.

"I'd like to place another series of pins. One representing where each of the victims worked." Joshua picked up the first pin and scanned the map. "The one thing about all of these women is their character. All are strong, fiercely independent women. Victim number one is an auto mechanic—clearly a male-dominated field."

He inserted the first marker in place.

"Torrence, who seemed to have the most contact with the perpetrator, was studying engineering."

Marker two made it onto the board.

"Victim three, Heather Allen, was a competitive body builder. I'm going to pin her workplace and her gym."

Joshua paused as he placed these two pins. "I haven't quite identified how Jacqueline would fit. She's a kindergarten teacher. But you must have some dominance raising four kids as a single mother."

"She was widowed," Nathan volunteered.

"Ah, interesting. And obviously, Lilly is not meek. She's a martial arts expert, weapons owner, and accomplished ER physician."

Joshua stopped his work and stepped to the side. "All these women represent his mother." Nathan's heart rate increased as he began to see a pattern emerging.

"It always goes back to the cradle." Brett smirked. "You're here to tell us something we can't figure out on our own."

"Unfortunately, our deepest wounds come from childhood. I'm not treating you as inferiors. A lot of our knowledge will overlap."

"Let me stop you right there." Brett held up a single hand while the other gripped the arm of his chair. "How long have you been with this unit?"

"One year."

"How many cases?" Brett fired the question without pausing.

"With BSU, this is my first field assignment. But surely you know what an accomplished agent you have to be to even get where I am."

"Joshua. Forgive me, but this is all part of Introduction to Rapist 101. Obviously, we will find that his mother is a domineering woman and treated him horrendously in some manner. He's likely married because all these creeps need a wife to look legit. Can you give us something that maybe we're not thinking of?" Brett asked, hands folded, index fingers tapping with expectation.

"This will be preliminary."

"Of course. We won't hold you to the fire if it doesn't pan out," Nathan said.

"I will," Brett replied, slamming his feet onto the tabletop.

Nathan studied the newly placed locations. He stood from his chair and shoved Brett's feet off the conference room table as he moved to the link chart. In the center of the pins was a blue circle with a white capital "H."

"He works at SMC." Nathan's fingers slid over the tops of the cool plastic push pins. "This is home base."

Joshua faced the board. "We know Lilly and Torrence had crossings at SMC. Lilly is employed there, and Torrence was a patient in the ER and was also being followed at that facility for her pregnancy. Your perp selects his victims from his work and play environments. He stalks them for long periods. He must do this in order to copy their keys and learn when it is best to attack. Your victims are widely scattered all around the city in nearly a sixty-mile radius. However, when I add these new points, you can see each of the victims falls, at some point, within a ten-mile radius of one institution."

Nathan turned to face Joshua. "He's a doctor."

Joshua's face was solemn. "Well respected and liked. Each of your victims already knows him by name, but the disguise he wears keeps them from realizing it."

Chapter 22

December 11

KADIN WORRIED AS he bounded up the steps to Lilly's townhouse. He'd received a frantic call from Dana begging him to do everything he could to clear his schedule and come immediately. Next to Lilly, or at least who Lilly had been before she became this shadow, Dana was one of the most level-headed people he knew, and her demeanor never rose above subtle joy at best.

He knocked softly on the door. Dana answered in mere seconds and pulled him by the elbow into Lilly's home. The scene before him was so foreign that he had to force himself not to back out the door and check the address.

The living room was dark. Only a faint glow from the gas logs provided any light. Lilly was supine on the couch dressed in underwear with a loosely fitted white blouse covering her upper chest. It was buttoned just below her breasts, exposing her belly. She held one of her firearms over her navel and did not meet Kadin's eyes.

Covering her coffee table were several empty wine coolers, beer bottles, and shot glasses. Her empty eyes threatened to pull him into an unrelenting void of despair.

He cursed himself silently for not coming by last week.

"What's going on?"

"Follow me."

Watching Lilly from the corner of his eye, he followed Dana up the stairs and to the bathroom that sat opposite Lilly's bedroom. Entering after her, he paused, attempting to interpret the scene before him.

Strewn in every conceivable nook were dozens of white sticks. They bloomed from the small white trash can that sat next to the sink.

"They're pregnancy tests."

"I know what they are." Kadin stepped closer to the vanity and leaned closer to see what the results indicated.

"They're all positive. I checked."

"I thought she took emergency contraception."

"She did."

"How long has she known?"

Dana sighed and plopped down on the toilet, the knuckle of her index finger gathering her sadness before it tumbled down her cheeks.

"I don't know. She hasn't returned any of my calls for over a week. Anderson cornered me in the ER to ask about her when I was down there for a consult. Said she's missed her last three shifts. She hasn't even called in to report her absence." She paused, tapping two fingers on the nearby toilet paper roll, tearing off several sheets, and dabbing her eyes. "When I got here, the door was open. She won't acknowledge me. It's freaking me out!"

Kadin could feel his heart heave beneath his ribs. "Do you think she's suicidal?"

"I don't know. I can't get her to talk."

He leaned down before her. "We'll get this figured out. We won't leave her alone."

Dana nodded weakly.

"Why don't you let me try." Kadin stood.

They returned to the lower level. Dana took the chair. Kadin sat at the end of the couch. He reached for the gun and slipped it from her listless fingers. He released the magazine and set it separate from the weapon on the floor next to him.

"Lilly, Dana and I are very worried about you. Can you tell us what's going on?"

Kadin feared falling into her cavernous depression.

"Obviously, we know about the baby. Do you want to talk about it?"

Lilly did not engage him.

Kadin turned to Dana, searching for a suggestion. She shrugged her shoulders haplessly. His soul tugged at his heart. Unsure what Lilly's response would be, he folded his hands and prayed.

"Heavenly Father, Dana and I come to you on behalf of our friend Lilly. We see she is in such deep pain that she can't seem to even speak of it. We know the Holy Spirit will pray for us when we don't have the words . . ."

"Do not pray for me, Kadin."

A pain cracked in his chest. He looked up. The voice was strong, free of slurred, intoxicated syllables.

"Unless you talk to me, I don't know how else to help you, Lilly."

"Do you think I deserve what's happened to me?" Tears fell freely, though her voice remained steady.

Kadin's mouth dried. "Of course not."

"Then why did God allow this to happen? Why do I have to carry this monster's child?"

Kadin tried to hide the shock from his eyes, but he couldn't keep it from his next question. "You intend to keep the baby?" Lilly looked away, and Dana's glance threw knives as she shook her head in disapproval. He placed his palms over his eyes and rubbed hard.

"It's hard for me to speak to you about this, Lilly. I fear whatever I say will be too much and send you in the wrong direction."

Lilly left her escaping tears untouched.

"What's been going on?" Dana asked.

"I don't know if I can talk about it."

"Do you want to kill yourself?" Kadin asked. "It was a little unnerving seeing you lying here with a loaded weapon."

Dana squirmed, struggling for words. She stilled, a determination straightening her posture.

"Lilly, you have to be honest with us on this. Otherwise, we're not leaving you here until we're sure you're safe."

"I think I would be better off dead than to live through this."

Kadin's breath stilled in the silence. Considering Lilly's lack of faith, he feared his words would drop her from the cliff as he held on with a shaky grip from the ledge. It was almost like she was opening up her hand so she would fall. Would shock help her hold on tighter?

"What's stopping you, Lilly?" Kadin challenged. From his peripheral vision, he saw Dana tilt in her seat, incredulous.

"I can't kill the baby."

The hand took hold. Motherly instinct kicked in. "Why not? You didn't care about the possibility before."

"Kadin, back off," Dana warned.

"That's before I knew it was real! Before I felt it moving!"

Kadin leaned back as Lilly sat up. Relief flooded through his body. Anger meant she could still fight.

"I've missed several cycles. I thought it was stress because I had some spotting the first couple of months after the rape."

They both remained silent.

"Denial is an extremely useful tool." She brought the back of her hand to her face and cleared each cheek. "I started to not feel well a couple of months ago. I would come home and immediately go to bed. I asked Anderson to split my shifts because I couldn't bear the thought of working two in a row."

Lilly settled her legs straight. Kadin took in the swollen abdomen.

"My last shift, I had this lady come and visit me."

"You specifically?" Kadin asked.

"Work seems to be a nice place to get messages delivered."

"What are you talking about?"

"When I got horribly sick, I was visited by a man name Gabe."

Dana sat forward. "Lilly, you already told me about this. The story he told you."

"Well, did I mention he told me I would have to make a decision about a life and it wouldn't exactly be a clear one?"

Kadin took her hands. "Try to calm down . . ."

"Then, my last shift, it was Sonya's baby shower. I didn't feel well at all—something weird in my belly like a dozen trapped butterflies, like weird muscle fasciculations. I was sick to my stomach. Eating didn't make it better. I nearly killed a patient! Then this woman comes to see me. She's dying of cancer."

It took everything for Kadin not to interrupt and clarify exactly what these odd happenings meant. But it was the most she'd ever opened up.

"She said she'd been having dreams from God. That he wanted her to give me a message."

"What was the message?"

"To not be afraid. That I needed to take a pregnancy test. That this baby would save my life. How is that possible when it will remind me every day of what happened?"

Kadin gripped her hands tighter. "Lilly, we're going to be fine here."

Her words clustered between sobs. "The baby's not going to be right, anyway. All of the drinking I've been doing. It's going to be damaged."

"That's not necessarily true, Lilly," Dana said.

"Lilly, I think God gave you this baby to make a way for you to be free. To understand how a child can save."

"Do not give me any line about how God won't give you more than you can handle."

"Lilly." Kadin leaned forward and placed both hands on her exposed abdomen. "I know I've probably said all the wrong things. My purpose is not to alienate you from God, and I beg his forgiveness every night if I do things that make him less visible to you. In my heart, I know this baby lives to give life back to you. I don't know how, but it will save you. Sometimes, God will bring you to the end of yourself so that all you can see is him."

Chapter 23

December 18

Touchdown was smooth, and it didn't take long for Nathan and Brett to gather their luggage and make it off the plane. It was midmorning in Las Vegas. They were scheduled to stay one evening. Nathan hoped they could wrap up this interview and he could have one night to rest from the stress of the case. To say that this was all-consuming wouldn't rise to the level of an understatement.

Nathan waited as Brett got their rental car. It seemed like such an outside shot that this vehicle and the woman who owned it would have anything to do with the case. Meanwhile, the task force was considering themselves lucky that there hadn't been a new attack and the rapist seemed to be veering off his normal pattern.

Then again, maybe there was another victim, and they just didn't know about her yet.

Brett neared him and jingled the keys in front of his face. "Ready?"

"Why not?"

They made their way through the terminal, exchanged paperwork with the rental car company, and neared the row of vehicles. After several failed attempts to locate it, Brett hit the remote entry, and a set of headlights flashed to their left.

"I thought you got a midsize?" Nathan asked.

"How can a car be that small?" Brett inspected it for damage and struggled to stow their luggage in the truck. "Why'd you bring so much?"

"Case files."

"There'd be less if you were a girl." Brett struggled to latch the miniature trunk. He finally gave up, took a high leap, and slammed his rear on top of the lid to close it.

"I hope we can get that open again. The weight of your buttocks probably broke the latch."

"Ooh, Mr. Funnyman today. You navigate, and I'll drive."

Getting inside their white compact car, Brett wiggled in the seat, pushing his feet into the floorboard.

"I think that's as far back as it goes." Nathan pulled his seat belt and locked it.

"You have got to be kidding me. My knees are touching the dash." More wiggling ensued.

"Brett, your seat is touching the backseat. Give it up."

He sighed as he turned around. "You cannot call that a backseat. You know there are a minimum set of dimensions."

"For you and a woman to have some fun?" Nathan opened a local map and checked the address.

"It's only American."

"Well, the problem is, I doubt this is American made."

"Whatever. Which way?"

"Take a left out of here."

The glory of the Vegas strip was lost as the sun rose high and whitewashed the landscape. Still, it seemed busy with foot traffic. After passing the major hotel attractions, they settled into residential areas that were calm and modest. A sharp contrast to the glitz of the main corridor.

"You said she lives in a gated community." Brett thumped his knee against the steering column.

"It should be about another five miles up the road here."

Nathan noticed the houses beginning to space out. A large stone-and-wrought-iron fence began, shielding the rich from the poorer citizens. A guarded gate was on their right. Brett turned the vehicle in, and the guard did not immediately open the window.

"He thinks we're in the wrong neighborhood. Doesn't like our car much." Brett cranked down his window. "Not even a power package." Nathan smirked as his partner twisted, attempting to reach his wallet. The car rocked back and forth.

"You're going to pop a tire, all that movement," Nathan teased.

"Shut up."

Pulling out his ID, Brett quick-flipped it at the guard, who slid the window open.

"We're here to see Meryl Stipman," Brett said.

"I'll have to ring her." He slid the window shut.

"I'm going to start feeling insulted," Brett said, the car jiggled more as he placed his wallet back.

"I'm already there."

The window slid open again. "She says she's expecting you. Take the large circle around, first right you can make, she's the second property on the right."

"Thanks." Brett eased the car through the gate.

"Can't wait to see this place. They don't even call it a house."

A long, winding street was lined with giant palm trees on either side of the lane. The road split into a circular drive; the center area was grass with a huge, gray stone fountain with a vase spilling water over a large pile of rocks. Brett parked their micro car in front of the marble staircase that led up to the front entrance of the property. Tiered fountains sat at the base of either side of the stairwell. The house was several stories of white stucco and black clay roof tiles.

"You know she has some money."

"I wonder where the pink Escalade is." Nathan said as they topped the staircase. There was a bell with a pull chain. Brett gave it a single tug. The black doors opened, and a young woman in a tailored pantsuit greeted them.

"Detectives, come in. Ms. Stipman is waiting for you in the sunroom."

They followed her clicking heels across intricate tile floors as she veered slightly left into a glass-walled room. The view out the back of the house was even more stunning. A large patio met a large oval pool lined with more palm trees that continued around the pool and made another small lane to a group of tennis courts.

"Do you play?"

"Tennis?" Nathan neared the older woman and took her hand in both of his. Ms. Stipman was nearly three inches taller than he was, with stylish gray hair and steel-blue eyes. "I rarely have time for sports. I'm Detective Nathan Long. This is my partner, Brett Sawyer."

She relinquished Nathan's hand, offering hers to Brett. "You?"

"I like to try every now and then."

"Honestly?" She pulled his hand closer to her, lowering her voice in a conspiratorial whisper. "You seem more the armchair-quarterback type."

Nathan could sense Brett didn't know if that was playful bantering or an outright insult.

"Maybe we'll play and you can judge for yourself." He dropped her hand.

"Seems crazy you boys had to come all this way to look at my silly vehicle." She walked away from them. Brett rolled his eyes at Nathan.

"We just need to ask you a few questions, and we should be on our way."

"I'm just curious about the color," Brett said. "Why pink? Seems like a dainty choice for a heavy-duty vehicle. I don't imagine you get much snow here in Vegas." He took a seat in a padded white wicker chair.

"Let's just say I had a small disagreement with a cosmetics company. Wanted to show off a little bit."

"Mary Kay?" Nathan replied.

"In turn, I started my own home-based cosmetics company to try to run them into the ground. As you can see, I've been quite successful with that."

"But they're still more prominent. Why not pick your own unique color?"

She seemed stumped. Nathan wondered what Brett's angle was. "Were you in Colorado around January 3 of this year?"

"Yes, I was visiting a relative for the holidays."

"Were you in an accident?"

"I'm not used to driving in inclement weather. It had snowed, and the roads were icy. I slid into a sign as I was trying to stop at a light."

"Did you report the accident?" Nathan asked.

"I didn't see a need to. No other cars were involved, and I figured the police were too busy doing other things."

Nathan smoothed his tongue on the inside of his cheek. Had he just caught her in a lie? "Where does your relative live?"

"In Lone Tree."

"Were you in possession of your vehicle the whole time?" Brett asked.

Meryl tapped her heels together where she stood, like Dorothy trying to go home.

"These questions seem to be going outside those for a minor traffic collision. I already said I was in the car at the time of the accident."

"Who were you visiting?"

"I said a relative."

"Mrs.—"

"Ms., please."

"Ms. Stipman, the more forthright you can be with your answers, the less likely we are to become suspicious that you're trying to hide something. Your vehicle was in the vicinity of a crime, and we believe that the person who committed it is responsible for several others."

"So there's been a rash of unreported stop sign collisions? That's why you're here?"

"No, of course not." Nathan closed his notepad and squared his shoulders. He took several steps in her direction. "There have been several rapes. Are you a mother?"

"Yes."

"Any daughters?"

"No, two sons."

"Is that who you were visiting? Your son?" Brett asked, picking up Nathan's dangling thread.

She eased away from Nathan and looked at Brett. "Yes, I was visiting him."

"So, I'll ask you again, Ms. Stipman, were you in possession of your vehicle the whole time?"

"That is like the airport baggage question. If you walk two steps away from your suitcase, are you still in possession of it?"

"So, either you're not sure, or you don't want to commit to any answer." Nathan blocked her between the two of them.

"I'm just saying it's technical. After the damage occurred, my son took it to a body shop. He said he was friends with the owner and could get a good price."

"But why would you be worried about money, considering your incredible resources?" Brett stood and inched closer.

"Just because I'm rich doesn't mean I'm not frugal."

"Why didn't you fly, Ms. Stipman?" Nathan asked. "Seems an awfully long way for you to drive."

"My son wanted to see the car."

"Why didn't he come here to visit?"

"He's a doctor. It's hard for him to get away."

"A doctor?" Nathan's heart dropped several beats as pressure swelled in his throat. "What hospital?"

"He covers several."

"Is Sage Medical Center one of them?"

"I believe so. Why?"

Nathan thought back to the link chart as Joshua's pins clarified the pattern in his mind. He'd been right.

A doctor.

Nathan tried to swallow past the viselike sensation.

"Ma'am, we'll need a recent picture of your son, if you have one."

Chapter 24

December 21

A Christmas storm swooped in over the Rocky Mountains. Visibility was a few feet at best in the darkness. The only things discernable were sheets of blowing snow pelting Lilly's windshield. She found it difficult to keep her car from fishtailing on the straight paths, let alone each turn. After she had parked, the frigid wind propelled her toward the ER entrance, and she leaned back into it to prevent herself from falling forward. Stomping the snow off her boots, she entered the hospital and slipped her coat off as she walked.

The department was quiet, although saying the *q* word out loud invoked community tyranny, as the volume of patients could quadruple in a matter of minutes. The halls were vacant, and most of the people were sitting at computers in the central work area, catching up on charts from patients they'd seen during the day. Lilly didn't mind working the night shift. Generally, the pace slowed as the night progressed. Fewer administrative personnel lurked to try to snatch you for meetings, chart clarification, and billing concerns.

After placing her coat in a locker with her purse, she buttoned up her new lab coat that she'd bought several sizes larger, rolling up the sleeves to her wrists. She was hopeful it would disguise her pregnancy enough so that if most people wondered about her recent weight gain, they would assume it was from other vices. Lilly wasn't sure she'd actually get away with it. Medical people were astute, and she found it hard not to exhibit the habits pregnant women subconsciously portrayed, like keeping a protective hand over her expanding belly.

Kadin called her daily, begging her to come in for an exam. Although it would have been her preference not to give up the sleeping pills and alcohol, there was a small maternal burden present to at least try to do her best to keep the baby healthy, and that was the only decision she'd made so far. She could see the questioning worry in both Dana and Kadin about what she was going to do in the end.

Maybe nine months of pregnancy was a blessing.

"Lilly, good to see you at work on time." Dr. Anderson approached her with several charts in his hands.

"Are these patients you need to turn over?"

"No, finished up. Oddly, you're starting fresh with new ones. There are a few that were just finished in triage. Minor complaints."

Lilly heard a nurse pick up the EMS phone, taking report from an ambulance crew. She beckoned Lilly closer.

"What's up?"

"They're bringing in a pregnant patient. She seems physically stable. Do you want her to go upstairs?"

"How far along is she?"

"They don't know, and I guess she's not saying."

"She's incoherent?"

"No, refusing to give the information."

Lilly brushed her hair from her eyes. "Well, unless we know for sure she's over twenty weeks, she needs to come here. We'll medically screen her. Who's on call for OB?"

"Dr. Maguire."

"Why don't you see if he can come down with an ultrasound machine and clear up how many weeks pregnant she is? What's their ETA?"

"They're pulling in. I told them Trauma 2."

Lilly made her way to the trauma bay. Just as she rounded the corner, she saw the crew coming in. One of the ER nurses trailed behind them.

"Hey, Lilly." Eric smiled, one eyebrow raised in that you're-going-to-love-this-patient sense.

"Having trouble staying on the roads?" Lilly watched as the crew placed the patient on the gurney, tilting the backboard to one side.

"We're not, but I guess this young lady is. I think she's in her twenties. Skidded into a tree, though I'm not sure how much of an accident it was."

"Oh?"

"She was sliding off the road, but the direction of the tire treads didn't initially send her in that direction. The officer on scene told me that he saw what seemed to be a lot of correcting in order to meet the tree intentionally."

"Has she said she's suicidal?"

"She really won't say anything. She's got some pretty deep lacerations on her hands and arms that look like they have glass embedded in them. She moves everything. Pupils are equal and reactive. I didn't see any obvious fractures. She was able to extricate herself from the vehicle. We found her wandering away from the scene toward the woods. The person that called in the accident kept tabs on her until we arrived."

"Was she dazed?"

"No, she seemed quite determined, like she didn't want us to find her. The man following her said she kept telling him to go away."

"What about ID?"

"Nothing in the car. No purse or vehicle registration. The police are close behind. They're running the plates and the VIN number. If we're lucky, the car will be registered to her or at least someone who knows her." Eric's partner approached, pushing the empty pram. "Let us know if you need anything else. We're on all night."

The nurses already had her connected to the monitor, and the patient's vital signs looked reassuring. Radiology had completed their films, shielding the patient's abdomen to the best of their ability. Lilly saw the nurses take off their lead aprons. After grabbing a warm washcloth, she approached the bed. A pair of green eyes peered through a tangle of red curls. Grass, blood, and dirt made her pale skin look darker than it actually was.

"Hey there," Lilly spoke, her words just above a whisper. "I'm Dr. Reeves." Lilly began to brush the dirt away with light strokes of the cloth. "What's your name?" The patient stared at her initially, almost fearful, but now averted her gaze. "Are you uncomfortable on this board?"

There was a slight nod in the affirmative.

"If you can answer my questions, I can get you off. Okay?"

Another nod.

"Name?"

"Annalisa."

"Annalisa, are you pregnant?"

A pause, the tip of her tongue smoothing over cracked lips. "Yes."

"How far along are you?"

"Twenty-eight weeks."

"We're going to have an OB physician come down and check you out. Are you feeling your baby move?"

Clearing her throat, Annalisa whispered, "Yes."

"Were you trying to hurt yourself?"

Again, she looked away. Sometimes avoidance was the only way to answer. Lilly stepped back, giving her some physical space, and reviewed the films of her spine.

"I'm going to examine you. If everything looks good, I'll get you off this board." Lilly stepped through the trauma exam quickly. Not seeing any neurologic deficits and noting that the spinal films were negative for fracture, she removed the C-collar from her neck and helped her to roll off the board. Lilly pulled several blankets from the warmer and placed them over her shivering patient.

"There's a problem with the baby," Annalisa said to Lilly's back. She turned to see her patient's eyes moist with tears.

"What sort of problem?"

"I don't want it."

"We can talk about options if you don't want to keep the baby."

The patient whipped her head from side to side, tear droplets flinging from her face. "No, the baby is evil! I don't want to carry it anymore."

Lilly approached the bed, placing her hands on the young woman's shoulders. "Annalisa, it's just a baby . . ."

"You don't understand!"

"I'm trying to, but I need you to calm down."

Dr. Maguire entered the room.

"Dr. Reeves." He pulled an ultrasound machine to the bedside.

"Thanks for coming," Lilly stood and straightened her lab coat. "This is Annalisa. We need the baby checked. She thinks she's seven or eight months."

"Who's your regular doctor?" He pushed the layers of blankets to one side and unbuttoned the patient's shirt. She slapped his hands away.

"Annalisa, it's okay. We just need to check the baby."

"I don't want him touching me."

"Here, I'll do it," Lilly offered. "We just need the bottom part up a bit." Annalisa allowed Lilly to expose her belly.

"This will be cold." Maguire left trails of clear jelly over her abdomen. He placed the transducer down and static swooshing overcame the beeping from her monitor. Lilly saw the images appear on the screen.

"Fetal HR 160. That's good."

"Do you want to see your baby?" Lilly asked. Annalisa was not looking at the screen. Her eyes were turned away, tears continued to flow down her face. Lilly grabbed some tissues and dabbed at Annalisa's cheeks. "What's wrong? The baby is healthy."

"I think she's just shy of twenty weeks," Dr. Maguire stated.

A look came across Annalisa's eyes that spoke of resigned hatred.

"He's lying!"

She was off the bed, making quick swipes at her stomach to remove the conducting gel, then shoved the machine away. Maguire backed up several steps. Annalisa stood there, breathing hard, her lips pressed so the color drained.

Lilly put herself directly in front of the patient. From the corner of her eye, she saw one nurse leave the room for security. Drake began to approach from the side, closing the gap. Annalisa grabbed a scalpel from the laceration tray that had been opened at her bedside and pulled off the protective cover, slicing several of her fingers. Tiny red droplets fell onto the white tile floor. Drake stopped his forward progression as she slashed the object at him.

"Annalisa," Lilly waved in her direction. "Look at me. Tell me what's going on."

"I know the baby's not twenty weeks."

"How do you know?"

"Because I know the exact day I conceived."

"It's not unusual to be off. We'll look again."

"I'm not off!"

"Annalisa, I meant the machine. We'll look with the machine again."

"He is not coming near me." She pointed the sharp at Drake.

"All right. He's not moving. See, he's still." The nurse had reentered the room with a security guard and additional ER doctor, Kurt Stephans. At least he could keep his cool. They hung toward the wall.

"I was raped."

The words were so small, encapsulated, spoken at the end of a dark tunnel that Lilly almost wondered if she had said them to herself.

"What?" Lilly asked.

"That's how I know the date. It's his baby."

Lilly's mouth dried, her words stuck in her throat. All of them were silent. Lilly wasn't sure she could speak the words out loud, but she didn't know how to diffuse the situation, either. She took a deep breath and closed her eyes.

"I know how you feel."

"You can't!"

"I do," Lilly added quickly. "I'm dealing with the same thing." Lilly slowly unbuttoned her lab coat and turned to the side, smoothing her hands on her protruding belly, exposing her secret to save this frail girl's life. If she didn't diffuse the situation, things were going to escalate, and likely not in Annalisa's favor. The room coalesced in disbelief. "It's not something I would lie to you about."

"It doesn't matter. I know what I need to do."

The motion was so quick that even as the arterial spray from Annalisa's neck hit her and Drake, Lilly wasn't quite sure what happened until she saw the red fluid flowing down Annalisa's chest and the scalpel drop to the floor. The patient still stood, swooning, her hand at her throat, her eyes filled with regret.

"Kurt!"

He rushed passed Lilly, nearly toppling her over as he slammed her shoulder. He caught Annalisa before she fell, scooped her up and laid her on the bed, grabbing a stack of gauze pads from the opened tray and began to apply pressure. Bubbles frothed from her throat as horrible gasps shuddered from her mouth.

"She cut through half her trachea. Someone get me an airway tray!"

The security guard hit the code blue button. Several additional nurses fled in.

Lilly turned to Maguire. His back was toward her. "Drake, you have to take the baby!"

"It's not viable!" he shouted back. Lilly stared at the scene before her. Something was not clicking. Something she shouldn't be missing. The monitor alarmed. Lilly noted the deadly heart rhythm on the screen.

"What harm will it do?" Kurt asked him as one of the ER techs stepped up on a stool to start chest compressions.

"Dr. Reeves, are you bleeding?"

Lilly looked down and saw the crimson streak across her chest. Glancing to her left, she saw Drake wiping his eyes. She grabbed his arm and hurried him toward the sink.

"Is it in your eyes? Drake!"

He seemed stunned, resisting her.

"Her blood could be infected. We have to wash your eyes."

Lilly shoved him hard against the metal edge. Popping the protective covers off the eye wash station, she shoved his head forward into the stream. He bucked, attempting to pull up. She bore down on his neck with her elbow and used her free hand to scoop water. As she reached into the sink to gather more, a contact lens fell from his eye.

A green-colored contact.

The other dropped into the sink.

He raised his head.

One blue eye. One brown eye.

Lilly's heart seized within her chest as she reached forward to grab his shirt, her hand clenched to the point where her fingernails drew blood from her palm even with the fabric serving as a barrier.

She yanked his scrub top down.

The tattoo. Three heads. A snake breathing fire.

"Looks like I have another baby on the way," he whispered, reaching down and placing his hand over her stomach. Lilly took one step back and punched him in the jaw. He fell against the sink, then slumped to the floor.

A security guard tackled Lilly from the side, sending them both into a light crimson pool of blood and water. Lilly scrambled out of his arms as he tried to contain her, stood, sliding in the water as she pointed an accusatory finger at Drake.

"Call the police and detain Dr. Maguire. He's the man who raped me!"

Chapter 25

NATHAN STOOD OUTSIDE of the interview rooms, looking at Drake Maguire through one window and Lilly Reeves in the next. She was huddled into her lab coat. Blood stained the front of her garment, and she stared straight ahead, unseeing. His whole case had just ignited, and he wasn't in a good mood about it. The late-night phone call summoning him to the office was the last thing he'd expected.

What is the world coming to?

This is where Nathan was. *The Twilight Zone.* A doctor accused of sexual assault on a fellow physician. An OB as a serial rapist.

It wasn't a situation he could comprehend.

Doctors, as well as peacekeepers, held an elevated place in society. They were trusted to make decisions that might irreversibly alter the course of another's life. A doctor could cure someone, yet in the next breath, that same physician could prioritize one critical patient over another, and someone could die.

These decisions played out every day in law enforcement, as well. A cop could send someone to prison, or give a guy a second chance to walk the narrow path. In the next second, a decision can be made to use deadly force in order to save a life or the future of another's. It was the expectation that law enforcers and life protectors were above reproach. They were the moral fiber that held the culture together in one, albeit dysfunctional, cohesive system.

Drake Maguire had cut a hole into that fabric. He crossed a line that he should not have breached. Not only did he hurt countless women, but he also betrayed the public trust.

These things were difficult to heal from.

"You're sure she's all right?" Nathan asked Brett, who stood next to him, raking his fingernails through several days of stubble.

"Physically or otherwise?"

Nathan couldn't still his mind. His approach to both Lilly and Drake was going to be tricky.

A rape case was always tricky. Especially when you had feelings for the victim.

He massaged his forehead with the palm of his hand, attempting to determine which interview tactic to use. "Both."

"She says it's not her blood. Evidently she was caught in the cross spray after the patient slit her own throat. So, physically, I guess okay."

"What do we know about the baby? Is it his?" Nathan motioned toward Drake's room.

"She's not said anything. We only have the accounts from the rest of the ER staff. None of them knew before today about this pregnancy."

"She's been hiding it from everyone? Do you think Daughtry knows?"

"Your guess is as good as mine."

Nathan glanced between the two individuals. Tradition and logic, as opposed to legal necessity, dictated that he talk to the victim first. It was the assumption that victims would be the honest ones with nothing to hide. Nathan exited the monitoring station, turned the corner, and opened the door to Lilly's room.

It was a typical government interrogation setup. The size of the room was determined by the recording devices it was equipped with. A larger table and bigger room would've meant more cameras and microphones. Instead, the small room had just one little, wooden veneer table sitting in the center. Along each edge, the laminate had been chipped by hand-cuffed suspects and bored cops using pens like schoolboys stuck in detention. Nathan smoothed his new shirt close to his chest so the pocked edge of the table wouldn't snag the fabric. The chairs in these rooms were the worst in the building, castoffs from people in search of a better one. The carpet was cheap and frayed.

This is detention for me.

Lilly pulled the edges of her lab coat tighter.

The air in the room was thick with his apprehension at not opening with the right words.

"Why didn't you tell me?" He moved his hand across the table to reach for her. She edged back. "Do you think the baby is Dr. Maguire's?"

She looked down; her foot kicked the leg of the table. His stomach twisted, nausea setting his gut on fire. The flames tunneled his vision.

"Lilly!" His voiced boomed in the small room. She stilled like prey in a hunter's sight. His heart sank with regret, his voice cracked. "He's filing an assault charge against you. It was witnessed by nearly the entire ER staff. Right now, all we have on him is your accusation—and unproven at that."

"Isn't my word enough? My identification?" she asked, finally looking up at him, eyes clear with determination.

"We're going to probably need a little more. Do you know him?"

"Yes."

"How?"

"He works at the hospital."

"Do you know him outside the hospital?"

"I honestly don't know much about him other than he's one of Kadin's associates."

"In his medical practice?"

"Yes."

"For how long?"

"I don't know. You're going to have to ask Kadin."

"So you're denying any type of relationship with him."

"Unequivocally."

"Tell me about the baby."

"It's his."

"Kadin's?"

If her glare could generate physical force, Nathan would have toppled over. Dropping his accusatory tone, he softened his voice. "How long have you known?"

"Not long, Nathan. I wasn't hiding it from you or anyone. It's only been a week or two."

"Good. I mean . . . Lilly, what do you think?"

"I don't know. I'm sure you've seen I've not been managing well. I was drinking, overusing sleeping pills. I still feel like I'm barely making it day to day. To think about this child and what I may have done to it scares me."

"Have you had the baby checked? How far along are you?"

"I haven't had the baby checked. The conception date seems obvious, but I haven't figured out my due date. I'm not ready yet." She pulled her hair from her eyes. "What are you going to do about Drake?"

"We'll bring in the rest of the victims and see if they can ID him as well. Get a DNA specimen of course, but it will take some time before we get those results."

"Are you letting him go?"

"I don't know. If enough of the victims say he's the guy, we'll have enough to get an arrest warrant signed. But in order to get a conviction, we're probably going to need DNA from this baby to establish paternity."

"I don't think you're going to need it."

"Why?"

"The patient we were all caring for. I think he raped her, too."

"What makes you say that?'"

"I don't think she recognized him, but she was fearful of him."

"Maybe she just had a fear of men in general. That's common after rape."

Lilly leaned forward, "The patient said she was twenty-eight weeks pregnant. When he did the ultrasound, he said she was only twenty weeks."

"What difference does that make?"

"Every woman knows when she is due," Lilly pressed.

"When are you due?" Nathan folded his hands.

Lilly punched her fists into the table. "What is wrong with you! This is you trying to help me?"

"I'm sorry. I'm playing devil's advocate. Not all your observations are absolute."

"Twenty weeks is considered a nonviable fetus. The cutoff for viability is generally twenty-four weeks. At that gestational age, we would try to take the baby if the mother was in distress. Maybe even a few weeks shy of that we would try. But there's no way anyone would grab a baby at twenty weeks if the mother was dying."

Nathan waited as Lilly drew breath, collecting her thoughts. She placed the palms of her hands together and pointed her fingers at him.

"He underestimated the age so we wouldn't grab the baby. He didn't want it to live. It's his MO to kill his offspring. Can't we remember Torrence being run off the road?"

"Lilly, there are several problems with this. First, you assume he knew she was going to kill herself in the ER and he was setting up a reason to let the baby die as well. He may be a criminal, but I doubt he's a psychic."

"I think he recognized her and was going to use the advantage of the hospitalization to take her out anyway. Having it documented in her chart that she had a nonviable fetus, no one would have attempted a C-section."

"I think it's a stretch, Lilly. Secondly, the patient's accusation of rape is essentially an unreported event."

"She reported it to me."

"But not to the police. And her reporting it to you is not going to hold credence with any judge. You're claiming this man raped you; you want him in jail; you'll say anything to get him there. It creates an obvious conflict of interest—a victim in a profession with a duty to report. Besides, what she said to you is hearsay, and she obviously won't be around to testify. These are two major problems that a defense attorney will have a field day with."

"I wouldn't lie."

"I'm not saying you're lying, but a judge will need more."

"I'm telling you Nathan, he raped that woman. That is his baby."

Nathan slumped in his chair. "Brett's already made a few phone calls to the patient's family."

"And?"

"The problem is she not only didn't report it to the police, she never confessed this crime to anyone else; not her parents, not her sister, not even her husband. The family was fairly stunned to hear of her suicide. They think the baby is her husband's child. He's not claiming otherwise."

"Nathan! It is Drake's—"

"Lilly, we can't go down this path."

She buried her face in her hands. "He touched me."

He reached out to her and laid his hand on her shoulder, relieved she didn't push him away. "I know, Lilly."

She looked up and grabbed his arm. "No, today. He rested his filthy fingers on my stomach and commented about how he had another child on the way."

Nathan's heart hammered with adrenaline-laced fear that his next words would cause any trust she had in him to disappear. "Do you think anyone else can verify that statement?"

Lilly's face was resigned, almost hopeless and she pulled her hand back.

He could see her bold facade start to fracture and her lower eyelids began to fill. "We're going to have to use the other women. It shouldn't be hard. After all, we do have a sample of his DNA from several victims."

"Something tells me that's not going to be enough."

"We'll have to wait and see. Unfortunately, I'm going to have to charge you for hitting him. Luckily, it's a misdemeanor assault, and I can give you this summons rather than booking you into jail. You have to sign it as a promise to appear in court. If you don't, you'll be placed in lockup. So sign this and make sure you show up."

Nathan slid the summons toward her. The look of betrayal in her blue eyes sunk his soul with despair. Lilly pulled it with her index finger and scanned it. He handed her a pen, and she took it and signed, sliding them both back to Nathan. He tore off the defendant's copy. She took it, folded it without looking, and placed it in the splotched red pocket of her lab coat.

"Just so I can clarify, I'm getting a ticket, and he's going to walk."

"At least you didn't break his jaw. Then it would be a felony and you'd be spending the night with us."

"Can I go now?" Lilly asked, standing from the other side of the table.

Nathan's throat dried as he watched her readjust her shirt over her expanding belly. There were so many things he wanted to say, but any expression of them would come across as weak. He stood as well. "Lilly, what can I do to help you?"

"You can make sure Drake Maguire gets the electric chair." She pushed past him and left.

Chapter 26

"So are we going to play this good cop, bad cop?" Brett asked as Nathan returned to the monitoring room.

"Absolutely not. We're going to play this bad cop and on-the-verge-of-homicidal-maniac cop. You get to play bad cop."

"But you know I love the maniacal, homicidal role better."

"Let's just do it cleanly. The last thing we need is this guy on the streets because we screw up. Lilly is convinced that her suicidal patient was one of his victims."

"Just that we'll never be able to prove it." Brett laid his hand on the two-way glass and drummed his fingers.

Nathan leaned into the wall. "If Lilly's right, don't you think it's odd to have so many pregnant victims? I mean: Torrence, Lilly, this patient—three altogether."

"Does seem high."

"So either he has intimate knowledge of these women and their cycles, which would be feasible being an OB, or he is victimizing a lot more women than we know about."

"Not good options, either way. A doctor in betrayal of the public trust or one of the worst serial rapists this department's encountered." Brett slapped the glass. "Since he's not under arrest, I didn't Mirandize him. I did ask if he wanted to call anyone, and he refused."

"No request for a lawyer?"

"None."

"Well, let's see what Dr. Maguire has to say about this whole situation."

Nathan allowed Brett to enter the room first. Brett took the single chair in front of Drake as Nathan hovered in the corner, searching the doctor's physical features for anything that would betray the evil within him. The diatribe of tall, dark, and handsome fit him to a tee. His hair was dark chocolate. The eyes off-putting at first: one blue, one brown. But the longer you looked, the more intriguing they seemed. The gym might be his second home as he was physically strong, well defined, and his posture expressed confidence. He was well groomed, and taking into account the earlier incident, he was dressed decently and had smoothed down his hair during his wait. Being a doctor, Drake made more money than Nathan did, which usually made up for every other shortcoming a woman might find fault with. He couldn't fathom Drake having difficulty getting a date.

But then rape was never really about that anyway.

Yet, he's chosen this path, and I have to figure out why so I can keep him from doing it again.

"Dr. Maguire. How are you doing? Is there anything we can get for you?" Brett offered. Nathan popped an antacid to keep the bile in his throat at bay.

"I'm fine. Thank you."

"I want to reiterate that you're not under arrest, though there are some questions we'd like to go over with you. The more information we have, the more easily we can clear up this little misunderstanding you have with Dr. Reeves."

"That's trite. She accused me of raping her in front of the whole ER staff."

"As I said, the more we know, the easier it will be to clear your name."

"Did you charge her?"

"Dr. Reeves has been served a summons, and she was released. That's common in an assault case such as yours."

"Good, then I don't see any other reason for me to be here. It's clear I didn't harm her in any way."

"Not today at least," Nathan said from his position in the corner.

"Not at any time." Maguire sat taller in his chair, glaring at Nathan. He folded his arms in defiance. Nathan had seen thousands of these attempts to establish superiority. The chess game had begun, and it was going to go quick. Nathan had struck early.

"I know women like Dr. Reeves can sometimes say things when they're confused, so any information you can provide will help us get you out of here," Brett offered. Drake seemed to consider his options. "We will videotape this, but again, you're not under arrest. Answer a few questions for us, and you'll be out of here."

"Whatever, let's just get on with it."

"How do you know Dr. Reeves?"

"She's an ER physician, and we work together occasionally. I don't know her personally."

"How often do you see her?"

"Only when she calls us on consults."

"Ever see her outside the hospital?"

"No."

"Never? Not even on the sly? Maybe pass her by in the cafeteria? The grocery store?"

"Not that I remember."

"So, you and Lilly never dated?"

"Never."

"Why do you think she would accuse you of raping her? I mean, a man she's merely an acquaintance with?"

"I don't know. You'd have to ask her."

"What's your theory, Doctor?" Nathan asked, stepping closer to the table. "You must have some thoughts as to why she would do this." Nathan knew posing a challenge to an intellectual would force him to say something. Drake wouldn't play dumb. It would be too self-degrading.

"There have been rumors," Drake offered.

"Of what?"

"Of the fact that she's not necessarily the most stable personality."

"In what way?" Nathan pulled up an extra chair and took a seat.

"That she's been drinking, missing work."

"Why would you care about hospital gossip? Aren't you in nearly different worlds? How would you know that unless you were keeping tabs on her?" Nathan pressed.

"It came to mind after she right-hooked me in the ER."

"This is confusing to me. Initially, she was trying to help you. Correct?" Brett asked.

"If that's what you want to call laying me out with a punch to the jaw."

"No," Nathan corrected, jamming his index finger into the table, "According to Lilly, you had that girl's blood in your eyes and she was trying to get it out. Can't you catch some pretty nasty diseases from an exposure like that?"

"Yes, disease can be transmitted that way."

"So, she was trying to help you."

"Whatever you want to think."

Brett leaned back, letting Nathan take the lead.

"Drake, did you have blood in your eyes from that patient?"

"Yes, but what does it matter?"

"This is where my confusion lies. Why would she initially be trying to help you, then suddenly, on the turn of a dime, have enough anger within her to punch you in the face?"

"Like I said, rumors have it that she's not stable."

"Lilly says while she was washing your eyes, your contacts fell out and she saw that your eyes were different colors. That's one of the identifying marks of her rapist, an assault she reported to us several months ago."

"I'm not the only man with eyes like this."

"No, but you're the first one I've ever seen. Must be pretty rare," Brett said.

"I don't know the statistics."

"Why are they different colors?" Nathan asked.

"I don't know. I was born with them this way."

"But you're not curious as to why? Being a doctor and all, you must have at least a few educated guesses," Brett followed.

"It is what it is."

Brett stood from the table, taking a position off to the side. Nathan inched closer to Drake. He was always drawing closer. His goal was to be inside Drake's personal space, but he had to get there without him noticing, slowly over time. Move the chair an inch closer as you pretend to adjust your own position. Lean in and lean out, but lean in more and scoot forward just a bit. Subconsciously, Drake was backing up, trying to get away from the invasion of his personal sphere. There was little room for retreat in these interview rooms. Brett had already seated Drake in the back corner, opposite the door and the camera. None of this was by accident.

"Why do you hide them?" Nathan leaned in, making it appear that he wanted a closer look, but nudging forward to close in farther.

"What do you mean?"

"Why do you wear the colored contacts to hide them?"

"Every day I work with anxious, pregnant women. I got tired of repeating myself all the time because they were looking at my eyes and not hearing what I was saying."

"So initially, you didn't wear the contacts."

"I can't remember when I started wearing them."

"Since you were a teenager?"

"No, it hasn't been that long."

There was a faint knock on the door, Nathan turned to see Brett step out.

"Where did you grow up?"

"That seems to be going a long way back for the incident today."

"The more we know about you, the more we'll know that you couldn't possibly have done what Dr. Reeves says."

Maguire scratched his arms before continuing on. "A small town outside of Las Vegas."

"Did you go to school there?"

"Yes."

"Public? Private?"

"Public."

"You have parents?"

"Obviously."

"Still living?"

"My mother, yes. My father, I don't know."

"Why don't you tell me about that."

He sighed. "It wasn't a great childhood. My mother ran my father off when I was little."

"Explain that more. What was going on in the house?"

"She was yelling all the time. Nothing was ever good enough for her. Everything had its place, its order. My father never earned enough money even though he worked all the time."

"How old were you when he left?"

"Little . . . three, maybe four."

"Do you know where he is now?

"I have no idea."

"Are you still in touch with your mother?"

"She comes here to visit every now and then."

"When was the last time she was here?" Nathan asked.

"Honestly, I can't remember."

"Any siblings?"

"I have one brother."

"Where is he?"

"I don't know."

"The only family you keep in touch with is your mother."

A low, faint hum sounded. "Essentially." Maguire looked down and glanced at his pager. "It's the hospital. I'll have to call in."

"I'll give you a few minutes."

Nathan stepped out and paced in front of the two-way glass like a caged tiger wanting to devour the visitors on the other side. Brett approached him, a piece of paper secured in his hand. "We have the warrant to obtain DNA samples. Crime lab guy is on his way over."

"I want you to call the OB unit. See who's covering for him. I don't want him to say he has to leave to take care of a patient." Brett did as he was asked. Nathan continued his observation. Drake seemed calm and relaxed on the phone, unflustered to be sitting in a police interview room on suspicion of rape.

He has no concern about any of this.

"They say Kadin Daughtry is covering. He's actually there now."

"Good," Nathan nodded, seeing Drake put his cell down. "Let me continue on my own. I know where I left off."

Brett acquiesced, and Nathan stepped in. "Everything all right?" He closed the door behind him.

"Fine. How much longer are we going to be?"

"All depends on you. Let's wrap up these questions, and we'll see about getting you on your way. Why did you decide to become a doctor?"

"To help people."

Nathan frowned. "You don't seem to like women very much."

"Why would you say that?"

"Because you referred to your patients as anxious pregnant women. That's derogatory."

"For one, that's a professional observation. Secondly, you can ask any OB to verify what I said."

"What are some of your hobbies?"

"I don't really have much extra time."

"So you never have any fun? What do you do to relax? I'm sure the demands of your job can be stressful."

"I don't see how this has any bearing on why I'm here."

"Then let's move on. I was curious about your tattoo. When did you get it?"

"It's been several years."

"Was it here in Colorado?"

"Yes."

"What's the story behind it?"

"Story?"

"Tattoos are symbols for many people. They represent something. I was curious as to what it meant for you. It's pretty dramatic. I mean a beast with three heads."

"It's a hybrid of many of the animals I admire."

"What do you admire about the serpent?"

"Excuse me?"

"Isn't that one of the components? A serpent? They don't exactly have a warm, fluffy reputation."

"Why are you so interested?"

"Your tattoo also happens to be an identifying characteristic of the man who assaulted Dr. Reeves and several other women."

"I'm sure I'm not the only one who has this design."

"That's likely true. However, how many men do you think there are with that tattoo and your distinctive eye characteristics?"

"I think with the advent of color contacts, the possibilities are endless."

"I see. Then you won't have any problem supplying me with the name of the parlor where you got that tattoo."

"Not at all. I'll have to check my records."

"Tell me about ketamine."

"What about it?"

"Do you have access to it?"

"All of the physicians at the hospital can get it."

"Including a podiatrist?"

Drake swept his hair from his eyes. "Most have access to it."

"Do you use it much in your practice?"

"It has limited benefits in obstetrics because of its normal side effects. We generally don't like pregnant women to have increased heart rates and high blood pressure. I've personally never used it."

"Is it secured in your area?"

"I don't know. I'd ask anesthesia."

Nathan felt his BlackBerry vibrate. He viewed the text. Brett was ready with CSI. Ignoring it for the moment, he placed a manila folder on the table and pulled out four pictures, placing them in a neat row in front of Dr. Maguire.

"Do you recognize any of these women?"

"What does this have to do with anything?"

"Please, just look at the photos."

Drake took a cursory glance before he settled back into his chair. "None of them are familiar to me."

Nathan pointed to Torrence's photo. "This woman was a patient at the hospital where you worked. You don't remember ever seeing her?"

"No, I don't."

"How about this woman?" Nathan slid Celia's pictures forward. "It seems you brought your mother's vehicle into the garage where she works after a minor fender bender."

"I don't remember ever meeting her."

Nathan gathered up the pictures and placed them back in the folder. He pulled out a sheet of paper with some annotated dates. "I want you to take this piece of paper with you when you leave. These are dates that I'm going to need an account of your whereabouts for. I'll also need a list of people that can verify your statements as to where you were on these dates."

"January 3? March 4? May 5? July 7 and September 3, as well? January was almost a full year ago."

"We wouldn't ask if it wasn't of the utmost importance to clear you of this accusation. The person responsible for Lilly's attack is also responsible for the victimization of the women in those photos I showed you. Prove where you were on those dates, and it's more likely we'll believe that you didn't have anything to do with the crime against Dr. Reeves."

Nathan stood. "I think that will do for now. I'd like to thank you for your willingness to cooperate. We'll contact you within the next couple of days to get that list back from you. We're probably going to have a few follow-up questions."

"Great," Drake said, standing as well.

"Oh, there is one more thing." Nathan turned and opened the door, motioning in Brett. He stepped in with another man carrying a large case; a camera swung from his neck.

"Dr. Maguire, we have a warrant to secure a DNA sample and photograph of you and your tattoo. Will you do this willingly?"

To Nathan's surprise, Drake Maguire didn't hesitate to pull off his shirt.

Chapter 27

KADIN'S PAGER VIBRATED on his hip as he finished up the last of the staples on his patient's lower abdomen from a successful, though emergent, C-section. He was relegated to the main OR due to a plumbing issue in the labor unit's OR. The baby's cries comforted him as he placed a dressing over the incision. Ripping off his gloves, he grabbed his pager.

"The nurse's station just called. They need you. Room 350," Barrett said.

"Where's Drake? He's supposed to be covering the unit."

"He's not answering his pages."

A page and a phone call meant a woman or baby in trouble. Maybe both. Kadin ran the list of patients through his mind, trying to remember who was in that particular room. Stephanie Nelson. He recalled the blonde hair with blue streaks. The last he'd heard, she was eight centimeters dilated.

"You guys got it covered here?" He pulled off the rest of his OR garments. Barely staying to see the affirmation, he raced up the stairs and used his badge to get through the door. He didn't see anyone at the main desk and made his way down the hall.

310. 320. 330.

A nurse waved from two doors up. "Dr. Daughtry. The baby's crowning."

Kadin entered the room. The patient was positioned on her left side, her hand tightening around the bed rail as another contraction hit.

"Don't push, honey, not yet. They don't want you to push." A nervous father smoothed his wife's hair. "Remember, like the nurse said. Think birthday candles."

"How much longer?" she screamed through her oxygen mask.

Darien, one of the unit's most experienced nurses, had the delivery tray set up. "Dr. Daughtry, this is Stephanie. This is her first pregnancy. She came in ruptured at 1500. Her strip is showing a nonreassuring fetal pattern and we suspect possible mal presentation. She's had an epidural.

OR on standby. Stephanie, this is Dr. Daughtry, he's covering for Dr. Maguire."

She grabbed the monitor strip for Kadin.

"I see it. Let's see what pushing does and we'll go from there."

Darien began to break down the bed and position the patient in the stirrups. Kadin squirted antiseptic spray into his hands. Another nurse waited for him with a gown unfurled. He pushed his arms into it as someone else tied it from behind. He grabbed the black rolling stool and positioned himself at the bottom of the bed. After placing a mask with a face shield over his mouth and eyes, he pulled on a pair of gloves. Kadin placed a comforting hand on the woman's lower leg, already positioned in the stirrups. He always felt at a disadvantage when he delivered another doctor's patient. You had a few seconds at best to build rapport.

"Stephanie, it's Dr. Daughtry, I met you not too long ago. Looks like your little one is in a hurry." He patted her foot. "I'm going to check the baby, but feel free to push with the next contraction." Kadin placed two fingers inside the birth canal, feeling the baby's suture lines. Sure enough, the baby wasn't in the best position. He looked at the fetal heart monitor and noted the up swell of another contraction. The patient cried, grabbed her knees and pushed. He could see the perineum bulge, the baby's head protruded slightly, then sucked back into the birth canal like a turtle hiding its head within its shell.

The baby's shoulder was stuck.

The heart rate monitor alarmed as the baby's heart rate dropped.

"Darien, lower the head of the bed." He placed his hand gently on the patient's knee as the top of the bed was lowered. "Stephanie, I need you to listen to me very closely. Your baby's shoulder is stuck and I need to help you get it free. Can you pull your legs out of the stirrups?"

He saw her attempt, but her legs quivered. The epidural had knocked out her motor function from the waist down.

He glanced at Darien.

"Epidurals off," she confirmed.

Kadin snapped his fingers at the husband. "Dad, I need you to grab a leg and help widen her legs apart. You." Kadin pointed to a nurse he was unfamiliar with. "Grab the other leg and do the same thing. Darien, I need you to apply some suprapubic pressure at the next contraction."

Kadin reached up and felt the top of the woman's abdomen. The muscle tightened beneath his hand.

"Stephanie, give me all you've got. Push past the pain." Kadin placed his hands on each side of the baby's head and reached in as far as he could to place gentle downward traction as Darien pushed from above, to pop the shoulder free. He felt a slight give and the baby's head popped all the way out. Although he'd hoped against it, Kadin felt the umbilical cord was wrapped once around the infant's neck.

Can I catch a break?

Supporting the head, he guided the cord gently over the top of the baby's head. He was relieved that it pulled easily and was not taut. Taking a blue bulb syringe, he suctioned out the mouth and nose.

"One more gentle push, Stephanie, and you'll have your baby."

He let the baby drift and cradled it as it slid into his arms. He knew his stress level was exceeded when the nurse announced the sex of the baby and he hadn't offered the father a chance to cut the cord.

The mother and baby cried in unison.

Darien took the baby from his arms and headed straight to the warmer. "Mom, we're going to take a quick look at her to make sure she's doing all right."

Thank you, God.

He finished with the patient and stepped out of the room, only to find Detective Nathan Long hovering in the hallway.

"You have a few minutes?" he asked.

Definitely not going to catch a break.

"Is this about Lilly?"

"Is there somewhere we can talk privately?"

He took Detective Long to the nearest private lounge. Kadin washed his hands and splashed his face several times with cool water, tasting the salt on his lips as he cleaned off the last several hours of worried tension. His stomach gnawed from both hunger and nerves. He halfheartedly offered a bag of potato chips from the snack bowl to the detective, who had shown up at the worst possible time. After Nathan waved him off, he took a soda and corn chips for himself and sat on the couch. Long took a nearby chair.

"It's nearly three in the morning. Seems awfully late, or early for that matter, for you to be doing police work. Is this about Lilly? Is she all right?"

"You haven't heard any hospital gossip?"

"Sadly, I've been working. Two crash C-sections and just finished an emergent delivery. Believe me, I've been too busy to pay any attention to the rumor mill."

"Do you know why Dr. Maguire asked you to cover for him tonight?"

"Actually, I didn't know he had left the building. Drake often has a need to find coverage for his night call." Kadin lifted the aluminum tab and took several swigs of the lukewarm caffeinated sugar.

"Really? You keep any records of when others cover for him when he should be working?"

"I have a log I keep for the practice."

"I'll need to take a look at it."

Kadin couldn't keep his annoyance at bay. He still blamed this man for the delayed public notification.

And for Lilly's attack.

"For what purpose? Detective, I run a private practice with obvious confidentiality issues. You're going to need a very good reason and warrant." His frayed nerves pushed aside his normally calm demeanor. "I don't want you thinking you can shut down my practice while you rifle through our office. Babies don't stop coming, ever. Your department couldn't afford the windfall of lawsuits that would come as a result of you blocking my patients' access to health care."

"Kadin," Nathan put his hand up. "Let me put my request into context. Lilly has accused Drake of committing her sexual assault."

As if a tornado had just taken out the walls of his house, Kadin felt everything within him shift. Everything he knew and trusted, in shambles. His associate was a rapist?

That meant Lilly was pregnant with Drake's child.

"Dr. Daughtry?"

He shook his head, trying to clear the debris. His mind struggled under a thousand thoughts. The ramifications. Consequences. He needed to say something intelligible.

"How did this happen? How do you know Drake is the one?"

"There was quite a ruckus in the ER tonight. A patient committed suicide. Maguire was splashed with some blood in his eyes. Lilly was trying to help him wash it out. Drake was wearing contacts to help cover up the fact that his eyes are different colors. When she irrigated them, the lenses popped out. Lilly checked for the tattoo. And well, she decked him because she thought her rapist was standing right in front of her. It was a mess, but she had security detain him, and they called us."

"Did Drake confess?"

"He professes his innocence."

"Do you believe him?"

"We took DNA samples under a court order and photos of his tattoo. It could take several days for them to run the tests. We're going to need to re-interview the other victims and see if they can identify any of his physical characteristics. This is why I requested to take a look at that log. I know you still harbor some resentment toward me, but both of our goals should be the same. What do you know about Dr. Maguire?"

Kadin acquiesced, feeling his anger subside. "He came on board with our group about three years ago. He's a competent physician, though not very compassionate. Sometimes I wonder why he picked this particular area of practice."

"Because he doesn't seem to like women very much?"

Kadin considered the question and realized it was a concise statement of how he'd felt about Drake for a while. He never seemed personally connected to his patients, more going through the motions. Not wanting to fulfill his call responsibility. Not knowing the sex of a baby he'd delivered minutes before. Was a competent physician more than someone who could just safely deliver a baby?

"I guess it would be hard for me to disagree with that statement. It's a difficult bridge though to cross from his dislike of working with women to outright violence against them."

"What do you know about his past? Where was he before he came here?"

"I know there was a period of about a year where he didn't work at all. He said he had cancer and required a bone marrow transplant that took him out of commission. I know he doesn't like being low man on the totem pole, either. He wants an equal share of the practice, but Melanie and I aren't sure we want to make him a partner."

"Why not?"

"It's hard to put a finger on it. More of a feeling, an intuition, that he's not a good fit."

"Has he ever had complaints of any kind?"

"Nothing formal. I have had more than one nurse pass along patient comments about his bedside manner, but never anything that overly concerned me and certainly nothing about his decision making."

"Do you know where he was before Colorado?"

"Las Vegas."

"Did he bring any issues with him?"

"There hadn't been any complaints filed with the Nevada Board of Healing Arts. He got favorable references. There were no red flags. We wouldn't take on a liability like that."

"What do you know about his family?"

Kadin opened the bag of chips, taking a few to munch as he considered the question. What did he really know about Drake's personal life? He'd only brought his mother around one time, and it had been a cursory introduction at best.

"He's not forthright about his personal life. I met his mother one time, just after the first of the year."

"January?"

"Exactly then. It was the day after New Year's—a Monday. I remember pulling into our lot and seeing this huge, obnoxious, hot-pink Escalade. It had snowed over the weekend, and the car just stuck out. When I went into the office, they were there together."

"Did you speak with her?"

"Only cordially, then I grabbed the things I needed for patient rounds."

"Are you aware of Dr. Maguire's genetic eye defect? That one eye is blue and the other brown? When I interviewed him last night, he said that it is something he hides from his patients because it tends to be distracting. Was he hiding it from you and the rest of the staff as well?"

"It was obvious he wore lenses because the color is not natural. But I didn't know he was hiding something. I thought it was vanity."

"Is there a medical cause for his condition?"

"In general, eye color is determined by the presence of melanin. A lot of melanin gives you brown eyes. Lack of it gives you blue eyes. There are several genes involved. I'd have to do some research."

"Can I get a look at his personnel file?"

Kadin considered the request. He struggled between balancing Drake's privacy over his need to see justice for Lilly. "Look, Detective, these are pretty serious allegations you have against my coworker. I'm sure you want to know everything about him, but I'm not going to jeopardize what I've built here by giving you unfettered access to my files. Get a warrant and I will fully cooperate with its requirements."

"Okay, Kadin. I understand where you're coming from. Can you meet me halfway and tell me what I need to ask for in the warrant, so at least I won't have to come back twice? Will you guarantee me that you'll protect all the documents in question? I don't want to have a race with Dr. Maguire to see who can get to his file first."

"Fine."

No breaks tonight. That's for sure.

No matter what happened, it seemed impossible for Kadin to believe that his business was not going to take a hit. News that an OB physician is a suspect in a serial rape case was like gasoline and flame, not only for local news, but national outlets as well. If what Nathan said was true, it would mean the demise of his professional practice altogether. What woman would ever go to a group where a man, even if it wasn't him, was accused of rape? How could he distance himself and his practice from these allegations and maintain his personal integrity? It was his nature to cooperate with law enforcement. But how did he do that without angering Drake, who could be covering his true nature from all of them?

And what if Drake was innocent? Nothing was proven yet.

"When you submit your warrant to the judge, make sure you ask for his employment application, his CV, and references."

"CV?"

"It's a little more detailed than your average résumé. It should include a list of any publications. Also, ask for his billing records and my log so you'll know when he says he was supposed to be working. As far as the security of the records goes, I'll just lock him out of the office due to the nature of the investigation, which is your idea by the way. In fact, you didn't get any of this from me. Are we clear on that? You just happen to be one smart, detail-oriented detective—which I think is the truth anyway."

"I don't mind being the fall guy if it helps take him off the street. Can you help me with setting up some interviews with others on your staff?"

"I can have the staff stay after work for a couple of hours. We can't shut everything down to help you out. Plus, if any patients get wind that our staff has been questioned by the police, they'll assume the worst, and the gossip alone will cost us business."

"That's great, Kadin. I couldn't ask for anything better, and you have my word I will bend over backward as far as I have to in order to minimize the impact on your employees."

Kadin watched as Nathan scratched down several notes.

"Do you believe her?" Kadin folded over the top of the chip bag, his appetite diminished.

"Lilly? Absolutely. You can't refute good evidence. Why would I not believe her?"

Kadin shook his head. It was hard for him not to let his own desire for self-preservation overshadow his need to believe Lilly.

"When do you anticipate this hitting the news?"

"We haven't officially arrested him yet. We need to conduct more interviews and wait for the DNA tests. We're playing it close to the vest, and it's not our practice to divulge a suspect until more evidence is gathered. We wouldn't do a press release until he's in custody. Anything sooner and we run the risk of turning him into a fugitive. If he is our serial rapist, we don't want to make any careless mistakes. This guy is not going to get off on a technicality."

"How's Lilly doing?"

"Physically, she's fine. Emotionally, I'm not sure. Drake has pressed charges against her for assault."

"What?"

"Unfortunately, we had to charge her. The incident was witnessed by several people in the ER. We'll need more to arrest Drake than just Lilly's accusation. Though Lilly did identify his tattoo as belonging to her assailant, as have other women. His mother's vehicle that you mention was noted to be in the vicinity of another victim as well. These should strengthen our case. We still have a lot of work to do."

"Where is she? And where is he for that matter?"

"Home . . . and I don't know. We're concerned for her safety since we had to let Drake walk away. We just don't have enough to hold him right now. If he is the rapist, he seems to like killing his pregnant victims. So I had an officer take her home and clear her residence before she went inside. The cops will be near her townhouse tonight, and I'm working on additional coverage for later. If you have any idea of how to keep her out of harm's way, I'm open to suggestions. Can you think of someplace for her to go?"

Kadin wanted to go to her. He wanted to protect her.

"She doesn't have any close family that I'm aware of. Of course, she's welcome to stay with me. I don't know if she would choose to do that. Dana, her closest friend, is a possibility as well."

"How has Lilly been over the past couple of weeks?" Nathan asked.

"A complete and utter disaster would be an understatement." Kadin threw his empty soda can into the wastebasket across the room. It sank into the middle of the trash with a muffled *kerchunk*. He felt his nerves beginning to settle.

"Want to expand on that?"

"She's been missing work, drinking too much, and taking sleeping pills. The baby seems to be helping her pull it back together, at least for now. She won't let me examine her or the baby."

"She will. Give her time. I think she feels she has a vested interest in keeping this baby alive."

"Why?"

"To prove that Drake is guilty."

"Well, the DNA will do that anyway."

"I hope you're right."

Chapter 28

December 22

Nathan was weary as he and Brett returned to the Center for Mental Healing where Heather was still a patient. They'd spoken to Dr. Jonas, who cleared his morning schedule so he could be available as well to support Heather during the interview.

According to Jonas, Heather had been doing well. Her OCD was improving, and she was filling fewer notebooks with the fractured reminiscences of her attack. They entered Dr. Jonas's office. He sat behind his desk, minus the orange-and-black striped bow tie Nathan remembered from their first encounter. For this meeting, he wore a white one with large red polka dots.

At least we're in sync with the holidays.

To the side sat Heather in a pine-green, overstuffed, chenille chair. She wore a tank top and skirt despite the cool weather, and the exposed areas of muscle showed striations of rediscovered muscle mass. Clear eyes returned Nathan's gaze as she stood and walked to him, giving him a confident hug. Before he could return the gesture, she pulled away but kept her hands on his upper arms.

"I always meant to send you a note. To thank you," she said, giving one of his arms a couple of strokes before stepping back, tucking her long, straight brown hair behind her ears.

"I haven't done anything," Nathan said.

"You were so kind to me when we first met. Other than Dr. Jonas, you were one of the first men I felt safe being around."

"She's done a lot of great work," Jonas said, still seated. "Shall we all sit?"

Brett took one of the chairs in front of Jonas. Nathan opened Heather's file and slipped out several photos. "Heather, that's kind of you to say. Did Dr. Jonas explain why Brett and I are here today?"

"He said you think you might have a suspect in my case."

"We believe that the same man who attacked you is responsible for crimes against several other women. The DNA sample collected from you matches that of another victim, which is good news. One of these women was able to identify him. We want our case to be as strong as possible. I know your memory is fuzzy, but you do have excellent recall of some of his physical characteristics like his tattoo."

"I do remember that."

"Can you explain it to me? The drawings in your journals are black and white. I'm looking more for the colors you remember, the approximate size of it."

She pondered his question as she tapped her foot on the floor and clenched her hands tight against her belly, a small crack in her calm demeanor exposing itself.

"The colors were bright, almost psychedelic. Like what you'd think of from the sixties. It was a beast with three heads. One breathed fire—that was red, orange."

"What about the size?" Nathan asked.

Heather held up her hand and splayed her fingers open. "Slightly larger than this. I put my hand over it to try to push him away. It's the last thing I remember, those three hideous heads peeking through the open spaces between my fingers."

Heather shuddered. Nathan took the knitted throw that lay on the back of the chair and placed it over her shoulders.

"I have some pictures I'd like to show you of some tattoos to see if you can identify the one you remember."

While Nathan had been interviewing Dr. Daughtry at the hospital, Brett had spent several hours with one of the department's computer specialists, finding different pictures of tattoos. The pictures were then cropped to show only the tattoo on a dermal background in order to limit anything else that might bias the witness. He handed the photo series to Heather that had been arranged on a single page. She pulled the wrap tightly around herself, fisting the layers together. She placed the paper on one thigh and studied them. Nathan watched her face as she scanned over the images and saw hints of recognition play on her features.

Tense lips. A slight raise of her eyebrow. An unconscious action of pulling away from the paper.

She stared at Maguire's tattoo.

"This is the one." Heather tapped the page, confirming Nathan's suspicion, and then flicked the edge of it, sending it gliding off her leg to the floor. She made no effort to grab for it and turned her head away as it flittered onto the carpet.

"Heather, don't worry. Let me get them. You're doing great," Nathan said. "I need to ask you a few more questions. Are you doing okay?"

She turned her head back to Nathan and nodded. Nathan looked to Jonas, who motioned for him to continue. Brett gave him a thumbs-up.

"You also mentioned in your report your assailant had different colored eyes. Do you remember the colors?"

"One was brown and the other was blue."

"Do you remember which was which?"

She shook her head.

"Have you ever sought medical care at Sage Medical Center?"

"I think I've been in the ER before."

"Did you see any other doctors other than an ER physician?"

"I don't think so. I was there for a few stitches after I caught my hand in a machine at the gym."

"Whom do you go to for female issues?" Brett asked.

"Dr. Minor."

That physician was not in Kadin's practice.

"Do you know a Dr. Maguire?" Nathan asked.

"Drake?"

Brett leaned forward. Nathan stood from his kneeled position and tucked the photo line-up back in his folder.

A cool calm washed over Nathan. "That's his first name. Do you know him?"

"Yes."

"How?" Brett asked.

"He was a client of mine. I was trying to save up extra cash for college, and I did some personal training over the summer."

"What did you think of him?"

"I felt, I don't know, weird around him."

"Why?"

"For one thing, I didn't really understand why he needed a trainer. I mean, I'd seen him in the gym a lot. He knew how to workout. He didn't need to lose weight. It was a waste of his money, and I felt like he used the opportunity to hit on me."

"How many sessions did he sign up for?"

"Only one."

"Was there anything odd to you about his appearance?"

"It was obvious he wore colored contacts. Nobody's eyes are naturally that green."

Nathan took a few deep breaths to slow his increasing heartbeat like a hunter preparing for the kill shot. "Do you remember anything strange happening around the time of his training session? Was your home broken into? Any strange phone calls?"

"My locker had been broken into that day at work."

"Was anything missing?" Nathan imagined the feel of a rifle in his hands.

"No, but it did look like someone had gone through my purse. My keys were out of it. They were sitting at the bottom of the locker when I opened it."

"When was your attack in relation to this incident?"

"It was that night."

All these details brought Drake into his line of sight and closer to a home behind prison bars. Nathan smiled as he pressed the trigger.

Chapter 29

December 26

THE GRAVES THRUST up from the sparkling snow like broken, gaping teeth. Lilly held the poinsettia plant in one hand as she consulted the map the caretaker had given her. The blanket of white powder covered her usual landmarks, and after twenty minutes of traipsing through the cold crystals, she'd surrendered and asked for help. Turning to her left, she began to brush the flakes off the faces of the chilled marble. On the fifth one she stopped, tracing her fingers in the grooves of the stone.

Samantha Reeves.

She cleared the remainder of the marker and set the plant down at its base.

"Hey, Mom, sorry I missed your birthday this year."

Flurries dotted the black, glossy surface.

Black and white.

Lilly pushed her hands into her pockets. Were there any clear-cut choices anymore?

"Someone I know visited Dad. He gave me your journal."

She tilted side to side, like a bell swaying in a gentle breeze. One of her childhood habits surfacing when she struggled to come up with the right words. Her eyelashes began to stick as tears froze in the biting wind.

"Why didn't you ever tell me that he was responsible for your death? That his selfishness took you away from me?"

Her body tensed as she heard footsteps crunch through the snow behind her. Turning, she blinked several times, attempting to convince herself it really wasn't her mother standing behind her.

"Aunt Savannah?"

The woman approached her and brought her arms up slowly, wrapping her in a cautious hug. Lilly felt her muscles stiffen as the protrusion of Lilly's belly limited the usual close embrace. Pulling away, Savannah held

Lilly's shoulders within her hands, bringing one up she placed her palm against Lilly's face. The warmth was comforting.

"What a Christmas blessing to see you," she said.

Lilly took a full step back, pulling away from her grasp.

It was as if her mother's features had been stamped onto her aunt's face. Savannah stood a couple of inches shorter than Lilly. Her black hair was shoulder length with streaks of gray, the natural wave giving it fullness. Just like her mother's eyes, Savannah's crystal-blue irises comforted Lilly. Business slacks and a button-up shirt had replaced the tracksuit and tennis shoes. More refined than Lilly remembered.

"How are you?" Savannah asked.

Lilly took her index finger and held it to her lower eyelid, a dam against the flood of tears.

"It's been a tough couple of months."

"You didn't come on her birthday this year."

"How would you know?"

"Because I come on that day, too. Mostly to watch you."

"You never spoke with me before. Why today?"

"Nosy, I guess. I was curious about the baby." She motioned toward Lilly's midsection. "Do you want to talk about it?"

"Did you know the real reason my mother died?"

Savannah pulled her boot through the snow. "Yes."

"Why didn't you ever tell me?"

"It was your father's wish. That's why he kept your mother's journal. You must be in possession of it if you're asking me these questions."

"Why would you, of all people, want to protect him?"

Looking directly at Lilly, Savannah pulled a stray strand of hair that clung to Lilly's eyelash.

"Growing up, you yearned for a relationship with him. If you knew it was his choice in refusing to give her his kidney, the chances of reconciliation between the two of you would be negligible."

"You hiding all of this from me was not the right choice to make! Whether or not I had a relationship with my father should have been my decision. All these years, I blamed her for not doing enough to live."

"You're right, Lilly. But which would have been easier for you to overcome? The thought that your father emotionally couldn't handle her wasting away from cancer, or his utter selfishness that he couldn't spare any part of himself for you or her to keep your family together, to keep her alive?"

"It doesn't seem to have made a difference anyway. He never tried to find me, so the reason for his leaving seems irrelevant."

"I'm not saying what we did was right; after all, I was complicit in the lie. You were suffering so badly. He begged me not to tell you that it was his fault. I made up the cancer story." Savannah paused, tracing more patterns in the snow. A star. A heart. "Maybe now would be a good time to reconnect with all of us."

"Because of this?" Lilly pushed her abdomen out and patted it. "The baby? Actually, no. It's not a good time to bring all of you back into my life. I don't want to have to explain any of it, and after I was kicked out of your house, you didn't really stay in touch, either."

"Lilly, you were an angry teen at that time. You chose to go. I didn't force you to leave. I kept tabs on you, but anytime I tried to reach out, you wouldn't have anything to do with it. You hung up on me, returned my letters unopened. I understand all of this. Your father left. Your mother died. You witnessed your uncle shot and murdered."

"How did my father even know when my mother died? I thought when he left he cut off all contact."

"I told him. One, I needed money to bury her. Two, we were talking all the time over our concern for your welfare. In his own way, he was watching over you."

"Just not in any way that mattered."

"Lilly." Savannah sighed. "These are wounds that are hard to heal. I want a relationship with you. I always have." She reached into her purse and pulled out a business card. Lilly did not immediately reach for it. "I sense you're in trouble. Obviously pregnant. No ring on your hand. You rarely stray from your routine, yet here you are, the day after Christmas, at your mother's grave. You have all this new information about your family, and you don't know how to process it. I can help you. I want to help you. I have money now."

"I don't need your money."

"I didn't mean for it to sound like you couldn't take care of yourself. You have for so long. Aren't you tired of that? Of being alone?

"It's my decision."

Savannah stepped past her and laid the card on the tombstone.

"You're right, Lilly. These are your choices to make. But I think you're also choosing to go it alone. It doesn't have to be that way. There are people like me who want to help you."

Savannah tightened her scarf as the wind picked up, and turned, the helpless resignation in her eyes tearing a hole in Lilly's soul. Lilly picked up the card and tucked it in her pocket.

Lilly wasn't sure if it was the appearance of Savannah or the weeks she'd spent mulling over the pregnancy, but she found herself driving to Kadin's office. Replaying her meeting with Savannah consumed her thoughts, and too soon for comfort, she was parked in front of his medical building.

There'd been an announcement in the press two days ago about the questioning of Dr. Drake Maguire concerning his possible involvement in the rapes of several local women. Her ob-gyn, Melanie Wells, encouraged Lilly to find another practice. Since Drake was free, she thought it better for Lilly's peace of mind to avoid any possible confrontation at the office. Why was Lilly's life so affected when Drake was the criminal? Lilly hoped Kadin would be in disagreement with his partner and refuse to turn her away. She didn't know if she could face another person, a stranger, knowing any of these details.

Lilly stomped the snow from her shoes as she entered. She headed toward the elevator and pressed the button for Kadin's floor. According to Nathan, Drake had shaken his police tail and disappeared, likely left the city. She had called the OB unit and learned Melanie was there and had two women ready to deliver. With Melanie tied up for hours, she should be unable to interrupt this visit Lilly had been putting off with Kadin. Still, Lilly's stomach flopped nervously. And the baby echoed her trepidation.

There was also this ache within her, a desperation to connect with him, maybe to connect with anyone. Kadin was the only one, other than Dana, who knew her whole story. She'd been dreaming of Gabe, her mysterious ER visitor, over the last several nights. Never having been exposed to a religious upbringing, the whole concept of prayer was foreign to her.

Is there really a God who created all there was and ever would be? Does this God care for me, as an individual? Doesn't he have more important affairs: war, famine, and disease? What is my life, really, to him in the end? What is worth praying over? A parking spot? A cancer diagnosis? Needing a kidney?

A child conceived during a sexual assault?
How do I say the words? What are the right words?

As she entered Kadin's medical office, Lilly found the reception area empty. The door automatically closed behind her, hitting her in the back and nudging her forward. She stood there, not knowing how many minutes passed, when Kadin walked through the lobby with several patient files in his hands. His mouth gaped open.

Chapter 30

KADIN FELT UNSURE about trusting Detective Long. On Christmas Eve, there had been a news report, albeit short and not the leading story, that Drake had been questioned in relation to the string of rapes that had plagued their city. It likely wasn't the leading story because they didn't have any photos of Drake in handcuffs, and no one could find him.

This announcement sent seismic ripples through the office their next business day. He'd been forced to place Drake on a paid leave of absence. Several of Drake's patients cancelled their appointments, and the remaining few Kadin volunteered to work into his schedule as Melanie had agreed to cover Drake's call that night.

He was reviewing the files of several of Drake's patients he'd seen that day since he hadn't had a lot of time to thoroughly read their histories. As he headed to the main reception area to make copies, Kadin saw Lilly standing there, her hands deep within her black overcoat, a green-and-red plaid scarf wrapped around her throat.

"I thought maybe you could take a look at the baby," she said, her voice quiet and unsure.

His heart stopped. "Yes, absolutely, follow me."

She did as instructed, entering a small room with a sonogram machine. She took off her coat and placed it on a nearby chair. He patted the table, and the waxed paper rustled under his touch.

"How have you been? I've been trying to call you." He pulled the machine closer to the bed and powered it up.

"I know." She hoisted herself up, pulling the pillow down to support her neck. "I was scared to come see you."

"Why?"

"How's the practice been?" she asked in avoidance.

"You mean in the wake of the news story about Drake?"

Lilly nodded as Kadin eased her shirt up. He rubbed his hands together for several seconds, the friction warming them before he placed them on her belly. "I just want to see if I can feel the position of the baby."

"You didn't answer my question."

He paused. "Right now, Drake's MIA. No one has seen or heard from him. A few patients have called to say they're leaving the practice. At this point, most are rescheduling with Melanie or me. We've talked about bringing in an interim person for the short term." Kadin pushed one side of her abdomen in, feeling with his free hand on the other side. There seemed to be an odd distribution of lumps and bumps.

"You really don't know where he is?"

"Hopefully the police are keeping tabs on him. I'm going to measure your fundal height." Taking a tape measure from his pocket, he felt for the top edge of her uterus and laid the paper strip vertically down, to the top of her pubic bone. "Were your cycles regular before?"

"Yes, why?"

"Since we know the baby was conceived on September 3, you should be about twenty weeks. You're measuring quite a bit larger than that. First pregnancy, right?"

"Yes."

"Let's see what we have."

Kadin squeezed several circles of heated gel over her abdomen. Despite the warmth, he could see her flesh raised in small moguls. Kadin angled the screen toward her, moving the transducer with practiced maneuvers over the length of her belly. Even though he knew Lilly was not well versed at reading sonograms, he felt her still as the images came up.

"Lilly, there are twins."

She made several attempts to speak, the words caught in her throat. Kadin continued in quiet study, taking measurements and photos. "Looks like they're fraternal. Do twins run in your family?"

"No," she choked, tears streamed and collected in small pools in her ears. "What about Drake's family?"

Kadin left the question unanswered as his own thoughts, fatigued from the day, struggled to come up with something comforting to say.

"They're a bit underweight. Heart rates are good. Do you want to know the sex?"

He was stunned when she reached up and grabbed his wrist. For several months he'd sensed that she'd yearned for his help, but fear had kept her silent and he'd prayed that something would bridge the divide between them. Was this the moment when she would finally feel free to come to him and lay her burdens at his feet?

Would he be enough to meet those needs?

"Kadin, please. I'm so freaked out! I need you to say something not medical!"

He eased his hand from her grip and set the transducer down, holding her hand within his. "Tell me what you want me to do. I'll do anything."

"The visitor I had . . ."

"In the ER?"

"Yes . . ."

"What?"

"He said . . ." she gulped. The apprehension that widened her eyes caused his heart to skip beats. Could she trust him with the thoughts that plagued her at night? Would she let him into that dark place?

"Pray for me."

Racking sobs seized her. She put her hands over her face and pressed the bottoms of her palms into her eyes. Kadin placed his hand over her stomach, forgetting the thin coat of transducer gel was still in place. He leaned over her and pulled her to his chest, closing his eyes. He tried to steady her shaking, pressing her to his chest and rubbing his thumb in calming circles over her back. He swallowed heavily.

"Heavenly Father, I come to you on behalf of Lilly and these babies." Her shaking worsened. "First, I ask that she know you in a real way. That she is assured of your love for her and that she know there is nothing left for her to do because you already surrendered your Son to save her. We need your help. Please provide peace for Lilly and clear thinking about these babies . . ."

Lilly pushed up and jumped off the table, grabbing a nearby towel to clean herself. "Kadin . . ."

He neared her. "Lilly, don't fight me," and though she resisted at first, she allowed him to pull her close. He ran his fingers through her hair, his fingers catching in the windblown tangles. She buried her face against his chest. "We're going to figure it out. I want you to come and stay with me."

She shook her head. "I can't do it."

"We have time."

She pushed away from him.

"I need you to take the babies."

"Lilly, I can't. I wouldn't. And besides, you're too far along."

"No, I mean I need you to find a home for them," she said as she backhanded the tears off her cheeks. "Someone to adopt them. Someone I don't even know. I need to hide them, or Drake will kill them. I can't deliver here, or any hospital."

"All right, we can look into it. But Lilly, the risks are too high to have them anywhere but a hospital."

"No, Kadin, I mean it! If you don't promise these things to me now, I'm leaving, and you won't find me. He's killed every baby."

His stomach tore at his own indecision. He wanted her safe, but her request could mean death for all three.

"Let's just wait and see."

"Promise me, or you'll never hear from me again!"

Chapter 31

January 2

THE CHRISTMAS AND New Year's holidays had slowed DNA results on Drake Maguire. But that was the least of Nathan's issues, as it seemed Drake had left the city and no one could locate him. He hadn't used a credit card, made an ATM withdrawal, or bought groceries as near as anyone could tell. No plane or bus tickets had been purchased in his name, even though his car remained parked outside his residence. To Nathan, that meant that he must have had cash stored up somewhere in the event he had to flee after an accusation. Nathan hoped this wouldn't top the list of his unforgivables.

Letting a serial rapist walk free.

He and Brett were parked in front of Jacqueline Randall's home. She'd been difficult to get a hold of. When their frequent calls broke through, the earliest she'd agreed to see them was after the holidays. She insisted they come after dinner.

Brett had been right on every account. The screen door was fixed. Alternating white-and-green Christmas lights hung on the eaves, and a blanket of snow lay over the cut lawn. The front window framed a pine tree, decorated with multicolored bulbs and silver tinsel. Faux snow frosted the inside edges of the panes of glass. The driveway and walk were shoveled.

"Why are we really here, Nathan? She doesn't remember anything. The only evidence we have from her that will help us in this case is the semen sample."

"You never know what might happen over time. We never did a follow-up interview from her inventory."

"I told you Grandma would put those boys to work," Brett said as they walked up the path. "Silent Night" played through the house as Nathan pressed the doorbell.

Jacqueline came to the door dressed in a bathrobe. She was emaciated, her eyes sunken into the dark moons of her lower eyelids. She stepped aside without saying a word and motioned them in. The house still reeked of smoke. Brett sputtered a few times, covering his mouth with his forearm. She took a chair at the kitchen table, and they followed suit; oppressive stillness was thick in the home.

"Where are your children?" Brett asked.

Jacqueline's hand shook as she took a cigarette from the cellophane-wrapped package. "My dead husband's mother took them in. I just couldn't do it anymore."

"Are you seeing that counselor?" Nathan asked.

Lighting the end, she took a long breath and slowly exhaled the smoke. She trembled as she pulled at the sleeve to her robe, exposing the white gauze dressing that was wrapped around her wrist. Nathan reached out to touch it.

"Jacqueline, did you hurt yourself?" Her lips quivered around the filter. "When?"

The words came in a whisper. "A couple of days ago."

Nathan wondered if this was the cause of her delay in seeing them. She hadn't figured on being here.

"Is your mom still coming by?" Brett asked.

"She's staying with me now. It's the only way they would let me come home."

"Where is she?"

"Since she knew you'd be here, she went to get groceries."

"We'll be sure to stay until she gets back." Brett stood to get her a glass of water from the sink.

"I don't know what to say. I'm sorry things are so tough." Nathan placed his hand over the one that rested on the table, her skin dry and coarse.

"There was a story on the news that you arrested someone." She took another drag; the end lit up like slow-burning lava.

Brett set the glass beside her. "We questioned someone but didn't arrest him."

"Why not?"

Brett remained quiet and let Nathan lead the interview.

"That's partly why we're here. We need to gather more evidence."

"But you got his DNA, right?"

"Yes, but the more evidence we have, the stronger our case will be. Have you ever been to Sage Medical Center for treatment?"

"No, but I see a couple of doctors there."

"Your gynecologist?"

"No. The kids' pediatrician and the psychiatrist I'm supposed to follow up with."

"Did you deliver any of your kids at that hospital?"

"No, they were all born out of state."

"Which state?"

"Nevada. I moved here several years ago."

"Do you have any family still in Nevada?"

"No."

"What about your father?"

Jacqueline swallowed hard; cigarette ashes fell onto the table. "My father is dead."

"How?" Brett brushed the ashes from the table into a yellow molded ashtray made by a child's small hands.

"He killed himself."

Brett placed the dish onto the table. "Do you have any siblings?"

"I had a sister, but she was killed when I was in high school."

Nathan wanted to escape this woman's pain. Why was it that some lives were plagued by tragedy?

"Jacqueline, I know talking about these things is very hard, but can you tell me what happened to your sister?"

"Kate was raped and murdered," she said, an ironic grin spreading over her face.

Even Brett, who was rarely overwhelmed with emotion, looked down and away. Her sorrow was piercing.

"Did they catch who did it?" Nathan asked.

"He's in jail. At least he's supposed to be unless they paroled him."

"What's his name?"

"Drew Stipman."

Nathan met Brett's gaze as he looked up.

Stipman?

"Did you know Drew's family?"

"They were our neighbors."

"What was his mother's name?"

"Meryl?"

"Does Drew have a brother?"

"Yes."

"What's his name?"

"Drake. Drake Stipman."

Nathan's inner cop threw up a red flag. His thoughts scurried at the implications.

Jacqueline's mother returned shortly after this revelation. Nathan's and Brett's shoes slipped on the ice as they hurried to Brett's vehicle. Climbing in, they slammed the doors. Brett turned the vehicle on and cranked up the heat.

"Is it possible he changed his name?" Brett asked as he turned the ignition.

"We need to check. Mommy Dearest refused to provide a picture or name. Now we know why."

"It's got to be Drake. Everything is falling into place. Now it makes more sense to me why he picked her, some odd obsession with this family. We need to get on the phone with Nevada State Police ASAP." Brett pulled away from the curb and fishtailed on the tight turn.

Nathan received a text. The chief wanted them in his office.

That was never good. The chief didn't like to stay late.

"What is it?" Brett asked.

"We need to get back. Chief Anson wants a meeting."

"Holy—"

"Don't say it."

The station was not far from Jacqueline's home. Snow had begun to fall in fat, heavy flakes that covered the recently brushed steps of the station house. They made their way to the chief's office. He was initially on the phone but disconnected when he saw them outside his door. He waved them forward.

"We've got some issues." He sat down and moved several papers off to one side as Nathan and Brett took chairs.

"What are those?" Nathan asked, trying to stem the gurgling in his gut. He reached inside his suit pocket. He'd left his antacids in his overcoat.

"Our prime suspect, Dr. Maguire, has re-emerged."

"Where's he been?"

"From what I can tell, meeting with a sleazy, high-priced defense lawyer."

"Not surprising," Nathan said.

"What is interesting is that he's filing a restraining order against Dr. Reeves."

"What!" Nathan started to come up out of his seat. Brett reached across and grabbed Nathan's arm to keep him in the chair.

"I have it here. I'm going to need you to serve her with it."

"You can't expect me to explain that insanity to her," Nathan protested.

"It's a temporary order, but on the emergency track. She'll have to appear in court tomorrow."

"Chief, we should have a restraining order against him."

"We've got bigger problems than that."

"Bigger than a rapist filing a restraining order against his victim?"

"Nathan, just cut your tone. I'm as frustrated as you are. But he may have valid reasons."

"What would those be?"

"The witnessed assault and now a false accusation."

"What are you talking about?" Nathan demanded.

"Drake's DNA tests came back. He's not a match."

"It's not possible."

"In fact, there is a match. Evidently, Las Vegas Metropolitan PD forensic lab has been catching up on their backlog of DNA specimens. They've been adding to CODIS samples of sex offenders that have already been convicted, just got some big private grant to complete it in the last couple of weeks."

"So who did it come up with?"

"That's the bad news. It came up with an inmate, now released, by the name of Drew Stipman."

"This is not happening," Nathan's voice was soft, incredulous.

"What was he in for?" Brett asked, easing his grip in Nathan's arm.

"Rape and murder of . . ." The chief rifled through some papers on his desk, snagging one and holding it a few inches from his face. "Kate Randall."

"Jacqueline's sister," Brett said.

"Something funny is going on here," Nathan added.

"I don't know," Brett said. "It makes some sense to me. Maybe this nut job came back to finish the sister."

"But she was the fourth victim."

"I bet we check out his physical characteristics and our mystery will be solved," the chief said, putting the paper down.

"Do you happen to know who donated the money?" Nathan asked.

"Looks like Drew's mother, Meryl Stipman."

How did any of this make sense?

Chapter 32

Lilly felt peaceful for the first time since her attack. She'd agreed to stay with Kadin in his small log cabin, which was nestled at the base of the foothills on a couple of acres that flourished with aspen groves dotted with ponderosa pine trees. She'd spent the last week in solitude, often by the fire catching up on medical journals. Kadin had left for the evening, stating only that it was in relation to her request to talk to someone about adopting the twins.

She was considering going to bed when she saw lights bounce through the darkened living room. Approaching the front door, she squinted her eyes against the beams, thinking it was too early for Kadin to have returned.

The headlights darkened. Two figures emerged from the vehicle. Lilly flipped on the porch light, shocked to see Nathan. She opened the door as he raised his hand to knock.

"We need to talk," he said. The stern look on his face, coupled with his lack of congeniality, caused her nerves to fire. They followed her to the living room. She returned to her seat by the fire; they remained standing.

"What's going on?"

The babies' squirming intensified her nausea. Nathan was apoplectic. Brett spoke first.

"The DNA results are back. It's not a match to Dr. Maguire."

Lilly gulped several times, trying to knock the vomit back to her stomach; her breathing quickened into shallow, ineffective respirations as her vision began to cloud.

"Dr. Maguire has also filed an emergency restraining order against you," Brett continued. "You'll need to appear in court tomorrow to defend yourself."

"I have a shift tomorrow," Lilly said. It had always amazed her that during an emergency resuscitation, relatives of the morbidly injured would say the most inane things, and she would always wonder if they comprehended the information she was trying to relay.

Now she knew how they felt.

"You'll have to make other arrangements," Brett said.

"It's not possible. Nathan?"

"It seems there *is* a DNA match." He wilted into a chair that sat across from Lilly.

"Who is it?"

"That's the first strange part. A match came from CODIS to a prisoner in Nevada who is now released. He was incarcerated for the rape and murder of a young woman. This murder victim is the deceased sister of another victim whom we think this man raped," Brett said.

"The problem is that this criminal was released in the last couple of years. We'll have to locate him." Nathan said.

"Who is he?"

"Drew Stipman."

"I've never heard of him."

"He's Drake's brother. At some point, Drake changed his last name. The interesting thing is that Mommy Dearest put up a bunch of money to get the DNA backlogs caught up for the state of Nevada."

"Why would a mother do that? Now they've found more cases her son could be charged with, and it'll put him back in jail. Why would a mother want her son to go back to prison?" Lilly rubbed at the knotted muscles in her neck.

"Maybe it's her keen sense of justice. However, I think that's a minor part of the mystery we need to solve," Brett said.

Nathan was disengaged. His stoic attitude began to wither her conviction. He couldn't look her in the eyes.

"Nathan, I know it was Drake. There is a logical explanation for all of this."

"It's not that I don't believe you, Lilly. Brett and I just finished interviewing two other victims who we feel could strengthen our case. The problem is going to be the courts. There isn't going to be a sane district attorney who is going to take on a sexual assault case where the DNA conclusively excludes our primary suspect and points to another. You have to bear in mind that Drew Stipman already has a conviction for another rape and murder. They're going to want us to find him and pin all these cases to him. We might be able to get Drake on one of the rapes where DNA wasn't involved, based on an ID of his mismatched eyes, but that is pretty thin considering that victim doesn't have clear recall of the events either because of the ketamine. Also, this particular victim has also been taking a drug that blunts her memory. Drake's hired a top-gun attorney who will fillet this charge considering these test results."

"What happens if I don't show up in court tomorrow?"

"Restraining orders are a civil process. Basically, if you choose not to appear, the judge can issue a default judgment and grant the restraining order if he agrees with Drake's argument as it's presented in the application."

"So if I don't go, he gets his restraining order automatically? I won't go to jail if I don't show up, will I?"

"No, not at all," Brett said.

"So besides the obvious, what does the restraining order entail?"

"They are usually pretty generic. Drake will have an opportunity to name several addresses, like his home and place of business, from which you are barred. To cover everything else, the judge will set a minimum safe distance that you must stay beyond, generally a hundred feet. The order will instruct you to refrain from any kind of contact with him. Not in person, not on the phone. No e-mails or third-party contacts. Are you with me so far?"

Lilly was silent as the anger built within her.

"If Drake perceives that you have violated the order, he can call the police, and a criminal investigation will be initiated in order to determine if there is probable cause that you violated the court's wishes. If the responding officer can establish probable cause, you will be arrested and booked into jail. That's state law, Lilly, and there's no discretion or consideration for your predicament. This will not be a serve and release like the assault charge."

"We work at the same hospital. What do I do about that?"

"In that case, the judge might set an additional safe distance, considerably shorter, which only applies to the workplace, but you can plan on never being in the same room with him."

"It's not feasible. I won't be able to care for my patients. It will disrupt the ER too much."

"Lilly, I think you should go to court tomorrow and state your case. Otherwise, Drake will get anything he wants within reason. You need to be there to help the judge make a good determination of that."

Lilly tried to pull her knees into her chest, forgetting her expanding belly prevented the comforting position. She let her feet flop to the floor. This piece of paper did nothing to protect her from Drake.

"Maybe I should just walk away from all of this and disappear to another state. Change my name and start over. How can it be possible that I, as the victim, am losing my livelihood?"

"Lilly, I believe you and these other women. I just don't know how to prove it. I need time, and I need you to stay in the fight with me," Nathan said.

"What are you going to do, then?"

"We'll have to take a look at Drew. Figure out where he's been and if he could have been responsible. Unfortunately, if we can't locate him, the assumption will be that he's the perpetrator. It will actually be easier to point the finger at Drake if we do find Drew, because he likely won't have these distinctive physical characteristics," Brett said.

"The DNA test is going to be our Achilles' heel. We need a workable theory to prove how Drake is responsible for these crimes yet the DNA rules him out. I just don't know how to do it," Nathan confessed.

It was at that point, when she saw the resignation in Nathan's eyes, that she understood the uphill battle ahead. Even if he did wholeheartedly believe her, which at this point he didn't present a convincing front for, what exactly was he supposed to do? Time and budgetary constraints were going to tie his hands as far as pursuing Drake as a viable suspect.

"This has been a little overwhelming for me. I think I need to rest. After all, I have a court appearance in the morning."

Brett took the hint and began to make his way to the front door. Nathan lingered a few moments before following him, eyeing her suspiciously. Lilly waited on the porch until they pulled away and the darkness engulfed their headlights.

It was up to her. She had to prove it. Something was wrong with Drake's DNA.

That's why all his pregnant victims met their demise. *It's about the children.*

The babies were the key.
That's why none of them could live.
That's why my babies have to be born.
Not just for me, but for all these women.

She rushed to Kadin's study and began to rifle through his documents. He'd brought Drake's personnel file home over concern that Drake would destroy it before the police could obtain it. Finding it amongst a multitude of manila folders, she marked the spot with a ruler and approached his combined copy/fax machine to make her own duplicate. She straightened the sheets and put it back in its proper order, pulling the wooden stick as she slid the drawer closed.

The file contained everything about Drake's past. His former employers and residences were listed. That's where she would start. Visiting every hospital in the area to see if he had a medical file and widening her search from there based on the information she found.

Even though it was dark, it was still early evening. If she hurried and packed her things, she could make it in time to her local bank and withdraw her money, leaving just enough in the accounts to keep them open. She hoped operating in cash would make it more difficult for Drake to find her, as she had no doubt that, with the police off his trail, he would feel comfortable hunting her and disposing of her with some convenient accident. Struggling out the door, clutching her belly with one hand, she dragged her suitcase down the snowy walk with the other.

Chapter 33

ELLIE BEGAN TO clear the dishes as Kadin mopped up the rest of his gravy with a homemade dinner roll. Several garbage bags full of newly made quilts for the neonatal intensive care unit waited by the door. His sister's husband was out of town on business, and Kadin thought it was a good opportunity to present the idea of adopting Lilly's babies. If Ellie felt it was something she couldn't do, he'd only planted the idea in one mind and not both.

He'd tried to broach the subject several times during dinner, his nerves getting the better of him. Since her miscarriage, Ellie and her husband had tried several times to adopt. Twice, the birth mothers had decided to keep their infants—one after the baby had been in their home for two weeks. After that experience, they tried an international adoption, but just as they were preparing to leave, they got word that that child had died. No explanation as to the cause of death was given. After the multitude of fertility treatments and three failed adoptions, they found their financial resources thin.

Ellie brought Kadin's favorite dessert, cheesecake with fresh berries, placing it in front of him with a fresh cup of coffee.

"So, Brother, are you going to tell me the reason for your visit?"

"Just coming for your fine food and company isn't enough of a reason?"

"Of course it is, and I wish you would do it more often. But since this is the first of such a visit, I figure there must be ulterior motives."

Kadin took a few bites, then wiped his lips with the pressed cloth napkin. He set the dessert plate aside and grabbed the coffee cup and eased back into his chair.

"You're too perceptive for your own good," he said, taking a sip. "The cheesecake is great."

"You don't lie very well. Never have." She ran her fingers through her blonde hair.

"True." He put the cup down and placed his elbows on the table, folding his hands underneath his chin. "I know a woman who is pregnant with twins and wants to give them up."

"Why?" Ellie brushed the crumbs off the top of the table.

"The pregnancy is the result of a sexual assault. On top of that, she's single and doesn't really have any family to speak of. She just doesn't think she can take care of them."

"How serious do you think she is?" A hopeful light brightened her eyes.

"Very. I think she wants a private adoption."

"It seems too good to be true."

Kadin laid one of his hands over hers. It trembled under his touch.

"Ellie, I know you feel like having your own children is never going to happen, but I know this woman. She's adamant about giving them up. She asked me to arrange this for her. Are you interested?"

"Of course I want these babies. I just don't know if I could handle it not working out."

"I know that I can't fully understand your fear, but I can sympathize with it. There are a couple of other things I should share with you before you make your decision."

"This is where the big heavy hammer drops." She pulled her hand away from his.

"That's up to you. After the rape, the mother was not functioning very well. She didn't receive any prenatal care during the first five months. She'd been using sleeping pills and alcohol to get through her grief. I don't think she was using anything in terrible excess, and she's not doing these things anymore, but the overall effect on the babies won't be known until after they're born."

"That doesn't bother me as much as you would think. No child is perfect, and there are no guarantees in life."

"The other reason my friend wants a private adoption is there is some concern her rapist might come after these infants."

"Why would he do that? Wouldn't it just put him more at risk of getting caught?"

"These are her feelings, and I'm not sure how grounded they are. She says her perpetrator is one of my associates, Drake Maguire."

"Is it true? Did he rape her?"

Kadin's pager buzzed; he checked the text. Nathan Long was trying to get a hold of him.

"I don't know. The DNA tests are pending."

"Do you believe her?"

"I want to. Part of me is dying inside, knowing I hired this man who victimized all of these women. I reviewed his file, even called the Nevada State Board of Healing Arts. Nothing came up as a red flag. He doesn't have the greatest bedside manner, but it's a stretch from that to being a serial rapist."

Ellie stilled like a small animal caught in the stream of a flashlight in the darkness. "Drake is the man on the news?

"I thought you would have known," Kadin said.

"I don't really know the other doctors in your practice. Living up north, I don't have any reason to keep tabs on the people at Sage. This must be having a horrible effect on your practice."

"It's not been as bad as I would have thought. Obviously, some of his patients have left. Melanie and I are absorbing the rest. What's a woman to do late in her pregnancy? Some don't want to hassle with finding another doctor at this point."

"So he hasn't been working?"

"No. And we haven't heard from him. We're just assuming that he's never coming back."

Kadin's pager went off again. He viewed the text.

"Ellie, I need to call this person back. It's the detective in charge of my friend's case."

He stepped into her living room and dialed Nathan's number on his cell.

"Detective Long?"

"Kadin, thanks for calling me back."

"You seem anxious to get a hold of me."

"It's Lilly. We've had some developments."

"Such as?"

"Can we meet in person?"

"It's not possible right now. I'm up north having dinner."

"Great. Listen, Drake has been cleared by the DNA tests."

"He has? Does Lilly know?"

"I went up to your place to give her the news and just got back. There's another issue, though. Drake has filed a restraining order against her."

"You've got to be kidding me."

"An emergency hearing has been filed. I just got done serving it to her. She has a court appearance tomorrow. Did she call you?"

"No, I haven't heard from her."

"When are you due back?"

Kadin glanced back toward Ellie, who had begun to clear the dishes from the table. "I could leave anytime, but I'm ninety minutes away. Why?"

"I think Lilly's going to run."

"Where?"

"I don't know. But I think she's going to try to solve this thing on her own. She believes that Drake is the one responsible despite the DNA test. I told her it was going to be a tough case to prosecute in light of that evidence."

"What's your take on it?"

"I believe Lilly, but I'm struggling. I'm an analytical guy, so it's hard to discount the test results. In the same light, these women describe some very unique physical characteristics that I would venture to say few men have. Regardless, the DNA evidence came back to a convicted criminal who's been out of jail a couple of years. Happens to be Drake's brother."

"He never mentioned that he had a brother."

"There's a lot we need to figure out. Just check on her, please. I've tried to call her a couple of times since I left, and it goes straight to voice mail."

"I'll finish up here and go."

"Do you know what she's doing about the baby?"

Kadin struggled with answering truthfully. Lilly must have kept the information back about having twins. Maybe she felt she couldn't trust Long with the information, and it wasn't Kadin's place to divulge the information, either.

"Arrangements are being made."

"So she's going to carry it."

"It's really too late in the pregnancy for her to do otherwise."

"Sounds like you have it under control. Let me know how she is when you get back."

Kadin helped Ellie finish the dishes before he left. Part of him delayed departure because he didn't know what he would say to Lilly. Had she made a mistake? Could all these women be wrong? Could he support her when his professional reputation had taken a solid hit based on her false accusation?

As Ellie walked him to the door, she promised to speak to her husband and give Kadin a final decision after he returned from his business trip.

After two hours, he neared his small home. Lilly hadn't answered any of his calls, either. Her car was gone. The house was empty, with a note left on the kitchen table.

Detective Long had been right.

Chapter 34

January 3

Lilly felt determined leaving Kadin's. After the messages from her strange visitor and the old woman, she knew protecting these babies was her first priority. The second one was figuring out why the DNA test had not proved Drake's guilt.

How many rapists could there be with mismatched eyes and a tattoo of a hideous creature on their chests?

Lilly knew that to ensure her freedom while she pursued Drake, she had to make herself electronically invisible. No credit cards or ATM drafts. She tossed her phone into the mountainside when she neared the city. She first went to her bank and withdrew as much money as she could without closing the accounts. Her next stop was her townhome. She collected her remaining firearm, as Dana had refused to give back the one she'd confiscated. Luckily, they'd left all of her ammunition behind, and she grabbed every box, placing them inside one duffel bag. There wasn't any use in packing most of her clothes, but she did grab all her scrubs, as the ties allowed her to still wear them as her belly swelled. A few roomy dresses completed her wardrobe. She'd have to buy more clothes in the morning. As she rifled through her medicine cabinet, she discovered one remaining vial of sleeping pills that Kadin hadn't thrown away. Her fist closed over the plastic bottle as she considered the ramifications of taking them along. The temptation to ingest them would easily supersede her desire to refrain, so before she could change her mind, she opened the container and threw them into the toilet.

Next, Lilly went to Savannah's home unannounced. Trying to disappear meant getting rid of her vehicle, at least for the interim. To her surprise, Savannah agreed to loan her a car that had been unused for several years and stated she would keep Lilly's hidden.

After checking into the cheapest hotel she could find near the courthouse,

Lilly could not sleep. The room felt subzero, and the thermostat wouldn't heat above sixty degrees. She tried a warm bath, but after seeing the tea-colored water spew from the faucet, she couldn't relax and abandoned the tub idea. The remainder of the night was spent shivering under two thin blankets; she shuddered to think what filthy stains a Wood's lamp would show. She folded the pillow around her head, trying to block out the sound of a TV and other guttural noises as she searched the darkness for her frosted breath.

As soon as morning broke behind the light-blocking drapes, Lilly threw the covers aside and got ready.

Her court appearance was at 9:00 A.M.

She decided to take a cab to the hearing, not wanting anybody to see the new vehicle she was driving. The courtroom itself was nothing she would have imagined. The judge's bench was a small, laminated table sitting in the front of a white-walled, brown-tiled floor. The chairs were formed plastic, and every movement against the floor, whether it was a chair scraping or high heel tapping, echoed throughout the chamber. Lilly sat at one table alone. Drake followed a few minutes after, his attorney in tow.

It was as if a clutch of spider's eggs hatched at the base of her spine, and thousands of new fledglings ran upward along her vertebrae to see who could be the first to nest in her hair. Drake didn't seem to have any trouble meeting her gaze. He was dressed smartly in a business suit, his mismatched eyes bore a searing look of certainty. Lilly pulled her hands closer against her stomach; the babies seemed to be sleeping despite the noise of her heart hammering beneath her rib cage like a jackhammer tearing apart concrete.

The judge stepped into the room, robe unzipped. To Lilly, he seemed too young to hold such a position. His baby face and relatively short stature made it difficult for her to feel like he could have any authoritative demeanor. He consulted several files and called their case to the forefront.

"Dr. Maguire, would you like to present your evidence as to why you feel you need a restraining order against Dr. Reeves."

Drake stood and buttoned his jacket.

"Your Honor, Dr. Reeves is a troubled woman, and it saddens me greatly that I have to come before you with this request. However, I feel my safety is paramount, and I cannot guarantee my safety any longer."

Drake paused, tugging the edge of each of his sleeves to straighten them. "She is obsessed with me, and since I have dismissed her sexual advances, she has chosen to undermine my business and reputation. She assaulted me in the emergency department at Sage Medical Center as I was trying to save a woman who'd slit her throat with a scalpel, which, I might add, Dr. Reeves carelessly left behind—"

"This is not a medical malpractice case, Dr. Maguire," the judge interrupted.

"Sorry, Your Honor, I was just trying to give you context."

"Just relay to me how she is affecting you personally."

"She has falsely accused me of rape. My attorney has the DNA reports that prove my innocence."

"Dr. Reeves, what is your response to these allegations?" the judge asked while he busied himself with papers.

"What Dr. Maguire says is true," Lilly said.

He looked up, stunned at her statement. "You did assault him and falsely accuse him of rape?"

"Your Honor, I can't explain the DNA evidence. I believe he is the man who raped me. I am carrying his child as a result of that assault. What can you expect a woman to do when she sees the man who violated her?"

"You mean when you assaulted him."

"Yes, I punched him in the jaw to help detain him until the police got there."

"Do you feel as if you're going to harm Dr. Maguire?"

Lilly considered the statement. Was it better to pretend to be submissive or just flat out confess her course of action?

"I don't have any plans to hurt Dr. Maguire."

"But you're convinced that this is the man who assaulted you."

"Yes."

"What are you going to do about it?"

"Prove his guilt."

"How?"

"I have a plan."

"Dr. Reeves, in light of your confession and due to the fact that it doesn't seem like you have the capacity to take these DNA results at face value, which makes me concerned about your level of reasoning, I'm going to grant Dr. Maguire his restraining order. You are not to go to his residence or his place of work, and you must maintain a distance of one hundred yards at all other times. Do you understand?"

"Completely."

Lilly left the hearing and took a cab to the hospital. She needed to gather a few things and speak to Anderson about taking an indefinite leave of absence. Making her way through the ER, she was stopped by Luther in the hall.

"Anderson's been trying to get a hold of you."

"Where is he?"

"His office."

She stopped by her locker and emptied its contents, doubtful that she would be working over the next several months. What she needed most was her lab coat, which would be essential in her quest to prove Drake's guilt. Leaving the ER, she spoke little to her coworkers and made her way to the medical office building where the department chiefs were housed. The moment Anderson's secretary saw her come through the door, she nearly toppled from her chair as she reached for the phone. Lilly had never seen the woman so flustered.

"Dr. Reeves! Dr. Anderson had been trying to reach you."

"So I hear."

"You can go down to his office."

Lilly walked past her desk, feeling the woman's eyes tracking her every step. Anderson waited by his open door and escorted her in, pulling a chair out for her to sit in.

"Lilly, how are you today?"

"I've had better ones. I hear you're anxious to speak with me." She set the duffel bag beside her. Anderson's eyes lingered on it as he took his chair.

"That's correct. I got a call from an attorney representing Dr. Maguire. He's made me aware that a restraining order was granted, prohibiting you two from working in the same building."

Lilly smoothed her tongue along the inside of her cheek.

"That was fast. I just came from that hearing and understand things may seem confusing right now. I wanted to speak to you anyway. I need to take a personal leave of absence."

Anderson fidgeted in his chair, rolling a pen under his fingers over the desktop.

"Lilly, you know . . . maybe you don't know. I think you're a fine doctor. I know I've been hard on you, but it was only to make you better, stronger. If I didn't care about you, I wouldn't have done those things." His voice cracked, and Lilly began to pity his position. "That being said, your performance over the last several months has been barely adequate. I've heard concerns from several staff members about you possibly abusing drugs and alcohol. I'm not sure what's happened between you and Dr. Maguire, but you assaulted him in front of the staff and publicly accused him of rape, besmirching his reputation in consideration of the DNA tests. In light of these issues, I can't take on the liability of keeping you on staff any longer."

"You're going to fire me?" The last string that held her to her life was snipped, and she felt herself freefalling into utter loneliness. What did she have to come back to? A job? A family? None of these existed. Losing employment meant no further cash to support her quest. All she possessed was next to her on the floor.

"Lilly, I don't have any other choice."

Even though her task was impossible, even though he had cleared the DNA testing, she felt it was her responsibility to prove Drake guilty. Now, nothing hindered achieving this goal. Maybe this was why she had been given this burden.

Chapter 35

January 15

THE LAST TWO weeks had been a firestorm for Nathan. Sitting alone, he brooded over the empty desk in front of him, the top clear of any belongings. Brett had requested and been granted fourteen days' vacation and seemed too eager to distance himself from Nathan, and he wondered if Brett would place a request for a new partner when he returned. Department backlash was not overt but subtle in its undermining of Nathan's position and authority. It wasn't the fact that Drake Maguire had been a suspect, but that Nathan continued to pursue him in light of the evidence.

Soon after they had learned about Drew Stipman, contact had been made to the Nevada State Police and the correctional facility where he'd been detained. The unique body marks that the women described were not part of Drew's biological makeup. He did have several tattoos, but none that matched the description of the women involved in his case. Drew's eyes were naturally green, and he had perfect vision. Nathan found it curious that Drake had chosen to wear contacts that matched the natural color of his brother's eyes.

He's trying to mimic his brother to frame him.

Nathan studied the photo he'd been sent of Drew Stipman. He and Drake were identical twins, but some of their physical characteristics made it possible to distinguish the two. Drake was taller and more physically defined, but otherwise they could be mistaken for the same person. Even though Drew didn't have any physical characteristics of their serial rapist, Chief Anson wanted him located and for the case against Drake Maguire to be dropped. He reasoned that the ex-convict could have gotten a new tattoo since his release and possibly was wearing colored contacts to pose as his brother.

Question being, what was Drake's motive for framing Drew?

Drew's photo had been released to the press in connection with the case, and a nationwide search was on. Even Drake was making the most of his position. He'd had several news conferences lending compassion to the victims, particularly Dr. Reeves, stating it was easy for him to understand her confusion in light of the resemblance between him and his brother. He urged his sibling to come forward and accept responsibility.

Nathan approached the DA on behalf of Celia Ramirez. There had not been a DNA specimen collected in her case, but she was able to ID her assailant based on eye color alone. As he suspected would happen, the DA scoffed at trying to garner a conviction based on this, even if it was an oddly distinct physical characteristic. With the advent of colored contacts, how could he prove it was Drake who'd committed these crimes and not just someone in disguise? He wouldn't take the case forward.

So far, Drew was nowhere to be found.

For that matter, Lilly was missing as well.

When he and Brett had left Lilly at Kadin's cabin, Nathan had slipped a tracking device purchased on the Internet under her vehicle. Brett was surprised at his lack of following the legal letter, but if Nathan lost Lilly and the baby, then there would be nothing to connect Drake to these crimes. He was as convinced as she was that the infant was the key to unlocking this mystery. Would this be the case that could knock DNA from being the gold standard in criminal prosecution?

It was clear Lilly had shown up for her court appearance and subsequently been fired from her job. That information was obtained from a few phone calls. After she left the hospital, her trail thinned out and disappeared. Nathan discovered she'd emptied her bank accounts of nearly every cent, which was quite a bit of money. He'd located her vehicle at the home of her aunt. Savannah wouldn't give him any information on her whereabouts. It wasn't too much later when he discovered Savannah owned two vehicles and located the one she'd loaned to Lilly at the airport. Nathan slipped another tracking device onto that vehicle and spent the day at Denver International, trying to figure where Lilly had gone.

She'd purchased an airline ticket to Montana and boarded the flight. Once she'd landed, there wasn't clear evidence of where she'd gone. She hadn't rented a car, no one with her description had purchased a bus ticket, and she hadn't boarded another flight.

Nathan's best guess was she had taken a bus somewhere in disguise or had purchased a vehicle in cash from a private seller and paid extra for that person to keep the plates registered in his name. He didn't believe Montana was her chosen destination. If he had to place a bet, he'd stake his reputation that she was in Nevada, looking into Drake's background.

Kadin seemed equally clueless, or at least that's what he professed. He swore Lilly hadn't reached out to him. The last thing they'd talked about was arranging someone to adopt the baby and her desire to have the baby delivered away from any hospital. Nathan surmised Lilly was planning on Kadin delivering the infant at the cabin. Of course, Kadin attempted to pull Nathan from that idea, stating it wouldn't be safe and he wouldn't put her at risk no matter how she felt about it.

Lilly has a way to make this happen.

Nathan scooped up his folders and his list of local tattoo parlors. On a map, he'd circled a two-hour radius from Drake's home and looked up every business within the circle. It was one of two things he could think to do, and Nathan was fortunate in that Drake had held only one primary residence since his move to Colorado. Next on this list was to try to find a geneticist to talk with about DNA testing.

He pulled up to one of the last facilities on his agenda. Nathan was used to the rundown habitations that encased most parlors. This structure was clinic-like. Inside was a large desk built from glass counters with soft under-lighting. A receptionist sat at the front, in conservative dress and makeup. The decor was soft hues of blue and plenty of real foliage. Comfortable leather chairs lined the other side of the waiting room, which was currently empty.

As he approached, the woman looked up. "You must be Detective Long."

"How did you guess?"

"Your appointment and that police vibe you give off. Let me get Lawrence for you."

It was one of the few tattoo places that required appointments. Lawrence came through a set of double doors. He was dressed in a simple white T-shirt and blue jeans minus any markings on his own skin.

"Why don't you come back, and we'll talk."

Nathan was ushered through the doors into the back. The business maintained its sterile feel, and he was shown into a small office.

"You're not quite what I expected." Nathan took a seat. The room contained two chairs and a row of file cabinets.

"Our clients tend to be more upscale."

"I'm sure any comment I make in response to that won't seem very cordial. Why don't you have any tattoos? At least none that are visible. Every other artist I came across was like a painted canvas with very little virgin skin remaining."

"Me?" Lawrence tapped his chest with the fingertips of both hands. "I'm horrified of needles, but I love the art form. It's the best way for me to express what I want to create."

"I was hoping you could look at several photos of a particular tattoo and give me your thoughts on it."

Nathan pulled out the same photo lineup he'd shown Heather and handed it over. Lawrence studied it, tilting it into the overhead light several times like a doctor examining X-rays.

"There's only one tattoo here that's not photo-shopped. This one," he said, pointing to Drake's tattoo.

"You have a good eye."

"It's my job. The tattoo is quite intricate. It has good color detail. It was done by someone professional, definitely not an amateur."

"Can you tell me anything about the creature itself?"

"Sure. It's a monster from Greek mythology, a chimera."

"You're a student of Greek mythology?"

"I know. You probably haven't come across many like me."

"You could say that."

"I was a literature major in a previous life. It was an interest of mine."

"What's a chimera?"

"In Greek mythology, it's a hybrid of different animals functioning as one monster."

"Have you ever known anyone to get this particular tattoo or anyone else who does this kind of artwork?"

"Actually, I did this design."

Nathan's heart stopped. He'd actually found the artist.

"Can you tell me who the recipient was?"

"I don't know about giving you a name. People don't like that information to be divulged. But he is a local physician."

Nathan crossed his legs and leaned back. Did he know about Drake's crimes?

"Did he happen to tell you why he wanted this design?"

"People get tattoos for all sorts of reasons. The stigma of having one has worn off. People don't feel like they'll be associated with prisoners, motorcycle gangs, and prostitutes if they get one. Some tattoos have a cultural basis. Other people use it to make a statement or advertise something they identify with."

"Is that what this doctor told you?"

"People are usually pretty open about sharing why the tattoo is important to them. He said it was an open expression of who he was inside, a clue to his exact nature."

"So he considers himself a combination of several different creatures functioning as one monster."

"In the literal sense I guess you could view it that way. He boasted about perpetrating a crime that he could never be prosecuted for. He said someone else was wrongly convicted and serving prison time in his place."

Nathan's mind reeled, the question quick from his lips. "Did he confess to you what the crime was or who that person might be?"

"He never mentioned anything specific, and honestly, I don't take any of the things people say to me very seriously. Clients brag all the time to appear to have more machismo when they're just trying to hide their fear of the procedure."

"Have you seen this doctor recently?"

"No, but he's been on the news."

"Did that concern you, considering his previous statements?"

"It certainly gave me pause, but in light of the fact that he didn't confess any crime and has subsequently been cleared by DNA, I didn't feel like I needed to do anything further. Again, I chalked it up to petty bragging. Something he was trying to do to impress me. Make it seem as if he was tougher than he really was."

"Do you remember when he got this tattoo?"

"It's been several years, two or three maybe."

"What about him stuck in your mind if it's been so long?"

"For one thing, this is the only tattoo like this I've ever done. He asked for it specifically. I had to draw up several designs for his approval. That process took weeks. He was very particular about the look."

"Anything else?"

"Yeah, he had the weirdest eyes. They were different colors."

Nathan returned to his vehicle and made several notes. The tattoo artist was further confirmation of what he knew in his heart was true. Drake was the one and only perpetrator of these crimes. How could Nathan get the chief on board with his theory and keep his job?

Chapter 36

January 29

AFTER LILLY HAD flown to Montana and purchased a nondescript, run-down vehicle, she'd driven back to the state of Colorado. Her plan was to search the medical records of every known hospital and clinic for information pertaining to Drake Maguire or Drake Stipman. It wasn't clear from his résumé when his name change occurred. When he originally practiced medicine in the state of Nevada, it could have been under Stipman. Lilly reasoned it was possible that Drake went back after his name change to have his Nevada records listed under Maguire.

To Lilly's dismay, these names weren't that uncommon. She looked at every record that matched Drake's birthday with either Maguire or Stipman. In Colorado, that netted ten records between the two. The other issue was that many of these files were stored on microfiche, and she'd have to return after they pulled and printed the files. Each record garnered in this fashion took several days—and in one case, two weeks—to retrieve. The only visit she found likely was for Drake Maguire receiving stitches at a clinic. Anything that was taken care of by a private physician wouldn't be accessible. In some instances, people refused to give her the records, either not buying her explanation that she was Drake's wife collecting his records for insurance purposes or questioning the forged medical release.

Currently, she was in Las Vegas near Drake's last address in Nevada as listed on his résumé. As in Colorado, she would hit the major medical centers first, then work her way down to the smaller clinics. Then she'd begin at the facilities closest to his previous residence and work her way outward.

Colorado had given her the opportunity to perfect her ruse. She'd dressed conservatively, but with a shirt she could unbutton to show cleavage if a young male was working the medical records department. If it was a young woman, she would pretend onset of contractions to hasten the interaction; an older woman, and she would talk about having the twins and how nervous she was, gathering several nuggets of grandmotherly advice along the way.

She stood in front of the mirror, putting the final touches on her hair and makeup. The once roomy lab coat was now tight around her belly and she'd given up buttoning it. Placing her stethoscope around her neck, she picked up her pocket holder that contained a penlight, scissors, and a set of hemostats.

It was never as difficult to get into the hospital as one would hope. Typically, if she were even stopped, she would claim she was a new physician on staff who had lost her badge. If they asked for further credentials, she'd show her Colorado license and feign how difficult it was working in a new facility to get away to spend hours at a slow government office to obtain a new driver's license. Generally, this garnered sympathetic nods, and she was on her way.

The medical records office was nearly as easy. As she made her way down into the bowels of this hospital, she discovered the door to medical records electronically guarded by a badge entry device. She knocked on the door and waited, leaning against the cement-bricked wall. An older gentleman opened the door.

Lilly pushed her way in. "I'm so sorry, I lost my badge. You don't know how hard it is to get around this place when you lose that thing." She approached the desk and grabbed a brochure to fan her face. "These babies are killing me. Is it hot in here to you?"

"Not in the least," he said, rounding to the back of the counter. "How can I help you today?"

An old curmudgeon. She didn't have a play for that.

Placing the brochure on the desk, she pulled her notebook out. "We got a call, a patient we're expecting in the ER, a referral from an outlying clinic, but they say he gets treatment here. I need to know if you have any records for Drake Maguire, birth date May 10, 1973. Oh, he may also be listed under Drake Stipman. If you don't find anything with that birthday, can you do a larger search? I guess he's had a head injury and is presenting with some confusion."

He paused, studying her. "What's your name? When did you start working here?"

Lilly surmised hiding her true identity would be difficult. No matter how much she changed her looks with a cut and store-bought hair dye, possibly even using color contacts like her nemesis, there was one characteristic she couldn't hide. The only benefit of giving a false name would be to hold people off her trail for a little longer.

"Misty Rainforth. I was hired in the last couple of weeks."

He tapped his fingers on the desk, playing with his upper set of dentures as he contemplated her statement. Lilly did her best to portray boredom and looked about the room, hoping that her elevated heartbeat wasn't evident at the side of her neck as she turned her head. Finally, he made his way to the back. It wasn't long before he returned with several thick files in his hands.

"Did you find more than one patient?"

"No, these are all his."

That was interesting, it meant his records weren't in storage and he'd likely had a recent visit. A file this thick, considering Drake's age, meant a serious health crisis.

"Is there somewhere down here I can look through these?" She smoothed her hands over her belly. "I don't want to haul this all back to the ER."

He acquiesced and carried the record to a small room with a single table and chair. The chart was divided into several sections. Lab work, radiology, MD notes.

She began flipping through the lab work, beginning with the most recent. For the last couple of years, Drake had a complete blood count, which looked at the makeup and number of cells in the blood. It wasn't unusual to have this test performed, but then the tests began to occur every six months. That was fairly odd unless the doctor was trying to track a chronic disease—a blood disorder like anemia, for instance. About four years ago, he was tested every three months, and then Lilly discovered why.

An abnormal CBC.

Lilly noted a critically high white count corresponding with increased levels of immature white blood cells. His red blood cells and platelets were critically low. She continued through the lab work. Bone marrow studies. Spinal fluid results. These confirmed her original suspicion.

Drake Maguire had cancer—leukemia to be specific. This diagnosis had occurred before his name change.

Continuing through the lab section, she noted the paternity tests and other results pertaining to the hunt for a donor match when she stumbled across an aberrance, a lab sheet for DNA matching from an anonymous donor several months after Drake's bone marrow transplant. It was buccal cells, obtained from a cheek swab. Whoever this person was, he wasn't a DNA match to Drake.

But why would Drake pursue testing for a DNA match after his bone marrow graft?

Lilly flipped to the doctor's notes, starting with the dates that corresponded with the abnormal lab work. This chart was before the advent of computer documentation, and the handwritten notes were a challenge to read. After Drake's initial diagnosis, he'd been started on chemotherapy. Per this physician, Drake had briefly been in remission and then relapsed within a few months, and the medical team had investigated the issue of bone marrow transplant early in the course of his treatment. The oncologist in charge of his case outlined that they tested his wife, mother, twin brother, and two sons.

After this doctor's note was a lengthy entry from a social worker. Her note included the following statement: "Wife and mother are not a match. DNA testing of the sons has proven that they are not biologically Drake's children. Spouse is very upset over these test results and is requesting further genetic testing. Patient does not want to place children under any more stress and is refusing wife's request. Seems unlikely further DNA testing would shed any light on the issue. Twin brother is currently incarcerated, but courts allowed testing for DNA matching since other family members prove negative. Brother, Drew Stipman, has proved to be a match for Drake and will be the donor for the bone marrow transplant."

Lilly flipped to the demographic information and jotted down Drake's address at the time of his diagnosis. It was interesting that he'd had issues with paternity in the past, and she wondered about the feelings of this woman, his previous wife, considering she wanted to pursue further DNA testing regarding her children.

She gathered the chart and returned the record to the man at the front desk. After leaving medical records, she made her way to the laboratory. A sliding glass window was utilized for the transfer of specimens. She pushed one side open and greeted the young woman who was seated at the desk.

"I was wondering if you could answer a question for me about how long you keep pathology specimens on hand."

"We keep them a long time. With medical malpractice the way it is anymore, we usually don't throw anything away."

"Can you see what you might have pertaining to Drake Stipman?" Lilly rattled off his date of birth as the woman typed.

"Looks like we have quite a bit; blood, bone marrow aspirate, and cerebral spinal fluid, as well. It might take a while to get it from our off-site storage."

"I don't need you to get it now. It's just good to know it's there."

Lilly left the building and walked to her newly purchased junker. Even though it was the desert, it was cool in late January. Once inside, Lilly picked up several maps from the passenger seat and found the section for the address she'd culled from Drake's medical record. She pulled out of the hospital parking lot, cranking up the heat. Cold air with the faint smell of antifreeze misted from the vents.

The community hid behind a gated wall. She waited several minutes for a car to pull forward that she could piggyback access behind. Earthtone stucco houses, each three stories with a pool in the backyard, sat on one- to two-acre lots. As she turned and entered into a cul-de-sac, she busied herself checking the numbers on the mailboxes. Based on these, Drake's old house should come next.

She looked up and punched the brakes.

The lot was empty. All that remained was a charred fireplace column and a murk-filled pool in the backyard. She got out of her car and walked the lot. Bits of old charred wood still lay in the frosted grass. A neighbor looked at her from the next home, and Lilly walked over to greet him.

"Hey," she said, extending her hand. "Misty Rainforth. I'm an old friend of the Stipmans'. I thought I would surprise them with a visit, but I see they're not home."

"You haven't been in touch for a long time. They haven't lived here for years, and they're not together anymore. It's tragic what happened to that family."

"Must have been a terrible fire."

He nodded. "Whole thing went up like a tinderbox. Never found who did it."

"They think the fire was set intentionally?" Lilly pulled her shoe through the grass.

"That's not in dispute. Only thing they don't know is who set it."

"Do you know where I can find Ms. Stipman?"

"She's probably the same place she's been for the last few years. After her boys died, she moved to a small apartment on the other side of town."

"Her children died in the fire?"

"Yep. Horrible. I can still remember it like it was last night. The mother was lucky to get out alive."

"Do you happen to have her address?"

"Probably. Wife's inside. She'll get it for you."

Chapter 37

February 14

DANA ENTERED HER small, cottage-style home and set her briefcase down on the hope chest that sat in the foyer. Her feet ached with each step, and pulling off her shoes didn't ease the pain. Unbraiding her hair as she walked to her living room, she stilled as she saw a man sitting in her chair, acting as if it was his name on the mortgage. He sat nonplussed, watching her TV, the back of his head visible and unmoving. The intruder had one of her beers popped open, the condensation leaving a ring on her cherry-wood table. Dana pulled up onto her stockinged toes and inched backward, at first thinking maybe he hadn't heard her clamoring into the house over the noise of the TV, but then her disbelief proved false when he turned his head around and leveled a gun at her chest.

Her unexpected visitor was Drake Maguire.

"Dr. Morrell, come and have a seat. There are a few things I'd like to discuss with you."

The knowledge of her impending death collided with her instinct for self-preservation, and she turned on her heel and lunged for the front door. She felt the pain first, a crack at the back of her right thigh, as her leg gave way beneath her. Her fingers brushed against the cool metal of the doorknob as she fell. Drake was next to her within seconds, scooping her up and throwing her over one shoulder, his gloved hand boring into her wound. In the few seconds she had, she pulled up his shirt and began to claw at his lower back. Drake didn't even flinch from the scratches, and he threw her onto the chair he'd vacated. He took a seat on the floor before her and wiped the blood from his glove onto her white Berber carpet.

"Do I have your attention now?" He twirled the weapon around his index finger.

Dana prayed a neighbor had heard the gunfire and would call the police. However, cool weather kept people indoors, and societal mores prohibited people from getting involved. In light of this, her sense of doom did not diminish. She pressed her right hand firmly against the back of her leg. It did little to stem the flow of blood, and she glanced down, watching the crimson pool spread on the camel moleskin chair underneath her. She could feel faint shock tremors begin to rattle within her as her skin tone faded. She tried to focus, but her normally crisp vision was fuzzy.

"I need to know where Lilly is."

She shook her head in response and leaned back in the chair, the flow of pain like heat waves rippling across her vision.

"Dana," he chided in singsong.

"I don't know where she is." Her tongue was like a wooden block in her mouth.

"Interesting." Drake pulled himself up onto his knees, obviously attempting to draw her line of sight back to him. She refused to look.

"Dr. Reeves has been making quite a pain of herself lately. It seems she's been to nearly every hospital here and in Nevada, looking into my old medical records. Thankfully, my mother has spies, and after Lilly visited one such place, my mother was alerted by a staff member. Unfortunately for me, it was too late to discern what information she gathered, if any. But at that point, Lilly sealed her fate."

"Why would you care about what she's doing if you're innocent?" Dana pulled her head up and met his gaze, seeing the cold stare as it drank from the well of evil within him. She regretted every moment she'd doubted Lilly's explanation of events. After Lilly's disappearance, Dana had made feeble attempts to try to locate her, but nothing that would rise to what a true friend should have done.

"Well, that's a curious question, isn't it? I'm sure you're realizing now that possibly I'm not all that innocent."

"I'm not sure what you're trying to accomplish here, but even if I had one iota of information pertaining to Lilly's whereabouts, I would never give it to you."

"Even if it would save her life? What about your life?"

Dana remembered the first time they'd met. Lilly had been entertaining a patient in the PICU, a young girl with a sick heart. There'd been a quiet tenderness in her interaction with the child. A vulnerability Dana felt was rare. A confidence that was strong and sure. The memory brought comfort. Dana shook her head to keep her darkening peripheral vision at bay.

"Do you recognize this weapon?" He raised it like a ceremonial chalice. "I do from searching Lilly's place. It's never good to have a victim surprise you with a firearm. Were you worried that she might use it to commit suicide? You were such a good friend to her, to try to protect her like that."

"How did you get in here?"

"The spare set of keys you gave Lilly." He reached into his back pocket and removed the ring, jiggling it from his fingertips. "She was nice enough to label them and everything. You should be more careful who you leave these with."

"She never told me they were missing."

Drake clicked his tongue against the roof of his mouth. "I'm sure there were too many other things on her mind for her to worry about such trivial matters." He walked toward her on his knees. "You see, Lilly's prints are all over this weapon. I'm going to shoot you with it and conspicuously place this set of keys she labeled right here." He tapped her end table. "I'm also going to leave this weapon behind and maybe a little note of confession. If I can't find Lilly, I'll get the police to hunt her for your murder. You won't be around to tell your version of events."

There is a moment of choice in each person's life to either stand firm or wither under the pressure. Dana's mind focused little on Drake's threat. She'd known his intent as soon as she became aware of his presence. What consumed her thoughts was her life as she led it and whether or not it had been enough.

Did I love my family enough?

Did I take care of my patients well enough?

Did I serve a friend in crisis to the point where she could see you, Lord, and not me trying to help her?

Dana was confident about two of the three answers. The last thought in her mind was a prayer of hope that the answer to the third question was also *yes*.

Chapter 38

February 16

THE CORONER MIGHT say differently, but the timeline suggested that it was about forty-eight hours before the body of Dr. Dana Morrell was discovered. Nathan surmised she was murdered when she arrived home from her shift on Wednesday. He paced around the living room as Brett discussed aspects of the crime scene with the first responding officer. So far, they hadn't found any evidence of forced entry. She was dressed in comfortable clothes, a set of soiled scrubs in a large tote bag rested against the door, her briefcase on a hand-painted hope chest a few steps away. Next to this was a small table where her keys sat on a saucer-sized china dish.

Dana had a scheduled day off on Thursday. A friend, Amber, had come forward saying they were scheduled to have lunch that day and Dana had missed the appointment. Amber stated she'd run by Dana's home to check on her. When no one came to the door, she assumed it was a work-related emergency, as had often happened before, and didn't think twice about it, claiming she'd expected a call from her in the next couple of days.

Friday, when Dana didn't come in for morning rounds, missed her first surgery, and failed to respond to her pages, the operating-room staff had called the police. As the first responding officer looked through the back windows, he could see the body through the thinly veiled glass, and thus came the call to Brett and Nathan.

Dana's body was on a chair and had two obvious wounds, one to the back of her right thigh and one to the right temple. Deceptively, most of the blood on the chair came from the leg wound. Her head was intact, but at the small entrance wound on her temple, some bruising, and misshapen features on her face left clues to the utter destruction within her skull. Nathan leaned in and shone his flashlight at the entrance wound. Some unburned gunpowder was embedded into the skin immediately around the wound site, which suggested a shooting at close range. A set of keys sat next to her, feminine writing annotated with Dana's name on a tag, likely a set she'd left behind for a neighbor. Thus far, they were canvassing her block to see if anyone would lay claim to the key being in their possession.

The initial point of attack seemed to be near the front door. Three small pools of blood had formed a few feet from the threshold. Then the droplets ran in a sporadic line into the living room, where they terminated at the chair. Several wide smears of blood stained the top of the carpet fibers as if someone had wiped a hand clean. The weapon was placed beside the keys, and a typewritten note was there, as well. All it said was "I'm sorry. Lilly."

Nathan called the crime-scene technician over and had her take a couple photos of the gun in place. Then, with gloved hands, Nathan picked up the weapon, careful to touch surfaces that would not be large or smooth enough to capture fingerprints. It was a smaller caliber, semi-automatic, which might explain the lack of an exit wound. Later, in a better environment, Nathan would drop the magazine out and record the type of ammunition in the gun. He expected some kind of hollow-pointed, expanding round, which would prevent the bullet from maintaining enough energy to break through the bony skull a second time. No one at the scene had found any high-velocity blood spatter or any sign of the round that killed Dana. Oddly, Nathan hoped the round was still in her head so they could have it as evidence.

Upon further examination of the weapon, Nathan noted it wasn't well maintained. Dust and fibers were stuck in every nook, and it lacked the distinctive smell of cleaning solvents that his own service piece carried. That told Nathan the shooter was probably not a gun enthusiast. Carefully turning the gun, he pointed it in his own direction; staying well away from the trigger, he asked the tech to shine a light down the barrel. The nose and the barrel's interior surfaces had blood, skin, hair, and other fibers crusted in place. Coupled with what Nathan had seen at the wound site, he knew this was an up-close-and-personal killing.

This was an execution.

"Snap a couple of shots of this blowback; then we'll bag it as is. Make sure the coroner bags the victim's hands. I don't want anything getting lost inside the body bag."

As the crime-scene technician continued to work, Brett approached Nathan, flipping his phone closed. A uniformed officer entered the home and zeroed in on Nathan as well.

"I've got some information from one of the neighbors," the officer said.

"What's that?"

"A Mrs. . . ." He paused and flipped through his notes, wetting his index finger at each turn of the page. "Davies. That's it. Anyway, she lives a couple houses down. She's a young mom with several kids in tow. She says when Dana moved in a couple of years ago, she offered to hold onto a set of keys for her. Dana had told her at the time she had a friend at work who already had a set."

"Did the neighbor happen to say who that friend was?" Nathan asked.

"The name wasn't volunteered when I spoke to her, and honestly, I didn't ask."

"Nathan, you know this is Lilly," Brett said.

"I don't know anything until I discover it during the course of the investigation, Brett."

The officer excused himself. The tension between Nathan and Brett was becoming difficult to hide. Brett was settled on the thought that Drew Stipman was the real threat and that when they found him, the case was over. Nathan continued to pursue Drake, mostly on his own time and as quietly as possible to prevent being thrown off the case entirely by the chief.

"I've contacted the ATF and started a trace on the weapon. The serial number on the gun doesn't come up through NCIC or CCIC as being stolen." Brett folded his arms across his chest. "However, this is the same make and model of a weapon that Lilly is known to have owned. We learned that from Kadin. That they had taken a gun away from her, fearing that she was suicidal. I'm sure we'll find her prints all over it."

Nathan turned and faced Brett squarely. "I know what this scene seems like. I'm not going to jump to the obvious conclusion, because everything seems a little too perfect to me."

"Don't be looking for zebras here."

"Let's assume it is Lilly. Let's start at the top. Where is she?"

"I don't know, Nathan. No one seems to know. She's off the grid, but that doesn't mean she hasn't been here." Brett pointed to the floor.

"What we do know is that she's had contact with one person. Kadin

Daughtry. She sent him a postcard in the last couple weeks from Nevada. All it said was 'Make sure the paperwork is ready.'"

"As I said, that could all be a sham."

"So let me sum this up. You believe Lilly committed this crime because these are likely the keys she was in possession of for Dana, and Lilly's weapon is on the premises because Dana had taken it from her to save her life. Tell me your theory of what Lilly's motive is. Why would Lilly want to kill this woman, her closest friend by all accounts?"

"We know Lilly's not right in the head. It's been said by more than one person that after her attack she unraveled. She accused an innocent man of rape. He had to file a restraining order against her—"

Nathan cut him off.

"Why Dana? Those would all be fine points if it were Drake Maguire in that chair, but it's not. It's her friend, her closest confidant."

"I don't know, Nathan. We can't always identify the motives of crazy people."

"Then explain a few aspects of the crime scene to me. We know the initial point of attack was right here at the front door." Nathan paced quickly in that direction and pointed with his pen to the hardwood floor. "There's a large pool of blood here, then just droplets forming a path until the chair. How do you think that happened?"

"She was shot in the leg, probably to disable her. It's likely she wouldn't have been able to walk. Someone carried her over here."

"How far along do you think Lilly is in her pregnancy?" Nathan asked.

"I don't know."

"She's probably close to six months."

"Whatever. Your point?"

"Well, how do you imagine a woman that pregnant carried Dana to the chair?"

"Maybe she had help."

"From who?"

"I don't know."

"And then the most important question is why she would want Dana dead and obviously point the police in her own direction? She leaves a weapon behind that she knows is registered in her name and a set of keys right next to the victim presumably with her handwriting. I'm not going to even entertain that insipid typewritten note. This could all be planted evidence."

"Then what is your alternative theory, Nathan?"

"Based on all we know thus far, I think we should consider that this was Drake's doing. It would be foolish to rule anything out this early."

"And what would be his motive?"

"Honestly, I think he's trying to draw Lilly out. We know that his pregnant victims haven't fared very well."

"Drake's been cleared by DNA."

Nathan ignored the comment. "I think Drake is looking for Lilly—and why would she not try to attend her best friend's funeral? Once he draws her out, she suffers some unfortunate incident and all his loose ends are tied up. We know Lilly believes he is guilty and wants the baby tested for paternity. She's going to push for it after the delivery."

"Nathan, in light of the DNA results, no judge will grant her request."

"I agree it's going to be difficult in light of the current evidence. I think we need to wait until the postmortem is completed on this body. Maybe there will be DNA. The killer might have left something behind or the victim might have taken it from him. Or her. Whether it's Drake, Lilly, or the bogeyman, we're going to have to collect more evidence. Whatever we decide on, the evidence had better support our theory."

Brett's shoulders slumped. The fighting between them added to Nathan's stress, but could Brett be opening up to other theories? "Regardless of that, Nathan, we're going to need to find Lilly. Are you sure you don't know where she is?"

"I don't. The transponder I planted indicates her car is in the same place, and I've been checking it frequently to make sure the batteries don't run out. The only people who might know her whereabouts are Savannah and Kadin. I guess that's our next stop."

"Let's make sure we're at the funeral. Maybe the killer will come to pay his respects."

Chapter 39

March 2

It had taken one week for the coroner to find Dr. Morrell's parents, who'd been on some exotic African safari, and additional days for them to travel back and arrange for their daughter's funeral.

Nathan stood next to Brett, surveying the mourners as they made their way to the graveside. They had approached two obviously pregnant women, suspecting one might be Lilly in disguise. Brett asked point-blank how far along they were. One of the women, not Lilly, was near delivery. The other woman was not pregnant. Brett handed her a card for the public relations officer when she requested one to file a complaint.

After rubbing the ice crystals from the end of his nose with his gloved hand, Nathan grabbed Brett's elbow and pulled him back into the distance, the snow crunching under their feet as they walked. The day was bright; fresh snow sparkled under the gleaming sun. Nathan pushed his sunglasses up the bridge of his nose and huddled into his coat.

It wasn't unusual to have these spring snowstorms in Colorado. In fact, some of the most devastating storms occurred in February and March. Nathan looked up the hill where the dirt dug for Dana's grave spotted the snow. Her polished gold casket posed at the edge of the six-foot hole as the preacher spoke words of comfort to her family and friends.

Lilly had been smart not to show up.

Nathan checked the time. He needed to keep an appointment that had taken him weeks to set up. He didn't want to miss it.

And he didn't want Brett to know about it.

The service lasted another twenty minutes. Once Nathan saw people break up into small groups, he made quick work of leaving Brett, without giving an explanation, and made his way to his vehicle before he got caught in the flood of the departing.

It was a short drive to the genetics clinic. Since Kadin was reluctant to speak with him, Nathan had spent the last month cold-calling doctors who specialized in chromosomal defects and DNA testing.

Dr. Kent Lockwood had agreed to meet with him.

The man was average height with brown hair and darker brown eyes, but his presence exuded calm, which Nathan thought was important when parents were told their unborn child might have a devastating genetic defect.

They sat in his office, which was more coffee chic than modern doctor decor. Several overstuffed chairs were arranged around a circular, gray, marbled table. Nathan was served tea, and Lockwood offered him his choice of three flavored coffee creamers: amaretto, hazelnut, or Italian sweet cream.

"Seriously?" Nathan asked.

"Don't knock it till you try it." He poured a good amount of amaretto cream into Nathan's steaming cup before settling back into his chair. "Coffee was always too bitter for me, and I have to say I like all the new varieties of tea they've come out with. My wife got me hooked, and now I find myself perusing the grocery store aisles, searching for new tea and creamers. You can't beat the peppermint mocha at Christmas."

Nathan sipped the light brown liquid and nodded his approval. "Not bad. It beats what they brew at the station, but I would never live it down if I made a cup of this in front of my coworkers."

"Well, above all keep yourself safe." Lockwood balanced his cup on the arm of his chair. "So you mentioned on the phone you had some questions about DNA testing. How can I help?"

"I have a case that I have some questions on. First of all, have you ever heard the term *chimera*?"

"Of course, but how does this relate to your case?"

"To be honest, this is a shot in the dark for me. I'll need you to keep our conversation confidential. Can you agree to that?"

"Absolutely."

"I have a suspect in several rape cases that has been cleared by DNA testing. I believe with my heart that he is guilty. He has this unique tattoo, and I found the artist who created it. The artist said that it was a chimera, which is evidently some creature from Greek mythology. Anyway, while he worked with this client, the man bragged that this tattoo was a clue to his exact nature and that he had perpetrated several crimes for which he could never be convicted. That got me thinking that a chimera had something to do with DNA and was the reason he was clearing all these DNA tests."

Lockwood took several sips of his tea before responding. Setting the cup aside, he grabbed a clipboard that had several sheets of blank paper.

"Interesting connection you've made. Let me start by explaining what a chimera is. A chimera is formed very early in pregnancy when two fertilized eggs come together and are essentially fused into one individual. A single person is born, but they often have some unusual physical characteristics."

"Such as?" Nathan prompted.

"Oftentimes it looks as if they've been stitched up the middle. I saw a case where a chimera was formed from a Caucasian male and African American female. Externally, the person resembled a man, but it was as if you cut in half a white person and a black person and stuck the non-matching components together. One side of his body was white, the other side black skinned, and a dark line ran up his middle. Internally, he had both male and female reproductive organs. Does your suspect have any unique physical characteristics?"

"He has different-colored eyes."

"That can certainly be part of it. Does he have this odd line that runs up his center?"

"No, I don't believe he does."

"There are other genetic defects—Waardenburg Syndrome, for example—that can cause a person to have different-colored eyes. Typically one blue and the other brown."

"That's what this gentleman has."

"Does he have white patches in his hair or any hearing loss?"

"I don't think so."

Lockwood crossed out a section on his notes. "Hmm, then it probably isn't Waardenburg's."

"What about genetically? Is there anything peculiar about the DNA of a chimera?"

"That's where it can get interesting. A chimera is a single person with two DNA fingerprints."

"Two?" Nathan's mind whirled. Was his theory false? The crime scenes showed one unique individual. Not two.

"Yes, I would imagine that if a chimera committed the crime spree you speak of and didn't prevent the transfer of his DNA from himself to the victims, it could prove difficult for the police to catch him."

"Why is that?"

"Well, it would look like two people committed the crime instead of just one."

Nathan struggled to clarify his thoughts. "Is it possible for the DNA of one of the individuals to be hidden?"

"It's not the most common expression, but it is possible. There was one documented case of a woman who needed an organ transplant. Her children were teens at the time so they tested these boys to see if either was a match. They came back to this woman and told her that her sons were not her children. Well, she scoffed at them. She was a woman of fine standing in the community. She hadn't received any in vitro fertilization, which is thought to increase the chance a chimera could be formed. There was no doubt in her mind that these were her boys."

"Was she able to prove that they were her children?"

"Eventually. Her case garnered the interest of a research physician. This doctor began by testing several different cell types, taking the most easily accessible ones first like hair, skin, and cheek cells. All of those samples tested negative."

"What did they do next?"

"Well, you have to understand that with a chimera, different cell lines can express these two individuals differently. For instance, a chimera is often picked up through blood typing because generally, both individual's DNA will be represented in the blood, but this isn't always the case. In some cell lines, only one individual is represented, and the other individual's DNA can be hidden in harder-to-get cell types. In this woman's case, she'd happened to have some tissue taken from her bladder for a biopsy several years prior, and that's where they found the DNA of the individual that mothered her children."

"What about sperm cells? Is it generally one or both DNA fingerprints?"

"It could be either. I mean, if the DNA test ruled out your suspect and you really thought he was a chimera, you would have to look at other tissue types to find the other person's DNA. In this case, I assume you have semen samples that you've used as comparison. How did you test your possible suspect?"

"A cheek swab."

"Did you test his sperm?"

"That's not going to happen."

"Why not?"

Nathan's eyes widened. It amazed him how intelligent people could have inverse common sense. "One, the suspect has already been ruled out based on the buccal cells. Two, exactly how would we obtain a sperm sample from an unwilling participant?"

"I see how that would be a problem."

"Three, the sperm samples from the victims are a match to another convicted criminal, so most people in the law-enforcement community feel like the case is solved."

"But you don't."

"No."

"Can I ask you? This individual that you suspect as having committed these crimes, does he have a twin?"

Nathan sat straighter, his throat tight with expectation. "He does. He has a twin brother."

"I think I may know what's happened."

Chapter 40

March 21

LILLY LEARNED OF Dana's death as she watched FOX News, and in the next instant discovered she was "a person of interest" in her murder. Though it had been more than a month, the daily news reports kept it fresh in her mind, and she found it hard to keep her sense of futility at bay. CNN's Nancy Grace held on to the case like a starved dog on a bone. It didn't take Lilly long to figure out how Drake had framed her for her dearest friend's murder. Considering Drake had had access to her townhome, he'd probably pilfered the set of keys Dana had entrusted to her. Somehow, he had found out the information that Dana had taken one of her guns, which was coated with Lilly's fingerprints and registered in her name. Even if the police thought she was innocent, the evidence would pull them to a conviction.

Hopelessness drained Lilly's spirit. Though she'd felt down at several points in her life, it was the first time she felt despair, as if she were sitting at the bottom of a drained well, the sides too slick with mud for her to get a foothold to climb out. In the aftermath of the rape, the depression and misuse of mind-altering substances were a bridge until she got her footing. She always felt there would be an end to these feelings, either by her own perseverance or formal therapy.

Now, there was no end.

Not only did she have to prove Drake's guilt, she had to prove her innocence.

The weight of her circumstances and the tragedy that had befallen those who loved her kept her at the bottom of this pit. Lilly sat motionless on the bed in her dank hotel room for hours at a time; the only movement was the twins repositioning themselves within her, the remote control that rested on her belly jiggling as they moved.

Should I call Nathan and profess my innocence?

Should I call Kadin to make sure he's ready for the babies?

Dana's funeral had come and gone, and it was all Lilly could bear not to go. It would be impossible to disguise herself from Drake and the police, and the risk to the babies was something she wasn't willing to chance. If she wanted to do justice for her friend, her absence was the only way to accomplish it.

Her room phone rang. There was only one person who would be calling her. Finding Drake's ex-wife had proven difficult. The address from the neighbor had been a false start. Lilly had garnered the services of a private detective, paid in cash, to help her find this woman and Drake's brother, as well. His information was short and to the point. He'd found Drake's ex. She would only see her today. Now that someone had found her, she was going to disappear again. Lilly only hoped that the woman she was meeting with didn't watch the news.

She neared the mobile home park that sat on the outskirts of Las Vegas city proper. The desert winds drudged up dirt from the compacted earth and put down further layers of grime against the metal siding. Few people were visible, and they were easily outnumbered by the cactus and tumbleweeds that blew through the development. The vehicle she drove blended well with the current occupants, and she didn't worry about being singled out. Exiting her car, she pulled her scarf over her mouth and nose as she climbed three rickety steps to the small threshold. As she raised her fist to knock, the door opened a few inches, then wider as the woman's shoulders eased in relief.

Lilly stepped into the trailer and pulled her coat off. The stale air was little improvement from the dusty gusts outside.

"You must be Lilly Reeves." The woman held out a hand in greeting. It was limp in Lilly's grip.

"Thank you for seeing me, Julie."

Julie Stipman was short statured, but the way she clenched her arms tightly into herself and jumped at the slightest sounds made her seem physically smaller and mouse-like. As the minutes passed, she became more comfortable with Lilly and transformed more into weary prey.

They sat in two threadbare recliners that faced a black-and-white TV, its picture distorted by jagged horizontal lines. The home was stifling hot, and Lilly felt sweat pooling in all her new pregnancy crevices.

"I knew this day would come," Julie said. "I just didn't think it would take this long."

Lilly rocked her chair slowly, hoping the movement would circulate the air. She hadn't explained to Drake's ex-wife the nature of her visit. Only that she desired to ask her about the death of her sons. After her private investigator swore to Julie that Lilly wasn't a member of the press or an associate of Drake's, the woman had agreed to see her.

"You thought someone would visit you about your boys?"

"No." She pointed to Lilly's belly. "I thought there would be a woman to come and ask me about Drake."

"Do you mind talking about your boys?" Lilly asked.

The woman picked up a needlepoint project and placed several stitches before continuing on. Lilly noted two packed suitcases against the wall.

"I don't mind. It's just hard."

Lilly felt they were each of the same emotional resolve. Both were too beaten down to shed a tear over their tragedies.

"I can't imagine. I would love to hear about them."

Julie pushed her fingers through her artificially colored coal-black hair; a skunk line of intermittent silver hairs showed at the roots. Her grief had aged her. Lilly guessed her to be barely thirty-five at this point in her life.

"They were amazing, but so different from each another. Austin was the oldest and the outgoing one. He loved baseball. Trevor was nine months younger and the soft-spoken introvert. The best thing about him was his huge heart. He had such empathy for other people. Just seeing someone else cry brought him to tears."

"They weren't that far apart in age. I'm sure you were busy."

"At the time, I would whine about how crazy it was. Now I would give anything to have them back, even for one day."

"I can't imagine how you must feel."

"It wasn't my idea to have them so close together." She clipped the thread and selected a new floss color. "Drake and I started dating when he started his freshman year in college. I was a sophomore in high school. We'd only been together a couple of weeks before the first time. Shortly after that, I hadn't been feeling well and my mother dragged me to the doctor. A few days later, she gets a call with the wonderful news. Health-care laws weren't what they are now, and they disclosed the pregnancy to her."

"I'm guessing that didn't go over so well."

"My mother was livid. I was scared. Meryl Stipman insisted Drake and

I marry or she would cut him off financially. The proposition seemed like an easy solution for everyone. After Austin was born, Drake didn't want to wait until I healed, and he refused to let me take birth control. I was pregnant at my six week check-up. I don't know if you know, but Meryl Stipman is a very wealthy woman."

"I've never met her."

"You're lucky. She puts the word *witch* with a *b* to shame. It was all so fast for me. Drake was the first man I ever dated, let alone slept with. Then I was a mother at sixteen with another baby on the way."

"How long were you married?"

"Until the fire. Then we divorced."

"How did you keep from getting pregnant again, considering his views on birth control?"

"Trevor was breech. I was taken for a C-section, and they couldn't stop me from bleeding. They had to do a hysterectomy. At the time, I considered it a blessing in disguise because I didn't know how to keep him off me."

"Was he abusive to you?"

"Depends on who you ask. People have different definitions of that."

"It only matters what you say."

"He was mean and controlling. I didn't have a car, so if I left the house, I would have to walk. With two small children, it was difficult to go anywhere too far. My money was limited, and I had to account for every penny. I was given a strict budget for groceries and clothing. Verbally, he would remind me every day of how worthless I was and that I was the worst mother around. That was the most terrible thing he ever said to me because in my heart I knew I was a very good mother."

Julie pulled a locket from beneath her blouse and began rubbing it between her fingers.

"May I see the picture?" Lilly asked.

Julie unclasped the lock and leaned forward.

"They're handsome boys." Lilly let the locket fall from her fingertips.

"Look like their father, don't they?"

Lilly nodded in agreement. "How did you survive those years?"

"Not every day was bad. When Drake finished med school and started his residency, he would moonlight different places to earn extra money. He wanted to show that he could be wealthy without his mother giving us handouts. We bought a bigger house. I got more allowances for clothing so me and the boys could wear brand-name designers." Julie paused, finding a new place in her sampler to sew.

"We hosted dinner parties, and of course, every good doctor's wife sits on some board and raises money for good causes. That became my life, and with Drake gone most of the time either working or away on any number of extracurricular activities, we really didn't see each other that often. When he was home, I would try to stay out of his way. Even though he was still controlling, it's hard to keep the reins tight when you're absent. That was the calmest time until his cancer diagnosis."

Lilly felt her heartbeat uptick. She tried to keep a calm exterior. It was better for Julie to volunteer this information than for Lilly to try to pull it from her.

"Tell me about that."

"Drake had just started his private practice. He was tired, but it seemed more than just fatigue. He was bleeding from his gums, and his body bruised easily. For weeks, I begged him to go get checked, but he would never do anything at my suggestion. One night, he collapsed at work. The labor nurses took him to the ER, and before he came to, they'd sent off all this blood work to try to see what was wrong. That's when they found out he had leukemia."

"How did he react?"

"It was strange. He never did have an emotional response, though I'd never seen any type of feeling from him other than anger. Even when the boys were born, he didn't seem very sentimental about it."

"What happened after that?"

"It was the usual cancer regimen. They started chemotherapy. He responded well in the beginning and went into remission. Unfortunately, he relapsed, and they suggested a bone-marrow transplant." Julie placed her project to the side. "That's when the trouble started."

"What do you mean?"

"We had to find a match. They gathered all of us up and took these cheek swabs and sent them to the lab. I felt okay testing Austin and Trevor. They were ten and eleven at the time. That's when I got the shock of my life. The testing showed not only were they not a match, but also that they weren't Drake's children. There wasn't any possible way for that to be true. I demanded the tests be redone."

"What was their response?"

"They refused, insisting the testing was sound. Drake, for the first time ever, plays the protective father and says he doesn't want them put through any more hell. He said he was going to leave me because of my unfaithfulness, and since the DNA tests proved they weren't his children, he was going to leave me penniless."

"But you hadn't been unfaithful."

"Absolutely not. Honestly, I couldn't make sense out of what was happening. I knew in my heart what the truth was, but how could I go against these tests?"

"What did you do?"

"While I was serving on the ethics committee, I became close with several physicians. There was a geneticist that I was a good friend with, and we would get together all the time. Though she never told me why, she wasn't a big fan of Drake's, and I got the feeling he'd done something inappropriate with her."

"Did you have these feelings often? That he'd been with other women?"

"All the time," she said, punctuating each word with a tap of her knuckles to her leg. "There were constant rumors of him sleeping with the nurses. One even claimed pregnancy, but then she died in this horrible car accident and that was the end of that."

Lilly shuddered. Drake's crimes were like cancerous tentacles, and she wondered what the family thought happened to this woman. "Did your geneticist friend have any suggestions?"

"She said we needed to look at the DNA of Drake's blood relatives. From those patterns, she would be able to determine that my sons' DNA came from that family. It was my job to gather samples from all the relatives that were biologically linked to Drake."

"How did you manage that?"

It was the first time a smile broached the corners of her lips. "It wasn't as hard as you might think. We had a sample from Drew, who was a match for Drake's bone-marrow transplant. I brought the boys to visit Meryl, and while I was at her place, I stole her hairbrush and toothbrush. Meryl has a brother who's considered the black sheep of the family, but we're kindred spirits so I always kept in touch with him. He let me take a swab from him. I brought them back to the geneticist, and she performed these tests on her own time at a private lab that her husband owned so that Drake wouldn't catch wind of it."

"And the results?" Lilly's heart stalled in her chest.

"The tests showed that Drew, his twin brother, was the father. However, Drew was in prison when Trevor was conceived. That's when she said Drake must be a chimera." "A chimera?"

"I wouldn't know how to explain it, but I presented the test results to Drake. I told him even if he left me, I was going to sue him for everything he had, and he would support those boys."

"What was his reaction?"

"The fire."

Lilly's vision clouded, heat rose within her. Her head pounded. "You think he started it?"

"Yes, I just can't prove it."

"How do you think he did it?"

Julie's hands began to shake. She clutched them together to still them.

"Another doctor covered for him. That happened all the time when he was sleeping around. His medical group was having trouble finding qualified doctors, and they didn't want him to get fired."

Julie stopped and pressed her lips together until her trembling eased.

"It was clear to the arson investigators that the fire originated in the boys' room. Gasoline poured over their beds." Julie collapsed forward in her chair, her face smothered in her hands as she tried to quiet her sobs. After several minutes, she sat up, brushing away her tears with quick flicks of her hands. Her words came between chopped hiccups. "We had a main-floor suite. The smoke detector woke me up. When I left my bedroom to get the boys, the staircase was in flames. I couldn't get to them."

Julie hugged herself, running her hands up and down her arms. Her voice cracked but was calmer. Quiet control set in.

"I don't think it would have mattered anyway. When I came out the front door, all I could see was flames shooting out every window on the upper level. When the firefighters got there, they broke in but couldn't make it to the second floor, either."

"Why do you think he did it?"

"He wanted those boys dead. He didn't want to take responsibility for them."

How could Drake deliver life and, in the next breath, kill his own sons? Go into their bedroom, gaze upon the peaceful look of sleep on their faces, and pour a toxic combustible over them to burn their flesh, one of the most excruciating deaths imaginable? It made her father's actions seem tame in comparison. Lilly wanted to vomit.

She changed the subject for both their sakes. "How did his brother end up in prison?"

"Like I said, the Stipmans are wealthy. Growing up, Drake and Drew were very popular at high school. Drake was the classic athlete, sports hero. Drew was more refined, captain of the debate team."

"Is that where you met Drake?"

"Yes, when I was a freshman, and he was a senior. I admired him like all the girls did, from afar. We lived close so I would watch for his comings and goings. It was just after our marriage that the girl turned up dead."

"Who was she?"

"Kate Randall."

Lilly's mind whirled. That name was familiar.

"What happened?"

"The whole thing was eerie. Her body was found on a golf course not far from where we lived, on the thirteenth green. She'd been beaten until she lost consciousness and left to die. Then a storm came. The police theory was that she was alive for a while because she bled through the snow that had fallen over her. Drew was a prime suspect because they were dating. They were both freshmen in college, home on Christmas break. They'd been out that night and been seen by several people."

"Where was Drake?"

"Not with me, that's all I can say."

"You suspect him?"

"You'd have to know Drew. He's complacent. Honestly doesn't have a mean bone in his body. He would avoid violence at every turn. During this time, I'd begun to see Drake for who he really was. There was this controlled savagery within him. He would try to cover it, but it was always in his eyes. Right after we married, he showed me the pet cemetery in his backyard."

The classic symptoms of antisocial personality disorder coalesced like bullet points in Lilly's mind. Lack of empathy. Pervasive lying. History of torturing animals. "He was responsible for these deaths."

"At first he said no. Then he claimed he would use them to learn more about medicine. Dissect them and perform surgery. Keep in mind, those animals were not anesthetized. Toward the end of our relationship when he was openly spiteful, he would go into long details about what he had done to those pitiful creatures. It was awful."

"What happened after Kate was murdered?"

"They arrested Drew right away. I was so concerned for him that I met with police and told them Drake could be responsible. I was close to delivering our first child, and it was obvious this detective didn't place much credence in my story. He wrote it off as the hysterical ranting of a pregnant woman. They liked Drew as a suspect and were testing some blood found on the victim."

"What did the results show?"

"At that time, they didn't do the extensive testing they do now. Once the basic blood type was a match, they stopped looking."

"But you thought they still needed to look at Drake."

"Yes. And that's when it became interesting. Drake should have the same blood type as his brother because they're identical twins. The police were nervous about testing my husband because they thought it would only complicate matters, and they didn't want to screw up their case. But then the victim's sister came forward and claimed that Drake had picked Kate up after Drew dropped her off. That put the police in a corner, and they tested Drake."

"And?"

"They showed that Drew was a match to the blood type, but something happened with Drake's specimen."

"What?"

"The results were inconclusive. They tried to test it again, and the same thing happened."

"Inconclusive." Lilly pondered the implications. Were the police protecting Drake? Was the lab complicit? Or was it a medical anomaly they couldn't decipher at the time?

"Yes. And after that, they didn't feel like they wanted to look anymore. The rest is history, as they say. Drew was convicted, based solely on the match of his blood type."

"Have you seen Drew since he's been released from prison?"

"No, but I know they're looking for him in relation to these rapes in Colorado."

Lilly glossed over the statement. "Do you still happen to keep in touch with that geneticist friend of yours?"

"Yeah, we talk often."

"Do you think it would be possible for me to speak with her?"

"About Drake?"

"That and her thoughts about Drew's case."

Lilly could see the fear in Julie's eyes as she considered her request. Would she put her friend at risk? "Can I ask you a question? Is this baby Drake's?"

The rocking motion of the chair increased Lilly's dizziness; she pressed her toes into the floor to keep the recliner still. "Yes."

"Did he rape you?"

A cool saliva filled her mouth. "Yes."

"Did you kill your friend?" Julie's voice was soft, as if the tone would soften the implication.

"You've seen the news." Lilly wiped the sweat from the base of her neck.

"Watch it every day. Listen, you don't have to answer. They know you're in Las Vegas. Meryl Stipman found me. Drake won't be far behind. I got a call from Meryl just today warning me not to talk to you. She knows you've been looking into Drake's medical records."

Lilly sat forward. The walls of the trailer closed in several inches. She glanced at the door, the sunlight under the frame a welcome relief. A shadow passed through the thin line. "How is that possible?"

"That woman has spies everywhere. Why do you think I live here, in hell? I thought I'd finally dropped off her radar, but your rummaging into Drake's past is causing Meryl to tighten her grip on anyone who could help the truth come out. Lilly, Drake's onto you. That's why he murdered your friend. He's looking for you. And he's not going to stop until he finds you. Your friends and family don't matter to him, either. Whatever it is you're doing, it better be enough to put him away, because if you don't, you'll be running forever."

Julie reached over for a pad and paper and scrawled down a name and number.

"I'm going to call her first and tell her to be expecting you. You're going to have to meet somewhere private. It wouldn't surprise me if someone is following her, too."

"Thank you."

Julie stood and tugged her shirt straight over her scrawny frame.

"I'll also be moving today. Probably leave the state this time. Your being here will bring Drake back, and I can't risk that."

Lilly attempted to stand, but her legs were weak and she leaned heavily against the arm. "I understand. If you're scared of him, why did you help me?"

Julie placed a reassuring hand on her shoulder. "Sometimes fear is worse than death. By meeting you, hopefully I'm helping to put him away so that I can live in peace."

Lilly stood, steadying herself on the chair as her vision clouded over, squeezing out droplets of sweat as she ran her fingers through her hair. Her stomach tilted.

"Are you all right?"

"I'm sorry. I'm not feeling well. The heat in here must be getting to me."

She stumbled as she made her way to the front door. Her vision darkened as she placed her hand on the knob. She pulled the door open, and even through her tunneled vision, she could see Drake Maguire standing in front of her.

Chapter 41

March 23

LILLY FELT THICK and heavy and literally tied down to the bed she'd been sleeping on. Moving her left hand over her belly, she felt four tight elastic bands. The movement of her right hand was restricted by an IV. Her vision remained blurred, and her tongue was heavy, coated with a thick, mucous paste that was unrelieved after several attempts to increase saliva in her mouth. Grabbing the rail on the side of the bed, she turned and saw a dark figure sitting in the corner. His posture was rigid.

Guarded.

Lilly felt through her covers for the nurse call light, trying to keep her fear at bay.

The man leaned forward as he saw her stir but did not approach.

"Lilly. I don't want you to be frightened. I'm Drew, Drake's brother. I'm not going to hurt you. I want to help." His voice was deep and gravelly, possibly marred by years of cigarette smoking.

Lilly eased back into her pillows, keeping the button for the nurse tucked in her hand.

"What happened to me?" Her heartbeat slowed with his revelation. Wouldn't she already be dead if he'd wanted to harm her? Her instinct told her to wait for an explanation.

"You passed out. I didn't think it was safe to take you to a major medical center with our names on the news. I know it was risky with the pregnancy, but I drove you about an hour outside the city to a smaller community hospital."

Smart choice. One that helped her stay hidden.

"What's wrong? Are the babies okay?" She closed one eye in an attempt to clear her double vision. No luck.

"The doctor says your blood pressure is too high. The babies are fine, but the medicine they put you on . . . Mag . . ."

"Magnesium sulfate."

"Right, that's it. They said it would make your vision blurry."

"It's to keep me from having a seizure. How long have I been here?"

"You've been in and out of it for two days. Do you remember anything?"

"Two days?"

"You haven't been taking care of yourself."

Concern for her welfare. Her wariness continued to ease.

"I've been busy."

"I know."

"Come closer."

"You're sure?"

She lifted her hand and waved him forward. He scooted his chair, the metal legs scraping against the tile as he pulled it. "I should tell you that I signed you in under an alias, told them we're married and that I was so worried about you, I left my wallet at home."

He turned his chair to face her.

"Are you dirty? I can't tell."

"Tattoos actually."

"Why so many?"

"When you're in prison, you have to find something to occupy your time. This is what kept me alive."

"Tattoos?"

"Well, providing them for other inmates. People respected my work so I could stay relatively independent. I didn't need a gang to protect me."

The bed swayed like a canoe in rough water. She gripped the side rail to steady herself against the vertigo. This unsolicited offer of assistance considering Drake's ruthlessness kept doubt in her mind. "Why are you helping me?"

He shifted in his chair, twirling his thumbs for several seconds before answering.

"I don't have a choice. They're looking at me for the rapes of these women in Colorado. I don't want to go back to jail. If Drake can be proven guilty of those crimes, maybe they'll look at the one I served time for."

Clarity began to ease her brain fog. "Were you ever close with him?"

"Sure, when we were younger."

"How can he ruin your life like this? Allow you to take the blame for his crimes?"

"Drake had a hard life growing up. Sometimes, I feel responsible for what he became because I didn't stop what was happening. I'm his older brother, even if it's only by a few minutes. I should have protected him. I was the stronger one."

"What did happen to him?"

"My father left when we were little. I don't know if he's still alive. My mother's an angry, domineering type. Everything had to be perfect. You know how hard it is for young boys to stay clean. Drake had a problem toilet training. Lasted until he was in grade school. I can clearly remember. When he would wet the bed, she would yank him from our room, throw him in a bathtub of cold water, and scrub him till his skin bled, shaming him the whole time about what an awful boy he was. She singled him out for abuse. I was spared. Drake feels my going to prison is retribution for his suffering, because I didn't protect him."

"Your mother has to be aware of his crimes . . . what she created."

"She's a smart woman."

"I mean the grant she gave to the state."

"What are you talking about?"

Lilly shifted. The fetal monitor toned then resumed the rhythms of the babies' heartbeats. "There was a large grant given to the state of Nevada so their crime lab could catch up on putting their DNA samples into CODIS. When they entered their backlog of specimens, that's how they fingered you for Colorado."

He smoothed his hand over his head.

"I knew she would protect him. I guess I didn't know how far she would go."

"Placing blame on her innocent son?"

"To absolve herself over how she tortured Drake." He reached for the pack of cigarettes in his back pocket; pulling one from the pack, he rolled it between his thumb and index finger. "Right after I went to prison, she paid me a visit. She seemed relieved that I was there. I was adamant about my innocence and begged her for help. I asked her to hire a top attorney for my appeal. After all, she was loaded with money. Her only response to me was that I was the strong one and that I needed to be where I was to protect Drake. She said if he went to jail, he would die."

"How did you take it?"

"It hurt a lot. But once I was in prison, it was clear I wasn't going to get any more help from her. I didn't have any money. The only thing she did for me was pay off my debt from the first trial. The evidence that led to my conviction seemed irrefutable, so there wasn't any chance another attorney would take my case pro bono. I dug in—survived. I was angry, but that began to slowly kill me. I kept my nose clean. Got early release and have been trying to start over. Now, Drake seems to be freelancing on my DNA."

Lilly's heart ached for his predicament. "Do you know about the evidence from your trial?"

"I couldn't tell you the ins and outs now. You'd think I would never forget, but you do. It's been a long time."

Drew placed himself at risk by helping her. The least she could do was trust his intentions. A small hope began to take seed in her soul. "We need to talk to Julie's geneticist friend."

A man entered the room. Drew pushed his chair back and stood, maintaining the part of the dutiful husband.

"Mr. and Mrs. Lane?"

The physician approached her bed and extended his hand. Lilly, impaired by her double vision, tried to estimate the location of the real appendage as she reached forward. He saved her from guessing and clasped her hand between his two.

"I'm Dr. Stone. Hayden, it's good to finally meet you. You've been pretty sick the last day or so. Your vision should get better in a couple of hours. The nurse has stopped your magnesium. Do you mind if we talk in front of your husband?"

She paused. Even though she didn't fear Drew, she didn't know him either and was unsure about how much information he should be privy to. Maybe the more information he had the better off both of them would be.

"Of course, it's fine."

"I should apologize. I think your husband was unaware of some aspects of your pregnancy." He pulled a rolling stool to her bedside.

"We've recently reconciled. I was working up to telling him more."

"That you were having twins."

"Exactly."

"One of each."

Lilly's heart leapt at the information. An unexpected rush of emotion caused tears to well in her eyes.

"Honey, that's great!" Drew reached down and grabbed her hand, placing a quick peck on her cheek. Was Stone buying Drew's acting?

Lilly swallowed over her nerves. "How are the babies doing?"

"They're well. We did give you a course of steroids to mature their lungs in case it was necessary to deliver them because of your high blood pressure. Your husband didn't know your due date, but based on the babies' measurements, you're about thirty weeks along so they could do well at this point. Does that sound about right?"

"Yes, I'm due in late May."

"Have you been getting regular prenatal care?"

"I'm unemployed and have been traveling, looking for work. I couldn't afford to see anyone."

"Are you settled someplace now?"

"Not exactly."

"Hayden, you need to have someone closely follow you and these babies. High blood pressure in pregnancy is very dangerous. Your labs are showing us that you have a condition known as eclampsia. Eclampsia is uncontrollable blood pressure in pregnancy. The only way to cure it is to deliver the babies, but at thirty weeks, we'd like them to stay tucked inside for a while longer."

"Dr. Stone, I really need to leave. There's some business my husband and I need to take care of."

"Hayden, your condition is critical. I can't impress that upon you enough. Both you and the babies are in grave danger."

Drew fingered her hair. She tried not to back away. "We will do whatever is necessary for the babies. Right, honey?"

"Can't you give me an oral medication I can take for my blood pressure?"

"Since we've stopped the magnesium, I've started you on some IV medication that, if it works, you can take orally. Even with that, you need to remain on complete bed rest. There will be no TV, cell phone, or visitors. You can't be out of bed for any reason."

"For how long?" Drew and Lilly asked in unison.

"As long as it takes. Additionally, we are not equipped to handle your care adequately here. I've put in for a consult in the city and we'll be transferring you there once you're stable. They have a top notch neonatal team. You'll be in great hands."

"No, I don't want to do that. I can't go—"

"Hayden, you must listen to me. This condition is very serious. I'm doing all I can to help but you are the only one who can determine the fate of these babies. I need to know if we are going to work together."

Drew clenched her hand tighter. "Whatever you tell her to do, she'll do it."

Stone searched Lilly's eyes. "I need to hear that from you."

"Fine." Her one word answer brought sudden memories of Nathan.

"Excellent. Let's see how it goes today. Any more questions for me?"

Lilly shook her head and felt her stomach tilt.

"Good." He stood and turned away from her. "Wow, I know you probably can't see them clearly, but one of our volunteers is here with an unusual bouquet of flowers." He turned back to her, rubbing her shoulder. "I'll check on you later."

He left. Drew took the arrangement from the older women dressed in a blue smock and signed for them. He placed them on Lilly's bedside table.

"Are those black?" Lilly asked.

"Yeah, kind of a weird color choice."

"The doctor is suspicious."

"I know, but what are we going to do? Aren't we banking on the babies proving that Drake is the father?"

Lilly swung the blankets off her body. She turned off her IV pump. "I'm getting a bad feeling."

"What are you doing?"

She pulled the bedside table closer to her body and felt through the thorns, numb to the pricks of pain, until her fingers landed on a stick of cool plastic. She ran her fingers up and yanked the card from the twines.

"What does this say?"

Drew took the envelope clenched between her thumb and forefinger.

"Lilly, you need to chill out." Drew tried to ease her back into bed. "Remember what the doctor said."

She pushed his hand away and pulled the tape off her IV. "Who would know where I am to even send these?"

Drew paused at her question. Under normal circumstances, getting a delivery of flowers in the hospital was expected.

Neither of them was living under normalcy. Drew ripped open the envelope and pulled out the card.

"What does it say?" Lilly asked.

"Found you. Love, Drake."

Chapter 42

April 2

MOMENTS AFTER THE flower arrangement and Drake's nefarious note had arrived, Lilly had left the hospital posthaste with Drew in tow. She'd pulled her IV and disconnected the fetal heart monitor, running from the facility because she knew that within minutes the nursing staff would come to check on her. Drew stole a prescription pad, and Lilly forged a script for blood pressure medication. When they filled the labetalol, she also purchased a home blood-pressure machine.

For the past week, they'd hidden in low-rate hotels, changing locations each night to throw Drake off their trail. They checked in under new names every day, sometimes together, sometimes separately, though always staying in the same room. Drew wasn't on board with their purchasing any weapons until Lilly showed him the one she carried and what an expert marksman she was. They were currently in the possession of four smaller-sized, semiautomatic guns.

Now they sat in a deserted parking lot at a roadside diner, awaiting the arrival of Kathy Everly, Julie Stipman's geneticist friend who had information about Drake's unusual DNA. The morning breakfast round was over, and a few stragglers remained inside enjoying coffee and conversation. Lilly wanted to be done with this meeting before the lunch rush started. Drew leaned over as the numbers displayed on her blood-pressure machine.

"It's 128/82. Is that good?"

"Not great, but fine for now." Lilly tore apart the Velcro and removed the cuff from her arm. "That's not what's worrying me."

"Then what is?"

"I'm having contractions."

"Regular?"

"How did you know to ask that?"

"My cellmate's wife was having a baby, and she told him to read *What to Expect When You're Expecting*. Bad thing was he was illiterate and was hiding it from her. I read that book to him every night and would quiz him about things to remember."

"You probably know more than I do then."

"You're a doctor, right?"

"An ER doctor. We try not to deliver babies." Lilly plopped the machine beside her on the seat. "They're not regular, but they're not going away. I need to get back to Colorado. I've made arrangements for the twins. Someone who can keep them safe while I'm working on getting Drake into jail will be taking them. I'm driving back tonight."

"That's twelve hours."

"Drew, I'm not sure what your endgame is. You've been very helpful to me, and Drake probably would have found me by now if it hadn't been for you. But this is not a group decision."

"I'm sticking with you. The only way to get my life back is to prove Drake guilty of these crimes. I just don't think it's wise, in your condition, to travel for that long."

"I can't deliver here. It has to be in Colorado, and I have a feeling these two aren't going to wait much longer. If we leave after this meeting, it will be dark when we get back. I have supplies I'll need to pick up."

A car pulled in that met the description the doctor had given them. Drew placed a soft hand on Lilly's forearm, delaying her exit from the vehicle until the woman entered the eatery and they had ensured she wasn't being followed. They reached her table and got to business after exchanging short pleasantries. Even sitting down, Dr. Kathy Everly was several inches taller than Lilly, with fair skin, blonde hair, and tense gray eyes.

"I'm a little nervous being here," she confessed. "I've been getting some strange phone calls. Hang-ups and the like."

"We don't have much time, so if you don't mind, we'll just get straight to business. What do you know about Drake Maguire?" Lilly asked.

"I know Julie told you he was a chimera. Do you know what that is?"

"I've been doing some research over the past week." Lilly pulled a small notepad from her purse. "It's a fusion of two separately fertilized embryos resulting in a single birth of a person that has two DNA fingerprints. Two people living in one body."

"Exactly, but Drake is a whole new ball of wax. Drake's chimerism, as far as I can tell, is undocumented. Obviously, with Drew here, you know that Drake is an identical twin."

"Yes, but there are some physical differences between them. Drake's eyes, of course."

"What occurred in Drake's case is that there were two eggs that were fertilized. Drew's egg split, forming identical twins. Then what happened is most unusual. After Drew's egg split, his identical twin fused with Drake's egg, forming a chimera. These criminal tests point to Drew because Drake carries Drew's DNA as well as his own. The nefarious part is that Drake has figured out which cell lines in his body point to Drew and which are his own. That's why Drake is the perfect serial rapist."

"Because his own DNA is not expressed," Lilly said.

"No, it's there. Let's go back to the first crime that landed Drew in jail. Fifteen years ago, a naturally occurring human chimera was unheard of. It's only been with the advent of widespread DNA testing that we've been able to identify a few rare individuals who carry this peculiar DNA pattern. Drew was convicted solely based on blood evidence."

"Only on blood type," Drew said.

"Right," Kathy said, motioning to Drew. "Your blood type matched the blood type found on the victim. However, blood type is much different than a person's DNA profile. Many people have the same blood type. However, each person has a unique DNA pattern that no one else has. This holds true for fingerprints, as well."

"Except in the case of identical twins," Lilly interjected. "They would have the same DNA profile but they do have unique fingerprints."

"That's true. When Drew was convicted, DNA testing was in a crude form and not widely used. Drew, your blood type was different from the victim's blood type so that's why they assumed it was from her assailant. When Julie pushed to have Drake tested, the lab couldn't determine his blood type. The reason the lab results came up inconclusive is that in Drake's blood there was an expression of two DNA fingerprints in his blood sample. It's why they couldn't type it, and they didn't have the wherewithal to pursue it. Drake must have been expressing two blood types at the time. Unfortunately for Drew, the police had him linked to the victim, and they had his blood type on the victim. That was enough back then to get him locked up."

"Why did you pursue it?" Lilly asked. She pressed her hand into her abdomen, her womb tight under her palm, the pain mild.

"You have to remember, I originally got involved in looking at Drake's DNA when the family was testing the boys to see if they were a DNA match for Drake's bone marrow transplant. It was those tests that showed Drake was not their father. This was only about three or four years ago and DNA testing had rapidly progressed. Julie was distraught. Drake was going to divorce her and leave her with nothing."

Lilly eased back in her chair as a waitress approached. Drew waved her off. Kathy waited until she was out of earshot before continuing on.

"Julie didn't have any skills and knew she had to prove Drake as the father to provide for her children. I'd heard about these rare cases where women had obtained maternity testing for different reasons and proved not to be the mother. They were later diagnosed as chimeras. That's when I thought Drake might be one. Drake has some of the physical characteristics of chimerism. The fact that his eyes are different colors is one of those. I had Julie gather up specimens from every biological relative of Drake's that she could think of. There were leftover samples taken from Drew in relation to the bone-marrow transplant. My tests showed that Drew was the boys' father."

"I don't understand why it's surprising that Drew showed up as the father of Julie's boys if they are identical twins. Drake and Drew's blood types are the same, and their blood has the same DNA fingerprint."

"When the hospital began screening everyone for their DNA profiles to see if someone would match Drake for the bone-marrow transplant, these samples were all done by cheek swabs, grouped together, and sent to the lab. Drake's cheek cells carry the second DNA fingerprint. That is why those tests showed he was not the boys' father."

"How were you going to prove that he was a chimera?"

"I was going to pressure the court for more tests. You see, it wasn't possible that Drew was the father of Julie's boys, because he was incarcerated at the time Julie conceived her second child. We knew genetically that the boys had the same father. I was going to present my chimera theory to the judge. We were going to ask the courts for a witnessed blood draw from Drake and have it tested for paternity. Since Drake and Drew have the same DNA fingerprint in their blood, this test would show that Drake was the father. The chimera theory would then be proven because two different cell lines that came from Drake, the initial cheek swab and the blood test, would show that he carried two DNA fingerprints. I mean, one test shows he is the father. The other doesn't. This would present a problem for the court. They would need a clear explanation of why their golden standard DNA test was showing inconsistencies with Drake's paternity. The assumption of the court is that every cell in a person's body carries the same DNA pattern. Well, for the chimera, this isn't true."

"But you were never able to take your evidence to court."

"No, because the fire happened and there were no boys to provide care for."

Lilly's muscles tightened again, stronger this time. "I looked through Drake's medical record during the time of his leukemia diagnosis. It didn't seem like they had any trouble typing his blood at that point."

"You're right; they didn't. And you know by now that Drew was his donor and saved his life. So it seems that Drew's DNA fingerprint was the only one present in Drake's blood at the time of his transplant. Chimerism isn't that straightforward. These individuals are often picked up during blood typing because both DNA fingerprints are often present. However, this may change over time, and one individual's DNA may become the more prominent one in certain cell lines. Particularly those that change over rapidly like red blood cells."

"So the children are the key." Lilly smoothed her hand over her side, her belly softened as the contraction eased.

"Drake is more sinister than either of you give him credit for. He is a smart man, and when I raised the issue of chimerism, he obviously did his own research."

"He did." Lilly scooted forward. "When I was looking through Drake's chart, I saw a DNA profile obtained from cheek cells from an anonymous DNA donor looking for a match to Drake's blood. The profiles didn't match. It didn't make sense to me then because Drake had already received the bone-marrow transplant. Drake must have provided his own cheek cells for the test. He wanted to know which of his cells would match Drew and which didn't. The paternity results gave him the hint. He used that test to verify it."

"That's why he's so vile. Drake knows his blood and semen will point to Drew. He's verified that his cheek cells are his own. He can commit these rapes at will, knowing that as long as he doesn't leave any saliva behind, the rest of the DNA evidence will point to Drew. What specimen do the police generally take to test a suspect?"

"A cheek swab," Drew interjected.

"That's why he bathes his victims," Lilly said. "To make sure he doesn't leave any saliva behind."

"He moves to Colorado. Changes his name. Gets that crazy tattoo, and begins his crime spree."

"Only after he knows I'm out of prison so that I'll be a viable suspect."

Lilly turned to Drew. "He does try to protect himself a little with the disguise and colored contacts. But what happens as soon as the heat is on him? Your mother steps in and ponies up the money so Las Vegas can get caught up in their CODIS database. Your blood from that crime fifteen years ago now is tested for a DNA profile, and lo and behold, the police in Colorado have a criminal to look for."

"I don't understand why he wants to kill all his offspring when the DNA swab of his cheek cells will clear him because it holds the second DNA fingerprint." Drew waved the waitress off again.

Dr. Everly pulled a thumb drive from her pocket and set it on the table in front of Lilly. "Drake is afraid of this. These are the DNA profiles from his boys. Drew was in prison when Julie conceived her second child. I've already proven that genetically the boys have the same father. I've worked in the judicial system quite a bit. The court is not apt to repeat any testing it has already done in relation to these rape cases in Colorado. Remember, DNA testing is the standard. There is little you can do to refute it. You're going to have to bring forth new evidence. When your children are born, you need to have their DNA tested against these boys who have already died. Those tests will show they all have the same father. Since Drew was incapable of fathering Julie's second child, a smart judge will scrutinize Drake and hopefully order further testing. You need to have witnessed testing of his blood and cheek cells. These tests will prove he is a chimera, the father of these babies, and your rapist."

Lilly grasped the thin stick in her hand. "I can't thank you enough for all your help."

"Just make sure you get him this time. The only thing that man leaves in his wake is death and destruction."

Lilly gathered up her purse. Everly came around the table to give her a quick hug. "Keep these babies safe. They're your only hope."

"I will, I promise."

Drew left ten dollars on the table for the waitress who only served them water but waited a few moments before following Dr. Everly out of the diner. Lilly climbed into their truck, another junker Drew had come across that they'd been using for the past week.

Backing out of the parking spot and approaching the highway, Drew paused before pulling out.

"What is it?" Lilly asked.

Their truck was sitting a comfortable distance away from Everly's vehicle.

"What is that?" Drew asked.

Lilly followed his finger and noticed the small object rolling along the ground. It was small and gray and came to a stop directly under the doctor's car. Surveying the landscape, Lilly did not see anyone.

"It looks like someone threw a rock."

The pulse wave from the explosion knocked out the windows and rocked the truck up onto its side. Drew threw himself over Lilly's body, sheltering her from the showering glass as the windows imploded. The truck slammed down on all four wheels, and Drew righted himself, stomping his foot on the accelerator. The tires squealed in protest as they shot out into the street. Lilly pushed herself up, brushing the shards of glass off her body. The wind blew heavily through the missing windshield.

"We have to go back!" Lilly screamed at Drew.

"No way!"

"We have to check on her!" Lilly turned around. Black smoke plumed into the sky. A single black car traveled in their wake. Pain gripped Lilly's belly, and she turned forward, pressing both hands into her sides to counteract the pressure.

"She's dead, Lilly. And we will be too if we go back. We've got problems of our own. I think we're being followed."

Chapter 43

NATHAN STRAIGHTENED HIS blazer over his button-up shirt, pulling the tabs of his collar over his suit jacket, brushing the lint off the tweed as he walked down the ER corridor at Sage Medical Center. Dr. Anderson had notified him that a rape victim had arrived via EMS. The victim's details of events were similar enough to Lilly's that Anderson called Nathan directly. Since Nathan and Brett weren't on chummy speaking terms, Brett had been notified through dispatch. His partner waited outside the victim's room, sitting in a chair, trying to smooth over his wrinkled clothes, as well. Though not unusual for Brett to present in such attire, Nathan knew his worry over Lilly and the stress over her case were wreaking havoc in his personal life and he struggled to keep up appearances.

Drew Stipman was still an unknown. There had been a few calls from rural areas in Nevada stating that he had worked for several different places. He generally stuck with those establishments who weren't too concerned about checking identification, staying no more than two months at a time, and then moving on. He always operated in cash and hadn't filed a tax return since his prison release. The people who Nathan spoke to consistently commented that he was the nicest, most congenial man they'd ever met. In the short time he'd spent in any particular area, there was story after story about how he'd helped people ranging from moving a coworker to donating his entire month's pay to a woman who had just lost her husband and was facing eviction from her home. He'd stayed in that place the longest, helping her find new housing and working to get her and her sons stable before moving on.

He was a ghost.

An unknown.

A benevolent entity to all who knew him.

Scattered reports had come in from multiple hospitals in early February from the Las Vegas area concerning a pregnant woman, posing as a doctor, who had requested medical files. Though the media did not list the name of what person this woman was seeking information on, one call to local law enforcement made it clear that it was Lilly searching for information on Drake Maguire. Then, for a couple of months, she was off the grid again until Nathan had received a call from a Dr. Stone.

Evidently, Stone had been watching a local news report about this peculiar pregnant woman scoping out medical charts. All the local media networks were airing a fuzzy image of Lilly at a hospital. He felt she matched the description of a pregnant woman who was recently brought to his facility after fainting. When she suddenly left AMA, he'd contacted Las Vegas police regarding the matter, and they then encouraged him to phone Nathan as Lilly remained a person of interest in Dana's murder. That's when an odd morsel of information came to light.

The physician stated that she had been accompanied by a man who claimed to be her husband. In response, Nathan faxed him a photo of Drew Stipman. It was moments after the photo went through that the physician called him back, confirming his suspicion.

Lilly and Drew were together.

Stone pleaded with Nathan to find Lilly. He said he couldn't divulge specific medical information due to healthcare privacy laws, but that her pregnancy was in jeopardy because of a medical condition she'd acquired. When Nathan pressed him for more information, he was reluctant to continue but made it clear that Lilly could die if she didn't deliver soon.

To Nathan, it meant she was likely on her way back. Kadin was the only person she trusted with her child. Nathan tried to assure Stone that he would know the moment she was back. He checked the transponder on her car religiously to make sure the batteries were changed and the unit was functioning properly. Savannah had been noncommittal when he begged her to call him when Lilly returned. He didn't know if his assurances to her that he was Lilly's only friend on the police force had eased her apprehension.

Their case was in disarray and would likely remain that way until Drew and Lilly were found and could give testimony to their locations and activities. Nathan didn't feel as if he could ever be himself again until he resolved this situation.

For Lilly.

For all of the women.

Brett stood as Nathan approached.

"You okay?" he asked.

"Fine. What do you know?"

"I mean your clothes and all . . ."

"Brett, it's the middle of the night."

"I know, but you don't look so good."

"Can we just focus on the victim?"

"Nathan, I'm worried about you. Once we find Drew Stipman, I think this whole thing will fall into place."

"Whatever. You have your theory of these crimes settled in your mind."

"And you're being completely objective?"

"At this point, no. I'm worried about a friend who's sick right now. I am in fear for her life."

"That's the whole problem, Nathan. Your judgment is clouded for that very reason. You never considered Lilly as a murderer, and I suspect you want to be more than her friend."

Kadin Daughtry exited the room, and Nathan took a step back. A police officer followed him with several evidence bags and gave a small wave to Brett as he left the building. Nathan fisted his hand inside his pants pocket at the dismissal from his coworker. He stiffened his shoulders and chest, preparing for Kadin's sharp criticism.

"Detective Long." He held his hand out. "Thank you for coming personally. I happened to be on call. I was requested by Dr. Anderson to do the rape kit. The victim had several significant injuries that needed consultation anyway."

Nathan took Kadin's hand, but held it firmly in his, grabbing his elbow to keep him close. "I need to know if you've heard from Lilly."

"Nathan, it's not something I'm going to divulge to you."

"She's sick."

Nathan felt a slight tilt in Kadin's posture at his statement and released his grip.

"What do you mean?"

"I'm not sure I should even be sharing this, but I got a call from an ob-gyn out near Las Vegas. I think that's where Lilly's been over these past couple of months, trying to get information on Drake. All he would really say was that she would die if she didn't deliver soon."

Kadin walked a few paces to the nurses' station and set down the chart.

"The provider is concerned? Then it's probably developed to be a little more than PIH."

"What's that?"

"Pregnancy-induced hypertension is high blood pressure that occurs during pregnancy. It can be common among first-time mothers. The process isn't well understood, but if she was in the hospital then she likely developed eclampsia."

"She could die?"

"One of the end-stage problems of this disease is that you can have seizures. If you can't control the seizures, then yes, the woman can die."

"How do you treat it?"

"The only cure is delivery of the baby. That's why that physician made that statement to you. I promise you, Nathan, I don't know where she is. We have a plan for the delivery, but now I'm even worried about that. If she has this condition, she'll need to deliver in a hospital."

"Let's focus on this victim, shall we?" Brett interrupted.

Kadin motioned toward the woman's room. "This is Latasha Diamond, though I'm not sure that's her real name. She's a high-priced escort. Works exclusively off the Internet—one of the upper-end sites. Her going rate is five hundred dollars an hour."

Brett let out a slow whistle. "Why so high?"

"According to her, it's for a 'disease free' guarantee. She gets regular testing for HIV and hepatitis. And the man has to use contraception."

"What happened to her tonight?" Nathan asked, grabbing his notebook.

"She got a call for a meeting at a hotel. She enters the room. He's sitting on the bed and requests that she undress. As she's doing this, he lunges at her and injects some sort of medication into her arm that incapacitates her."

"Was he wearing a disguise?" Brett asked.

"No."

"No? Can she provide a description?" Nathan followed.

"I think so. Despite the drug, she is pretty clear on some details. I told her to save that part for you two. Anyway, per EMS, they got a call when a concerned coworker had gone to check on her after she failed to make contact for several hours. She was found in bed, naked, posed, alive, but unresponsive."

"Do you think you found anything from the exam?"

"Clearly, she was raped. There is significant trauma. There was a semen sample left behind. I've already given the kit to one of the officers. I need to ask her some follow-up questions," Kadin said. "Give me a few minutes, and you can come in. I'll stay with her. She doesn't have any family here, and I'm sure you can understand why her coworkers aren't here, either."

"What do you think?" Brett asked, turning to Nathan.

"I'm certainly interested in her description of this man. Sounds like our guy."

"I agree."

"I think this could be good news for us." Nathan shrugged out of his coat. "Obviously, our perp feels like the heat is on. He's not able to follow his normal routine anymore."

"And who would be watching the good doctor?" Brett asked. "Considering he's been cleared as a suspect."

"Not sure on that one," Nathan said, not making eye contact. "I think this guy is destabilizing. The lack of disguise is evidence of that. At best, he's becoming sloppy, or at worst he's too confident to think he can be caught."

"Which can be good and bad for us," Brett said.

"Shall we?"

Nathan followed Brett into the room. Kadin stepped back and allowed Nathan to take his chair at the bedside.

"Latasha, this is Detective Long. He's a friend of mine. You can trust him."

Nathan tried to prevent his surprise from showing. "Ms. Diamond. I'm a detective with the police department."

Her eyes were transfixed on the television.

"Ms. Diamond? Dr. Daughtry has told us you may be able to provide a description of the man who did this to you."

No response. Nathan waved a hand in front of her face. The woman batted it down, her eyes never leaving the TV screen.

"Latasha?" Kadin asked.

Nathan waved him off and turned to the TV himself. FOX News was airing a story about a car explosion, speculating that it might have been a bomb, which had killed a local physician outside a small diner near Las Vegas late this morning. The woman was a geneticist whose specialty was DNA profiles. A pregnant woman and man were seen entering the diner shortly after this doctor. According to the waitress who served them, all three had met and talked for nearly an hour but never ordered anything.

"Could it be that someone was unhappy with a paternity test result?" the anchor asked before popping up a video taken of two "persons of interest" the police were looking for.

The video was not grainy and showed Lilly with another man walking into the restaurant. As Nathan watched, Latasha raised her arm and pointed to the screen.

"That's the man who raped me."

"What?" Brett asked, turning as well.

"I swear that's him," she insisted.

"But that guy was in Las Vegas this morning," Brett said after listening to the story unravel over the next few minutes.

"It's Drew Stipman," Nathan said.

"Then he couldn't have done this crime. Las Vegas is at least twelve hours. The doctor was attacked around ten o'clock."

"We need to check Drake's whereabouts," Nathan said.

At that moment, Nathan received two text messages. The first started with the numbers 911. A message from Savannah: "Lilly's back. She's sick. She's in labor."

The second text was automated from the transponder Nathan had planted on Lilly's vehicle. Her car was on the move.

Nathan turned to Kadin. "I have to go, and I need you to come with me."

"I'm on call."

Nathan showed Kadin the text, and he nodded in understanding.

"I'll call Melanie to cover for me. Tell her it's an emergency."

"Brett, you need to find Dr. Maguire. Detain him if you can."

"I need to gather up some supplies," Kadin said.

"Meet me in the parking lot in ten minutes," Nathan said.

Nathan checked the contents of his trunk. He'd prepared for this day ever since Lilly had disappeared. Kadin approached him from the side, carrying a large duffel bag, and Nathan began to rearrange the trunk's contents to make room.

"Do I even want to ask what all this is?"

"Weapons, rope . . . yeah, you probably don't want to know." Nathan grabbed the bag from Kadin and secured the trunk. "I need to make one stop."

"I know where she's going."

"Things may have changed. We need to find out if she is still with Drew. If she is, Savannah may know if he's a friend of hers or not. She'll have a feeling if Lilly's being coerced."

"Who's Savannah?"

"Lilly's aunt."

"She has family?"

"Look, Kadin, There're probably things I know and things you know. Let's just put it aside for now and find Lilly. Make sure her baby is okay."

"Whatever you want."

Savannah's house was close to the hospital. Nathan exited his car, and Kadin followed up to the porch. Savannah was waiting for them on the threshold.

"Good to see you, Savannah." Nathan embraced her to calm her trembling. He wasn't sure if it was the cool night or her nerves. "When did she leave?"

"About thirty minutes ago."

"Was there anyone with her?"

"A man."

"Do you know him?"

"No, but he looked a lot like that officer who's been coming by to check on Lilly's car."

"What officer?" Nathan pushed her back so he could look into her eyes. "What do you mean?"

"Well, there's been a policeman coming by every so often, like you do, to check the tracking device on Lilly's car."

"And he looks like the man who's now with Lilly?" Nathan's muscles tensed. His heart dropped into his feet. His precautions for her safety had been breached. It was like a shark coming into a diver's protective cage.

"Yes." Fear crept into her eyes. "You didn't send him?"

"No."

"Then who was it?"

"Savannah, if this man comes back, I need you to call the police. Don't let him inside."

Nathan stepped off the porch, grabbed Kadin, and pulled him back to the vehicle. As soon as they were secured inside, Nathan backed out, checking the most recent coordinates on Lilly's transponder.

"What's going on?"

"When Lilly disappeared, I put tracking devices on her car and the one Savannah let her borrow."

"What are you freaked out about?"

"For one thing, it's illegal to place these devices on a person's car without a warrant."

"And you didn't have one."

"Correct. Secondly, there's only one person who knew about what I had done. Even if Brett doesn't like me right now, he would never betray my trust. That officer Savannah spoke of is Drake. Once you know the make and model of the device, you can figure out a way to track it. And now, Drake is following Lilly."

Chapter 44

LILLY WAS SICK, and Drew didn't know what to do to help her other than find this cabin in the woods. Problem was, even Lilly wasn't sure of its exact location. He glanced at her in the passenger seat. She was bent over, clutching her abdomen, breathing through another contraction. He placed a reassuring hand on her forearm, which was moist with sweat. The contractions were frequent, occurring every several minutes, and seemed to be intensifying as the hours wore on. After the explosion at the diner, it hadn't taken Drew long to shake their tail, but it had taken a few hours to find another vehicle to purchase. Stealing one was sure to attract the scrutinizing eyes of the police.

They already had enough of those.

The stop at Savannah's for Lilly's car had been short.

Lilly eased back into the seat. She would communicate with him only out of necessity, and he'd given up on comforting her with platitudes hours ago.

"Can you help me find the turn?" Drew asked.

"I've never been here before. I only know the name of the street."

"Deer Valley Drive?"

"Yes."

"How far do you think it is?"

"Drew, I don't know!" Her hand clenched the dashboard like a vise. Headlights loomed in the rearview mirror and were gaining distance. Lilly must have sensed his concern, as she turned to look behind them.

"Pull over," she said.

"I don't think that's an option."

"Just let them go by!"

Drew placed a protective hand over her belly as the lights filled the backseat and they were struck from behind. It sent them into the guard-rail, and sparks blazed against Lilly's window as metal met metal. Drew swerved the car into the oncoming lane.

"How did he find us?" Lilly asked.

"There must be a tracker on this vehicle."

"Give me a weapon."

"No, you need to stay in your seat belt. I don't know if I can shake him."

Drew pressed the accelerator to the floorboard and eased back into their lane. Ignoring his request, Lilly unbuckled her seat belt and grabbed the gun from the backseat. She hooked her arm around the headrest to steady herself, and took one shot, blowing out the back windshield. The second bullet caught the trailing vehicle, and it eased back a few yards in response. Lilly screamed and dropped the weapon, her breath jagged through clenched teeth. She turned and sat, her arms tight around her midsection.

The vehicle gained speed and pulled up beside them. Drew turned to look. The fallen night and tinted windshield made it impossible for him to see the driver, but he sensed who it was. The vehicle slammed into theirs, pinning them up against the guardrail. A flurry of sparks cascaded next to Lilly's window, the smoke from metal grinding against metal filled the interior compartment. Lilly shielded her face with her arm. Drew hit the brakes, and the other vehicle shot forward, but as soon as they reached the end of the rail, the momentum carried them onto the loose shoulder.

There was a moment of reprieve when the car stilled, up on two tires. He turned to Lilly. She pulled her arm down from her eyes, a hint of hope in her blue eyes before the car groaned and pitched. Her scream pierced his ears as they tumbled side over side, every loose object in the car a deadly projectile. The wind whistled through the broken glass. His limbs bounced uncontrollably, and he was unable to reach out and grab Lilly. Suddenly, they stopped, a pine branch punched through the window behind Lilly. The resinous scent of pine filled his nostrils. Dust and smoke clouded the air, and Drew coughed as the particles invaded his lungs. He reached to his side, feeling for Lilly.

She wasn't moving.

"Lilly?"

The vehicle was tipped up, the driver's side higher than the passenger's. The interior was dark. Drew unclipped his seat belt and edged closer to her. He placed his fingers against her neck. Her pulse was strong and steady. Reaching into the back, he patted around for the flashlight he had stowed. Finding it, he gripped his fingers around the cool metal and flipped it on. He began to brush the debris from her face.

"Lilly!"

He shook her gently.

Her eyes rolled back as her arms and legs pulsed in rhythmic contractions.

Chapter 45

"I THOUGHT YOU were going to meet her at your place?" Nathan checked to see if the latest coordinates for Lilly's vehicle had transposed to his PDA.

"We didn't want it to be obvious. A friend has a cabin not too far from mine. He only uses it in the summer. We were going to meet there."

"The most recent download has them heading straight there."

"I thought you got updates every five minutes."

"I do."

"Well, hasn't it been longer than that?"

Nathan pushed a button on his watch; the iridescent light shone. Kadin was right.

"Something must have happened to the transponder."

"Like what?"

"I don't know, but they should be on this road."

"Do those look fresh?"

"What?"

Kadin pointed to the long, black strips of rubber melted into the gravel. "Those skid marks."

Nathan pulled his car to the shoulder and stepped out. The night air cooled the sweat on his forehead. Kadin followed, and Nathan handed him a flashlight.

"How far are we from your friend's place?"

"Not far."

Nathan stepped into the roadway, scanning his flashlight to and fro. His heart thundered in his chest as he silently prayed to find Lilly alive and unharmed. He started walking the way they had come. He noted damage to the guardrail. Glass sparkled under his flashlight beam. Kadin concentrated on the car's forward progress. Nathan looked his way. He was still at the roadside.

Nathan's lungs tightened with dread, and he began to think through his options. If he summoned search and rescue, the lit-up scene would be a beacon for Drake. If he delayed, he risked losing Lilly. How did he know she wasn't already dead?

"Nathan! Something's down here!"

He ran to Kadin's position. Joining his flashlight beam with Kadin's, he could see a car halfway down the slope, pinned against a pine tree. There didn't seem to be any movement within the vehicle. The faint smell of smoke in the air hinted that they had not been too far behind what had happened.

"I'll go get the rope."

Nathan ran back to his car. Popping the trunk, he grabbed the multi-colored climbing rope and two weapons, placing one gun behind his back. Kadin helped him secure one end of the line to the guardrail.

"I'm going first," Kadin insisted.

"No, I'm going."

"She's probably injured."

"We don't even know it's her yet. Let me take a look first," Nathan said. He handed Kadin the spare revolver. "I need you to keep an eye out. If you see anything suspicious, fire a warning shot into the air."

Nathan faced his back down the slope. He took even steps backward, making sure his foot was secure before leaning his weight to take the next step. From the top of the hill, the slope didn't look that bad, but the farther Nathan descended, the harder it was to keep himself from sliding. Making it to the vehicle, he secured the rope around himself. The driver's window remained intact. The front windshield was shattered. Nathan pulled his weapon and eased his way to the front of the car.

He peered in.

Lilly was there, slumped in the passenger seat. The rush of blood in his ears overcame every other sound. He aimed his flashlight beam directly at her chest and watched for movement.

Please . . . please.

Lilly's chest rose. The tightness in Nathan's chest eased.

He looked up the hill. "Kadin, it's Lilly! I need you down here!"

The vehicle hadn't nudged with his weight against it. Feeling confident it would maintain its position, he climbed up onto the hood and laid himself flat, inching across until he could reach in and feel Lilly.

"Lilly? Can you hear me?"

Kadin was next to him quickly and up on the hood as well. He climbed into the driver's seat. A moan escaped her lips.

"Well?" Nathan asked.

These were the moments where Nathan felt inept. He watched as Kadin checked her pulse and shone a light into her eyes. Lilly pulled her head away at the insult.

"Lilly?"

Her scream lit Nathan's nerves. Kadin placed gentle hands over her belly.

"Nathan, we need to get her out of here. She's in labor."

Chapter 46

THE FIRST SENSATION Lilly had was of distant voices clamoring, distressed. Thick fluid slid down her temple. She reached to her face with her right arm, but it didn't respond to her brain's command for movement. The left hand obeyed, and she eased it up and felt leaves encrusted in drying threads of blood. Her lungs rejected the first deep breath she took with several racking coughs. She batted the light away and opened her eyes. A figure in front of her was on the hood, and someone sat beside her.

"Drew?"

"Lilly. It's Kadin. Nathan's here, too."

"Where's Drew?"

Her vision cleared. Nathan was visible to her now, lit by the flashlight he held in his hands. "I'll look to see if he was thrown from the car."

"Can you move?" Kadin asked her. A contraction hit, and she doubled over. Kadin was silent but offered quiet expressions of comfort. He pulled the matted hair from her eyes and smoothed his hand over her back until the contraction eased.

"How long have you been having these?"

"All day."

"Are you hurting anywhere else?"

Lilly was beyond herself with pain, but no singular injury seemed to be life threatening. Her hands and feet moved at her brain's request. No numbness. The explosion had left hundreds of small cuts and scrapes on every exposed surface of skin. Dirt and pine needles covered her hair from being run off the road, and the right side of her body ached from slamming into the door when the car had crashed into the tree. Lilly was ambivalent as to whether this suffering was worth mentioning.

"I can't do this anymore."

"You don't have a choice."

Kadin looked around the inner compartment with his flashlight, finally testing the door and opening it after several hard shoves. Nathan returned and hoisted himself back onto the hood of the car.

"I don't see anyone around."

"I think he's gone," Kadin said. "There's no blood on this side. Steering column is intact."

"Damage is significant. Looks like they rolled a couple of times."

"She wasn't wearing her seat belt."

"Someone ran us off the road."

"Well, I don't think Drew wanted to stick around for whatever reason." Kadin patted his back pocket for his cell. He came up empty. "Nathan, I need you to call an ambulance. She needs a hospital."

Lilly shoved Kadin back. "I'm not going there! We're keeping with what we arranged. With what you promised me."

"No. Absolutely not! You were unrestrained. This pain could mean your placenta has torn away. It's too dangerous, Lilly." Kadin looked through the broken windshield to Nathan. "I need you to make that call, Nathan. This isn't smart."

Lilly leaned forward and groped for Nathan over the glass that littered the dashboard. She found his hand and held tight. "Nathan, please, don't. I'll be fine."

Kadin shook his head. "She could die, Nathan. I'm not joking about this."

In Nathan's eyes was the sure resolve that he was in her corner. Lilly's heart swelled with gratitude.

With his free hand, Nathan pulled his weapon and pointed it at Kadin.

Kadin raised his hands. "What are you doing, Nathan?"

"I'm giving you an out. If things go wrong, you can testify your actions were under duress. I'll take the fall. I'll go to jail. But, we're doing as Lilly asks."

Lilly reached for Kadin. "Please, trust me."

"Both of you have lost your mind." Kadin stepped out. "Let's get her out of this car."

The progress up the hill was painful and slow. Lilly stopped every few yards as the contractions continued to build in pacing and intensity. If Kadin was worried, he didn't let on, which was every physician's learned trick, but she could see the distress in Nathan's face as he glanced at Kadin for reassurance every time she nearly buckled to her knees in agony.

"Can't you give her something?" Nathan asked.

"Not in the middle of the forest, in the dark, climbing up a hill. Go ahead and call for that ambulance like I asked."

Lilly pulled away from them and slid a few feet back down the hill. Nathan grabbed her hand to keep her from falling. Kadin's eyes were wide in disbelief.

"You really can't expect to keep the plan. You have eclampsia." Kadin argued.

"How did you know?" Lilly crossed her arms over her chest.

"Nathan told me."

She looked up at him, his grip firm on her hand. "How did you know?"

"Dr. Stone called."

"It's my decision!" She wanted to be strong, but the tears betrayed her.

"Everyone . . . this is not helping," Nathan said. "What we know for sure is that we don't know where Drake is. Being out in the open is not an option." Nathan smoothed his thumb over the back of her hand.

"Fine. Let's get her to the cabin so I can assess her."

Once they made it to Nathan's car, the drive was short. The first thing Lilly did, without asking Kadin's permission, was find and lock herself in a bathroom, undress, and sit at the bottom of the bathtub, letting the hot water from the shower and soap steam away the aftermath of her hellish day. A soft knock at the door beckoned her eyes open.

Kadin's voice was muffled through the wood. "Lilly, it's been fifteen minutes. Are you okay?"

Lilly watched rivulets of dirt, pine needles, and blood swirl down the drain as the water washed each particle from her skin. Being in solitude and safety was a comfort she hadn't known in far too long, and it was easier for her to manage the contractions, actually breathing through several without feeling the need to scream at the top of her lungs. Kadin banged on the door, giving up his gentle questioning, and she reached and turned off the water. As she stood up, a large flow of fluid, warm and thick, gushed between her legs. She wrapped a towel around herself, the length not enough to cover her protruding belly as Kadin made his way into the bathroom with a key in his hand.

"Are you all right?"

"My water broke." Tears leapt over her lower eyelids.

"You're going to do fine."

"Why did I ever think this was a good idea?"

"People give birth at home all the time."

"Twins?"

"There weren't always hospitals, Lilly. Let's get you settled."

Leading her by the hand, Kadin brought her to a room that looked like a mini hospital. There were two bassinets with tables set on either side full of medical equipment. Several large, metallic green oxygen tanks sat in the corner.

"You're sure Drake didn't find his way here?"

"I haven't seen any sign of him yet," Nathan said, keeping vigil by the window.

Lilly eased herself onto the bed. Kadin worked at checking her blood pressure and started an IV. He placed cool jelly on her abdomen and began searching for fetal heart tones with a small, hand-held Doppler, finding them quickly.

"They're strong. You want to tell me about your hospital visit?"

"I passed out. Drew took me in. I was on mag sulfate."

"Did the doctor say anything else to you?"

"I think I had a seizure when we had the accident."

"You know the best cure is to get these little ones out." Kadin grabbed a small machine about the size of a large laptop and sat next to Lilly. "Looks like they agree with me."

"Did you steal that from the ER?" she asked, referring to the ultrasound machine he held.

"No. A friend of mine from school is working in medical equipment development and loaned one to me. It's not going to do anything fancy, but I want to check the position of the babies. Pray they are both head down."

Lilly appreciated Kadin's calm demeanor, but she realized now how much she had missed Nathan.

"At least these two are behaving themselves. They're in good position. Hopefully, they'll stay that way."

"I feel like I have to push."

"Let me check you."

"No, I mean it."

"Me, too. Let me look."

She felt his hands gently ease her knees apart. "Nathan, I'm going to need you over here."

Nathan looked away from the window. "Why?"

"I need your help."

"That's why I brought you here."

"I'm going to have my hands full," Kadin said. "Lilly is having twins."

"Twins! No . . . no . . . no . . ."

"That's right, Nathan. Maybe we should have talked more about the things I know and the things you know."

A stabbing pain shot over Lilly's abdomen. She sat up and grabbed her knees.

Chapter 47

THIS WAS THE moment Kadin still relished as a physician, holding a new, perfectly formed life in his hands. People often took this miracle for granted, how DNA spelled out a code, whose transcription led to the formation of cells, which differentiated and began to form into organs, coming together to form an individual with a unique set of eyes, of fingerprints—a unique identity, yet in the image of their Creator.

"It's a girl!" Kadin cradled the infant in his hands and laid her on the bed. With deft skill, he clamped then cut the cord, grabbed several towels, and began rubbing gently, coaxing her to take breaths to clear the amniotic fluid from her lungs.

"She's not crying," Lilly edged up.

"She's not crying, but she's smiling. Want to hold her?"

Lilly hesitated. She reached forward and took the baby from Kadin, bringing her close to her chest.

"She's beautiful," Lilly said.

Nathan leaned over and caressed the baby's cheek. "What did you expect? Her mother is, too."

Kadin raised an eyebrow at Nathan's statement. It was easy to see the comfort between the two of them, and Kadin felt he'd let Lilly slip away by not fighting for her more. Nathan shared her unwavering belief in Drake's guilt, and he was willing to put himself professionally on the line in all respects.

Setting his troubled thoughts aside, he watched Lilly bond with her infant. Even though Lilly had decided to give the babies up for adoption, she exhibited all the behaviors new mothers possess. First, they'd gently stroke the face, and then open up the covers to verify that there were ten fingers, ten toes, two ears. In all the time he'd known Lilly, this was the first moment he'd seen her express true joy.

Not too long after the delivery of the first placenta, the second amniotic sac broke. Lilly fell backward onto Nathan as another contraction hit.

"Nathan, take the baby from her."

He stood and eased Lilly back into a bank of pillows.

"Oh, geez," he said, taking the small infant into his hands, holding it away from his body like one would a smelly sock.

"Nathan, you have to bring her close, into your chest."

At first Kadin didn't understand what was happening. Just as Nathan tucked the infant closer, he almost dropped her as his whole body spun. Nathan fell to his knees, looking as blood spilled from his left arm. He half handed, half tossed the baby girl to Kadin.

"What are you doing?"

"I've been shot!"

"What?"

Glass shattered and broke. Kadin saw dark indentations form on the wall just above Lilly's head as Nathan killed the lights.

"Get her on the floor!" Nathan ordered.

Lilly cried out, racked with another contraction. Kadin took the child and slid her under the bed. He groped for Lilly, his eyes still not adjusted to the darkness.

"Nathan, you're going to have to help me."

Kadin grabbed her feet as Nathan secured her with his good arm around her chest and they lifted her onto the floor.

"I have to push," Lilly said.

"No! I have to see if the baby turned. He may be breech."

"Kadin . . ."

"Let me check the baby. Nathan, are you all right?"

"I think it just grazed me. I'm going to take a look outside."

"That's not a good idea. We're secure in here."

"Let me do the police work! You handle the delivery!"

Kadin eased Lilly against the wall.

"Lilly, I'm going to feel for the baby's head."

"Hurry . . . he's not going to wait."

"All right. Just breathe through the next contraction."

Another window shattered, the cool night air evaporated the sweat that collected at the nape of Kadin's neck.

"This might bother you a little bit."

What met his fingers was not the smooth surface of a head, but the small pebbles of five tiny toes.

The baby was breech.

"Nathan, I need you over here."

No response.

"Nathan!"

"What is it? What's wrong?"

"He's breech."

Kadin heard the fine pitch of a bullet graze past his ear and shatter the plaster on the wall to his right. Lilly began to cry, and he wasn't sure how long he could hold it together himself. He began thinking through Bible verses he'd memorized about the Lord's promises, but at this juncture, he felt his faith wavering under the responsibility of bringing Lilly, these babies, and himself through this alive.

Grabbing several pillows from the headboard, he placed them behind Lilly. Now that his eyes had adjusted to the dark, he saw her fear and worry as he positioned himself, holding her knees in each of his hands. She was shivering and slick with sweat; racking sobs were making it difficult for her to breathe.

"Lilly. We're fine."

"The baby's going to die."

"Breech presentation is not a death sentence."

"I'm going to die."

"Lilly, please, listen. Just breathe with me. Come on, now. Deep breath in through your nose." It took several attempts before she would follow his lead. "Good. That's great! Now hold it and blow it out through your mouth."

More glass breaking. Upper level.

Heavy footfalls on the floor above.

"Next contraction, I want easy, gentle pushing. Nothing too dramatic."

"Aren't you going to pull him out?"

"No. You're going to do this."

"His head is going to get stuck. He'll suffocate."

"Lilly, if I pull on the baby, that will cause your cervix to become more irritable and cause it to clamp down on the baby's neck. Just give me easy, gentle pushing."

A heavy thud shook the house.

Kadin supported the infant's lower body as Lilly pushed. She was making slow, steady progress with each contraction.

"You're doing great. We're almost there. Whatever you do, don't stop pushing."

Kadin heard someone coming down the wooden steps. The lights turned on. His vision flashed white, and he waited for the pain of a bullet snapping into the back of his head.

"Just push, Lilly."

She delivered the head. It was then, as Kadin held the baby boy in one hand and reached up to the bed for several towels that he paused, looking at the gun-wielding tattooed man that stood in the room. Kadin's throat froze in fear, and he was unable to speak.

"I'm Drew. I've been helping Lilly. Thought Drake might show so I was hiding outside waiting." He pointed with the tip of his gun. "What's wrong with her? She did that right after the accident."

Kadin turned.

Lilly was having another seizure.

Chapter 48

April 3

THE AIR WAS heavy and thick, like trying to breathe during times of high humidity. Lilly felt a tight band around her finger and heard a faint, constant, annoying beep in the distance. In the background, a voice beckoned her, calling her name with soft reassurance. A pressure on her cheek brought her fingers up to determine the cause. The pressure lightened, and soft fingers caressed her eyelids.

"Lilly. Wake up."

She didn't want to obey at first, but then the thoughts tumbled through her mind. There was a shooting. Nathan was injured.

The babies.

She opened her eyes and found Nathan lying beside her. He pulled the bed covers up and tucked them around her shoulders. The cabin was chilly as the wind blew through several broken windows. Lilly smoothed her hand over her belly; she felt a cord inhibit her progress and the blips picked up pace. At first, she didn't know why the tears came so quickly, considering she'd prepared for this moment for months and intellectually felt that giving the twins away was in their best interest. But the emptiness of them not being part of her brought unexpected grief. Nathan placed his hand on her cheek, wiping her tears away with his thumb.

"Are they alive?"

"Yes."

"Where are they?"

"Kadin took them. Isn't that what you wanted? For them to be safe?"

"Are they?"

Lilly felt Nathan move to sit up. She grasped his wrist, and he eased his head back onto the pillow. The tears became uncontrollable sobbing, and before she realized or could deter his action, Nathan had gathered her in his arms, placing gentle kisses on her face. His tenderness calmed her anxiety, and she felt herself ease into his embrace until the tension within her passed.

"Why did Kadin leave?"

"Do you remember last night?"

Yesterday had been never-ending. The murdered physician. Driving back to Colorado. Being run off the road. Going into labor.

"You were shot."

"It's fine. Just a flesh wound, as they say. Kadin stitched me up before he left."

"Why is he not here?"

Nathan pulled away. "Kadin was worried. The first baby, a little girl, was delivered okay. That's when everything hit the fan. Though I can't prove it, Drake was trying to finish you. Your missing friend intervened. Drew was watching the cabin from a distance when he saw the shooting start. We chased Drake off after a bit."

Nathan lifted the small machine that was attached to Lilly's finger and removed the clip.

"During the ruckus, you delivered the second baby, but he was breech. He came out all right but required some extra breaths to get him going. You were having a seizure, and Kadin gave you Valium to stop it. He felt like he had to move the babies to a more secure environment. Said he had someplace set up, like here, where he was going to try to take care of them unless he was forced to admit them into the hospital."

Peace settled over Lilly. She'd accomplished her main goal, delivering the babies and getting them somewhere safe. "Where's Drew?"

"He went with Kadin to provide an extra set of hands. Security if needed. Then he was going to disappear until we got everything ironed out."

"Why didn't you go?"

"I wanted to be here with you. I can't tell you how crazy I've been. I know things are not supposed to happen this way. You probably think I'm misconstruing my feelings because I'm trying to help you, but the thought of you dying or being injured has left me paralyzed. I realize now what I was feeling was different than worry. It was fear of losing someone I loved and never seeing her again and leaving things unsaid that should have been spoken a long time ago."

"Nathan, I'm a mess."

He eased himself beside her and cupped her chin in his hand, searching her eyes until she stopped trying to look away. "It's okay. I'm not expecting anything from you, but I am in love with you, and I'm not letting you leave me again."

Chapter 49

April 17

LILLY SAT IN her car in a darkened corner of the hospital parking lot. The faint green glow of the vehicle's digital clock cast a sickly shadow on her pale skin.

Ten minutes to go.

It didn't take long for Lilly to hear of Kadin's beating, likely at the hands of Drake but as yet unproven. Nathan had delivered the news in person, shaking his head often and slamming his fist into the table. Drake was just beyond the grasp of law enforcement, even though the noose around his neck was inching tighter day by day. Most of Nathan's co-workers still felt Drew was the most viable suspect. Now Drew was off the grid, and Lilly knew they would never see him again until Drake was in jail.

As Nathan focused on Drake, Lilly's fear was the safety of the twins. It had been two short weeks since their delivery. Kadin hadn't worked since their birth, and in her heart she knew he'd been caring for them. The attack on Kadin meant Drake was seeking the babies. She had to find them first.

She didn't reveal this conviction to Nathan. His coworkers still doubted him, and she didn't want him putting himself in a position where his job would be at risk.

Lilly knew early morning would be the best time to execute her plan. The night was warm as she left her car, but she could see thunderstorms brewing over the mountains, lightning strikes flashed within the gray cotton mounds. She walked around the corner to one of the side entrances to the hospital, waiting for someone to leave through a door that was inaccessible from the outside. She was trying to avoid entrances with security cameras.

Thirty minutes passed, and the door opened, slamming against the side of the building as a janitor pushed through a rolling cart burdened with several trash bags. As he cleared the entrance, she slipped in and faced a concrete maze in the bowels of the hospital. This area was rarely visited by any member of the medical staff unless someone was bringing a body to the morgue.

She walked down the hall. Her footsteps echoing along the corridor competed with the sound of her own heartbeat rushing in her ears. Finding a stairwell, she took the steps to the floor where the ICU bays were housed. She'd not even asked Nathan for Kadin's room number, wanting to keep him off the scent of her plan. The problem with this ICU was that it was split up into four different bays, and finding Kadin would not be that easy. It was almost three in the morning, which served her purpose well because oddly enough, that's when this unit's nursing staff changed hands.

Sneaking into a patient's room, she pulled up the computer screen, hoping it would have the unit list open. She would have to find someone who hadn't logged off, because her computer password and login had been disabled after her firing.

This user had logged off.

It took her two more tries before she found a computer with the patient list open. Making her way to Kadin's group of rooms took longer than she would have liked. The next shift would be starting soon.

She eased through his door without garnering even one glance thus far at her presence. The nurses were still busy with patient hand-off report at the desk. During her time as an emergency physician, she had seen many people injured beyond recognition, but it didn't prepare her in the slightest for seeing Kadin cocooned in his bed, beaten and unresponsive.

His head was shrouded in gauze, with a bolt screwed into his skull that monitored the pressure in his brain. That number was borderline high; his gray matter was at risk for being shifted into areas it wasn't meant to go. That amount of compression meant brain cells would die and oxygen would be cut off under the atmosphere of diminished blood flow. She could feel her knees shake as she neared his bedside. The only sound in the room was the quiet noise of machines keeping him alive. A breathing tube in his mouth was secured with a blue plastic device to keep it in place.

His injuries were confined to his face. Both eyes were beaten and swollen closed. The right cheek was fractured, giving a caved-in appearance that even with the swelling was obviously different from the left. The medical team had placed a central line into his chest so his arms were free of IV lines. She took his hand in hers, letting the tears fall, dripping onto his sheets.

"Kadin?"

The weight of his choice overwhelmed her. How could anyone sustain such cruelty to protect the lives of others? He'd placed himself on the brink of death to keep her and the babies safe. She knew he'd kept her secret; otherwise they would all be dead. He didn't stir to her voice, but she did notice his heartbeat rise slightly.

"I told you that you had to leave a way for me to get to the twins. Drake is hunting them. I have to keep them safe."

His heartbeat remained elevated. She supinated the arm she held, rubbing her fingers along the underside of his forearm. There was a bandage that seemed out of place as there was no blood that seeped through the gauze and it would have been an unusual site for an earlier IV. She bent down, looking closer, and could see what appeared to be ink through the haze of the plastic tape. She picked at the edge with her fingers and pulled the dressing off.

It was a tattoo of a quilt with a date in the center.

The date of the twins' birth.

It was then that a conversation she and Dana had on the night of her attack came to the forefront of her mind. Hastily, she left his bedside, made her way to the stairwell again, and traveled a few flights to the neonatal intensive care unit.

Lilly beckoned to a lone parent to let her in the locked unit. Once inside, she could see what Dana meant. Over each Isolette was a quilt that would help maintain a calm, soothing environment against the harsh light and sound of their artificial womb. Lilly walked by a few babies, fingering their quilts as she went. Blue for the boys, pink for the girls, but beyond simple patchwork. There were stars and intricate square designs. She was drawn to one blanket that had a figure at the top with an oversized hat so you couldn't see the face. Appliquéd hearts showered down from his hands

Kadin's tattoo was a replica of this quilt.

A nurse approached her with one eyebrow raised.

"Can I help you?"

Lilly took the nurse's hand and shook it eagerly.

"I'm one of the new nurse practitioners. I got off work late, but I always like to peek in on the babies before I go home. I hope that's all right."

"Sure. It's just odd to have someone here at three thirty in the morning."

"Wouldn't it be nice to have normal hours? It's probably why I visit them, because I'm always working and never have time to meet a man and settle down."

"Tell me about it."

Lilly placed her hand gently over the quilt. "These blankets are amazing."

"Aren't they? The whole thing is quite tragic."

"What do you mean?"

"You probably haven't met Dr. Daughtry, but he's an OB on staff here. Did you hear about his beating in the news?"

"He works here?"

"Yeah. Anyway, his sister makes these quilts, all of them. She lost a baby several years back, and this is her therapy, I guess. But there's always a silver lining. This is the baby boy she just adopted."

Lilly's fingers froze on the quilt surface. She moved her hand and lifted up the edge of the quilt that draped over the side. Her son lay on his stomach nestled in a sheath of soft lamb's wool, his head rested on one arm. She brushed away the welling tears.

"Are you all right?"

"Dr. Daughtry's sister adopted this baby?"

"It's even more amazing than that. He's a twin. Sister is at home with Mom. It's strange how everyone seems to want to peek in on him tonight. He's been getting lots of visitors."

Lilly's stomach burned. "Really, who else but a crazy, lonely person like me would be visiting these little guys so early in the morning?"

"Dr. Maguire stopped by."

"And saw this baby?"

"Though I never was a fan of his, it's terrible him being falsely accused of rape. He ended up opening a practice of his own to get a fresh start. He came in for a delivery."

Lilly's heart tempered up a notch and she fingered her dyed blonde hair then shoved her fashion frames higher on her nose. Was the nurse astute enough to discover her ruse?

The nurse continued. "He's really concerned about what happened to

Kadin. They used to work together. When I told him Kadin's sister adopted this little one, he wanted her address so he could stop by and visit."

"Wow! That is sweet. Did you happen to give him that?"

"Yeah, he said he was going by right after he got off call."

Chapter 50

LILLY LEFT THE hospital in a hurry, expecting Drake to be close behind her. Her heart stammered in her chest, her body bathed in cool sweat. Lightning strikes flashed in the rain-blackened sky, the stars hidden by angry storm clouds, and she jumped as a crash of thunder hammered at her nerves.

It began to pour.

Once inside her car and protected from the sheets of water, Lilly pulled out the piece of paper that held Ellie's address. She'd quickly accessed an untended computer and was able to find the baby's records. Reaching for her phone—a prepaid one she'd picked up at a local Wal-Mart—she dialed Ellie's number. The phone rang, and she waited with her breath still for an answer.

None.

She peeled out of the parking lot. Ellie lived north of Denver, and it would take Lilly over an hour to reach her. Lilly hoped she could make it ahead of Drake and get her and the baby out of the house.

As she pressed the speed limit, she was thankful she was traveling in the opposite direction of rush-hour traffic. The roadway became clogged with workers making their way into the city. Her thoughts raced as to what her plan was going to be when she actually reached Ellie's house.

Lilly glanced at herself in the rearview mirror. She looked like she'd been sleeping in the mud. The rain had washed her mascara off her eyelashes, leaving dark heavy lines down her face. Licking her finger, she began to scrub off the trails with her spit. The heavy rubbing was able to remove the make-up, but left red blotches behind. She smelled like she'd showered after a work-out without using any soap and sighed at the fact that there wasn't anything she could do about that. How was she going to get Ellie to trust her when she looked like a homeless person? Lilly opened the case beside her and took out the weapon, keeping it near her on the console.

Lilly drummed the wheel incessantly with her fingers, the song on the radio driving them faster. She didn't know a safe place to hide Ellie and her baby girl. Nathan had put his job on the line by not arresting her for Dana's murder, and hotel hopping from night to night was not going to be an option for a preemie infant. Perhaps it was best to leave the state entirely until the DNA testing on the babies proved Drake's paternity. Nathan was working behind the scenes with a private lab to get that accomplished. All she knew was she had to get them out of the house and out of the city. She'd figure everything else out later.

The craftsman-style home sat up off the street, nestled back on the top of a gentle slope surrounded by oak trees. Grabbing her gun and exiting the car, Lilly jogged up the steps and rang the doorbell.

A blonde woman peeked through the side window, then scurried away. Lilly tested the knob. Locked.

She slapped the glass several times. "Ellie!"

Lilly took the gun out and held the barrel in her hand, using the handle to break the glass. Reaching through, she unlocked the door and entered the home, closing it behind her. She saw a formal dining room off to her left and grabbed one of the chairs to brace it under the door to prevent Drake from coming in.

She wasn't planning on leaving that way, anyway.

"Ellie! I know you're afraid, but I need to talk to you."

Lilly saw her at the top of the stairs, holding the baby in her arms.

"You can't have her."

Lilly tucked the gun into her pocket, trying to ease Ellie's fear with the downward motion of her hands.

"Ellie, listen. I'm Lilly. I don't know if Kadin ever told you who I was but I am the mother—"

"I'm their mother now!"

Lilly pulled her wet, tangled hair from her eyes.

"Ellie, I don't want to take the babies from you, but I'm not leaving this house without both of you with me. Drake is on his way. He's going to kill you, her, and me if we don't leave before he gets here."

Ellie tightened the baby to her chest. "I'm not going anywhere with you."

Lilly bounded up the stairs. Ellie backed into a bedroom. Lilly found the twins' room. Rifling through the closet, she looked for something to pack away the baby's clothing. Finding a suitcase, she flipped it open and pulled out one of the dresser drawers.

Boy's clothing.

She checked another drawer, seeing a sea of green and pink. She began to empty the dresser into the suitcase. Returning to the closet, she grabbed two packages of unopened diapers, retrieved the clothing, and made her way back downstairs. In the kitchen, she spotted Ellie's purse and dumped out the contents, grabbing the house keys. After several false starts, she found the garage and loaded her supplies into the car. She noticed several gallon jugs of water and placed three in the trunk beside the suitcase. Making her way back into the kitchen, she found the stock of formula and grabbed several canisters and bottles and stowed them, as well.

She paused at the bottom of the stairs, wiping the sweat, rain, and dirt from her face. Slowly she walked up. The twins' door remained open, but the door to the master remained closed.

That's when she heard sirens in the distance. Ellie must have called the police, which meant they'd likely apprehend Lilly, which would leave Ellie and the baby an open target for Drake's eventual arrival.

Lilly tested the knob. The door wouldn't budge.

Stepping back, she kicked it open. Ellie was huddled on the bed, the phone at her side, the baby clutched in her arms.

"Ellie, I know you're afraid. I'm not here to hurt you, but Drake is coming, and I swear to you none of us will be alive if we're here when he gets here."

"Why should I believe you?"

Someone pounded on the front door so hard that the whole house vibrated. Lilly looked out the front.

Not the police, but Drake.

Three successive bangs, like the sound of a car backfiring, reverberated through the structure.

She turned to the frightened woman and grabbed her arm, the sounds a convincing blow to Ellie's will. As they came to the top of the staircase, the damage to the front door was obvious but the chair remained in place and Drake wasn't visible at the moment.

Where had he gone?

Lilly pulled Ellie down the stairs and into the garage.

"Get the baby secured," she ordered, and made her way to the driver's seat.

Once Ellie was in the passenger side, Lilly laid the weapon in the space between them. Turning, she grabbed the spare blanket she'd thrown in the back and placed it over the baby's car seat.

"What are you doing?"

"I need you to stay low once we open the garage door. He's going to shoot at us. I need to protect the baby from the glass."

Ellie began to tremble. Lilly took her hand and tried to still it.

"It's going to be all right."

"Is it?"

Lilly punched the garage button and as soon as she felt she could clear the bottom of the garage door, she pushed her foot into the accelerator and shot backward into the driveway as if they were loaded on the end of a catapult. The front door of the house now stood open. The car launched into the street. Lilly threw it into forward just as Drake made his way out the front. As they drove away from the home, the back windshield imploded, glass raining down into the interior compartment. Ellie screamed. Lilly watched through the rearview mirror, seeing Drake bound down the stairs and retrieve his black Hummer.

He gained on them quickly.

The rain sheeted over the windshield. Even with the wipers at max speed, it was difficult to keep the glass clear. Ellie had unbuckled her seat belt and was flipped around, checking on the baby.

The grill of Drake's Hummer was zooming up on their rear bumper.

"Ellie, sit down and get buckled."

"He's gaining!"

"Ellie—"

She flopped back in her seat and complied. "What are you going to do?"

That was the question, wasn't it?

Lilly took the next left turn she could make. The car fishtailed to the right, hitting the curb with a jolt before continuing on. Drake cut the corner, not even slowing down to make the turn.

Now he was closer.

"Where is the nearest police station?"

"I don't know."

"The closest major street."

"Turn right!"

Lilly cranked the wheel and controlled the slide of the vehicle a little bit better. She saw the intersection ahead, but there wasn't any way she could get into the flow of traffic. She slammed on the brakes. Her decision was Drake's opportunity to pounce, and he rear-ended their car, sending it into oncoming traffic.

All Lilly saw was a blur of red. Then glass, air bags, and dust filled the inner compartment of the vehicle. Lilly's head hit the air bag that unfurled from the driver's window, but it was not the soft pillow she imagined, and her vision darkened.

Ellie's screams broke through the haze, and Lilly lifted her head. She groaned and reached for her neck as Ellie began to shake her ruthlessly from her position in the car.

"Faith!"

"What?"

"The baby! She's not here!"

Lilly unclipped her seat belt and turned to the back. The car seat was gone, and the driver's-side back-passenger window was punched out. She checked her door and found it easily opened. She grabbed the gun and stepped out.

Chaos ensued in the street. A man was checking the driver of the vehicle that had T-boned them. She could see Drake's Hummer at the intersection, but he was not inside. Traffic was stopped. People exited their vehicles. The roar of rain and thunder made it difficult for her to hear.

That's when she saw Drake, just a few paces away from her, holding the infant's carrier, a gun pointed at the baby's head. Ellie had made her way from the vehicle through the driver's door as well and dropped to her knees, begging heaven for mercy as she witnessed the dire straits her daughter was in.

Lilly raised her weapon, positioned herself, and placed Drake's forehead in her sights.

"Well, well, well. What a quandary we find ourselves in," he chided.

Lilly checked her peripheral vision. It seemed as if each passerby was either talking on their cell phone or taking stills and video of the scene.

"I think you're at your endgame, Drake."

"That's probably true, considering this little one has a brother I didn't quite know about. Fertile, aren't you?"

"Just put her down and walk away."

"And let you shoot me in the back? I don't think so."

"What do you want, Drake? Haven't you destroyed enough lives as it is?"

"I might as well finish my work. Don't you think?"

"Then kill me."

It was after she uttered those words and placed her arms wide, with visions of Kadin's broken and battered body in her mind, that Lilly finally understood what life was about.

Having a love so powerful for another that your own life didn't matter anymore.

Sacrifice.

A man giving up his life as a payment so others could be saved.

Her willingness to put her own life aside, to meet whatever was beyond, made it possible to understand why Christ chose death on the cross.

And as she looked at Drake, her conversation with a stranger began to replay in her mind, a conversation about making a choice for a life.

At first, she thought it was about her babies.

But her visitor had said one life.

Drake's life.

In that moment she felt a vibration swell up within her and a voice, crystal clear, speak a thought in her mind.

What you see before you is what I saw when I died on the cross.

A criminal.

A person who left utter destruction and broken lives in his wake.

A life left better to rot in the depths of hell than for another to lay his life down for it.

As I came for you, I also came for him.

And as she looked at Drake, she understood the weight of that truth. It broke her.

"What are you going to do, Lilly!"

A car horn blared.

Drake turned his head.

Lilly took aim and fired her weapon.

Chapter 51

IT WAS TRUE when they said the wheels of justice were slow to turn. Lilly fingered the gold cross that hung around her neck as Nathan clutched her other hand. Kadin sat on the other side, his arm around Ellie as each of them held squirming eighteen-month-old infants on their laps. The babies were happy and healthy, seemingly unaffected by Lilly's abuse of alcohol early in her pregnancy. Lilly felt a smile tug at the corners of her lips, as Ellie's eyes met hers and she gave her a thumbs-up.

The media storm would come to an end, and hopefully the relentless playback of the video of that fateful morning would become a distant memory in a society that craved new media and found it difficult to follow a story for more than a couple of days. She had to give them credit.

Her story seemed cemented.

With Ellie's account of events, they were able to arrest Drake on a host of charges. That put him in jail until the initial DNA tests showed the father of Lilly's twins was genetically related to his two sons that had died in the fire. After that, they were able to pressure the courts for a witnessed blood draw that showed Drake was the father of the twins. Since it was documented that Lilly's pregnancy was the result of rape, the door opened up for an additional slew of charges. It also called into question the crime that Drew had been imprisoned for all those years ago. Meryl Stipman had also been arrested and jailed on accessory charges for her attempts to cover up her son's crimes.

Kadin had recovered from his injuries and was slowly making his way back into private practice. When he was able to finger Drake for the beating, most people considered him a hero for defending Lilly's secret to the brink of death. Of course, the two-hour *Dateline* special cemented his stature, and he was currently turning clients away.

Then there was Nathan.

The one man who had stood by her without question.

Who defended her, despite the odds.

The one who had placed an engagement ring on her finger.

Happily, they were all family, and Lilly felt blessed that Ellie allowed her to have a relationship with the children: Faith and Levi.

The members of the jury were ushered in and handed the court clerk their findings. Having already been found guilty on a myriad of crimes, Drake stood, his arm limp at his side from the nerve damage caused from the gunshot wound to the shoulder he'd suffered when Lilly shifted the aim of her weapon away from his head.

The death penalty.

The gavel fell.

Jordyn Redwood has served patients and their families for nearly twenty years and currently works as a pediatric ER nurse. As a selfprofessed medical nerd and trauma junkie, she was drawn to the controlled chaotic environments of critical care and emergency nursing. Her love of teaching developed early and she was among the youngest CPR instructors for the American Red Cross at the age of seventeen. Since then, she has continued to teach advanced resuscitation classes to participants ranging from first responders to MD's.

Her discovery that she also had a fondness for answering medical questions for authors led to the creation of Redwood's Medical Edge at http:// jordynredwood.com/. This blog is devoted to helping contemporary and historical authors write medically accurate fiction.

Jordyn lives in Colorado with her husband, two daughters, and one crazy hound dog. In her spare time she also enjoys reading her favorite authors, quilting, and cross-stitching. Jordyn loves to hear from her readers and can be contacted at jredwood1@gmail.com.